SALAMANDER

'LET ME SEE it.' Pyriel reached out with an open palm and took up the chest reverently as Dak'ir handed it over.

Now he turned that omniscient scrutiny upon the artefact held in his hand.

'This is Vulkan's mark,' he uttered after a few moments. 'It is his icon, a unique brand borne only by the primarch and his forgefathers.' Pyriel's fingers traced subtle grooves and engravings now suddenly visible on the chest's surface, touching it delicately as if it was fragile porcelain, despite the fact of the chest's hardy metal construction. 'It is sealed,' he went on, although now it appeared he was speaking to himself. 'No skill I possess can open it.' The Librarian paused, as if unlocking some clandestine facet of the chest. 'There is an origin stamp…'

Pyriel looked up, as if struck dumb.

'What is it, brother? Where does it come from?'

Pyriel uttered a single word, as if it were the only sound that could pass his lips at that moment. It was one tha̶̶̶̶̶̶̶̶̶̶ well, and held the heavy weight of proj̶̶̶̶̶̶

'Isstv̶̶

A WARHAMMER 40,000 NOVEL

SALAMANDER

Nick Kyme

For mum. For being you and always believing.
With love.

A BLACK LIBRARY PUBLICATION

First published in Great Britain in 2009 by
BL Publishing,
Games Workshop Ltd.,
Willow Road, Nottingham,
NG7 2WS, UK.

10 9 8 7 6 5 4 3

Cover illustration by Cheoljoo Lee.

UK ISBN13: 978 1 84416 740 1
US ISBN13: 978 1 84416 741 8

See the Black Library on the Internet at
www.blacklibrary.com

Find out more about Games Workshop
and the world of Warhammer 40,000 at
www.games-workshop.com

Printed and bound in the UK.

IT IS THE 41st millennium. For more than a hundred centuries the Emperor has sat immobile on the Golden Throne of Earth. He is the master of mankind by the will of the gods, and master of a million worlds by the might of his inexhaustible armies. He is a rotting carcass writhing invisibly with power from the Dark Age of Technology. He is the Carrion Lord of the Imperium for whom a thousand souls are sacrificed every day, so that he may never truly die.

YET EVEN IN his deathless state, the Emperor continues his eternal vigilance. Mighty battlefleets cross the daemon-infested miasma of the warp, the only route between distant stars, their way lit by the Astronomican, the psychic manifestation of the Emperor's will. Vast armies give battle in His name on uncounted worlds. Greatest amongst his soldiers are the Adeptus Astartes, the Space Marines, bio-engineered super-warriors. Their comrades in arms are legion: the Imperial Guard and countless planetary defence forces, the ever-vigilant Inquisition and the tech-priests of the Adeptus Mechanicus to name only a few. But for all their multitudes, they are barely enough to hold off the ever-present threat from aliens, heretics, mutants – and worse.

TO BE A man in such times is to be one amongst untold billions. It is to live in the cruellest and most bloody regime imaginable. These are the tales of those times. Forget the power of technology and science, for so much has been forgotten, never to be re-learned. Forget the promise of progress and understanding, for in the grim dark future there is only war. There is no peace amongst the stars, only an eternity of carnage and slaughter, and the laughter of thirsting gods.

'In war, a Space Marine has no equal. He is the epitome of the warrior, a martial specimen of vast strength and dauntless courage. The Space Marine does not feel pain as other men do, he does not experience fear. He is master of both. But such inviolability must be honed, refocused before every campaign. It is here in battle-meditation that he girds himself, here that he finds the warrior spirit within.

In isolation do we find our true strength. Through self-sacrifice and endurance beyond all others do we become inviolable. These are the credos of the Promethean Cult; these are our tenets; these are our laws. From the fires of battle are we born, brothers. Upon the anvil of war are we tempered.'

– attributed to Tu'Shan, Chapter Master of the Salamanders

PROLOGUE

Tsu'gan screamed as he plummeted from the stone parapet towards the temple floor below.

'No!' The word was wrenched from his throat.

He heard rasping laughter as he fell.

Nihilan had planned this doom. He had fooled them all. It was this, the cold realisation of his failure, which sat like ice in Tsu'gan's gut.

He remembered the armoured shadow, closing in from where he should have been; where, as a loyal Salamander, he should have stayed sentry. Hubris and arrogance had impelled him to disobey. Tsu'gan had believed glory was worth the risk.

The world passed by in a blur as Tsu'gan traversed the short distance to the ground. In his maddened urgency, he'd lost sight of the ambusher who was closing on Kadai. His captain was alone, standing before the pooled remains of the warp creature he had just vanquished, and he was weakened…

Blinding light ripped into the darkness like a jagged knife, careless of the damage it wreaked. Tsu'gan kept his balance, a few seconds extending into lifetimes as he followed an incandescent beam searing through the gloom. He saw Dak'ir glanced by it, his battle-helm corroding, his pain at the beam's malign caress emitted as a wail of agony. The force of it, surging from the multi-melta, spun him away from certain death. Undeterred, the beam sped on and struck Kadai. The captain's body was lit up like an incendiary. Terrible light engulfed him. Kadai screamed and the wrenching sound echoed Tsu'gan's own as he landed in a crouch, shattering rockcrete beneath his Astartes bulk.

Heart thundering in his chest, Tsu'gan was on his feet and running, heedless of the danger presented by the shadows around the edges of the temple. The distance to his captain seemed so impossibly far, the chances of Kadai's survival so remote. Yet he hoped.

It was only when he closed and he saw Kadai's armour fold in on itself that he realised his beloved captain was dead. He skidded to a halt, not wishing to touch the corroded remains, and slumped to his knees. Tsu'gan hung his head, even as he heard the cries of N'keln and his battle-brothers returning to reinforce them. Only, they were too late.

'Salamanders! Slay them!'

Barking bolter fire brought a crescendo of noise. Tsu'gan was dimly aware of the bucking forms of dying cultists – the followers of the debased cult that had brought the Salamanders to this graven place – as N'keln and the others tore them apart. He felt hollowed, as if a dagger had been thrust into his gut and all of his innards carved away. Physical agony, more painful and invasive than any torture, spread through his bones to his very core. It was as if he had ceased to exist in the world and merely watched as it revolved around him.

A solid shot *spanging* off Tsu'gan's pauldron brought him to his senses. Grief and denial became rage. Shaking hands became fists grasping his bolter. Tsu'gan was on his feet again. He looked to the dark, but Kadai's murderer had fled.

A cultist came at him, seen from the corner of his eye. The wretched creature's stitched mouth prevented a battle cry. He wielded an eviscerator in bone-thin fingers. Ragged robes flapped around a withered body like a corpse.

He would have to do.

Tsu'gan ducked the clumsy swipe of the chainblade, hearing the churning teeth as they raked over his head. In the same motion, he brought up his fist into the wretch's stomach, felt ribs crack and then the soft meat of his belly. With a bestial roar, Tsu'gan ripped out a fistful of viscera and finished the cultist with a heavy blow from his bolter stock.

Tsu'gan barely registered the skull collapsing beneath his wrath when he turned and drilled three robed figures fleeing off into the dark. The muzzle flare from his bolter lit up their escape and they danced like doomed marionettes before the ammo storm. He found another, snapping its neck with a blade-like hand. Two more fell to his weapon's retort, their chests exploded as the volatile rounds did their gruesome work; another crumpled beneath an elbow strike that shattered her neck and left it sagging.

Green-armoured forms were moving around him too – his battle-brothers. Tsu'gan was only vaguely aware of them as he killed. He never moved far from his captain's side, maintaining a cordon of protection that none would breach and live. The cultists were many and he revelled in their slaughter. When his bolter ran dry, Tsu'gan cast it aside and lifted the still whirring eviscerator, torn from the dead cultist's grasp.

A red haze came upon him. He cut and cleaved, and rent and slashed, and gored and sundered until a grisly wall of body parts surrounded him. When the cultists thinned at last and the final few were chased down and executed, Tsu'gan felt the strength in his mighty legs fail him. He fell again, once more to his knees, in a pool of enemy blood. With the tip of the eviscerator's blade, he carved a long groove into the stone floor so the tainted vitae would not touch his captain. Tsu'gan then closed his eyes and despaired.

'Brother-sergeant,' a voice came to him through a grief-filled fog. 'Tsu'gan,' it insisted.

Tsu'gan opened his eyes and saw that Veteran Sergeant N'keln stood before him.

'It is over, brother. The enemy are slain,' he said, as if it was any comfort. 'Your battle-brother will survive,' he added.

Tsu'gan looked nonplussed.

'Dak'ir,' clarified N'keln. 'He will live.'

Tsu'gan hadn't even realised he was there. Kadai was all that mattered. Tears were streaming down his face.

'Kadai...' said the brother-sergeant, his voice barely a whisper. 'He is dead. Our captain is dead.'

CHAPTER ONE

I
The Old Ways…

DAK'IR STOOD ABOVE the lake of fire, waiting to let his captain burn.

What was left of Ko'tan Kadai's corroded power armour was chained to a pyre-slab along with his half-destroyed body. Lava spat and bubbled beneath it, wafts of flame igniting in it before being consumed, only to flare to life again in another part of the molten flow. The black marble of the pyre-slab reflected the lava's fiery glow, the veined stone cast in reds and oranges. Two thick chains were piston-drilled to one of the short edges, and the rectangular pyre-slab hung down long-ways. Ceramite coated its surface, so the pyre-slab would be impervious to the magma heat. It would take Kadai on his final journey into the heart of Mount Deathfire.

Inside the vast cavern of rock, Dak'ir recalled the slow and solemn procession to that great volcanic peak. Over a hundred warriors, marching all the way from the Sanctuary City of Hesiod, had made the pilgrimage. The mountain was immense, and tore into the fiery orange heavens of Nocturne like the tip of a broken spear. Ash drifts had floated from the crater at its peak, coming down in slow, grey swathes.

Deathfire was at once beautiful and terrible to behold.

But there was no pyroclastic fury, no belligerent eruption of rock and flame this day, just lamentation as the mountain took back one of her sons: a Salamander, a Fire-born.

'Into fire are we born, so unto fire do we return...' intoned Dak'ir, repeating the sombre words of Brother-Chaplain Elysius. He was speaking rites of interment, specifically the *Canticles of Immolation*. Despite the Chaplain's cold diction, Dak'ir felt the emotional resonance of his words as they echoed loudly around the underground cavern.

Though ostensibly rough rock, the cavern was actually a sacred place built by Master of the Forge T'kell. Millennia old, its artifice and functionality were still lauded in the current decaying age. T'kell had fashioned the vault under the careful auspice of the progenitor, Vulkan, and had been amongst the first of his students upon his apotheosis to primarch. These skills T'kell would impart to future generations of Salamanders, together with the arcane secrets learned from the tech-adepts of Mars. The Master of the Forge was long dead now, and others walked in his mighty stead, but his legacy of achievements remained. The cavern was but one of them.

A vast reservoir of lava dominated the cavern's depths. The hot, syrupy magma came from beneath the earth and was the lifeblood of Mount Deathfire. It was held in a deep basin of volcanic rock, girded by layers of reinforced heat-retardant ceramite so that it pooled briefly before flowing onwards from one of the many natural outlets in the rock. There were no lanterns in the cavern, for none were needed. The lava cast a warm and eldritch glow. Shadows flickered, fire cracked and spat.

Chaplain Elysius stood in the darkness, despite his prominence on an overhang of rock that sat on the opposite side of the cavern to Dak'ir. A spit of lava threw harsh orange light across the overhang. It was long enough for Dak'ir to see Elysius's ebony power armour and the ivory of his skull-faced battle-helm. It was cast starkly, the light describing the edges of its prominent features. Eyes glowed behind the lenses, red and diabolic.

Isolationism was a fundamental tenet of Promethean creed. It was believed this was the only way a Salamander could find the reliance and inner fortitude he needed to prosecute the Emperor's duties. Elysius embraced this ideal wholly. He was insular and cold. Some in the Chapter reckoned in place of his primary heart, the Chaplain had a core of stone. Dak'ir suspected that might actually be true.

Even though Elysius was often distant, in battle he was completely different. His barbed zeal, as tangible and sharp as a blade, as furious as a bolter's voice, brought his battle-brothers together. His fury, his fierce adherence to the Promethean Cult, became theirs too. Countless times in war, the Chaplain's faith had dragged hard-fought victory from bitter defeat.

A symbol of devotion hung from his weapons belt, a simulacrum of a hammer. It was Vulkan's Sigil and had once been carried by the famed Chaplain Xavier. Long dead now, like so many heroes, the legacy of Xavier as keeper of this badge of office had passed to Elysius.

There in the highest echelons of the cavern, the Chaplain was not alone.

Salamanders from the 3rd and 1st Companies were watching too from a ridge around the edge of the cavern, where they stood to attention in darkened alcoves, their red eyes ablaze. This ocular mutation affected all Salamanders. It was a genetic defect brought about by a reaction to the radiation of their volatile home world. Together with their onyx-black skin, it gave them an almost daemonic appearance, though there were none amongst the Emperor's Astartes more noble, more committed to the defence of humanity than the Fire-born.

Chapter Master Tu'Shan observed the ceremony from a massive seat of stone. He was flanked by his bodyguard the Firedrakes, warriors of the 1st Company, *his* company. Honour markings covered Tu'Shan's noble countenance, a physical legacy of his deeds writ into his ebon flesh. They were the branding scars that every Salamander had, in keeping with Promethean ritual. Few amongst the Chapter, only the most distinguished veterans, ever lived to have them seared upon their face. As Regent of Prometheus, Tu'Shan wore a suit of ancient power armour. Two pauldrons sat upon his hulking shoulders, wrought into the image of the snarling fire lizards from which the Chapter took its name. A cloak of salamander hide, a more venerable and honour-strewn version of that worn by the Firedrakes, was draped across the Chapter Master's broad back. Tu'Shan's bald pate shone with the reflected lustre of the lava, the shadows of its undulations creeping up the walls like fingers of dusk. His eyes were like captured suns. The Chapter Master brooded, chin resting on his fist, as inscrutable as the very rock of the mountain itself.

After acknowledging his Chapter Master, Dak'ir's eye was drawn to Fugis. The Apothecary was one of the Inferno Guard, Kadai's old retinue, of which only three now remained. He had removed his battle helm and clasped it in the crook of his arm. It was stark white like his right-side shoulder armour. His sharp, angular face was haunted by lava-shadows. Even through the rising heat shimmer emanating from below, Dak'ir thought he saw Fugis's eyes glisten.

Ever since Dak'ir had won his black carapace and become a battle-brother, throughout his forty years of service, he'd felt Fugis's watchful eye. Before he became Astartes Dak'ir had been an Ignean, an itinerant cave-dweller of Nocturne. That fact alone was unprecedented, for no one outside the seven Sanctuary Cities had ever been inducted into the vaunted ranks of the Space Marines. To some it made Dak'ir unique; to others, he was an aberration. Certainly his connection to the human side of his genesis was stronger than any the Apothecary had ever known. During battle-meditation, Dak'ir *dreamed*. He remembered with unerring clarity the days before he became superhuman, before his blood and organs and bones were reshaped forever into the iron-hard cast of the alpha-warrior. Biologically, he was a Space Marine like any other; psychologically, it was hard to tell just what potential lay within him.

Chaplain Elysius had found no taint in Dak'ir's spirit. If anything, the Ignean's strength of mind and purpose was remarkably pure, to such a degree that he had achieved the rank of sergeant especially swiftly given the slow and methodical nature of the Chapter.

Fugis, though, was curious by his very nature and unshackled by the extreme views that afflicted the Chaplain. Dak'ir was an enigma to him, one he wished to fathom. But the Apothecary's watchful eye did not scrutinise him this day. His gaze was turned inward instead, mired in grief-ridden introspection. Kadai had been Fugis's friend as well as his captain.

Unlike his brothers, Dak'ir wore the garb of a metal-shaper, the nomadic smiths who worked the iron found deep beneath the mountains and sweated over heavy anvils. The vestments were archaic, but then on Nocturne they still believed in the old ways.

In the earliest millennia of civilisation, when the native tribes of the planet lived in caves, worshipping the fire mountain as a goddess and its scaled denizens as objects of spiritual significance, metal-shaping was regarded as a noble profession and its masters were tribal leaders. The tradition held thousands of years later, after the development of primitive technologies and the nascent art of metal shaping became forging, after the coming of Vulkan and when the Outlander had taken him away again into the stars.

A pelt of salamander skin covered Dak'ir's loins. Thick sandals were lashed about his feet. The Astartes's bare chest shone like lacquered ebony, onyx-black and harder than jet. In his hands he clasped one of the thick chains that held Kadai's corpse steady above the lake of fire.

Promethean tradition demanded that two metal-shapers would guide the passing of the dead. Across from him, standing upon a plinth of stone that jutted out above the lava much like Dak'ir's own, was Tsu'gan. He too wore a similar garb. But where Dak'ir's Ignean heritage was obvious in his rugged and earthy face, Tsu'gan's noble bloodline, passed down from the tribal kings of Hesiod, made his countenance haughty and cruel. His glabrous skull was fastidiously shorn, and he wore a narrow crimson beard like a spike. It was as much a statement of his arrogance and vainglory as it was simple affectation. Dak'ir's hair was dark, characteristic of subterraneans like the nomads of Ignea, cut simply and close to the scalp.

Accusation and thinly-veiled contempt burned coldly in Tsu'gan's gaze, when their eyes met briefly. The fiery gorge between them spat and bubbled in sympathetic enmity.

Anger rising, Dak'ir looked away.

Tsu'gan was one of few amongst the Chapter that found Dak'ir's singularity deviant. Born into comparative wealth and affluence, as such were possible on a volcanic death world, Tsu'gan had found himself instantly at odds with the idea of Dak'ir being a worthy candidate for the Astartes. The fact of his humble birth, his lowborn origins, and the levelling effect of them both as Space Marines, vexed Tsu'gan greatly.

Heritage was merely the undercurrent of acrimony that ran between them now. The bitterness that divided the two sergeants so cruelly had been set in motion as far back as Moribar, their first mission as neophytes, but its colour and acerbity had changed forever with the recent undertaking to Stratos.

Moribar… The thought of the sepulchre world he had visited over four decades ago unearthed bitter memories for Dak'ir. It was there that Ushorak had lost his life, and that Nihilan's vendetta had been born.

Nihilan who had…

Old memories surfaced from Dak'ir's subconscious like pieces of sharpened flint. He saw again the looming dragon, its red scales glistening like blood in the light of the temple to false gods. The melta flare filled his vision like an incandescent star, angry, hot and unstoppable. Kadai's cries smothered all of his other senses and for a moment there was only blackness and the sounds of his accusing anguish…

Dak'ir snapped to. Sweat laced the grooves of his enhanced musculature; not from the lava heat, Salamanders were resistant to such things, but rather from his own inner pain. His secondary heart spasmed with the sudden increase in respiration, fooled into believing the body was entering a heightened state of battle readiness.

Dak'ir fought it down, mastering his own capricious biology with the many mental and physical routines he had been conditioned with as part of his rigorous Astartes training. He hadn't endured a vision like that since Stratos. By Vulkan's grace, it had lasted only seconds. None amongst his gathered brothers had noticed him falter. Dak'ir felt the impulse to suddenly cry out, and curse whatever fates had led them down this dark path to this grim moment of mourning and sorrow, this grief for a captain beloved.

Kadai's death had stained them both. Dak'ir wore his openly, a white patch of scarification from a melta flare that covered over half his face. He had seen it again in his vision, the self-same blast that had ended Kadai's life so grievously. Tsu'gan, however, carried his wounds inwardly where they ate away at him like a cancer. For now, their feud was kept hidden so as not to arouse the suspicion or displeasure of either Chaplain or, indeed, Chapter Master.

Brother-Chaplain Elysius had almost completed the ritual and Dak'ir shifted his focus back to his duty. It was a great honour to be chosen, and he did not wish to be found wanting under Chapter Master Tu'Shan's fiery glare.

At last the moment came. Dak'ir had carried the weight of the pyre-slab for several hours. His shoulders did not even feel this exertion as he fed the chain down slowly, hand-over-hand. Each of the vast links, twice as large as an Astartes's fist, was etched with the symbols of Promethean lore: the hammer, the anvil, the flame. Though the chain links would not dissolve when they touched the lava, they were still red-hot from the rising heat. As each link fed through his palm, Dak'ir gripped it and felt the symbols being slowly branded into his flesh.

Steam issued from every grasp. Dak'ir did not even flinch. He was focused on his task and knew that every link in the chain must be gripped in precisely the same way so that the three symbols were burned into the same place on his palm. Any mistake, however slight, would be obvious afterwards. The ruined mark would be scoured away by brander-priests, shame and disgrace left in its stead.

Though they never made further eye contact, Dak'ir and Tsu'gan worked in concert, passing the links, one over the other, in perfect unison. The metal chain clanked from its rig hoisted in the penumbral dark of the cavern's vaulted ceiling, and Kadai was gradually lowered into the lava. The pyre-slab was soon submerged. The captain's armour and the remains of his body were quickly ravaged. The intense heat would render the last vestiges of him to ash. Then he would sink, returning to the earth and Nocturne.

The scoured pyre-slab came into view again as the chain was hauled back up. Its mortal cargo was gone, its surface steaming. When the slab had at last reached its apex, the rig above was locked off and Dak'ir released it, his duty done.

A votive-servitor shambled forward. The part-flesh, part-mechanised creature was bent-backed from the weight of the massive brazier it carried. The dark metal cradle was fused to the servitor's spine, filled with the gathered ash of offerings. As it approached, Dak'ir plunged his hand into the ash and with a thumb daubed a skull-like symbol upon his right arm.

Turning away from the creature, Dak'ir smacked his hands together allowing the flakes of burnt skin from his palms to cascade into the lava below. When he looked back he found a pair of robed brander-priests in the brazier bearer's place.

Even without his armour, the Astartes towered over the serfs. Heads held low, they carried burning staves and used them to sear fresh honour-scars into Dak'ir's skin. The Salamander accepted the heat, scarcely acknowledging the pain it caused, but embracing the purity of it all the same.

The silent exchange with Tsu'gan was distracting him. Dak'ir barely noticed the brander-priests as they withdrew. Nor did he see at first the three serfs that came after, carrying a suit of power armour between them.

Remembering where he was, the sergeant bowed as the serfs proffered his MkVII battle-plate. He took each piece of armour in turn, slowly re-donning it, casting off the mantle of metal-shaper and becoming Astartes again.

A deep voice issued from the dark when Dak'ir had almost finished.

'Brother-sergeant.'

Dak'ir nodded to the armoured Salamander that emerged, the serfs scurrying past him and back into shadow. The mighty warrior, almost two heads taller than him, was clad in the green battle-plate of the Chapter, a blazing orange salamander icon on his left shoulder pad against a black field denoting him as a battle-brother of 3rd Company.

'Ba'ken.'

Trunk-necked and slab-shouldered, Ba'ken was a fearsome sight. He also held the rank of Dak'ir's heavy weapons trooper, and was his most trusted comrade.

Ba'ken's arms were outstretched. In his gauntleted fists he clasped an ornate chainsword and plasma pistol.

'Your arms, brother-sergeant,' he said solemnly.

Dak'ir mouthed a silent prayer as he took up his weapons, relishing the familiarity of their touch.

'Is the squad in readiness?' asked Dak'ir. He gave a side-glance to Tsu'gan across the lake of fire, as he too was re-armouring. Dak'ir noticed that Iagon, Tsu'gan's second, had dressed his sergeant. *'Beneath you, is it?'* His muttered words were edged with venom.

'3rd Company await only you and Brother Tsu'gan.' Ba'ken kept his expression and tone neutral. He had heard his brother-sergeant's veiled remark, but chose not to acknowledge it. He knew well of the discord between Dak'ir and Tsu'gan. He also knew of the approaches Dak'ir had made in an attempt to ingratiate the other sergeant and the fact of their falling on deaf ears and a closed mind.

'When I was in my youth, a mere neophyte,' Ba'ken began as Dak'ir sheathed his chainsword and holstered his plasma pistol, 'I forged my first blade. It was a gleaming thing – sharp-edged and strong – the most magnificent weapon I had ever seen because it was mine, and I had made it. I trained with the blade constantly, so hard it broke. Despite my best efforts, the hours I spent in the forges, I could not repair it.'

'The first blade is always the most precious, and the least effective, Ba'ken,' Dak'ir replied, intent on mag-locking his battle-helm to the weapons belt of his power armour.

'No, brother-sergeant,' answered the hulking Salamander, 'that is not what I meant.'

Dak'ir stopped what he was doing and looked up.

'Some bonds, they cannot be made however much we want them to be,' Ba'ken told him. 'The metal, you see. It was flawed. No matter how long I spent at the anvil, I could not re-forge it. Nothing could.'

Dak'ir's expression darkened and his red eyes dimmed in what might have been regret.

'Let's not keep our brothers waiting any longer, Ba'ken.'

'At your command,' Ba'ken replied, unable to keep the hint of melancholy out of his voice. He had neglected to mention that he had kept the blade, in the hope he would one day restore it.

'Or our new captain,' Dak'ir concluded, stepping off the plinth and stalking away into the darkness.

II
Grief

DAK'IR PASSED DOWN a line of warriors, Ba'ken in tow, until he reached those of his own squad. Several of the other sergeants of 3rd Company acknowledged him with a nod or mutter of approval – Salamanders like Lok, Omkar and Ul'shan, Devastator squad leaders who had shared in the tragedy of Kadai's death on Stratos.

He briefly locked eyes with Battle-Brother Emek, who clasped his shoulder with a reassuring hand. It was good to be amongst his brothers once more.

Others were less genial.

Tsu'gan had many supporters. In every sense, he was Promethean perfection: strong, courageous and self-sacrificing. Such warriors were easy to like, but Tsu'gan had an arrogant streak. His second, Iagon, was no less conceited, but his methods were entirely more insidious. Tsu'gan glowered from across the opposite side of the temple. The glances of his partisans were no less scathing. Dak'ir felt each and every one like red-hot daggers.

'Brother Tsu'gan still protests.' Ba'ken had followed the other Salamander's eye line, and whispered the remark to his sergeant.

Dak'ir's reaction was pragmatic.

'He is certainly fearless, defying the will of the Chapter Master.'

It was no secret that the appointment of Captain Kadai's successor had not been met with universal approval. Some amongst the sergeants openly contested it. Tsu'gan was the chief detractor. He and others like him had been silenced by Tu'Shan. The Chapter Master's decree was law. His eyes and ears, however, could not be everywhere.

'Doubtless, he expected his own name to be called,' Dak'ir continued with a trace of rancour.

'It's possible. He regarded Kadai as highly as you, brother-sergeant. He may not think his heritor worthy,' said Ba'ken. 'There's talk that Iagon has begun to gather support for his patron amongst the other sergeants.'

Dak'ir jerked his head towards Ba'ken abruptly.

'He would challenge the leadership of the company before Kadai's replacement is even sworn in?'

A few heads amongst the gathering on Dak'ir's side turned as he spoke a little too loudly. The sergeant lowered his voice.

'If enough of the sergeants support him, he could argue for Tu'Shan to make him captain instead.'

'It's a rumour. It may be nothing.'

'He wouldn't dare.' Dak'ir bristled at the thought of Tsu'gan's lobbying for power. It wasn't that the sergeant was unworthy. Dak'ir acknowledged Tsu'gan's prowess and courage, his tactical acumen. But he was also a glory hunter who sought advancement aggressively. Ambition was laudable, it drove you to excel, but when it was at the expense of others... Moreover, Dak'ir was annoyed because he had heard no inkling of this. Unlike Ba'ken, he was not so well liked. In many respects he was the outcast that Tsu'gan described. He could inspire his men, lead them into battle, and they would die for him as he would for them. But he lacked Ba'ken's common touch, his broad empathy with the warriors of 3rd Company. Sometimes that left him on the periphery where internal politicking was concerned.

Dak'ir felt his ire for the sergeant anew, his burning eyes echoing his belligerent mood. Tsu'gan caught his gaze and returned it, proud and imperious standing amongst the Firedrakes and Tu'Shan himself.

Something sharp and insistent pricked at Dak'ir's senses and he averted his attention from Tsu'gan to search for its source.

Clutching the hilt of his sheathed force sword, Librarian Pyriel regarded Dak'ir intently. A student of Master Vel'cona, Pyriel was an accomplished Epistolary-level psyker. Arcane power armour, accented by green robes and esoteric sigils, encased his body. The circlet of a psychic hood arced around the back of his skull. Tomes and scrolls were chained to his battle-plate, which was deep blue in the manner of the Librarium, and he wore a long drakescale cape. A faint trace of psychic resonance crackled cerulean blue across his eyes as Pyriel's gaze narrowed.

Whatever his interest in him, Dak'ir found the examination unsettling. Perhaps Pyriel had taken up Fugis's mantle as watcher, given the distraction of the Apothecary's grief. Determined he would not be cowed, Dak'ir stared back, inwardly squirming beneath the Librarian's intensity. In the end it was Pyriel who relented, smiling thinly first before looking away.

Dak'ir followed his eye to a long narrow walkway above the ridge of stone where he and his brothers now stood. A robed figure was standing in the centre of the dais at the end of the walkway, his features shadowed by a heavy cowl. Only the fire in his eyes was visible. From the darkness behind him, a pair of brander-priests emerged silently. As one, they gripped the rough fabric of his apparel and pulled it to the ground.

Veteran Brother N'keln stood before them, head upraised. He was naked apart from the tribal sash preserving his dignity. Fresh scars were burned into his bare skin; they were the marks of a captain, seared onto his chest and right shoulder by the brander-priests.

The dais was not merely as it appeared. A disc was sunken into the rock, the internal circuitry within it concealed behind stark grey metal. As the serfs retreated, a pillar of fire erupted from the dais, engulfing the ascendant completely. The inferno lasted seconds, and as the flames died away N'keln was crouched on one knee with his head bowed. Smoke rose from his coal-black body but he was not burned, rather he shimmered with inner strength.

Chapter Master Tu'Shan stirred from his throne and stood.

'Through elemental fire is our mettle gauged and our devotion measured,' he declared. His voice was deep and resonant, as if it had come from the soul of the earth. It held a molten core of inspirational passion, and carried such power and authority that all who heard it were instantly humbled. 'Endurance and fortitude are the tenets of our lore and creed. Sacrifice and honour are the virtues we Fire-born uphold. With humility do we guard against hubris and our own vainglory.' Tu'Shan focused all of his attention on N'keln, who had yet to lift his gaze.

'Vulkan's fire beats in my breast...' the Chapter Master began, thumping his plastron with a gauntleted fist and making the sign for the hammer.

N'keln looked up for the first time since his fiery baptism.

'With it, I shall smite the foes of the Emperor,' he concluded.

Tu'Shan smiled broadly, and its warmth spread to his blazing eyes.

'Brother-sergeant no longer...' he intoned, brandishing a massive thunder hammer in one huge fist. 'Rise, brother-captain.'

THE VAULT OF Remembrance was all but empty. Echoing footsteps reverberated off the walls from solitary Salamanders going about their rituals or serfs performing chores. From the catacombs below came the sound of forges, as anvils were struck and metals honed, travelling through the rocky core of Hesiod's Chapter Bastion as a dulcet ring.

Hesiod was amongst the seven Sanctuary Cities of Nocturne. These great colonies, their foundations bored deep into the earth and rooted in the hardest bedrock of the planet, were based on the seven settlements of Nocturne's tribal kings.

Each of the seven Salamander Chapter Bastions resided in one of these cities. Devoted to the seven noble companies, they were austere and hollow places.

Gymnasia provided for the rigours of the Astartes' daily training regimen, and a Reclusium, presided over by the company's Chaplain, saw to their spiritual needs. In the lower levels were the solitoriums, little more than stark oubliettes used for battle-mediation and honour-scarring. Dormitories were sparse and mainly inhabited by serfs. Armouries held weapons and other war materiel, though these were mainly for neophytes – seasoned battle-brothers often maintained their own arsenals, situated at private domiciles amongst the populace of Nocturne where they could better act as their custodians and protectors. Refectories provided repast, and in the great halls rare gatherings could be held. An Apothecarion saw to the wounded. Oratoriums and Librariums were the seats of knowledge and learning, though the culture of Nocturne stressed greater importance on the experience and the tempering fire of the battlefield.

Catacombs ran through a vast undercroft where the emanating swelter of the forges could be felt, the soot of foundries and the hard metal stench of smelteries absorbed into every pore. The great forges, temples of iron and steel, where an anvil not an altar was the pillar of worship, were ubiquitous across all of Nocturne. The hours of devotion spent in the cloying heat, through the lathered sweat and thickening smoke, were as crucial to a Salamander as any battle-rite.

It was in the highest echelon of the Chapter Bastion that two warriors in green battle-plate chose to reflect and offer supplication, in the Vault of Remembrance, in memoriam for their slain captain.

The temple was a vast, echoing space. The harmonies of phonolite-chimes echoed off its darkened walls. Hewn from volcanic aphanite, they rose up like geodesic intrusions and tapered off into a craterous aperture that lay open to Nocturne's fiery-orange sky. Black and fathomless obsidian formed a hexagonal expanse, serving as the massive chamber's floor. Stout columns of deep red felsite buttressed the half-ceiling, shot through with veins of fluorescent adamite.

The rare volcanic rocks and minerals used to fashion the magnificent temple were harvested after the Time of Trial, and the stark and frigid winter that followed in its wake. Such artefacts of geological beauty could be found throughout Nocturne. The most precious were protected within the stout walls of the Sanctuary Cities and their void shield generators.

Iron braziers around the chamber's edge gave it a fiery cast, flickering in the lustrous faces of the polished rock. It appeared luminous and abyssal in the light's reflection – a diabolic temple raised from the bowels of the world. At its nexus a giant pillar of fire roared, tendrils of flame spilling and lashing from a core of white heat. The two warriors knelt at it, insignificant before the conflagration.

'As Kadai passes, so does N'keln ascend,' Dak'ir uttered solemnly, his onyx skin tinged in dark amber by the memorial flame. In his gauntleted fist he clutched a votive offering that he threw into the fire. It ignited quickly, and he felt the heat of its immolation briefly against his downcast face.

'History will remember him,' Ba'ken replied in a reverent voice, burning his own tribute.

The ceremony of Interment and Ascension had ended with N'keln accepting his captain's battle-plate. Tradition held that whenever an old captain died and another took his mantle, the ascendant would wear the previous incumbent's armour. Ordinarily, the slain Salamander would be incinerated in the pyreum, a massive crematoria forge beneath the mountain. According to Promethean lore, the essence of the departed would be passed on into the armour when his ashen remains were offered up on the pyre-slab and he was returned to the mountain. Ko'tan Kadai had met his end before a traitor's multi-melta. There had been little left of him to salvage, so his armour was given unto the mountain instead. It seemed a fitting offering. N'keln's armour then was forged anew, an artificer suit fashioned by Brother Argos, Master of the Forge.

After N'keln had been reborn from fire as captain and clad in his battle-plate, the congregation of Salamanders had disbanded. Tu'Shan and the few Firedrakes that had been present for the ritual boarded Thunderhawk gunships idling on the Scorian Plain beyond the mountain. Tearing into the sky, they were bound for Prometheus and the fortress monastery stationed upon Nocturne's sister moon where the greater matters of Chapter and galaxy were Tu'Shan's chief concern.

For the others there was the slow pilgrimage back to Hesiod and a return to their duties.

3rd Company had earned a brief respite from campaign until their next mustering. Tempering of spirit and the remoulding of purpose was needed in the battle-cages, chapels and at anvils. Before the resumption of their training routines, Dak'ir and Ba'ken had come to the Vault of Remembrance. Like many others of 3rd Company, they did so to pay their respects and honour the dead.

'These are grave times.' Ba'ken appeared morose. It was unlike him.

A hot wind was blowing off the northern Acerbian Sea, bringing with it the stench of burning ash and the acrid tang of sulphur. Eddies swirled the blackening parchment Ba'ken had placed before the flame, slowly pulling it apart and turning it into ash. It reminded him of the deep fractures within their company left in the wake of Kadai's death.

'As one life ends, another begins. As it is before the forge flame, metamorphosis is existence in transformation,' a calm and thoughtful voice answered. 'Where is your Nocturnean pragmatism, Sol? You led me to believe you hailed from Themis.'

Ba'ken smirked away his melancholy.

'Pragmatism, maybe, but the sons of Themis are no philosophers, brother,' he offered dryly, a flash of fire lighting his eyes as he craned his neck to acknowledge Emek. 'We are warriors,' he added, clenching his fist in mock machismo. Themis was another of the Sanctuary Cities, well-known for its warrior-tribes and the tall, wide stock of men it produced, a trait augmented through the genetic process of becoming a Space Marine.

Emek smiled broadly showing his teeth, stark white against his onyx skin, and knelt down beside his brothers.

'Would you prefer a verse from the Promethean Opus, instead?' he countered.

Brother Emek, like his late captain, hailed from Hesiod. He had a noble, slightly studious bearing. His hair was carmine red and shaved into thin chevrons that extended across his entire skull and arrowed down to his forehead. Younger than Ba'ken – who had served almost a century in the Chapter but had no ambition for advancement – and even Dak'ir, Emek had an eternal look of curiosity in his eyes. Certainly, he possessed an impressive capacity for learning and an even greater desire. His knowledge of Promethean lore, its philosophy and history, and the culture of Nocturne, was lauded even by the Chapter's Chaplains.

'As worthy an account as that is, brother,' replied Dak'ir, 'I think that now is not the time for a recitation.'

Chastened, Emek lowered his head.

'My apologies, brother-sergeant.'

'None are necessary, Emek.'

Adopting an attitude of penitence, Emek nodded and cast his own offering into the fire. For a few moments, the three were joined in silent reverie, the crackling of the votive flame a chorus to their solitude.

'My brothers, I…' Emek began, but whatever he was about to say caught in his throat when he looked past the flame to the figure standing beyond it.

'Kadai's death has hit us all hard, brother,' Dak'ir told him, having followed Emek's gaze, 'Even him.'

'I thought his heart was cut from stone.'

'It would seem not,' offered Ba'ken, mouthing a silent litany before rising to his feet.

'This enmity with the renegades has exacted a heavy toll. Do you think this is an end to it?'

Dak'ir was interrupted before he could reply.

'Not for us,' snarled Tsu'gan, his belligerence unmistakable.

Dak'ir got to his feet to face his fellow sergeant, who was stalking towards them across the obsidian plaza.

'Or for them,' Dak'ir added, eyes narrowing when he saw Iagon following behind, the ever faithful lackey.

Iagon was gaunt and slight, his face etched with a perpetual sneer. He blamed this affectation on an encounter during the Gehemnat Uprising on Kryon IV when, during the cleansing of a genestealer infestation, a brood creature's bio-acid had severed some of the muscles in his face, leaving his mouth permanently down-turned.

Dak'ir thought it appropriate for one such as Iagon. He kept his gaze on the two approaching Salamanders, vaguely aware of the immense presence of Ba'ken at his back.

'This retribution is old, Emek,' Dak'ir told the other battle-brother. 'It goes back to Moribar when Ushorak died. I don't think Nihilan or the Dragon Warriors will easily lay the death of their captain to rest. I doubt even Kadai's destruction would have slaked their thirst for vengeance. No,' he decided, 'this will end when one of us is dead.'

'Annihilated,' added Tsu'gan unnecessarily, by way of elaboration for Emek's benefit. 'The entire Chapter – them or us.'

'Are you expecting a long war of attrition then, Brother Tsu'gan?' Dak'ir asked.

Tsu'gan's lip curled in distaste.

'War is eternal, *Ignean*. Though, I would expect no less from one of your craven ancestry to desire eventual peace.'

'There are many upon this planet and others across the Imperium who would welcome it,' Dak'ir returned, his ire rising.

Tsu'gan sniffed his contempt.

'They are not warriors, brother, like *us*. Without war, *we* are obsolete. War is my clenched fist, the burning in my marrow. It is glory and renown. It gives us purpose. I *embrace* it! What would we do if all the wars were to end? What use are we to *peace?*' He spat the last word, as if it stuck in his mouth, and paused. 'Well?'

Dak'ir felt his jaw tighten.

'I shall tell you,' Tsu'gan whispered. 'We would turn on one another.'

Silence followed, charged with the threat of something violent and ugly.

Tsu'gan's smile was mirthless and goading.

Dak'ir's hand went almost of its own volition to the combat blade sheathed at his hip.

The smile turned into a malicious grin.

'Perhaps you have some warrior's blood in you after all, Ignean…'

'Come now, brothers.' Iagon's voice dispelled the red haze that had settled over Dak'ir's vision. He spread his arms in an expansive gesture, ever the ostensible conciliator. 'We are all kin here. The Vault of Remembrance is no place for recusation or rancour. The temple is a haven, somewhere to absolve one's self of guilt or self-recrimination, isn't that so, Brother-Sergeant Dak'ir?' He added the barb with a viper's smile.

Ba'ken bristled, poised to act, when Dak'ir extended a steadying hand to placate him. He had already released his grip on the combat blade, seeing the act for what it was – a simple taunt. Emek, uncertain what to do, merely watched impotently.

'It is more than that, Iagon,' Dak'ir replied, side-stepping the snare Iagon had laid for him. He turned his attention back to Tsu'gan, making it clear that the lapdog was beneath his concern.

Dak'ir drew close, but Tsu'gan held his gaze and didn't flinch.

'I know what you are doing,' he said. 'N'keln is a worthy captain for this company. I warn you, do not besmirch Kadai's memory by opposing him.'

'I'll do what is best for the company and the Chapter, as is my right and duty,' Tsu'gan returned vehemently. Stepping closer still, he snarled through clenched teeth, 'I told you once I would not forget your complicity in my brother-captain's death. Nothing has changed. But question my loyalty and devotion to Kadai again, and I *will* cut you down where you stand.'

Dak'ir knew he'd gone too far with that last remark, so capitulated at once. Not out of fear, but shame. To challenge Tsu'gan was one thing; to call his fealty and respect for their old captain into doubt was unfounded.

Satisfied he'd made his point Tsu'gan backed down too and went to move around his brother.

'How long has he been here, like that?' he asked, looking beyond the memorial flame. There was the faintest trace of sadness in his voice.

The Vault of Remembrance was laid bare to the elements at its north-facing wall. An archway of white dacite engraved with the effigies of firedrakes led out onto a long basalt promontory that overlooked the sun-bleached sands of the Pyre Desert. Silhouetted in the evening glow was Apothecary Fugis, as motionless as a sentinel.

'Since we arrived,' said Dak'ir, and felt the spark of belligerence between them ebbing, if only for a few moments. 'I haven't seen him stir even once.'

'His grief consumes him.' Emek had turned to watch the Apothecary too.

Tsu'gan's face creased into a disdainful scowl and he looked away. 'What use is grief? It affords us nothing. Can grief smite our enemies or protect the borders of our galaxy? Will it resist the predations of the warp? I think not.' With barely concealed contempt, he nonchalantly cast the votive scroll he had clutched in his fist into the memorial fire. It slipped and fell out of the flame's caldera where the rest of the ash gathered, only half-burnt. For a moment, Tsu'gan almost went to retrieve it but then stopped himself. 'I have no use for grief,' he muttered quietly. Then he turned and left the Vault of Remembrance, Iagon following in his wake.

When Tsu'gan's back was turned Dak'ir did it for him, mouthing a silent oath of remembrance as the parchment was consumed.

Fugis stared out across the vastness of the Pyre Desert. He was standing upon an overhang of dark rock that was often used as a natural landing pad for the Salamanders' gunships and other light vessels. The strip was empty today, apart from the Apothecary, and Fugis welcomed the solace.

To the north beyond the arid desert region was the Acerbian Sea. Fugis saw it as a dim black line where the tall spire of Epimethus, Nocturne's only ocean-bound Sanctuary City, jutted like a dull blade. It was surrounded by other, much smaller satellites, the numerous drilling rigs and mineral harvesting platforms that raked the ocean floor or mined its deepest trenches for ore.

Out on the barren sands of the Pyre, he witnessed a sa'hrk, one of the desert's predator beasts, stalking a herd of sauroch. The lithe, saurian creature slithered low across the desolate plain, scurrying from the scattered rock clusters to draw close enough to its prey to strike. Oblivious to the danger, the sauroch herd ploughed on, their bulky, gristle-thick bodies swaying as they marched in file. The sa'hrk waited for the end of the cattle trail to reach it, then pounced. A bull-like sauroch was wrestled bodily to the ground, hooting plaintively as the predator levered aside the bone-plates encasing its neck to reach the soft flesh beneath. It gorged itself quickly, tearing strands of bloody meat with its iron-hard jaws and chugging them down its bloated gullet. The rest of the herd mewled and snorted in panic. Some of the cattle-beasts stampeded; others merely stood petrified. To the sa'hrk, it mattered not. It took its fill and merely sloped away, leaving the carcass to rot in the sun.

'The weak will always be preyed upon by the strong,' uttered Fugis. 'Is that not correct, brother?'

Dak'ir stepped into the Apothecary's eye line. Carrion creatures were already flocking to the dead sauroch, stripping it of whatever sustenance the sa'hrk had left them.

'Unless those with strength intercede on behalf of the weak, and protect them,' he countered, turning to regard his fellow Salamander directly. 'I didn't realise you were aware of my presence.'

'You've been standing there for the last fifteen minutes, Dak'ir. I was aware. I merely chose not to acknowledge you.'

An uncomfortable silence followed, filled only by the low, insistent thrum of Hesiod's void shield generators. Those of Epimethus to the north and Themis to the east added to the dull cacophony, audible even across the expanse of the desert and the shelter of the mountains.

'On Stratos, we were weak.' Fugis couldn't keep the spite out of his voice, as he said it. 'And the strong punished us for it.'

'The renegades were not strong, brother,' insisted Dak'ir. 'They were cowards, striking from the shadows whilst our backs were turned, and cutting him down–'

'Without honour,' snapped Fugis, turning on Dak'ir before he could finish, a mask of rage drawn over his thin countenance. 'They slew him, as that sa'hrk slew the sauroch, like swine, like cattle.'

The Apothecary nodded slowly, his anger usurped by bitterness and fatalism.

'We *were* weak on Stratos… but it began on Moribar,' he rasped. 'I curse Kadai for that. For *his* weakness then, that he did not see and end the threat Ushorak presented, the loyalty he had instilled in Nihilan, when he had the chance.'

Dak'ir was taken aback by Fugis's reaction. He had never seen him like this before. The Apothecary was calm, clinical even. It kept him sharp. To hear him speak like this was unsettling. Something had died inside him, burned along with Kadai's remains on the pyre-slab. Dak'ir thought it might be hope.

Fugis closed on him. It was the second time that one of his battle-brothers had approached him like this today. The brother-sergeant didn't care for it.

'*You* saw it, brother. You dreamed of this danger for almost four decades.' Fugis gripped Dak'ir's pauldrons intensely. The Apothecary's eyes were wide, almost maddened. 'I only wish we had known then what we know now…' Fugis's voice trailed away. Whatever grief-fuelled vigour had seized his body ebbed with it, as he let his arms fall back to his sides and faced the setting sun.

'Perhaps you should visit Chaplain Elysius. There is…' Dak'ir stopped talking. Fugis wasn't listening to him anyway. His eyes were glassy like rubies as he stared across the desert.

'Brother-sergeant.'

Dak'ir exhaled his relief at Ba'ken's voice. He turned to see the burly Salamander standing a few metres away.as if he had been there a while, not approaching out of respect.

'Brother-Captain N'keln is here in Hesiod,' Ba'ken continued. 'He wishes to speak with you.'

'Stay with him until you are called,' Dak'ir husked beneath his breath on his way back into the Vault of Remembrance, with a half-glance in the Apothecary's direction.

'Of course, brother,' Ba'ken replied and waited on the Thunderhawk platform for his sergeant's return.

SURROUNDED BY DARKNESS, Tsu'gan bowed his head and beckoned the brander-priest with an outstretched hand.

'Come,' he uttered, voice echoing inside the close confines of the solitorium. The reverberation faded, swallowed by the stygian black and the shifting of fire-wrapped coals beneath Tsu'gan's bare feet.

Iagon had already removed his power armour, securing it in an antechamber where he awaited his sergeant's return.

Tsu'gan stood bare-chested, wearing only a pair of training fatigues borrowed from the Chapter Bastion gymnasia. Steam cascaded off his body in waves, diffusing the blood-red gleam from his eyes. Fresh scarification throbbed against his seared skin where his brander-priest had already applied the rod. Still, Tsu'gan beckoned for more.

'Zo'kar!' he snapped, gesturing agitatedly with his hand. His voice came out in a harsh whisper. 'Burn me again.'

'My lord, I...' the brander-priest quailed hesitantly.

'Obey me, serf,' Tsu'gan hissed through clenched teeth. 'Apply the rod. Do it, now.' His tone was almost imploring.

The Space Marine's mind was in turmoil. He regretted not going back, on seeing to the offering he had so casually discarded into the memorial flame. Kadai was worthy of his reverence, not his scorn, however it might be directed. He recalled the moment in the temple on Stratos when he had confronted Nihilan.

You fear everything...

The remembered words were like cold steel rammed into his flesh. For in some hollow of his heart, some hidden vault the Dragon Warrior had uncovered and cruelly opened, Tsu'gan knew them to be true. He hated himself for it. He had failed his lord and thereby realised his greatest fear. Purgation was the only answer to frailty. Kadai was dead because...

Pain filled his senses, together with the stench of his own tortured skin. It was clean and pure – Tsu'gan revelled in it, sought solace in flagellation by fire.

'Scour it away, Zo'kar,' he husked. 'Scour it all away...'

The brander-priest obeyed, afraid of his master's wrath, searing again the lines of the Salamander's old victories and past achievements. It had gone beyond ceremony. There was no honour in what Tsu'gan was deliberately subjecting himself to. This was masochism; a shameful act brought about by his guilt.

By the time Zo'kar was finished and the rod had almost cooled, Tsu'gan was breathing hard. His body was alive with agony, the heat of the brand's attentions coming off him in a haze. The entire chamber was redolent of burning, and scorched flesh.

Masochism was becoming addiction.

Tsu'gan saw again the moment of his captain's demise. Watched his body immolated by the multi-melta's bright beam. His eyes hurt at the remembered sight of it.

Dragging air into his chest, Tsu'gan could only rasp. 'Again…'

In his half-delirium, he didn't notice the other figure in the room watching him from the secrecy of shadows.

DAK'IR FOUND HIS captain in one of the Chapter Bastion's minor strategium chambers. It was an austere room, bereft of banners, triumphal plaques or trophies. It was hard-edged, practical and bleak, much like N'keln himself.

Leaning over a simple metal altar-table, the captain scrutinised galactic maps and star-charts with Brother-Sergeant Lok.

Lok commanded one of 3rd Company's three Devastator squads, the Incinerators. A Badab War veteran, he carried black and yellow slashes on his left kneepad to commemorate the armour he had worn during the conflict. Lok was hard-faced and grim, two centuries of war calcifying his resolve. A long scar ran down the left side of his face from forehead to chin bisecting the sergeant's two platinum service studs. This he had received fighting a boarding action on an Executioner's battle barge, *Blade of Perdition*, during Badab. The bionic eye on the opposite side of his grizzled visage was implanted much earlier after the scouring of Ymgarl when he was only just a full-fledged battle-brother. Lok had been 3rd Company then, too, assigned as part of a small task force to assist 2nd Company who were mustered for the campaign in their entirety.

Lok reminded Dak'ir of an old drake, its skin chewed by the ravages of age, and as tough as cured leather. To see his dour expression, one might think he felt like one too.

The veteran sergeant's left arm was encased in a power fist. Lok rested the cumbersome but brutal looking weapon on the altar-table as he attended to matters of tactics with his captain. What campaign or mission they might be masterminding, Dak'ir didn't know. Many in the Chapter believed Lok should have been promoted to the 1st Company by now, but Tu'Shan was wise and knew that he was more valuable to 3rd Company as an experienced sergeant. To Dak'ir's mind, that decision had proven an astute one.

Lok looked up at Dak'ir as he entered and gave a near imperceptible nod of his head.

'Sir, you summoned me,' the sergeant said to his captain, after bowing.

Disturbed from his planning, N'keln appeared distracted at first. As he straightened, the captain's full panoply of war was revealed. Close up, the artificer armour he wore was rarefied indeed. Encrusted with the sigils of drakes and wrought with super-dense bands of adamantium that bound its reinforced ceramite plates, it was a masterpiece. A gorget lay discarded on the altar-table, evidently a portion of the suit N'keln had removed for improved dexterity in his neck. The battle-helm rested next to it, traditional MkVII in style but sleeker with the mouth grille replaced by a fanged drake snout. A mantle of salamander hide, the armour's last concomitant element, was hanging reverently in one corner upon a nondescript mannequin.

'Thank you, Sergeant Lok, that will be all for now,' said N'keln at last.

'My lord,' Lok replied, adding, 'brother-sergeant,' for Dak'ir's benefit on his way out.

N'keln waited until Lok was gone before he spoke again.

'These are inauspicious times, Dak'ir. To assume such a heavy burden as this was… *unexpected*.'

Dak'ir was lost for words at the sudden frankness.

N'keln went back to his charts for a moment, searching for a distraction.

Dak'ir's gaze strayed to the sheathed sword at his captain's side. N'keln caught the look in his sergeant's eyes.

'Magnificent, isn't it,' he said, drawing the weapon.

Master crafted, the power sword hummed with an electric-blue tang rippling along its gleaming face. Consisting of two separate blades, conjoined at points along each inner edge, it was unique. The hilt was masterfully constructed with a dragon claw guard and drake-headed pommel, plated in gold.

As august as the power sword was, it was N'keln's right and privilege to take up his old captain's weapon too. Dak'ir's understanding was that Kadai's thunder hammer was repairable. He wondered why N'keln had refused it.

'I confess, I prefer this.' After sheathing the blade and setting it back down, N'keln patted the stock of his worn bolter, lying opposite. A great many kill-markings were etched along the hard, black metal of the gun and the skull and eagle hung from its grip on votive chains.

'I know of the discontent amongst the sergeants,' he said suddenly. His eyes were flat as he regarded Dak'ir. 'Kadai's legacy casts a long shadow. I cannot help but be eclipsed by it,' he admitted. 'I only hope I am worthy of his memory. That my succession was justified.'

Dak'ir was taken aback. He had not expected his captain to be so forthright.

'You were Brother-Captain Kadai's second-in-command, sir. It is only right and proper you succeeded him.'

N'keln nodded sagely, but at Dak'ir's or his own inner counsel the brother-sergeant could not tell.

'As you know, Brother Vek'shan was slain on Stratos. I am in need of a Company Champion. Your record, your loyalty and determination in battle are almost peerless, Dak'ir. Furthermore, I trust your integrity implicitly.' The captain's eyes conveyed his certainty. 'I want to promote you to the Inferno Guard.'

Dak'ir was wrong-footed for a second time. When he shook his head, he saw the disappointment on N'keln's face.

'Sir, on Stratos I failed to protect Brother-Captain Kadai and that mistake cost his life and damaged this company into the bargain. I will serve you with faith and loyalty, but with the deepest regret I cannot accept this honour.'

N'keln turned away. After exhaling his displeasure he said, 'I could order you to do it.'

'I ask you not to, sir. I belong with my squad.'

N'keln regarded him closely for a few moments, making his decision.

'Very well,' he said at last, chagrined but willing to concede to his sergeant's request. 'There is something else,' he added. 'The other sergeants will hear of this soon enough, but since you are already here... I wish to heal the wounds in this company, Dak'ir. So, we are returning to the Hadron Belt. There we will scour the stars for any sign of the renegades. I mean to find them and destroy them.'

The Hadron Belt was the last known location of the Dragon Warriors. There it was that the Salamanders fought them on Stratos, or rather were ambushed by them and their former captain assassinated.

'With respect, sir, our last encounter with Nihilan was months ago. They will be far from there by now, likely returned to the Eye of Terror.' Dak'ir looked down at the maps on the altar-table and saw the dense and expansive region of the Hadron Belt. 'Even if, for some inscrutable reason, the Dragon Warriors still linger there, the Belt is a vast tract of space. It would take years to search it all with any certainty.'

N'keln allowed a brief pause, deciding if he should say anything further.

'Librarian Pyriel has been probing the star clusters out in the Belt and detected a resonance, a psychic echo of Nihilan's presence. We will use that as our marker.'

Dak'ir frowned.

'It is a slim hope to find them on such evidence. This remnant Brother Pyriel has found could be weeks old. What makes you think they will still be lurking in-system?'

'Whatever was begun on Moribar with Ushorak's death, it continued with the assassination of Kadai. Both planets are part of the Hadron Belt, which suggests that the Dragon Warriors have some lair situated there, from which they can launch their raids. Without the Imperium and the forges of Mars to sustain their war materiel, the renegades will need to get it from somewhere else. Piracy and raiding is the only way.'

'A slim hope – yes, I agree,' added N'keln. 'But a solitary flame when kindled can become a raging conflagration.' The captain's eyes flared with sudden zeal. 'It isn't over, Dak'ir. The Dragon Warriors have cut us badly. We must strike next and without restraint, so we are not blooded again.'

N'keln's final words before he dismissed Dak'ir sounded slightly desperate, and did nothing to assuage the brother-sergeant's own burgeoning doubts.

'We need this mission, Dak'ir. To heal the wounds of this company and restore our brotherhood.'

Dak'ir left the strategium feeling uneasy. The meeting with N'keln had unsettled him. The captain's candour, the admission of his own failings and deep-seated doubts, though masked, was disquieting, for no other reason than he now believed that despite his arrogance and vainglory Tsu'gan might be right. N'keln was not ready for the honour that had already been bestowed upon him, and he was brother-captain in name alone.

CHAPTER TWO

I
Dragon Hunting

THE DREAM HAD *changed*.

Blood soaked the walls of the Aura Hieron temple, giving off an abattoir stink. It was copper and old iron tanging the tongue, and something else, something just beyond Dak'ir's reach…

Silence, as deafening as an atomic storm, filled the empty pantheon devoted to false idols. Dak'ir thought he was alone. Then in the distance, a span that seemed impossibly long for the small temple, he saw him.

Kadai was fighting the daemon-spawn.

And he was losing.

Lightning thrashed around his thunder hammer, streaking from its head and roiling down the haft. It coursed over Kadai's armour in a rippling wave, but was curiously quiescent. The daemon-spawn was indistinct, the edges of its reality blurred into a tenebrous void of clawed tendrils and raw malice.

Dak'ir was running noiselessly, crossing what felt like kilometres, when the thunder came. Faint at first, it built as a

45

tremor until eventually it shook the heavens and sound rushed back in a cacophonous crescendo.

Through the conceit of hallucination, Dak'ir reached Kadai in time to see him smite the hell spawn down. Lightning arcs blasted its repugnant form until its grasp upon the material realm slipped utterly and it was claimed back by the warp.

The feat had taken its toll. Kadai was hurt. Breath wheezed in and out of his lungs, the genetic augmentation of his body failing to restore him. Armour, rent and torn in dozens of places, hung slack like shed skin about to crack and fall away.

'Stand with me, brother…' Kadai's voice was like gravel scraped over rock. There was the faintest gurgle of blood in the back of his throat.

He held out a trembling hand.

'Stand with me…'

Dak'ir went to reach for him when the stench of something on a sudden breeze pricked at his nostrils, making them burn.

It was sulphur.

A feeling, alien and inchoate, gnawed at the back of Dak'ir's mind.

Fear?

He was Astartes. He did not feel fear. Dak'ir quashed it beneath a resolve of steel.

Something was moving at the periphery of his vision. A sound like cracked parchment and worn leather filled Dak'ir's senses. Twisting, he saw a shadow slithering low and fast through the dark alcoves that surrounded the temple. An impression pressed at the fringe of his mind… incarnadine scales, a long serpentine body.

Dak'ir spun, trying to follow the spectre's path. A barbed tail – huge, like that of some primordial lizard – disappeared from view.

A crackle of embers, the reek of burning from behind him made Dak'ir turn. A spit of flame died: a silhouette of something large and monstrous lurking in the alcoves faded with it.

'Stand with me...'

Kadai had to heave the breath into his lungs to speak. He had slumped to one knee, using his thunder hammer as support. Blood eked from the cuts in his armour, staining it an ugly dark red. Still he reached out for his battle-brother.

Dak'ir's gaze flicked back to the creature. He felt its malice like a tangible thing, tracked its position from the shifting shadows and the reek of its foul breath, like old blood and decay.

He cried out –

'You shall not have him!'

– and rushed in to face it.

Chainsword whirring, Dak'ir barrelled into the darkness, tracking the monster's forbidding shadow. It shifted slightly as he came at it. There was the suggestion of a maw, blade-long fangs, settling wings...

Then it was gone.

White heat flared in his mind and Dak'ir turned, knowing in his heart that he was already too late.

The monster was behind him, looming over Kadai who was still reaching, seemingly oblivious to the danger.

Red scales shimmered like blood, immense membranous wings unfolded like old, dark leather. A thickly muscled body squatted slovenly, its barrel-chest expanding with a wheezing, sucking breath. Thin plumes of smoke trickled upwards from a long snout, its maw filled with sharp and yellow fangs. Hot saliva dripped from the beast's mouth, a slowly widening crack as its jaws parted, splashing against the ground with an acidic hiss.

Dak'ir ran, desperate to put himself between this monster and his stricken captain.

The dragon opened its jaws fully and Kadai was engulfed by an inferno, a blazing wall of fire thrown up in Dak'ir's path.

Through the haze Kadai and the beast became rippling heat shadows, dark brown and indistinct. Slowly the silhouette of *the dragon changed, becoming humanoid. It was now a vast armoured warrior, a fallen Angel of Death, a renegade, and the raging flame was the incandescent beam of a multi-melta.*

Kadai roared in agony and Dak'ir's anguished cry joined it, merging into a unified bellow of pain.

'Nooooooo!'

Dak'ir ran on – at least he would claim his vengeance – but found he was encumbered by his armour, so slow and heavy that the ground gave way beneath his feet and he fell…

The temple bled away, replaced by darkness and the sensation of crippling heat against his face. His skin was burning, alive with fire. The pain was intense, tearing at the left side of Dak'ir's face. He tried to cry out but his tongue had become ash. He tried to move but his arms and legs were blackened bones. As the last vestiges of his mind gave in to agony, he realised he was on Kadai's pyre-slab with the fire raging around him. He was sinking into the river of lava. The pain was almost unbearable as Dak'ir was fully submerged below the surface. Utter blackness swallowed him.

Then nothing. No heat, or fire, or pain. Merely silence and the absence of being.

A slash of red, the rancid whiff of decay in his nostrils. Kadai's face flashed before him, bloody and gaunt, half destroyed by the melta's beam.

His ghastly eyes were shut; his ruined mouth pinched as if stapled.

Kadai's voice emanated from the gloom, assailing Dak'ir from everywhere at once, yet his ragged lips did not part. 'Abandon hope, all ye who enter…'

Then the dead captain's eyes flicked open, revealing hollow sockets. His jaw gaped, as if the muscles holding it shut had been abruptly cut.

'Why did you let me die?'

DAK'IR JERKED AWAKE. Cold sweat veneered his face behind the hard plate of his battle-helm. Blinking, he caught fragments of his surroundings through his optical lenses.

Biological data, relayed from his power armour's internal systems and linked to his Space Marine physiology, materialised on his helmet display. Grainy crimson resolution revealed heightened breathing, accelerated blood pressure and a spiking heart rate. Myriad screens of diagnostic information flickered by between Dak'ir's slowing heartbeat, his ocular implant absorbing it all and storing it subconsciously.

Engaging a series of calming routines, hypno-conditioned for automatic and instinctive activation, Dak'ir fought his body back to equilibrium again. It was only then that he realised where he was.

The cool darkness of the Chamber Sanctuarine enveloped him. Re-scanning the battle-helm's data array, he accessed mission schemata and encoded briefings through a series of sub-vocal commands.

Dak'ir was aboard the *Fire-wyvern* on long-range reconnoitre in the Hadron Belt. The strike cruiser *Vulkan's Wrath* was several hours behind them in the gulf of realspace.

Engine noise of the gunship crashed back into being. Impelled by the on-board fusion reactor, the raucous din of turbofans assailed the Salamander's auditory canals. Dak'ir filtered out the worst of it via his Lyman's ear implant until he had readjusted a few seconds later. He was now fully aware. The dream-vision faded like dispersing smoke, though he caught fragments still – the dragon and Kadai's ruined face lingering like dirty splinters embedded in his subconscious.

Secured in a grav-harness, Dak'ir saw he was surrounded by his battle-brothers. Their eyes glowed faintly in the gloom like hot coals. Fully armed and armoured, the Salamanders' green armour shone dully. Bolters and blades were secured alongside them in reinforced steel racks. The heavier weapons – multi-meltas, flamers and heavy bolters – were stored in the Thunderhawk's armoury locker.

Nocturne was months away. Brother-Captain N'keln had assembled his sergeants, just as he told Dak'ir he would, and outlined his plan to return to the Hadron Belt. Librarian Pyriel had been present, explaining to the officers of 3rd Company that he had detected a faint but distinct psychic echo out amongst the debris and star clusters of the system. Brother-Captain N'keln conveyed his belief that this would lead them to Nihilan, the Dragon Warriors and a much needed victory.

Dak'ir remembered the look of disapproval on Tsu'gan's face as the mission was described. Though he kept his feelings well guarded from N'keln, Dak'ir knew that his fellow brother-sergeant thought the captain's gambit was desperate and a waste of time.

Tsu'gan hadn't decried him openly this time; his objections to N'keln's captaincy had already been heard twice over and rebuked by the Chapter Master on both occasions. No: despite his misgivings, Tsu'gan was loyal to the Chapter and ultimately respected command. Any reservations he had were kept to himself, for now.

From the collective mien of some of the other sergeants, notably those of the Tactical squads, barring Dak'ir's own, it was clear that Tsu'gan was not alone in his displeasure either. Dak'ir had thought again of the rumours to discredit their nascent captain, impeach him before Tu'Shan himself and sue for another to be installed in his place. Tsu'gan's ambition was voracious; Dak'ir was convinced that he did indeed covet command of 3rd Company.

'Restless, brother-sergeant?' inquired Bak'en, as if penetrating his thoughts, shifting slightly in his grav-harness to turn in Dak'ir's direction. Two blazing ovals of deep red loomed above him.

Deep space transit required that they wear their battle-helms at all times in case of a hull breach, their enclosed power armour suits combined with their mucranoid gland enabling survival in the vacuum of space until they could be recovered.

'I am, brother.' It wasn't a lie. Dak'ir simply didn't elaborate further. He'd caught Emek's attention too, the Salamander's gaze burning behind his ocular lenses as he regarded his brother-sergeant closely. 'Restless for combat,' he said to them both. 'There is no cause for concern.' Now Dak'ir lied.

The dream-visions had at first only surfaced during battle-meditation. They were rare, occurring once or twice every few months. Usually he dreamt of his childhood, of his life on Nocturne before becoming one of the Emperor's Astartes and venturing into the stars to bring flame and retribution to mankind's enemies. Many Space Marines didn't remember their existence prior to donning the black carapace. Recollection was often fragmentary and clouded, more a series of impressions than any distinct or ordered catalogue of history. Dak'ir's memories of his humanity were lucid and could be recalled with absolute clarity. It awakened a yearning in him, a sorrow for what he'd lost and a desire to reconnect with it on some fundamental level.

Occasionally he would remember Moribar, and his first mission. With the passing of years, these remembrances grew ever more frequent, violent and bloody. They were focused on death, but then Moribar revelled in the certainty of death. Mortality and the veneration of the fallen were its stock in trade. Dak'ir had been merely a scout back then, one of 7th Company. The grey sepulchre world had stained the Salamander somehow, a patina of grave dust coating him like a veil; it had wormed its way under his skin like the parasites consuming the rotten flesh of those buried beneath

Moribar's dark, forbidding earth. The deeds wrought on that terrible world had tarnished him deeper still, and like the unquiet dead they would not rest.

Nihilan would not rest.

At the thought of Moribar again, Dak'ir looked directly in front of him to where Tsu'gan was harnessed. Iagon was alongside him staring intently, his thoughts inscrutable. For once his brother-sergeant seemed far away and unaware of the brief exchange in the Thunderhawk's troop compartment. Twenty battle-brothers filled it, two squads of ten. Though the *Fire-wyvern* had alcoves for five more, they went unused. Venerable Brother Amadeus took up the advanced positions in the gunship's forward hold. The massive Dreadnought rocked quietly in his scaffold, subconsciously reliving old victories.

Crackling static fought for dominance over the thrumming of the Thunderhawk's engines as the internal vox-link attached to one of the gunship's bulkheads came to life.

'Brother-sergeants, report to the flight deck immediately.' Librarian Pyriel's silken voice was clipped, but unmistakable even above the din of rocket boosters. 'We have found something.'

Tsu'gan responded immediately. Unlocking his grav-harness by punching the release clasp, he levered the frame above his head and moved through the crowded chamber in the direction of the access stairs to the flight deck. He said nothing as he passed Dak'ir, who had just released his own harness with a hiss of escaping pressure.

Dak'ir wasn't about to question his brother's taciturnity. He was glad of the respite from Tsu'gan's choler. Instead, he followed swiftly in the brother-sergeant's wake and met both he and Pyriel in the upper forward section of the gunship.

The Librarian had his back to them, the clawed tips of his long salamander cloak just touching the floor. The curve of his psychic hood was starkly apparent above the generator of the power armour that dominated his upper back. Skeins of wires protruded from the arcane device and fed into the hidden recesses of his gorget. It reminded Dak'ir of the Salamander's exceptional talents and the precarious line that psykers, even those as accomplished as Pyriel, walked when they communed with the unknowable forces of the warp. The Epistolary's earlier scrutiny of Dak'ir during the ceremony of Interment and Ascension came to the forefront of the Salamander's mind. Had he been communing with the warp then, using his prodigious abilities to know his thoughts? There had been recognition in Pyriel's eyes when Dak'ir had met his gaze. Since that moment, and confronted with him again, the sergeant's sense of unease in the Librarian's presence hadn't lessened.

'It is incongruous,' said Pyriel, staring at something visible though the *Fire-wyvern's* occuliport.

The cockpit itself was a small space, made smaller still by the presence of the Librarian and two sergeants. Four Space Marine crew worked at the vessel's controls: a pilot sat in a grav-couch situated in the *Fire-wyvern's* stub nose; a navigator carefully monitored sensor arrays and complex avionics; a co-pilot and a gunner filled the other two positions. Each wore power armour but with their back-mounted generators removed – all of their suits' internal systems were maintained by the Thunderhawk's reactor.

Tsu'gan and Dak'ir came forward together to stand either side of Pyriel to see what had caught the Librarian's attention. Though still distant, but closing all the time, the sheer size of Pyriel's discovery almost filled their view. It was a ship, not a small fighter like the *Fire-wyvern* but a vast cruiser, akin to a floating city of dark metal.

The ship was evidently of Imperial design: long, but bulky like a long-hafted mace and with a slab-ended prow like a clenched fist. There was obvious damage to the hull, charred and laser-blackened as it was by munitions fire. Several of its numerous decks were breached. Ragged wounds in the metal were like the bites of some insect that had become infected, the vessel's flesh sloughed away by the contagion. Dormant weapon systems still held a threat, however – vast banks of laser batteries bowed down as if crestfallen along its ruined flanks. Auto-turrets, forward-arc lances and much larger ordnance made up the rest of the ship's guns. It was a fearsome array, but one laid low by some unknown enemy.

Clusters of factorum and munitoria comprised the vessel's hard-edged core, and gargantuan foundry-engines filled its belly. Deep crimson and black, and displaying the symbol of the cog, the cruiser had clearly originated on Mars. It was an Ark-class forge-ship, a vessel of the Adeptus Mechanicus.

'No energy signature from the shields or engines. No radiation reading from the reactor.' Pyriel's voice sounded tinny and echoing beneath his battle-helm. He exhaled a long breath, as if cogitating what might have befallen the stricken ship.

'The ship is dead.' Tsu'gan's tone betrayed his impatience.

'For some time, judging by the damage sustained to its port and aft,' added Dak'ir.

'Indeed,' Pyriel replied. 'But no enemy in sight, no plasma wake or warp signature. Adrift in realspace for us to find.'

'Have we tried hailing it?' asked Tsu'gan, clearly suspicious.

'No response,' Pyriel told him flatly.

'And is this the source of the psychic resonance?'

'No,' Pyriel confessed. 'I have not felt that for some time. This is different entirely.'

Tsu'gan's reply was pragmatic.

'Whatever the cause, vessels of that size don't simply appear in realspace crippled and without power. It's possible whoever did this is still lurking in-system. Pirates maybe?'

Dak'ir was only half-listening. He'd stepped forward to get a closer look.

'There is something on that ship,' he muttered.

The slight incline of Pyriel's head in Dak'ir's direction betrayed his interest.

'What makes you say that, brother?'

Dak'ir was taken slightly aback, though he kept the reaction from affecting his body language; he'd not realised he'd spoken out loud.

'An instinct, nothing more,' he confessed.

'Please elaborate.' The Librarian turned his scrutinising gaze upon him fully now. Dak'ir felt it like probing tendrils peeling back the layers of his subconscious, trying to get at the veiled secrets of his mind.

'Just something in my gut.'

Pyriel lingered for a moment, but then seemed content to leave it there and turned back to stare through the occuliport.

Tsu'gan's tone suggested a scowl.

'My gut is telling me we should not waste our efforts further. The Dragon Warriors are not here on this drifting husk. We should move on and let the *Vulkan's Wrath* decide what to do with her.'

'We should at least search for survivors,' Dak'ir countered adamantly.

'To what end, Ignean? The vessel is nothing but a floating tomb. There is no time for this.'

'What time do you think we need, Brother Tsu'gan?' asked Pyriel with a slight tilt of his head in the sergeant's direction. 'It has been weeks since we translated in-system, a few hours exploring this vessel won't–'

'*Archimedes Rex…*'

Pyriel turned slowly at the interruption.

'What did you say?' Tsu'gan snapped.

Dak'ir was pointing through the occuliport.

'There,' he said, as if he hadn't even heard his brother's words. He was indicating the vessel's port side as they slowly came abeam. The vessel's designation was stamped there in massive letters. 'It's the name of the ship.'

Tsu'gan was nonplussed as he turned on his battle-brother.

'What of it?'

'It's… *familiar.*'

'Meaning what, exactly – that you've seen it before? How is that even possible?'

Pyriel broke the sudden tension, evidently having come to a decision.

'Return to the Chamber Sanctuarine and prepare your squads for boarding.'

'My lord?' Tsu'gan could not see the logic in that, his pragmatism allowing him to put his issue with Dak'ir aside whilst he dealt with this latest concern.

Pyriel was disinclined to explain it to him. 'It's an order, brother-sergeant.'

Tsu'gan paused, chastened. 'Should we not at least wait for the *Vulkan's Wrath* and deploy via her boarding torpedoes?'

'No, brother-sergeant, I want to breach the Mechanicus ship quietly. Sensor arrays have discovered an open fighter bay, we can dock there.'

'I see no need for caution, Brother-Librarian,' he pressed. 'As I've said, the ship is dead.'

Pyriel's penetrating gaze fell on Tsu'gan.

'Is it, brother?'

* * *

II
Archimedes Rex

THE FIRE-WYVERN'S LANDING stanchions extended as the gunship came to rest in the darkness of the forge-ship's fighter bay.

Winking emergency lighting was strobing up and down the massive lozenge-shaped hangar, washing it blood-red. Squadrons of small vessels were revealed in the sporadic, visceral light.

The Salamanders deployed quickly, the rear embarkation ramp engaging as soon as they had docked. It hit the steel deck with a resounding clang, followed by the thunder of booted footsteps as the Space Marines dispersed. Mag-locks on the soles of their boots allowed them to traverse the plated floor in the absence of gravity, albeit in slightly syncopated fashion, and assume defensive positions. The manoeuvre was done by rote, but proved unnecessary. Aside from the host of dormant Mechanicus fighters, the hangar was empty. Only the echo of the Salamanders' approach, resonating off the stark, buttressed walls and up into a high, ribbed ceiling, gave any indication of life in the massive expanse.

'Leaving their fighter bay open and unsecured, someone must have fled in a hurry.' Emek's voice came through the comm-feed in Dak'ir's battle-helm. The two squads and the Librarian were synched with it in order to stay in constant contact.

'I doubt it,' growled Tsu'gan, already inspecting the many rows of small vessels. 'There looks to be a full complement here, all in dock. Nobody left this vessel. Or if they did, they didn't use any of these craft to do it.'

'Perhaps they were in the process of leaving,' offered Ba'ken, standing alongside one of the fighters. 'This glacis plate has been disengaged.'

It wasn't the only one. Several of the fighters had the glacis shields of their cockpits left unsecured; some were even wide open. It was as if the pilots, getting ready to launch, had left their posts and marched away to only the warp knew where.

'No pilots, no flight crew of any description,' added Dak'ir. 'Even the control consoles are empty.'

'It begs an obvious question–' Bak'en's query was left unspoken, as he was interrupted by the front embarkation ramp of the *Fire-wyvern* opening and easing to the deck with a metallic *clunk*.

Pounding footfalls announced the armoured form of Venerable Brother Amadeus. The Dreadnought was an imposing sight.

The mechanised exoskeleton that framed the armoured sarcophagus of Brother Amadeus was fraught with ribbed piping, cables and whining servos. Two broad and blocky shoulders sat either side of the Salamander's casket. Brave beyond measure, Amadeus had fallen at the siege of Cluth'nir against the hated eldar. Such were his deeds that the wreckage of his mortally wounded body was taken from the battlefield and interred within a suit of Dreadnought armour, so that Amadeus might fight on in the Chapter's name forever.

Looming over five metres in height and almost as wide, it wasn't just the sheer bulk of Amadeus's cyborganic body that made him formidable – both of his mechanised arms carried a potent weapon system. The left was a massive power fist that crackled with electrical discharge; the right bore a multi-melta, its barrel nose scorched black.

Ba'ken shifted uncomfortably at the sight of the Dreadnought, though only Brother Emek noticed it.

'*In the name of Vulkan,*' Amadeus boomed in automated diction, having only recently been awakened.

The Salamanders saluted as one, rapping their plastrons with clenched fists to show their veneration and
respect.

'*What is your will, Brother Pyriel?*' added Amadeus,
stomping over to the Librarian. '*I live to serve the Chapter.*'

Pyriel bowed.

'Venerable Amadeus,' he uttered, before straightening
again. 'Your orders are to remain sentry here and guard
the *Fire-wyvern*. The *Archimedes Rex* is obviously damaged. There will likely be little room for one as mighty
as you, brother.'

'*As you command, sire.*' The Dreadnought clanked back
towards the perimeter of the gunship, weapons whirring
into position as he adopted overwatch.

'Sergeants, form up your squads,' said Pyriel over the
comm-feed, facing his battle-brothers, 'and follow me.'
He was walking towards a pair of immense bulkhead
doors at the far end of the hangar when he intoned. 'In
the name of Vulkan.'

Twenty voices echoed back.

THE HANGAR LED into a smaller, but identically shaped,
airlock. Emek, who had disengaged the bulkhead and
then sealed it back behind them, worked at the room's
only access terminal, setting the entry protocols in
motion. Oxygen flooded the chamber, amber warning
beacons rotating whilst it was repressurised. The Salamanders stood stock still and silent until the process
had finished and the icon on the far bulkhead door
turned from red to green.

Upon interrogating the *Archimedes Rex*'s maintenance
logs and ship schemata, Emek was able to discern that
much of the Mechanicus vessel's structural integrity was
still intact. Deck by deck scans revealed that there was
also still limited oxygen on board, the admittedly weak
atmosphere perpetuated by reserve life support systems.

Most of the damage the Salamanders had seen outside during their approach appeared to have only affected the ship's ablative armour. Internal puncturing of the hull was restricted to only a few locations, and those areas had been sealed off.

With ponderous momentum, the vast bulkhead doors split and opened into the *Archimedes Rex* proper.

A WIDE AND gloom-drenched hall stretched out before the Salamanders. The Space Marines switched on the luminators attached to their battle-helms. Several grainy, white beams strafed outwards like lances to alleviate the darkness. Scads of expelled gases clung to the deck plates in a roiling, artificial smog. Recessed columns ran the entire length of the hall. They were linked by sepulchral arches that framed stygian alcoves, seeming to go on forever as they disappeared into the thickening shadows ahead.

Pyriel gave the order to advance, invoking a faint glow in the blade of his force sword.

'No life signs,' uttered Iagon through the comm-feed after a minute had elapsed. He glanced down intermittently at the auspex clutched in his gauntlet, scanning for bio-signatures.

'It's deserted,' rasped Tsu'gan, combi-bolter held at the ready, stalking along one side of the hall in front of his dutiful brother.

'Like a tomb…' hissed Brother Ba'ken from the other side, adjusting the weighty multi-melta he held, unknowingly echoing Tsu'gan's earlier words on the flight deck.

'Let's hope it stays that way,' Dak'ir muttered, taking point opposite Tsu'gan.

After several minutes, Brother Zo'tan articulated what they were all thinking. 'Feels like we're heading down.'

'We're in one of the ship's entry conduits,' offered Emek, flamer low-slung as he panned it back and forth with smooth sweeps. He had been promoted to special weapons trooper after the campaign on Stratos. The previous incumbent, Brother Ak'sor, had died during the engagement. He had been one of several Fire-born lost on that world. 'It leads into the bowels of the *Archimedes Rex*,' Emek continued, using the data he'd accessed from the ship's schematics and then stored in his eidetic memory to ascertain their exact location. 'At this pace we should reach the end of it in approximately eight minutes.'

Eerie silence resumed with only the dull thud of the Salamanders' footfalls disturbing it.

THE EMPTY SOCKETS of a Mechanicus skull glared at them when they reached the end of the conduit, another massive bulkhead door impeding the way ahead.

'Brother Emek,' invited Pyriel, a brief flare erupting along the blade of his force sword as he readied his power.

Emek allowed the flamer to loll against its strap as he went to the bulkhead's control panel and prepared to engage the access mechanism. Behind him, all nineteen of his battle-brothers took up battle positions. 'Disengaging locks,' he reported, and fell back quickly to join them.

A crack split the immense door, hermetically sealed from the outside, dividing it into two. Shrieking mechanisms were immediately smothered by an intense clamour spilling out from the chamber beyond, filling the conduit with raucous noise. After the silence they had just experienced, the din was like a physical blow and the Salamanders reeled as one. Only Pyriel was unfazed.

Adapting quickly, the Salamanders filtered out the crashing wall of sound, just as Dak'ir had done aboard the *Fire-wyvern*. Maintaining vigilance, they awaited the slow, inexorable process of the bulkhead opening.

Massive forge-engines loomed in the next chamber, banks and banks of pistons, foundries, kilns and smelting vats filling an expansive machine floor. Conveyors chugged with monotonous motion, steam spat in sporadic intervals from pipes and vents, unseen gears churned noisily.

It was a hive of industry, a slow-beating heart of metal and machines, oil and heat. Yet, for all its labours, the forge-engines had achieved nothing. The vast machineries were merely turning over and over, going through their production cycles bereft of raw materials. Spent bolts piled up on the floor beneath an array of heavy-duty riveting guns, their ammunition long spent; hammers pounded the vulcanised rubber tract of a running belt, their concussive force impotent without plating to beat; oil spilled across the deck and seeped down through cross-hatched grilles, no joints for the empty needle-dispensers to lubricate.

With no independent servitors in sight, no adepts to instruct them, the many and multifarious apparatus continued in their various indoctrinated routines uninterrupted. The only creatures in the forge were those servitors attached physically to the machines, but they too merely worked by rote, implementing their protocols like automatons. There was no evidence of crew or even skitarii armsmen or Martian praetorians, either – wherever the inhabitants of the Ark-class vessel were situated, it was not here.

'Tiberon,' barked Tsu'gan into the comm-feed, 'shut it down.'

The Salamander saluted and broke from formation, bolter held low and ready. He disappeared briefly amidst the forge-machines. A few moments later the machines slowed and began to power down, the din receding gradually into silence.

Brother Tiberon returned and rejoined his squad.

Dak'ir tested the reaction of a slaved servitor with the tip of his chainsword, watching it slump back as if its invisible strings had been cut by the weapon's teeth.

'We must find out what happened here.' He looked to Pyriel for some guidance, but the Librarian was still and appeared pensive.

Instead, Dak'ir looked around and noticed a console independent of the forge-machines.

'Emek, see if you can access the onboard maintenance logs. Perhaps it will provide some clue as to what happened.'

Emek went to work again, using the surplus power available from the shut-down forge-engines to activate the console. Dak'ir at his shoulder, the other Salamander brought up more ship schematics, this time with maintenance logs appended alongside. He read quickly, assessing the information display and absorbing it like a savant. Emek's capacity for knowledge and aptitude at applying it was impressive, even for a Space Marine.

'Records are incomplete, possibly as a result of the damage sustained to the ship,' he said, whilst reading. Touch sensitive screens allowed Emek to call up specific decks and areas, digging deeper for answers as he zeroed in on the salient information the vessel did still possess. 'There's an alert for a minor hull breach to the aft, starboard side.'

'We entered via the port side,' muttered Dak'ir. 'How close to our current position is it?'

'Several decks – potentially an hour's travelling through the ship, assuming a clear route and walking speed. It's too small to be weapons damage.'

'An internal explosion?'

'It's possible…'

'But you don't think so, brother?'

'This ship has been drifting for a while, any incendiary reaction from inside would have occurred before now,' Emek explained. 'There is a fading heat trace associated with this breach, which suggests it's recent.'

'What are you telling me, Emek?'

'That the breach was caused by external forces and that we are not the only ones exploring this ship.'

Dak'ir paused to consider this then slapped Emek's pauldron.

'Good work, brother. Now find us a route through the ship that will take us to the bridge. We may need the *Archimedes Rex*'s log to ascertain what tragedy befell them.'

Emek nodded and began examining the ship's layout in detail relative to the Salamanders' position in its bowels and the bridge situated in the upper decks.

'Brother-Librarian,' Dak'ir said to get Pyriel's attention after he left Emek to his task.

Pyriel faced him and his eyes crackled briefly with psychic power.

'So it seems we are not alone, after all,' he said.

Dak'ir shook his head.

'No, my lord, we are not.'

THE SALAMANDERS PROCEEDED with caution, following the route established by Brother Emek and inloaded to Brother Iagon's auspex. They passed through cargo zones, abandoned crew quarters and vast assembly yards fed by the forge-engines from below decks. The further into the ship they travelled, the more frequent the discovery of servitors became. Unlike those on the foundry floor in the bowels of the *Archimedes Rex*, these automatons were independent of engines or other machineries. Some lay slumped against bulkheads, others hung slack like wretched cybernetic dolls over benches or cargo crates, many were simply frozen stiff, locked in whatever perfunctory task they had been performing when the ship had been attacked. Whatever had crippled the Ark-class cruiser had acted swiftly and to devastating effect.

Despite its disrepair, the iron majesty of the Mechanicus still came through and intensified the deeper the Salamanders went in the ship. Symbols of the Machine-God were wrought into the walls, the holy cog of the Martian brotherhood prevalent throughout the upper echelons of the *Archimedes Rex*. Alcoves recessed into the walls punctuated regimental lines of bulkheads and were minor chapels of devotion to the Omnissiah. Incense burners hung from chains looped under the vaulted ceilings, emanating strange aromas reminiscent of oil and metal. Designed to appease and mollify the machine-spirits, these lightly smoking braziers were ubiquitous throughout the *Archimedes Rex*'s many upper halls, chambers and galleries.

Skulls set into the walls were mistaken as some form of reliquary at first, but the circuitry and antennae jutting from bleached bone exposed them as cyber-skulls, the sanctified craniums of pious and devoted servants of the Imperium. The entire ship was a monolith of religio-metallurgic fusion, the spiritual alloyed with the mechanised.

Tsu'gan stooped over the collapsed body of a servitor. There appeared to be no external damage, and yet it was lifeless and unmoving. Its staring eyes, milky orbs of glass, were bereft of animus.

'No putrefaction, no decay of any kind,' he reported from the head of the group. Brother Honorious watched the dingy route ahead of his sergeant, flamer at the ready.

The ship's corridors had narrowed, becoming almost labyrinthine, devolving into a myriad of tunnels, conduits and passageways like the multitudinous neural

pathways of a vast mechanised brain. Only Emek's route
to the bridge had kept them on course. The Salamanders
had to advance in pairs, one squad at the fore, the other
guarding the rear. Tsu'gan had been quick to establish
his dominance, eager for action, and taken the lead.
Librarian Pyriel had seemed content to let him, occupying a position at the centre of the two squads. The longer
they spent on the ship, the more seldom Pyriel spoke.
He interrogated his psionics constantly, trying to ascertain some thread of existence of the other intruders on
the vessel, but the machine presence on board, though
slumbering or inert, was hindering his efforts.

'These creatures are not dead.' Tsu'gan got back to his
feet. Though the majority of their bodies were mechanised, even servitors required biological systems to
maintain the integrity of their human flesh parts and
organs. Without them they would not be able to function. 'It's like some kind of deep hibernation,' the
brother-sergeant added.

'A defence mechanism, perhaps?' offered Emek, alongside Dak'ir who was just behind Pyriel.

Tsu'gan didn't have time to answer before Iagon spoke
up.

'I have a life form reading, two hundred metres east.'

Looking in that direction, Tsu'gan grunted.

'Weapons ready.'

Together, the Salamanders followed the quietly flashing signal on Iagon's auspex.

TWO HUNDRED METRES east led the Salamanders to a large
Mechanicus temple. Octagonal in shape and with an
archway leading off from each of its eight sides, here the
blending of machine and religiosity was even more
prevalent. There were iron altars, burning brazier pans
and devotional statues; cyber-skulls wound around the
temple's ambit like eternal sentinels. An inscrutable

sequence of ones and zeros, doubtless some esoteric equation relating to Mechanicus science, filled the plated floor. Huge, bulb-headed battery units spat arcs of electricity across flanged conductor fins fixed to a thin torso of metal. The ephemeral sparks filled the chamber sporadically, illuminating it in a harsh white glare.

In the centre of the room, encircled by the cog symbol itself, a robed figure knelt in supplication.

Tsu'gan was the first to enter, Honorious and Iagon at his back with weapons drawn. The figure seemed still to the brother-sergeant, though after he'd stared at it long enough he detected the slightest tremor of movement as it rocked back and forth. As it faced away from them, hooded by a heavy cowl, Tsu'gan was unable to discern its features or physical disposition. Combi-bolter readied cautiously, he battle-signed for his fellow squad members to fan out around him. In a few short seconds, the entire complement of Salamanders was in the large room and poised for immediate assault.

'A magos, by the look of it,' uttered Pyriel. His eyes flashed cerulean blue behind his helmet lenses and then died again. 'I see nothing,' he added in a hollow voice, 'Nothing but mental static. It is as if its mind is shut off somehow, or merely waiting for some trigger to ignite it.'

The Librarian looked to Brother Iagon, who was adjusting the auspex trying to get a more detailed reading.

'The biorhythms appear normal, all circadian functions are perpetuating as expected. Heart rate, respiration, they are consistent with a deep sleep.'

Brother Emek shook his head. 'It isn't sleeping, as such,' he observed, his curiosity coming through via the comm-feed. 'Its movements are acute, but exact and repeated, as if locked in some kind of holding pattern or mechanised catatonia. It is irregular.'

'Explain, brother,' Dak'ir returned.

'Magos are sentient: they are unlike servitors, dependent on doctrina wafers or pre-programmed work protocols. Cold and inhuman, certainly, but they are not slavish automatons. Some trauma must have afflicted it in for it to behave in this way.'

Tsu'gan had heard enough. He levelled his combi-bolter, taking careful aim.

Dak'ir put out a hand to stop him. 'What are you doing?' he snapped.

Though he couldn't see Tsu'gan's eyes behind his battle-helm, Dak'ir felt the heat in his fellow sergeant's glare.

'Listen to your battle-brother. It's a trap,' he growled, looking over at Dak'ir's gauntlet on his bolter stock. 'Step aside unless you want to lose your hand, Ignean.'

Dak'ir bristled at the slight. He had no issue with his lowborn heritage, he only objected to the way that Tsu'gan used it as a derogatory barb.

'Desist,' he warned him, through clenched teeth. 'I won't allow you to shoot a man in cold blood. Let me approach him first.'

'It's not a man, it's a *thing*.'

Still Dak'ir would not yield.

Tsu'gan's finger lingered near his bolter trigger for a few seconds more before he lost the battle of wills, lowered the weapon and stepped back.

'Proceed, if you wish,' he growled. 'But as soon as the creature turns – and mark me it will – I shall fire. You'd best be out of the way when I do.'

Dak'ir nodded, though the gesture went unheeded so was scarcely necessary. He glanced behind him at Ba'ken, who gave an acknowledgement of his own, though this one indicated that he was watching his sergeant's back. Before he turned away, Dak'ir noticed Pyriel looking on. The Librarian had observed and, doubtless, heard the entire exchange between the feuding sergeants but had said nothing. Dak'ir wondered then whether Pyriel's presence on this mission was more than merely simple command. Had Master Vel'cona, at Tu'Shan's bidding, instructed him to assess how far the enmity between the brother-sergeants went and act appropriately or even report back? Or perhaps there was another imperative guiding the Librarian, one related to his careful observations during the ceremony on Nocturne? Now was not the time to consider it. Dak'ir slowly drew his chainsword and approached the magos.

His bootsteps sounded like thunderclaps through his battle-helm as he walked tentatively towards the centre of the temple. As Dak'ir moved he panned his gaze slowly back and forth, interrogating the deeper shadows lurking in the recesses of the room. Cycling through the optical spectra afforded by his occulobe implants and combined with the technology of his battle-helm's lenses, Dak'ir felt certain there were no hidden dangers.

Within an arm's length of the kneeling magos, he stopped. Listening intently, he made out a susurrus of meaningless sound seeping from the supplicant's mouth. Close up, the tremors in the magos's body seemed more pronounced, though whether this was merely proximity or the fact that it had somehow detected his presence, Dak'ir was uncertain.

'Turn,' he said in a low voice. It was possible the magos was in some kind of trance or deep meditation. Perhaps he had lost his mind and was fixed in some catatonic state as Emek had suggested. In any case, Dak'ir had no desire to alarm him. 'Have no fear,' he added when a response was not forthcoming. 'We are the Emperor's Astartes, here to rescue you and your crew. Turn.'

Still nothing.

Dak'ir took a firm grip on his plasma pistol, still holstered for now, and reached out with the tip of his dormant chainsword.

The blade had barely brushed the crimson robes, when the magos turned, or rather its torso rotated as if on a gimbal joint, and it faced the intruder defiling the sanctity of its temple.

'*Abandon hope, all ye who enter…*' it barked, the chattering phrase it had been repeating made audible at last and vocalised in a grating, machine dialect.

Kadai's words in the dream came back at Dak'ir like a hammer blow and he almost staggered.

The phrase continued in an uninterrupted loop, speeding up and increasing in pitch and volume until it became an unintelligible whine of noise. Dak'ir brought his chainsword up into a guard position and retreated one step.

The sound of tearing cloth followed as the magos's robes flared out in shreds at his back and two mechanical arms sprang out like the pincers of some insect. A chainblade affixed to the end of one of the arms roared into life; on the other a vibro-saw shrieked. Pale, gelid skin, sutured with wires and metal, possessed no life. Sightless eyes held neither pity nor anger, only a simple function: eliminate the intruders. A nozzle protruded from its mouth like an obscene tongue forcing its way from the cold, dark crevice. It was the tip of an igniter, and spat a thin column of flame.

Dak'ir used his free forearm to shield himself, and intense heat washed over him. Radiation warnings spiked in his battle-helm's display. In the same movement, he parried the sudden dart of the vibro-saw blindly with his chainsword. Powerless to stop the magos's chainblade, it churned against his left pauldron hungrily. Spitting sparks, it retracted and came about again.

Bolter fire thudded behind him and Dak'ir half expected to feel the shots penetrate his suit's generator and then his back, but the aim of his battle-brothers was true and he did not fall. Instead, he felt the crackle of electricity and detected the stink of ozone in his nostrils. A secondary flash lit up his battle-helm, lenses struggling to compensate as the blades whirred towards him again. Dak'ir realised that the magos was force-shielded.

'Hold your fire!' barked the voice of Tsu'gan behind him. 'Encircle it, find its shield generator and destroy it.'

Dak'ir was aware of movement in his peripheral vision as his brothers sought to open their trap. Between searching blows, its mechanised limbs lightning fast, the magos reacted to the threat. Servos whining, its robed form began to rise on cantilevered legs until it loomed almost a metre over Dak'ir. Its mouth widened like the rapidly expanding aperture of a pict-viewer as a second and third flamer nozzle took their place alongside the first. Panning its head left and right like a scope, it spewed white-hot fire around the fringes of the room, keeping the Salamanders back. Molten deck plates and iron altars rendered to slag were left in its wake.

Dak'ir caught the vibro-saw as it came at him again, and cut it off with a brutal sweep from its chainsword. The magos's own chainblade struck the Salamander's generator on his back and found itself at another impasse. Dak'ir swung around, dislodging the weapon with his momentum, and hacked down the piston-driven arm two-handed. Issuing a metallic screech, the magos recoiled, the severed chainblade arm spitting oil and sparks. Exploiting his advantage, Dak'ir ripped his plasma pistol from its holster and blasted a hole through the magos's torso. Something within the voluminous folds of its shredded robes flared and died. Still, the firestorm cascading from its distended mouth continued, keeping Dak'ir's battle-brothers at bay, their only avenue of attack blocked by the brother-sergeant himself.

A flash of metal registered briefly in Dak'ir's restricted vision. Pain lanced his armoured wrist, forcing him to drop the plasma pistol, and he looked down to see a churning drill trying to impale his arm. Wrenching himself free, he gripped the twisting tendril fed from the magos's robes that had impelled the weapon towards him. Dak'ir was about to cut it off when a second mechadendrite sprang from the creature's torso, sporting some kind of mecha-claw. Dak'ir blocked it with the flat of his blade and pushed it down. Locked as he was, and acutely aware of the battle-brothers behind him, he started to try and manoeuvre his body to the side.

'Ba'ken!' he cried, seeing the vague form of the hulking Salamander in his peripheral vision.

'Hold it steady,' a booming voice returned.

It took almost all Dak'ir's strength to force the magos around and keep him steady as Ba'ken wanted.

Intense heat and blinding light filled Dak'ir's senses. His ears rang with the shriek of expulsed energy and he fell. For a fleeting moment as the radiation of the fusion beam stroked his battle-helm and power armour, Dak'ir was thrust back to Stratos and the instant of Kadai's death. The jarring impact of iron-hard deck plates against his body brought him quickly back around. The dull report of sustained thunder echoed around the room as the rest of the Salamanders unleashed their bolters. Sporadic muzzle flashes lit up the magos like some macabre animation, its body jerking and twisting as it was struck and demolished.

The munitions fire died and with it so did the magos, clattering to the floor in a disparate melange of wrecked machine parts and biological matter, the components of his former existence scattering across the deck like metal chaff. Oil slicked it, reflecting the dim light of the brazier pans like iridescent blood.

Bizarrely the head remained intact, rolling from its eviscerated body until coming to rest next to Ba'ken. The end of his multi-melta still exuded vaporous accelerant created during the chemical reaction engaged to fire the heavy weapon. He looked down at the decapitated head, his body language suggesting repulsion. The flamer nozzles had since retracted into the thing's lipless maw. Ba'ken shifted uncomfortably as a stream of binaric, the machine language the Mechanicum primarily used to communicate, barked from it like a torrent of ceaseless profanity.

Without waiting for orders the Salamander brought down his booted foot and smashed it to pulp and wires.

Dak'ir, now back on his feet, nodded his appreciation to Ba'ken, who immediately returned the gesture. Once the chattering had ceased, he turned to Tsu'gan who was making sure no life existed amidst the wreckage of the magos.

'I owe you a debt of gratitude, brother.'

Tsu'gan didn't even look up.

'Save your thanks,' he returned flatly. 'I did it for the good of the mission, not your well-being.' He was about to turn away, when he paused and looked Dak'ir in the eye. 'You'll doom us all with your compassion, Ignean.'

Dak'ir knew Tsu'gan was right to an extent; his desire to save the magos had endangered them, but he was adamant given the same situation again, he would make the same choice. The Salamanders were protectors, not merely slayers. Let other Chapters revel in that dubious accolade. Dak'ir wanted to enlighten his brother to that very fact, but the steady voice of Pyriel prevented any riposte.

'The battle is not over.' The Librarian's eyes flared cerulean blue behind his helmet lenses. 'Fire-born, prepare yourselves!' he called as one consciousness became many.

The dull sound of movement echoed from the corridor ahead as something shrugged itself awake.

'Multiple heat signatures,' reported Iagon as his auspex lit up a moment later. 'And rising,' he added, securing the device away and hefting his bolter. 'All entrances.'

The Salamanders spread out, covering ingress into the temple.

'Something comes...' shouted Brother Zo'tan. 'Servitors!' he added, the glare from his luminator casting one of the lumbering creatures starkly.

A lobotomy plate was riveted to the servitor's roughly shaven skull. It was dressed in dark labour overalls, scorched by fire and muddied by oil and grime. Its skin was grey as if swathed in a patina of dust or merely bled of all life and left to wither. One of its arms was curled up into a rigor-mortised fist, and fixed to a torso bloated with wires and fat, ribbed cables; the other arm ended in a mechanised pincer, puffs of hydraulic gas ghosting the air as it flexed.

Dak'ir recalled the slumped automatons they had encountered on their way to the temple. He could not be accurate, but he knew there had been hundreds.

'Another here, second right!' yelled Brother Apion.

Dak'ir heard Brother G'heb bellow after him.

'Targets spotted third left corridor.'

The Salamanders had formed two semi-circles, one per squad, with Librarian Pyriel as the link between them. Each faced outwards, one or two bolters levelled at an opening. Flamers took one portal each. That left Ba'ken's multi-melta and Brother M'lek, from Tsu'gan's squad, carrying a heavy bolter. Dak'ir hoped the combined firepower would be enough.

Brother Emek was standing to his left in their battle-formation.

'The death of the magos must have been the catalyst for some kind of activation code,' he said over the comm-feed, testing the igniter on his flamer with a short spit of fire.

'How many could there be?' barked Tsu'gan, itching to destroy this new foe.

'On a ship this size… thousands,' Emek returned.

'It matters not.' Ba'ken's deep voice was like dull thunder, on his brother-sergeant's right flank. 'We'll send them all to their deaths.'

Dak'ir only half heard him, having already picked up on Tsu'gan's line of thought.

'Wait until they've closed to optimum lethal range. Short controlled bursts,' he ordered over the comm-feed. 'Conserve your ammunition.'

Pyriel's force sword burst into cerulean flame, reminding the brother-sergeant of the Librarian's potency. His voice took on an unearthly timbre as an aura of power coursed over his armour in miniature lightning storms.

'Into the fires of battle,' he intoned.

'Unto the anvil of war!' his Salamanders replied belligerently.

The servitors emerged from the gloom with slow, monotonous purpose, like a horde of mechanised zombies. Their pallid faces were vacant masks, their only compulsion to execute the intruders on the ship. They were armed with the tools of their labours: chainblades, pneumatic drills, hydraulic lifter-claws, even acetylene torches burning white hot, heralding their advance from the darkness.

The Salamanders waited until the first wave of the servitors had made its way into the temple before unleashing hell.

Blood, oil, flesh and machine-parts cascaded in a visceral miasma, the automatons punished with the wrath of the Salamanders' weapons. But like their slayers, these creatures of melded skin and metal felt no fear; they experienced no emotion, and came forward implacably.

Where one fell, another two servitors took its place, funnelling from the depths of the *Archimedes Rex* like a tide.

Drone-like, they flocked to the temple and the interlopers within. As their numbers increased, so too did they begin to close on the Salamanders; for despite their prodigious abilities, the Space Marines could not maintain an unbroken wall of fire to hold the servitors off. With every metre gained, the fury of the Salamanders' response intensified and Dak'ir's earlier conservatism had to be abandoned.

It wasn't long before this desperate approach took its toll.

'Down to my last rounds,' voiced Brother Apion.

His report spurred a slew of others over the commfeed as, throughout the squads, Salamanders started to run out of ammunition.

'Flamer at seventeen per cent and falling... Switching to reserve weapon... Ammunition low, brothers...'

The circle of fire was failing.

'I'm empty,' replied Brother G'heb, the hollow *chank* of his bolter starkly audible as it ran dry.

Dak'ir reached across and shot a drill-armed servitor with his plasma pistol while his battle-brother drew a reserve weapon. Bolt pistol bucking in his grasp, G'heb nodded his gratitude.

'Endure it, brothers!' yelled Pyriel, impeding a servitor's mecha-claw with his force sword as it sought to remove his head. The automaton was one of the few that had made it through the bolt storm. The Librarian opened his palm. With gauntleted fingers splayed he engulfed the servitor in a blast of psychic fire from his hand, burning out its eyes, rendering its flesh to charred hunks and scorching machinery black.

Crushing the smoking husk of the servitor with a blow from his force sword, the Librarian moved out of formation, a hot core of crackling fire building inside his now clenched fist. Battle-brothers S'tang and Zo'tan covered him as Pyriel went down on one knee, head bowed, focusing his power.

The servitors converged on the Librarian but S'tang and Zo'tan kept them back with the last of their ammunition. They had enough for Pyriel to raise his head, his entire body now swathed in an aura of conflagration. It sped from his hunkered form in a violently flickering trail, its head that of a snarling firedrake that arced around the Salamanders, encircling them as the elemental swallowed its own fiery tail.

'Brothers...' Pyriel's voice crackled like the deepest magma pits of Mount Deathfire, '...go to your blades... Now!' he roared, and the wall of flame exploded outwards with atomic force, the nuclear fire burning all within its path to ash. The servitors became darkened silhouettes in the haze, only to disintegrate like shadows before the sun.

Dak'ir felt the prickle of Pyriel's psychic backwash at the edges of his mind, and he smarted at the unfamiliar sensation. He holstered his plasma pistol, which was down to its last energy cell, and drew his combat blade, wielding both it and his chainsword in either hand. Several of his battle-brothers had done the same, some preferring bolt pistols; others with no choice but to unsheathe their short blades.

Pyriel's unleashed holocaust had drained him, and Brothers S'tang and Zo'tan maintained guard as the Librarian returned to the cordon of green battle-plate in order to marshal his strength. Scorched metal, the forlornly dripping remnants of votive chains and the ashen corpses of servitors littered the ground around the Salamanders allowing them time to adopt fresh tactics.

The conflagration had been devastating. Hundreds of automatons were dead. It provided but a few moments' respite.

'They come again!' hollered Ba'ken, the booming laughter that followed echoing loudly around the vast chamber. 'They come for death!' He had stowed his multi-melta via a mag-lock on the back of the heavy weapon's ammo rig. It was cumbersome, but Ba'ken was strong enough to bear it without much deterioration of his close combat abilities. In its place he wielded a piston-driven hammer of unblemished silver, a weapon he had fashioned himself, all hard edges and promised destruction.

'Restrain your bull, Ignean,' snapped Tsu'gan, releasing a gout of fire from his bolter's combination flamer. There was only enough chemical incendiary for one shot, so the brother-sergeant used it to gain a few extra metres in order that his fellow battle-brothers could see him.

'Head for the bridge,' he declared, ripping out his combat blade and letting his combi-bolter hang by its strap. 'We'll use the narrow cordon to our advantage, deny them their numbers.'

Pyriel was still debilitated from his psychic exertions and could only nod his assent.

Moving off in pairs, the Salamanders made for the exit that, according to Emek, would lead them eventually to the bridge. As they fell back, snap shots executed the first automatons to come from the other seven portals.

Already, their exit was clogged with servitors, emerging from unseen maintenance hatches and hidden access conduits.

Seeing the danger that the plan might fail before they had even gained the corridor leading off from the temple, Dak'ir sped over to the conductor array still throwing off flashes of electricity.

'Hold, brothers!' he bellowed, just as the first pair of Salamanders, Apion and G'heb, were about to start cutting with their combat blades.

Obeying through conditioned reflex, they arrested their advance as Dak'ir crashed his chainsword against one of the conductor pylons. The first batch of servitors was emerging through the portal as an unfettered lightning arc erupted from the shattered conductor array. Dak'ir was thrown back by the resulting blast, as the bolt of electrical energy earthed into the servitor forms, exploding circuitry and burning through clumps of wiring. The arc spread, leaping from body to body, hungrily devouring the automatons who jerked and shook as the artificial lightning wracked them.

Smoking corpses and the stench of charred meat and hot metal were left in the wake of the electrical storm. Apion and G'heb rushed into the void it had created, crushing husked bodies with their booted feet and clearing a path for their battle-brothers.

Dak'ir was hauled up by Ba'ken, who then turned surprisingly quickly given the weight on his back, and crushed the skull on an oncoming servitor with his piston-hammer. When he turned back, tiny ripples of electrical charge were slowly dispersing over Dak'ir's power armour.

'Ready to move out, brother-sergeant?' he asked.

'Lead the way, brother.'

Fully half the Salamanders had entered the portal and were chopping through the hordes of automatons coming at them from deeper in the ship. As Dak'ir entered the darkness of the narrow corridor, he wondered briefly whether there was a vast factorum at the heart of the *Archimedes Rex* churning out entire battalions of the creatures in an unending cycle.

'Emek, what's the status of your flamer?' asked Dak'ir through the comm-feed. The battle-brother was one of the last out of the temple, with only Tsu'gan lingering behind him intent on taking on the entire horde himself it seemed.

'I'm down to six per cent,' Emek replied, between short roaring bursts.

'Hold the rear of the column as long as you can, brother.'

'At your command, sergeant.'

TSU'GAN REVELLED IN the act of righteous slaughter. He killed with abandon, seeking out targets even before he'd despatched the last. Every servitor that came within reach was cut down with ruthless efficiency. He decapitated one with his combat blade, a spinal column of wires and rigid cabling left protruding from the servitor's ruined neck. Another he gutted, tearing out a handful of lubricant-wet wires like intestines. Tsu'gan used his fist like a hammer, brutally pounding bone and metal with every wrath-fuelled blow.

Let the Ignean flee, he thought, derision creasing his face behind his battle-helm as he glanced in Dak'ir's direction, *I expect it from one such as he.*

A ring of carnage was rapidly growing around him, his combat blade so slick with oil and blood that it was almost black. These soulless creations were as nothing matched against the mettle of a Fire-born.

But for all his slaughter, the attacks did not abate and the servitors kept on coming.

A heavy blow rapped his pauldron, forcing him to step back. Tsu'gan cut his assailant down but was struck again, this time in the torso before he could get his guard up, and he staggered. Certain victory suddenly bled away, replaced by the prospect of an ignominious death. Tsu'gan craved glory; he had no desire to perish in some forgotten mission aboard a Mechanicus forge-ship.

Another thought crept into his mind, this time unbidden.

I have over-extended myself, cut off from my brothers…

Tsu'gan tried to fall back, but found he was sur-rounded. He balked at the realisation that his bravura might have doomed him.

A spear of flame erupted to his left, singeing the edge of his pauldron and setting warning icons flashing on his helm display. Tsu'gan was half-shielding his body when he saw the servitors engulfed by the blaze, slump-ing first to their knees and then collapsing in a smouldering heap. He recognised Brother Emek, releas-ing his flamer as the last of the promethium was spent. Tsu'gan also saw that the way to the corridor was now clear.

'Call your trooper back, Dak'ir,' he snapped down the comm-feed, outwardly lamenting his scorched armour, 'Unlike you, I don't want my face burned off.' He grunted a reluctant thanks to Brother Emek as Dak'ir returned:

'Then retreat with your fellow Fire-born. You over-stretch yourself, brother.'

Tsu'gan took out his frustration on a servitor that had strayed ahead of its pack, pummelling the creature with a blow from his fist. Inwardly, the brother-sergeant gave a sigh of relief – he knew were it not for Dak'ir's contin-gency, he would probably be dead. That admission alone burned more than the thought of perishing unher-alded on the *Archimedes Rex*. Tsu'gan was determined that the debt would not last.

STORMING THROUGH THE tightly-packed corridors of the Mechanicus ship, the Salamanders fought in the way they were made for – up close and eye-to-eye. Though they had exhausted both flamers, their zeal and wrath more than compensated for it. Blood and oil ran thick as they held their lines and won metre by gore-drenched metre, the tally of dead servitors in the hundreds. Tena-cious and unyielding, they epitomised the Promethean ideal – they were Fire-born, Salamanders. War was their temple; battle the sermons that they preached with bolter and blade.

Their violent efforts took them as far as a wide gallery, possibly an inspection yard given the ranks of assessment tables lining either side. Stout metal columns etched in binaric and the sigils of the Omnissiah punctuated each of the empty bays where armour, weapons and other materiel would normally be logged, examined and approved by inspection servitors. The barren bays were overlooked by broad steel gantries that hung fifty metres up. Any details were lost in shadow, but they were supported by angled stanchions enabling them to take a considerable mass.

Servitors spewed from blast doors that were opening in three locations around the yard. Tsu'gan, who had slashed and bludgeoned his way to the front, met them with a furious battle cry. He clove the arm off one automaton, spilling fuel and releasing sparks as Dak'ir bifurcated another from sternum to groin. A clutch of wires slopped from the ragged wound like intestines as the brother-sergeant swept past it looking for another foe, before Ba'ken followed in his wake and crushed the stricken wretch with his piston-hammer.

An organised retreat had turned into a melee. The Salamanders fought in groups of two and three, watching their brothers' blindsides as they brought fire and fury to the relentless enemy. Only Pyriel fought alone. None dared approach the Librarian, his force sword carving irresistible death arcs through anything it touched. Psychic fire spilled from his eyes like an optical laser, tearing through a line of servitors and severing their mechanised torsos. A clenched fist, and the summoned firedrake roared into being, the elemental burning down automatons as it swept over them in a fiery wave.

'In the name of Vulkan, repel them! Fire-born do not yield!' Pyriel bellowed a rallying cry as the servitors closed inexorably.

With their ammunition all but spent, many of the Salamanders had turned to close assault weapons. Some carried the traditional combat blade, akin to the Ultramarine spatha; others wielded hammers in homage to the blacksmith, and Vulkan's adopted father, N'Bel or in tribute to the primarch himself who had first taken up the weapon to defeat the xenos plaguing Nocturne and liberate the planet.

Honour, for all its noble intention, meant precious little as the Salamanders were slowly enveloped. At distance, the servitors were no challenge. Bereft of ranged weapons, the automatons could be vanquished with ease. At close quarters, they were a different prospect. Though slow and cumbersome, their claws and drills and hammers were deadly, easily capable of chewing through power armour. Attacking in such numbers with no sign of respite; unless something changed, the Salamanders could not hope to prevail...

The rash of fatalism flashed across Dak'ir's mind as he put another servitor down. Despite his training, the many hours of drills, the constant honing of his skills and building of his endurance, the brother-sergeant was beginning to tire. They'd sustained casualties. Brother Zo'tan was limping; S'tang had a fierce dent in his battle-helm that had probably cracked his skull; several others nursed shoulder or arm wounds and fought one-handed.

Tsu'gan raged against the inevitable, easily killing twice the servitors of any of his battle-brothers. Even Pyriel, with all his psychic might, was hard-pressed to keep pace with the rampant brother-sergeant's tally. Fatigue, to Tsu'gan, was an enemy just like the automatons. It had to be fought and bested, denied at all costs.

It was little wonder he carried such sway amongst the other sergeants of 3rd Company. But even Tsu'gan's will had its limits.

Something hard and heavy struck Dak'ir across his unguarded left flank. White heat flared behind his eyes as he felt his rib plate crack. Blood was leaking down the side of his power armour, black and thick like the oil of their adversaries. Darkness clawed at the edges of his vision. As he fell back, he saw the face of his killer – pitiless eyes stared back at him from above a mouth obscured by speaker-grille, framed by skin with a deathly pallor. Dak'ir thought of the robed figure in the temple as his body met the ground, his inevitable death playing out in slow motion.

With its final, indecipherable words the magos had damned them all.

MUTED THUNDER BROUGHT Dak'ir around. He'd been out for a few seconds before his body's physiology staunched his wound and clotted the blood, repaired his bones and sent endorphins to his brain to block the pain. He wasn't dead, and with that realisation others followed.

Muzzle flares lit the gloom in the vaulted ceiling above, the *thud-crack* of bolter fire emanating from the gantries. Something heavier accompanied it, a dense *chug-chank*, *chug-chank* of a belt-fed cannon, the grind of tracks rolling against steel and the creak of metal stanchions pushed to their limits.

Dak'ir was back on his feet before he had even told his body to rise, and in the killing mood. His chainsword hadn't stopped churning even as he fell, and the teeth found fresh flesh to chew as the Salamander fought.

Through snatched glimpses in the melee, Dak'ir caught the flash of yellow and black armour, the snarl of a painted skull, predator's teeth daubed down the edges of a coned battle-helm. As the barrage of enfilading fire continued from either flank, ripping up servitors, a further epiphany materialised in Dak'ir's mind.

Their saviours were Astartes.

Caught between such forces, the servitors finally began to thin out and fall back. Not out of fear or even any remote sense of self-preservation; they did it because some nuance in their doctrina programming had impelled them to. Emek would later theorise that the casualties the combined Space Marines had inflicted were such that they endangered the minimum output capacity of the forge-ship and this protocol, entrenched in one of the Mechanicus's fundamental paradigms, overrode any others and resulted in capitulation. The machines simply lowered their tools, turned and retreated. Some were slain as they retired from the fight, the last vestiges of battle-lust still eking out of the blood-pumped Salamanders. But the majority left intact, shuffling back to slumber until they were called upon by their masters to engage in their work routines once more. It was an order that would never come – for Dak'ir was certain now that the magos in the octagon temple had been the last aboard the *Archimedes Rex*.

As the bolter fire of the mysterious Astartes died, so too did the light cast by their muzzle flares and they were thrown back into obscuring shadow. Dak'ir considered utilising his optical spectra to penetrate the gloom and get a better look at them, but decided to wait as they marched heavily down the gantry. A pair of lifters stationed at either end of each one brought the Space Marines down to yard level, where the Salamanders could see their allies clearly for the first time.

Dak'ir was right; they were indeed Space Marines – ten of them, broken into two combat squads reunited when the lifters hit deck-plate, plus a Techmarine who manned a battle-scarred mobile gun platform. The war machine rumbled on steel-slatted tracks, cushioned on a bed of vulcanised rubber. Its design was narrow, ideally suited to the close confines of the Mechanicus ship that had prevented Brother Argos's much-needed, as it transpired, inclusion in the mission. The STC used to construct the gun, a pair of twin-linked autocannons with a modified belt-feed, looked post-Heresy but pre-Age of Apostasy. Similar in essence to the Space Marine Thunderfire cannon, the platform also bore the hallmarks of a Tarantula-cum-Rapier-variant mobile weapons system – something the Adeptus Astartes hadn't used in either form for many millennia. The example before the Salamanders was evidently based on archaic designs.

The Space Marines themselves appeared to be just as archaic. Most wore MkVI Corvus-pattern power armour, stained yellow with a black cuirass and generators, the left pauldron studded with fat rivets. The armour's plastron was bereft of the Imperial eagle, and carried only an octagonal release clasp, unlike the modern suits of the MkVII Aquila-pattern. Every suit amongst them, bar none, was patched and chipped. The rigours of battle were worn proudly as marks of honour, in the same manner as the Salamanders' branding scars. It was armour that had been made to last, not in the sense of its superior forging or exceptionally durable craftsmanship; rather, it was battle-plate that had seen hundreds, perhaps thousands, of victories and been strung back together and hammered into shape by any means necessary in order that it saw another.

Bolters were no different. Lengthened stocks with the extended shoulder rest were an antiquated version of the Godwyn pattern MkVb carried by the Salamanders – albeit with Nocturnean refinements. Drum-fed and carrying sarissas – a saw-toothed bayonet-style blade affixed to the gun's nose – the bolters hefted by the yellow-armoured Astartes were the sorts of outmoded weapons best left to museums.

But these warriors were hard-bitten veterans, every single one. They didn't have the forges or the technological mastery of the Salamanders. They were seldom re-supplied or their materiel restocked or replenished. They knew only war, and fought it so relentlessly and without cessation that their equipment was battered almost to destruction. As the leader of the Astartes stepped forward, his honour markings indicating he was a sergeant, and proffered a hand, Dak'ir was struck by a final revelation:

These were the other intruders aboard the *Archimedes Rex*.

'I am Sergeant Lorkar,' the yellow-armoured Astartes spoke in a grating whisper, 'of the Marines Malevolent.'

CHAPTER THREE

I
Malevolence

'Brother-Sergeant Dak'ir, of the Salamanders 3rd Company,' replied Dak'ir, who found he was facing Sergeant Lorkar. After a moment's hesitation, he gripped the other Space Marine's forearm in a warrior greeting and nodded his respect.

'Salamanders?' said Lorkar, as if seeing them for the first time, 'Of the First Founding? We are deeply honoured.' The Marine Malevolent bowed, then stepped back to remove his battle-helm as his battle-brothers looked on.

There was a strange manner about them, Dak'ir thought. The Marines Malevolent appeared edgy. All of Lorkar's ostensible bonhomie, his deference, seemed faked, as if they had not expected company and now they had it, resented its presence.

With the gorget clasps disengaged, Lorkar lifted off his battle-helm and cradled it under one arm. Like the rest of his armour, it was chipped and scratched. Much of the yellow staining had worn away, revealing bare ceramite beneath. Black hazard markings striped the metal, which Dak'ir assumed indicated veteran status. Lorkar's grizzled visage clinched that suspicion.

Two platinum service studs were drilled into the Marine Malevolent sergeant's skull. His skin was dark and rugged as if the centuries of battlefield dirt and enemy blood were ingrained in it. Scars crosshatched his chin, jaw and cheekbones, a veritable map of old pain and remembered wars. His hair was shorn short, but done so crudely as if by shears and without care or the assistance of a serf. But it was his eyes that struck the most – they were cold and empty, as if inured to killing and bereft of compassion or regard. Dak'ir had seen flint with more warmth.

Not wishing to cause offence, Dak'ir removed his own battle-helm, mag-locking it to his weapons belt. A tremor of surprise ran across Sergeant Lorkar's face, which then spread to his cohorts, as he regarded the Salamander's visage for the first time.

'Your eyes and skin…' he began. For a moment, Dak'ir thought he saw Lorkar's hand straying to his bolter, hanging on its strap by his side. The gesture was instinctive. Clearly the Marines Malevolent had never seen an Astartes with a melanochromatic defect before.

'As our primarch made us,' Dak'ir responded evenly, aware of his own brothers' restiveness around him, and meeting Lorkar's gaze brazenly with his burning red eyes.

'Of course…' The look of thinly-veiled suspicion in Lorkar's face suggested anything but placation.

Tsu'gan's voice broke the uncomfortable silence.

'Marines Malevolent, eh? Do you find malice to be a useful tool on campaign, brother?'

Lorkar turned on the Salamander sergeant, who was obviously goading him.

Tsu'gan decided he didn't like the way their new found 'allies' looked at Dak'ir. Their manner smacked of disgust and repellence. His intervention was not for the Ignean's benefit, Tsu'gan's contempt for him went deeper than the flesh, it was because the Marine Malevolent's slight tarred all of Vulkan's sons and that was something he could not abide.

'*Hate* is the surest weapon,' Lorkar replied with all seriousness. So vehement was his stress on the first word that if the sergeant had had the power to kill with it then Tsu'gan would have keeled over in his power armour there and then. 'You are the commanding officer here, Salamander?'

'No,' Tsu'gan answered flatly, taunting having now turned to outright belligerence.

'That honour is mine.' Pyriel stepped forward from the throng of Salamanders, authority and certainty never more evident in his voice and manner.

'*A warp dabbler!*' Dak'ir heard one of other Marines Malevolent hiss. He carried a twin-linked combi-bolter and wore a beak-shaped battle-helm made to look like a shark's mouth with painted fangs either side.

Lorkar interceded before Tsu'gan's promised violence was enacted.

'Excuse Brother Nemiok,' he said addressing Pyriel, who exhibited no reaction. 'We are unaccustomed to Librarians in ranking positions,' Lorkar explained somewhat thinly. 'The Marines Malevolent still adhere to some of the tenets laid down at Nikea.'

'An outmoded set of edicts some ten thousand years old, fashioned by a council arraigned before your Chapter was even formed,' countered Tsu'gan, his mood still truculent.

'Communion with the warp is perilous,' Pyriel intervened. 'I can understand your Chapter's caution, Sergeant Lorkar. But I can assure you that I am master of my abilities,' he declared, to defuse the situation and suspend the trading of insults before they devolved into threats and then violence. 'Perhaps we have lingered here long enough?'

'I agree,' replied Lorkar, with a dark glance at Tsu'gan before he replaced his battle-helm. He paused a moment, bowing his head slightly, and seemed to be listening intently to some private instruction. 'We should continue on together,' he said at last, surfacing from whatever discreet confabulation he had been engaged in. 'The servitors in this section of the ship are dormant now, but we can't know how long that will last and what other defences we might face.' Lorkar then turned on his heel, his warriors parting like a yellow sea to allow him through.

'Worse than Templars,' muttered Ba'ken to Emek, who was grateful that his battle-helm masked his amusement.

Dak'ir saw nothing humorous in it. The encounter with the Marines Malevolent had put him on edge. There was an air of frustrated superiority about them, suggesting they thought themselves uniquely worthy of the appellation 'Space Marine'. Yet here they were faced with a progenitor Chapter. Such evidence was difficult to refute, for even the most zealous-minded. They had an agenda, of that Dak'ir was certain. And if that conflicted with the Salamanders' mission, violence would surely follow.

THE ROUTE DEEPER into the *Archimedes Rex* was conducted largely in silence. Before they had headed out after the Marines Malevolent, Brother Emek had examined the wounded Salamanders using what rudimentary medical craft he possessed and declared all injuries minor, and the recipients fit for combat. Mercifully, there had been no further encounters with the forge-ship's guardians.

For now, it appeared that Lorkar was right – the servitors had returned to slumber.

Dak'ir sat beside an iron bulkhead in some kind of expansive storage room. The room contained numerous metal crates, caskets and munitions cylinders – all of which had already been ransacked. Dak'ir was sitting on one of the empty crates, methodically engaged in weapons maintenance rituals. He glanced up sporadically at the Marines Malevolent's Techmarine, who was using breaching tools and a promethium torch from his servo-harness to prise open a sealed blast door impeding their further progress into the forge-ship. It was the first barrier of its kind they had discovered which wouldn't open through a console or operational slate, suggesting the heart of the ship lay beyond it.

The other Salamanders were locked in similar routines to the sergeant. Once the room had been made secure, many had removed their battle-helms, taking the opportunity to be free of their stifling confines if only for a few minutes – for the Marines Malevolent's part, any reaction to the Salamanders' facial appearance was kept hidden. Pyriel was silently meditative, eyes shut whilst he channelled the reserves of his psychic energy and shored up his mental bulwarks to guard against daemonic possession. Tsu'gan paced impatiently, waiting for the Techmarine to complete his task. Dak'ir had learned the Astartes's name was Harkane, though that was all the taciturn Techmarine had disclosed.

They had already deviated from Emek's route. Sergeant Lorkar insisted that he and his combat squad had already tried that way and it was blocked. Harkane had mapped another course, and it was this which they now followed. Tsu'gan had been the most reluctant to accede. Pyriel's order had made it impossible for him not to.

'We are heading away from the bridge,' Emek whispered to Dak'ir, one eye on their battle-brothers in yellow. Brother Emek was the only one not engaged in weapons maintenance, instead using his time to conduct brief examinations of his wounded brothers. He had lingered by Dak'ir on his rounds in order to converse without drawing too much suspicion. 'Whatever they are here for, it is not to find out what happened to this ship, or to search it for survivors, either. I thought you should know, brother-sergeant,' he added, before moving on his way to check on the wounded.

Battlefield surgery was one of the Salamander's many skills, useful in the absence of Fugis. Seeing Emek work reminded Dak'ir of the Apothecary and their last exchange before departing for the Hadron Belt and his assignment to reconnaissance aboard the *Fire-wyvern*. Fugis had remained with the rest of 3rd Company on the *Vulkan's Wrath*. Though his place was with N'keln, it was unlike him to eschew frontline duties. Dak'ir wondered if Fugis had lost more than just his captain when Kadai had been killed; he wondered if the Apothecary had lost a part of himself too.

The hot glare from Brother Harkane's plasma-cutter spat suddenly, arresting Dak'ir's reverie. The Techmarine made a slight adjustment and the intense beam returned to normal, the light it cast flickering over Dak'ir as he checked and reloaded his pistol's last energy cell. Despite the Salamanders' obvious paucity of ammunition, the Marines Malevolent had neglected to supplement them. The fact that their guns were so antiquated that neither the drum-mags nor the individual shells would have been suitable for their bolters made the point moot.

'Their weapons are practically relics,' whispered Ba'ken.

Dak'ir masked his sudden start – he hadn't even heard the bulky Space Marine approach. Ba'ken eyed the Marines Malevolent warily as he set his multi-melta rig down, enabling him to sit with his brother-sergeant. The Marines Malevolent showed equal distrust, swapping furtive glances and watching the Salamanders through the corners of their helmet lenses.

'The old drum-feeds are prone to jamming,' Ba'ken continued. 'I'm surprised one hasn't misfired in their faces before now.'

'They are certainly not wasteful,' agreed Dak'ir, 'But aren't all our weapons relics to one degree or another?'

Ba'ken was one of those who had removed his battle-helm during the brief abeyance and his lip curled up in distaste.

'Aye, but there are relics and there are *relics*,' he said, obliquely. 'These guns should have been stripped down for parts and re-appropriated years ago. A warrior is only as good as his weapon, and these dogs with their patchwork armour and archaic ideas are ragged at best.' He paused, turning to look his brother-sergeant in the eye. 'I don't trust them, Dak'ir.'

Dak'ir agreed, reminded of Emek's suspicions, but was not about to voice the fact aloud. Whether they liked it or not, the Marines Malevolent were their allies for now – tenuous ones at that. Any comment that supported Ba'ken's views would only foster greater dissension between them.

'I wonder what their purpose aboard this ship is.' Ba'ken concluded his line of thinking during his brother-sergeant's silence. Again, he echoed Emek's unspoken thoughts.

'I suspect they would ask us the same thing,' said Dak'ir.

Bak'en was about to reply when he noticed Sergeant Lorkar approaching and kept quiet.

Lorkar waited, battle-helm clasped beneath one arm, until invited by Dak'ir to sit down with them. He nodded gratefully before setting his helmet on an adjacent crate.

'The earlier hostility,' he began, 'was regrettable. We acted with suspicion and without honour. Such behaviour is beneath fellow Astartes. Allow me to make amends.' It was an unexpected move. Certainly not one that Dak'ir had foreseen.

'Unnecessary, brother. A misunderstanding is all.'

'Even still. Our blood was up and things were said not befitting one Astartes to another.'

'Apology accepted, then.' Dak'ir nodded. 'But we were as culpable as you.'

'I appreciate your magnanimity, Brother...' Lorkar leaned forward and tilted his head slightly as he searched for the name, '...*Dak'ir*?'

The Salamander nodded again, this time to indicate that Lorkar was correct. The Marines Malevolent sergeant eased back, perpetuating a mood of camaraderie, but it was strained and false.

'Tell me, brother,' he said, his tone leading, and now Dak'ir knew he would get to the motivation behind Lorkar's sudden contrition. 'There is no campaign in the Hadron Belt, what brings you here?'

Lorkar was cunning. Dak'ir couldn't tell for certain if the sergeant's enquiry was merely to idle away time and build confidence or if something deeper lurked behind his words. He wanted to say that his timing was uncanny, but kept it to himself.

'Retribution,' returned Tsu'gan, his voice like a blade as he approached them. Evidently tired of his pacing, the Salamander sergeant had fixed upon the conversation between Lorkar and Dak'ir. 'We seek assassins, those who slew our captain in cold blood – renegades who call themselves the Dragon Warriors.'

'A matter of legacy. I see.' Lorkar rapped his plastron. 'This section of plate came from my dead sergeant's armour. I wear it to honour his sacrifice. Two of my slain brothers once wore this vambrace and pauldron–' He held up the pieces in turn '–before my own were shattered beyond repair.'

Tsu'gan stiffened at some unseen slight, but allowed Lorkar to continue.

'Do you bear your dead captain's armour still?' he asked.

Dak'ir weighed in on his fellow sergeant's behalf: 'No. It was incinerated, rendered to ash in keeping with our native customs.'

Lorkar looked nonplussed. 'You destroyed it?' His tone suggested consternation. 'Was the battle-plate entirely beyond repair?'

'Some could have been salvaged,' Dak'ir admitted. 'But instead it was offered to the mountain of fire on Nocturne, our home world, so that Kadai could return to the earth.'

Lorkar shook his head. 'My apologies, brother, but we of the Marines Malevolent are unused to such profligacy.'

Tsu'gan could restrain himself no longer. 'Would you have us bastardise our captain's armour instead, as you do?'

The Marine Malevolent glared back at him sternly. 'We only mean to honour our fallen brethren.'

Tsu'gan straightened as if stung. 'And we do not? We pay homage to our slain heroes, our lamented dead.'

The churning report of the blast door finally prising open prevented any caustic reply from Lorkar. Instead, the sergeant merely got to his feet and went to his Techmarine.

'And what is *your* business here, Sergeant Lorkar? You haven't told us that,' said Dak'ir as the Marine Malevolent was leaving.

'My orders stay within the Chapter,' he replied tersely, ramming on his battle-helm and rejoining his battle-brothers.

'It is more than protocol that stays his tongue. They are hiding something,' muttered Tsu'gan, before turning away himself, a dark look directed first at Lorkar and then Dak'ir.

Once Tsu'gan had gone, Dak'ir whispered, 'Keep your eyes open.'

Ba'ken's gaze was fixed on the departing yellow-armoured sergeant. He nodded, releasing his grip from the piston-hammer.

A THIN MIST drifted over the deck of the cryogenic vault like the slow passage of a tired apparition. A gaseous amalgam of nitrogen and helium combined to produce the chemical compound that would catalyse the cryogenic process, it rolled languidly off a series of semi-transparent tanks situated at one end of a large metal room. A high ceiling still carried the ubiquitous censers and there were small Mechanicus shrines set into alcoves in the walls. Exposed hosing, cables and other machinery were also prevalent. It was as if they were the excised innards of some mechanical behemoth, and this room was part of its mech-biology. The dense agglomeration of pipes and wires extruded from the room's perimeter and fed to a series of cryo-caskets that dominated a pair of raised, arc-shaped platforms in the centre. Both platforms were approximately two metres off deck level and reachable via a grilled metal stairway on two sides. A deactivated lifter plate was also evident, delineated by a rectangle of warning chevrons. The natural passageway between the two platforms led to the vault's only exit, a huge blast door sealed shut by three adamantium locking bars.

Brother Emek wiped his gauntleted hand across the thick plexi-glass of one of the cryo-caskets, breaking up a veneer of hoarfrost.

'No outward vital signs,' he muttered after a few moments. 'This one is dead, too.'

The liquid nitrogen run-off pooled around the Astartes's armoured boots, curling around his greaves. It spilled off the edge of the platform where Emek was standing to hang a few centimetres above the lower deck of the vault like a ghostly veil.

At the aft-facing end of the room Harkane worked at releasing the blast door, the low hiss of his plasma-cutter a dulcet chorus to the machine-hum of the stasis tanks. Half his Marines Malevolent battle-brothers were clustered around him – Lorkar's combat squad – intent on the Techmarine's endeavours as if whatever lay beyond the door was of profound interest to them. The brother-sergeant was locked in almost constant conference with his battle-helm's comm-feed now. Whoever he was getting his orders from was issuing regular instruction and demanding progress reports. The rest of Lorkar's troops were silently guarding the forced entry point and, unless Dak'ir's instincts were off, watching him and his battle-brothers.

The Salamanders' first concern was the possibility of survivors. The Marines Malevolent's disregard in this had not gone unnoticed, but was left unchallenged. Whatever the other Astartes' mission, the Salamanders were not privy to it and it was not the place of one Chapter to question another for such flimsy reasons when all the facts were not known. Pyriel was deter-mined it would not affect their own rescue efforts, however.

Two groups of five Salamanders, chosen from each of the two squads by their respective sergeants, were tasked with investigating the forty cryogenic chambers. Emek

led one group; Iagon the other. Two ranks of twenty
dominated the raised deck space, situated opposite the
blast doors against either wall. Within were human
adepts. Some had amputated limbs, fused stumps trailing insulated cables and wiring; others had hollow eye
sockets, ringed with pink scar-tissue and tiny puncture
marks where the installation pins had gone in and then
been retracted. The crew's constituent mechanical components – bionic eyes, arms, mechadendrite clusters
and even a half-track for a double leg amputee – were
locked away in transparent armour-plas receptacles,
stamped with the Mechanicus cog and fastened to their
individual cryo-caskets. So far, eighteen of the forty
were dead.

For one the freezing process had malfunctioned, atro-
phying his body, ice crystals infecting his lifeless skin
like a contagion; another had simply drowned in the
solution that had failed to catalyse when the casket was
activated, the adept's eyes wide with frozen panic, a forlornly beating fist held for eternity stuck to the
inner-glass. The others had succumbed to cardiac
infarction – possibly brought on through shock during
the cryogenic process or at the separation of their mechanised limbs and augmentation – hypothermia or
other, unidentifiable, mortalities.

One thing was clear. The steps taken to preserve the
crew, what few still lived, had been conducted in haste.

'Brother-Sergeant Dak'ir,' Emek's voice came over the
comm-feed in his battle-helm.

'Go ahead, brother,' Dak'ir returned. He was standing
on the lower deck alongside Brother Apion who was trying to raise the *Vulkan's Wrath* through a ship-to-ship
comm-device set up in the room. Thus far he'd had no
success – the strike-cruiser was obviously still out of
range.

'I need you to see this, sir,' Emek replied.

Dak'ir instructed Apion to continue. A self-conscious glance at Tsu'gan revealed his brother-sergeant to be intent on Lorkar and his warriors at the blast door. A cursory examination of the Salamanders' other forces showed that Pyriel was similarly engrossed, though Dak'ir suspected the Librarian's awareness went far beyond that of his fellow brother-sergeant. Those battle-brothers not engaged with checking the cryo-caskets were keeping sentry. The Salamanders mixed with the Marines Malevolent directly and the tension between them was almost palpable. Ba'ken, in particular, caught Dak'ir's attention positioned next to a Space Marine who was almost his match in sheer bulk. The Marine Malevolent bore a skull-faced battle-helm, the beak nose sheared off and sealed in order to promote the cranial analogue. Not like a Chaplain's, masterfully wrought to resemble bone, the battle-helm's decoration was painted on. He also carried a plasma gun, and held it with the sureness of a warrior born. The two massive Space Marines were very alike, but stoically refused to acknowledge one another. Dak'ir hoped it would stay that way as he reached the top of the stairway and the cryo-caskets.

Emek was a third of the way down the sub-group of four he was analysing when he saw his sergeant approach. Evidently, it was slow going.

Most of the associated instrumentation of the cryo-caskets was damaged, so there was no way to tell how long the stasis-sleep had lasted. It also retarded the assessment of vital signs, but the Salamanders engaged in that duty did so exhaustively and methodically. The majority of the bio-monitors situated beneath the caskets were no longer operating, either, or were simply too encrusted with ice to be readable. From the corner of his helmet lens, Dak'ir noted Iagon using his auspex to ascertain life signs in certain cases. The battle-brother acknowledged him from across the small gulf between the platforms, and Dak'ir felt his guard go up instinctively.

'Sir,' said Emek with a slight nod, once his sergeant had reached him.

'Show me, brother.'

Emek stepped back to allow Dak'ir to move in and get a better look.

'See for yourself, sergeant.'

Emek had smeared away the rime of ice crystals obscuring the view through the casket's plexi-glass frontis. Dak'ir peered through the ragged gap in the frost and saw the remains of the adept inside. It was difficult to discern at first: the nitro-helium solution was tainted with blood, lots of blood. Other things floated in the tank too, held fast in the stagnant liquid.

'Flesh,' Emek said from behind him. 'Bone chips too, if I'm not mistaken.'

'Mercy of Vulkan…' Dak'ir breathed. His voice was made even hollower through his battle-helm.

'Self-mutilation, sir.' The explanation was hardly necessary. Deep lacerations ran down the adept's torso, arms and legs, four-pronged as if dug by fingernails. The stark evidence of the adept's hands supported that theory – they were stained with blood. Three of the nails had been ripped off, revealing the soft red membrane beneath; the rest were clogged with shreds of flensed skin.

'This one had ocular implants?' Dak'ir asked.

'No, sir.'

The eyes, then, had been torn out. Gore streaked from the ruined sockets that were deep and red and visceral. Dak'ir regarded the abomination sternly.

'Assessment?'

Emek paused, weighing up his words, until his sergeant faced him to demand an answer. 'I believe the ship turned on itself, though I don't know how or why,' he said.

Dak'ir remembered the view of the *Archimedes Rex* through the *Fire-wyvern's* occuliport; in retrospect, the weapons damage was strange. It was possible that the ship's crippling had been self-inflicted. It might also explain why they had encountered one single magos – he was the last standing, having killed the rest. The cryo-vault was sealed, not against foreign invaders, but to keep the rest of the ship's inhabitants out.

'What about the servitors?' Dak'ir followed his line of reasoning out loud.

'They aren't sentient like the magos and the other adepts. Perhaps they weren't affected in the same way.'

Dak'ir took one last look at the mutilated adept in the tank. His salvation had come too late. Sealed in the cryo-casket, and with nothing to attack, he had evidently turned on himself.

'Keep looking for survivors,' he said, turning, glad to avert his gaze from the gruesome spectacle.

As he walked back down the access stairway, Dak'ir's comm-feed crackled to life. It was on a closed channel with himself and Tsu'gan.

'Brother-sergeants…'

Dak'ir looked over at the sound of Pyriel's voice. The Librarian maintained his vigil over their dubious allies. The cause for his words was obvious. The Marines Malevolent had opened up the blast doors. When he reached the Librarian, Dak'ir saw inside the chamber the other Astartes had been so fixated on. It was a massive storage room, akin to the one they'd discovered earlier only much larger. Also unlike the smaller munitions store, this one had a vast cache of manufactured arms and armour: MkVII battle-plate hung in suits from overhead armatures; bolters sat in racks like parade soldiers, pristine and unfired; ammo crates brimming with sickle mags for the guns were piled in pallets of a hundred, a thousand clips per crate. Materiel spanned the hangar-like room in an unending slew of grey-black.

The Marines Malevolent were already emptying it, positioning guns, ammunition and power armour directly outside the chamber within an invisibly delineated area.

Dak'ir then realised what Lorkar and his battle-brothers were doing on the *Archimedes Rex*. The fledgling weapons were the perfect replacements for their arcane militaria. The Marines Malevolent were re-supplying; appropriating the materiel cache from the forge-ship for their own purposes.

One of the yellow-armoured warriors, the shark-helmeted Brother Nemiok, had been in brief concert with his sergeant and afterwards removed something from a large belt pouch. It was a bulky device, hoisted into position atop the centre of the small arms cache by a thick handle, and consisted of a narrow-necked tube with a lozenge-shaped tip that contained a beacon, appended with small pistons that powered a ribbed compression cylinder.

Though crude and out-dated, Dak'ir recognised it at once. It was a teleport homer. En route to the *Archimedes Rex*, the Salamanders had neither seen nor detected another vessel. Dak'ir could only assume the *Fire-wyvern's* sensor arrays lacked the range to discover it, for he was sure now that the Marines Malevolent had a cruiser nearby, its teleportarium primed for the stolen Mechanicus haul.

Tsu'gan stormed towards the ring of yellow-armoured Astartes that had formed just in front of the teleportation zone.

'What do you think you're doing, *brother*?' he growled, ignoring the others and addressing Lorkar directly.

The sergeant was directing two of his battle-brothers hefting the equipment out of the storage room and didn't look at Tsu'gan when he answered.

'What it looks like, Salamander. I am re-supplying my Chapter.'

'You steal that which is not meant for you,' he countered, clenching his fists. 'I did not realise the Marines Malevolent were honourless pirates.'

Now Lorkar turned, and his previous nonchalance crumbled away.

'We are true servants of the Emperor. Our integrity is beyond reproach. We seek only the means to prosecute His wars.'

'Then honour the pact made between He and the Mechanicus. We Astartes have no call to pillage and ransack the stricken ships of Mars. You are no better than carrion snapping at the flesh of a corpse.'

'What concern is it of yours, anyway?' Lorkar returned, a slight tilt of his head suggested a glance at something behind the Salamander. 'Stay out of it.'

Tsu'gan felt the lightest pressure on his pauldron when he turned swiftly, seizing the wrist of the Space Marine attempting to surprise him and twisting until the bones snapped and he forced his assailant to one knee.

'Attempt to rise and I shall shatter your kneecap,' Tsu'gan promised, addressing the skull-faced Marine Malevolent with the plasma gun. Despite the obvious pain he was in, the yellow-armoured Astartes looked to his sergeant before he would relent.

Ba'ken stirred from his sentry position, as did the other Salamanders on overwatch, together with those manning the cryo-caskets.

'Remain where you are.' Pyriel's curt command arrested any further escalation.

Ba'ken seemed about to press anyway, when a glance from Dak'ir warned him off and he merely watched instead. Of the Marines Malevolent, only Brother Rennard had broken ranks, doubtless in response to an earlier directive from his sergeant.

Lorkar's fists were clenched as he considered what to do next. It was as if time had frozen. The tension in the room was strained; a little more pressure and it would break out in bloody violence. Dak'ir noticed that Harkane had switched the gun platform from dormant to active, the red targeting matrix hazing in the cryogas.

He thought about disabling the Techmarine. He still had enough charge in his plasma pistol for a wounding shot. It took less than a second for Dak'ir to decide against it. So delicately poised as the situation was, any unexpected move could be disastrous. Tsu'gan had the lead for now and he had to be content with that. A degree of insurance would be prudent, though, and it was with this in mind that Dak'ir issued the sub-vocal command into a closed channel of the comm-feed.

'Do you really want to do this?' Tsu'gan still had his back to Lorkar, glaring down intently at the Marine Malevolent under his control.

Lorkar exhaled slowly and released his clenched fists. 'Brother Rennard, stand down,' he ordered reluctantly, and the skull-faced Astartes relaxed. Tsu'gan let him go, facing Lorkar again, an awkward stand-off in prospect.

'These weapons can either gather dust on this wreck or be put to use destroying the enemies of mankind. We will not abandon them.'

Pyriel's voice invaded the deadlock. 'You are wrong. They will be returned to the Mechanicus for proper allocation,' he said. 'You are outnumbered by a superior force. Neither of us wants a conflict here. Relent at once or face the consequences.'

Harkane shifted, about to do something he would later regret, when he staggered a little as if stunned.

I would collapse your mind before your finger squeezed the trigger!

Dak'ir heard the psychic impel that was meant only for Harkane, and it chilled him.

Lorkar, who had not been privy to the mental threat, continued undeterred, nodding with assertion. 'The weapons and armour *are* leaving this ship–' he paused mid flow, slightly bowing his head again as instructions were relayed through his comm-feed.

'Let us all hear your orders, *Malevolent*,' Tsu'gan growled contemptuously. 'Or is the voice on the other end of that comm-feed too craven?'

Rennard had got to his feet and was supporting his broken wrist, when he spoke up. 'You disrespect a captain of the Astartes!'

Tsu'gan turned on him next.

'Show me this captain,' he demanded. 'I hear only a whispering coward hiding behind the pauldrons of his sergeant.'

Ba'ken loomed suddenly behind the belligerent Rennard, who was slightly crouched with his injury and wise enough to make no further move, merely seething behind his macabre battle-helm.

Dak'ir nodded to the bulky Salamander, who returned the gesture.

'Well then?' Tsu'gan pressed, focused on the Marine Malevolent sergeant. 'Where is he?'

Lorkar stalked forwards, the ring of armour parting to let him through as he unhitched an item from his belt and came face-to-face with Tsu'gan. Going to his fellow brother-sergeant's side at once, Dak'ir noticed Pyriel making a similar move as Lorkar whispered:

'As you wish…'

Brace yourselves!

* * *

II
Purgatory

IT WAS THE last thing Dak'ir heard as the cryo-vault disappeared in a brilliant magnesium flash. Then came pain, so raw and invasive it was as if his organs were twisting inside out, as if the very molecular structure of his being was breaking down in a nanosecond, atom by atom, reforming and disintegrating again a moment later. Sulphur and cordite wreathed his nostrils, so overwhelming he couldn't breathe. The acrid taste of copper filled his mouth as all notions of time and existence bled away into a soup of primal instinct, like being born. The tangible gave way to the ethereal as all meaning fled from his senses.

The light subsided as an image slowly resolved around Dak'ir. The actinic stench remained, as did the blood lining his teeth and in his mouth. He saw metal, felt it concretely beneath his booted feet. A sensation of nausea followed, supplemented by a bout of sudden vertigo making Dak'ir stagger as the corporeal world re-established itself.

He was on a ship. The device in Lorkar's hand had been a homing beacon, through which he'd teleported them aboard.

'The nausea will pass,' a grating voice Dak'ir recognised as Sergeant Lorkar's assured them.

Dak'ir was standing in a large circular room. It had a vaulted ceiling that led away into unfathomable darkness, and was poorly lit by sodium simulacra-lamps. Around its vast circumference, the room was papered with cloth banners describing numerous victories with rubrics daubed in High Gothic script, yellow-and-black armoured Astartes holding skulls and other grisly talismans aloft to the adulation of a horde. A hundred campaigns or more were arrayed across the chamber's ambit, each devoted to the Marines Malevolent Chapter's 2nd Company. The Marines Malevolent were not a First Founding Chapter, they had not fought in the Great Crusade, bringing thousands of worlds into compliance, but on the evidence of their laurels, one could be forgiven for thinking otherwise.

Accenting the self-aggrandising banners were other trophies – the actual macabre totems depicted on the cloth. Dak'ir saw the flayed skulls of xenos: orks, their jutting jaws and sloped brows unmistakable; the tyranid bio-form he recognised from the Chamber of Remembrance on Prometheus and the wing devoted to 2nd Company recounting their exploits on Ymgarl, when they cleansed the moon of a genestealer infestation. The bleached cranium of a hated eldar also sneered down at him, its countenance as haughty and disdainful in death as it was in life. The graven battle-helms of the Traitor Legions were also present, hollowed out and staring balefully. Disturbingly, he caught sight of a battle-helm that did not bear any Chaotic hallmarks he could discern, though it sparked a pang of remembrance in him. It was difficult to tell in the gloom and he was still fighting off the unpleasant lingering sensation of the recent teleport, but it appeared to be stygian black with a bony protrusion punching through the apex of the helmet like a crest.

'Idiot – you could have killed us all with that stunt.' Tsu'gan's voice arrested Dak'ir's attention. His fists were bunched as he directed his wrath at Lorkar. The Salamander sergeant was shaking, though Dak'ir couldn't tell if it was with anger or if he too was still acclimatising to their sudden transition from the *Archimedes Rex.*

Tsu'gan was right, though. Teleportation was a dangerous and inexact science. Even with the benefit of a homing beacon, the chances of becoming lost in the warp or translating back as a gibbering morass of fleshy blubber as your insides became your outsides were still uncomfortably high. To engage in teleportation when those translating had not been primed or were not wearing Terminator armour to protect them from the physical rigours of the process was even more hazardous.

'I did it to make a point.' The voice was hard like iron, full of power and self-confidence. It echoed from the edge of the room where the gloom gathered, and the Salamanders followed it to its source.

Bisecting the circle of glory was a steel dais holding up a black throne upon which sat a figure in the manner of a recumbent king. Only the tips of the figure's boots were visible, together with the suggestion of a yellow greave cast in the corona of light issuing from a nearby simulacra-lamp. His identity was swathed in shadow for now.

He was evidently a student of war history. Above the throne were numerous maps of ancient conquests and crusades. There were weapons, too: esoteric firearms, blades of unknown origin and other strange devices. The throne room was a proud boast, designed to promote the captain's obvious sense of vainglory.

'I am Captain Vinyar and this is my ship, the *Purgatory*. Whatever control you think you have here, you are wrong. The Mechanicus vessel is mine, I lay claim to all its contents.'

'*Lay claim*? You may lay claim to nothing, and will release the *Archimedes Rex* to our charge in the name of the Emperor,' said Tsu'gan.

'Cool your temper, brother-sergeant,' Pyriel warned in a low voice, a spectator until now. 'You are addressing a captain of the Astartes.' Dak'ir noted that unlike him and his brother-sergeant, the Librarian showed no outward signs of discomfort from their enforced journey.

'You are wise to rein your sergeant in, Librarian,' said Vinyar and leaned forward into the light in order to show his face.

The captain's countenance was as adamantine as his voice. Callous eyes glared out from an almost square head sat on broad Astartes shoulders. Bald, apart from the sporadic tufts of closely-shaven hair infecting his scalp like hirsute lesions, Vinyar had a stubbled chin with a jaw like a hammer-head. Three platinum service studs punctuated a line across his brow above a blood-shot left eye.

Vinyar wore the yellow and black battle-plate of his brothers. Both pauldrons carried chevrons, the veteran 'hazard' markings of the Marines Malevolent, and a ragged cloak of black ermine unfurled from his shoulders like old sackcloth. His left arm ended in a power glove, though the fingers looked to be fused, indicating they could no longer be opened. Dak'ir sensed that Vinyar had no use for gripping with it anyway, and needed it only as a hammer with which to brutalise his enemies.

A trace of amusement curled up his top lip in the approximation of a smile, but there was no mirth in it. If Lorkar was grizzled, then Vinyar was positively leaden by comparison.

Dak'ir noted that the hard-faced captain did not bother to ask Pyriel's or, indeed, any of their names. The fact was evidently unimportant to him.

'He makes a valid point, though, Brother-Captain Vinyar,' Pyriel asserted, stepping forward as Lorkar was dismissed by his superior.

'Oh yes…' invited Vinyar.

Dak'ir noticed armoured figures lumbering in the penumbral shadows at the edge of the throne room, just beyond the walls of victory banners. He recognised the forms as Terminators, but wearing an ersatz variant of the modern Tactical Dreadnought Armour. It was bulky with raised pauldrons surmounting a sunken, box-shaped battle-helm that had a rudimentary mouth-grille. The armour was much less refined with restricted dexterity, though it carried a fairly standard weapons array consisting of a power glove, but with a twin-linked combi-bolter in lieu of the more usual storm bolter. Despite their archaism, the Astartes wearing those suits were still deadly.

Pyriel went on undaunted.

'That you will leave the *Archimedes Rex* at once and render the forge-ship to us.'

'You are welcome to it, brother.' Vinyar grinned. Dak'ir likened it to the expression a shark might make if ever amused. 'I only desire its contents.'

'Which you will also yield to us,' Pyriel replied, not rising to Vinyar's facetiousness.

Vinyar leaned back and was lost to shadow again, evidently tiring of the game he was playing.

'Bring it up on the screen,' he said into the ship's voxlink, situated on the arm of his throne.

A small antenna poked its way up insidiously from between the cracks in the deck plate a short distance from Vinyar's throne. Once it had reached two metres in height it stopped and expanded into three metre-length prongs at its apex, between which a holographic image was revealed. It showed the *Archimedes Rex*, or rather a close up view of a section of its generatoria unseen from the *Fire-wyvern's* angle of approach. The pict threw off grainy blue light, and cast Vinyar macabrely in the half-dark.

'The generatoria you see in the holo-cast provides power to the forge-ship's life support systems, amongst some others.'

The image panned out swiftly, showing the end of a scorched cannon turret. 'One of the *Purgatory's* many,' Vinyar revealed. 'Master Vorkan, do you have a firing solution?'

A disembodied voice replied from the vox-link.

'Yes, my lord.'

Vinyar turned his attention back to the Salamanders.

'A single lance salvo will critically damage that generatoria, destroying the life support systems and with it any chance of rescuing any survivors aboard.'

Tsu'gan bristled with barely contained rage. Dak'ir felt his knuckles crack as he subconsciously made fists. Such an act was unconscionable. To treat human life with such flagrant disregard; it made him sick to the stomach, so much so that his objections came out in a grating rasp.

'You cannot mean to do this. To appropriate arms, to steal from a crippled ship is one thing, but *murder*?'

'I am no murderer, brother-sergeant.' Vinyar's eyes were dark hollows pinpricked by tiny spots of malice as he regarded Dak'ir. 'Murder is an assassin's bullet or a hiver's blade in the back. I am a soldier, as are you. And in battle, sacrifices must be made. I act out of necessity, in order that my Chapter should prevail. It is your hand that forces mine, not the other way around.'

'Do that and I will have no other recourse but to order my Astartes aboard the *Archimedes Rex* to take custody of yours, the outcome of which would not end favourably for you,' said Pyriel, re-entering the fray. 'Would you condemn your warriors to that fate?'

The holo-pict shut off, killing the light as the broadcast antenna retracted.

Vinyar leaned forwards again, scoffing. 'Of course not, they would be extracted before the attack even took place.'

'How?' Tsu'gan's tone was scornful. 'Even the Raven Guard couldn't perform such a manoeuvre.'

Vinyar turned his attention to the brother-sergeant. 'In the same way we extracted you. Teleportation is much easier going out than coming in, hence the reason I favoured boarding torpedoes for our initial breach.'

The arrogant captain allowed a pause. In it, his mood of vainglory seemed to gloss over for a moment, replaced by a veneer of sincerity.

'We Astartes are brothers. We should not come to blows over this. There is no malice here; it is only war. I have fought in over a hundred campaigns, over hundreds of worlds and hundreds of systems. Xenos, traitors and heretics, witches and daemons of all forms – they have died by my righteous hand. Humanity owes a debt of gratitude to my Chapter, as it does all the Chapters of the Astartes. It is by our will and strength of arms that they are kept safe, ignorant of the terrors of Old Night.' He made an expansive gesture with his arm as if to suggest the universe was contained in his very throne room. 'What are the fates of a few balanced against a galaxy of trillions?'

'Bad deeds are bad deeds,' countered Dak'ir. 'There is no scale upon which they can be weighed against your victories, brother-captain, no measure that can account for monstrous acts.'

Vinyar held up his hand, his voice never more serious.

'I am no monster. I do what I must to serve the Emperor's light. But make no mistake...' And like a harsh wind blowing away the ash from a smothered fire, his plaintive demeanour came away. '*I* am the master here. And it is I who shall dictate what–'

The crackling of the vox-link on the arm of his throne interrupted him.

'Yes.' Vinyar hissed with impatience.

'My lord,' the disembodied voice issued from some other unknown part of the ship, 'a vessel is hailing us.' There was a short pause before the voice continued. 'It is an Astartes strike cruiser.'

Vinyar raised an eyebrow as he turned to regard the Salamanders. The exchange between them remained unspoken, and as he suddenly felt his dominance slipping away like earth from a sundered hill, he issued a reluctant command.

'Broadcast it into my throne room.'

The link was cut and a new rain of static began as the ship's communications patched in from another source.

'Yours, I presume,' Vinyar muttered with bitter disdain.

Pyriel didn't even have time to nod as Captain N'keln's voice rang powerfully throughout the room from concealed vox speakers in the walls.

'This is Brother-Captain N'keln of the Salamanders 3rd Company, aboard strike cruiser *Vulkan's Wrath*. Release my men at once or face the consequences.'

Dak'ir smiled behind his battle-helm. Evidently Brother Apion had managed to establish contact with their ship.

'You address Captain Vinyar of the Marines Malevolent, and we do not respond to demands.' Vinyar was bullish, despite the precarious position he was in.

'You will respond to mine,' N'keln replied curtly. 'Escort my men back to the *Archimedes Rex*. I will not ask a third time.'

'Your men are free to go when they choose. It was they that requested an audience.'

'You will also hand over the forge-ship to our authority.' N'keln pressed, ignoring what the other captain had just said.

Vinyar scowled, clearly not liking where this was going.

'The ship is ours,' he hissed, his expression dark as he surveyed the three Salamanders before him, foisting all of his anger upon them in lieu of their absent captain. 'I will not relinquish it.'

There was another pause before the vox-link crackled again and the disembodied voice from before issued out.

'My lord, we are detecting weapons priming on the *Vulkan's Wrath*.'

Vinyar whirled to confront the vox-link as if it were an enemy that could be threatened or intimidated to change its report.

'What?' he snapped, flashing daggers at Pyriel. 'Confirm: the Salamander ship is bringing weapons to bear?'

'A full broadside of laser batteries, yes my lord.'

Vinyar hammered the arm of his throne with his power fist and crushed it. With the remnants of shattered circuitry and other detritus dripping to the ground from his fist, he glared at the invaders in front of him.

'You would fire upon a fellow Astartes vessel, but rail at me for threatening to execute a gaggle of human serfs?'

The Salamanders remained stoic in their silence. The confrontation was all but over now; they only needed to wait it out.

Vinyar slumped back heavily in his half-demolished throne, all arrogance and superiority having bled away from his expression and his body language – in its place was seething annoyance. The air was charged, and for a moment it seemed as if the Marine Malevolent captain was debating whether or not to engage the *Vulkan's Wrath* anyway and slay the interlopers aboard his ship. In the end, he relented.

'Take the vessel, if you must. But mark me: this misdeed will be remembered, Salamanders. None who raise arms against the Marines Malevolent do so without consequence or reply.' Vinyar turned away from them then to quietly brood in the shadows. When he did speak again a few seconds later, his voice was little more than a hate-filled whisper.

'Now, get off my ship.'

NOT WISHING TO risk the capriciousness of the *Purgatory's* teleportarium or its captain's spite, Pyriel transported the errant Salamanders back aboard the *Archimedes Rex* by psychically opening a gate of infinity into the immaterium. Invoking such power was not without risk, but Pyriel as an Epistolary-level Librarian was accomplished in his craft. The three Astartes arrived back in the cryovault aboard the forge-ship without mishap.

Though still uncomfortable, Dak'ir found the experience much less disconcerting as the metal walls of the room slowly resolved around him. An eldritch storm heralded their arrival as the veil over the material realm was peeled back to allow the Salamanders through. Re-emerging into reality, they found themselves encircled by their battle-brothers, weapons ready in the event of something unnatural coming across with them, seeking access via the breach in the fabric of reality that Pyriel had torn in order to effect their crossing.

Upon transition back aboard the *Archimedes Rex*, and after the dispersal of their vigilant battle-brothers, Dak'ir noticed that the Marines Malevolent were gone. Vinyar had evidently made good on his promise to haul his warriors out of the ship. But that wasn't all that was missing. The modest cache of arms the Marines Malevolent had piled up ready for teleport was absent too.

'When did this happen?' Tsu'gan demanded to know as soon as he'd realised the weapons and armour were missing.

'Upon extraction, no more than a minute before your arrival,' offered Brother S'tang, 'Men and materiel fled as one.'

S'tang was one of those keeping sentry and who had reacted upon his errant sergeant's return.

Tsu'gan shook his head in disgust and turned to Brother Apion, who was stationed farther away by the ship's vox-link. It was he who had re-established contact with the *Vulkan's Wrath*.

'This cannot stand. Raise Captain N'keln at once. We must chase these curs down and take back what they've stolen.'

'With respect, brother-sergeant, Captain N'keln has already been informed.'

Tsu'gan's wrath was stayed a moment.

'And what is to be done?'

'Nothing, sir. The captain is content that we have the ship and the bulk of its arms. He does not wish to press the issue with the Marines Malevolent any further.'

'For what reason?' Tsu'gan asked, his anger abruptly returned. 'They are pirates, tantamount to renegades in my eyes. Vinyar and his whoresons must be brought to account for this.'

Brother Apion, to his great credit, was unflinching in the face of the sergeant's ire. 'Those are the captain's orders, sir.'

'Given without explanation?'

'Yes, sir.'

Iagon's voice insinuated its way into the debate.

'I am certain the captain would have had his reasons, brother-sergeant. It is likely he did not wish to risk the lives of any potential Mechanicus survivors.' He had not been amongst the sentry party, and was standing just below the raised platform having recently descended following his duties and cast his gaze over the cryo-caskets. '*Few* as that may be. The company is also sore from its previous campaign. We are still licking our wounds. He may not have favoured conflict with another strike cruiser bereft of the element of surprise.'

'You should hold your tongue, Iagon, forked as it is.' Ba'ken loomed over the other Salamander. 'The captain's orders are not for you to discuss.'

Iagon tried not to balk in the face of the massive warrior's presence. He merely made a plaintive gesture and backed away a step, before feigning interest in cryo-casket readings patched in to his auspex.

Dak'ir took up the baton for his heavy weapons trooper.

'Captain N'keln is wise enough to know any fight with a fellow battle-brother, albeit from a Chapter as arbitrary as the Marines Malevolent, is a foolish and futile one.'

'Your opinion is neither warranted nor asked for, Ignean,' Tsu'gan replied darkly. The mood around the gathered Salamanders was becoming strained. It was as if the Marines Malevolent had never gone.

'Let it rest, brother-sergeant,' Pyriel's voice was as stern and uncompromising as an anvil. A faint aura of power was dying in his helmet lenses, and Dak'ir assumed the Librarian had been telepathically communicating with their distant brothers. 'The *Vulkan's Wrath* is already en route to us. We are to regroup in the fighter bay where we'll be met by a Thunderhawk. The survivors and their cryo-caskets are to be made ready for transport.'

Tsu'gan was ready to object, clearly incensed at what he saw as capitulation in the face of an enemy. Pyriel steered him back on target.

'You have your orders, brother-sergeant.'

Tsu'gan's body relaxed as he found his composure.

'As you wish, my lord,' he returned and went to organise his squad.

Dak'ir watched him go, seeing the anger linger upon him like a dark stain. Tsu'gan was poor at hiding his feelings, even behind the ceramite mask of his battle-helm. But Dak'ir sensed his displeasure was not directed at the Librarian, but at N'keln instead. Suddenly the ugly spectre of dissension with 3rd Company loomed once more.

Trying to put it out of his mind, he focused on the other Salamanders who were now busy securing the cryo-caskets for immediate evacuation and transit, disengaging them from the ship's onboard systems and allowing the internal power source of each to maintain it. A risky procedure for sure, and one not without casualties, but it was the only way any of the still living adepts were going to make it off the *Archimedes Rex*. Much like the initial assessment of the cryo-inhabitants' condition, careful extraction from the forge-ship was a slow process. Gradually though, Emek and Iagon – who had subsequently returned to his original duties – led their teams to work through each and every casket. The report at the end of it was bleak: only seven survivors.

It seemed small recompense for such an arduous journey. Dak'ir was reminded again of the doubt expressed in N'keln's judgement in insisting on this mission. The fallow results aboard the forge-ship could only serve to justify that doubt. He wondered briefly how many more of these cryo-vaults were situated around the ship and if it was even possible for the Salamanders to reach them and secure additional survivors. Those seven that still lived, when brought aboard the *Vulkan's Wrath* when it eventually reached them, would need to be taken to a nearby Imperial medical facility until the Mechanicus could recover them. That was assuming the Martians were even interested in collecting them. Whatever the case, upon revival and restoration, they would be pressed back into the service of the glorious Imperium.

'Glad to see you've returned to us in one piece, with your entrails inside your armour and all limbs attached,' said Ba'ken in a low voice, intruding unknowingly on Dak'ir's thoughts.

'Your relief is second only to my own, brother. Vinyar, their captain, was like no Astartes I have ever met. He was utterly ruthless – the antithesis of a Salamander. It is good to be back amongst my Chapter. It set me thinking, though. Whether or not we are too compassionate and if it is the very fact we value human life, perhaps more so than any of our brothers, that hampers our effectiveness as warriors.'

Ba'ken laughed quietly and without mirth. 'Chaplain Elysius would tell us that Astartes do not experience doubt, that they are sure in all things, especially war. But there is a difference between dogma and reality, I think. Only by questioning and then knowing the answers are right can we truly obtain certainty. As for compassion being a weakness… I don't think so, sir. Compassion is our greatest asset. It is what bonds us as brothers, and unites us towards a righteous and noble purpose,' Ba'ken replied, as sure and steady as the rock of Mount Death-fire itself.

'Our bond feels strained of late.' The implication at the discord in 3rd Company was obvious by Dak'ir's tone.

'Aye, and this latest mission will have done nothing to alleviate it.'

As those dark thoughts were churning through Dak'ir's mind, some unknown imperative at the edge of his sub-conscious made him turn towards the gaping blast doors that led into the storage room. The Marines Malevolent had escaped with only a meagre percentage of the materiel within, but Dak'ir felt compelled to see what they had left behind anyway.

'Brother-sergeant?' Ba'ken's voice invaded the sudden introspection.

Dak'ir looked back at him.

'Is something amiss?' Ba'ken asked.

Dak'ir hadn't even realised he'd started walking away from him. As if drawn by a siren's song, he had drifted towards the storage room and was almost at its threshold when Ba'ken had hailed him.

'No, brother.' Though truthfully, Dak'ir did not even know. 'The remaining arms cache must be inspected before transit; that is all.'

'Then let the serfs do that upon our return to the *Vulkan's Wrath*. It is no task for an Astartes, let alone a brother-sergeant.'

'A cursory examination only, Ba'ken.' Even to Dak'ir, his explanation sounded weak. He felt oddly detached, like when the teleportarium had wrenched them from the material realm and returned them aboard the *Purgatory*. Only this was somehow different, almost ethereal as if a layer of fog had manifested over the world around him, giving some sensations clarity whilst dampening others, and heightening his awareness.

'Do you require assistance? I can assign G'heb and Zo'tan.'

'No, Ba'ken, that won't be necessary. I can do this alone.' Just before he turned back, Dak'ir added as an afterthought, 'You are wise, Ba'ken, and would make an excellent sergeant.'

'Ah, but some are meant to lead and some are just meant to fight, brother,' he replied. 'I know I am of the latter.'

If he could have seen his face behind his battle-helm, Dak'ir felt sure that the heavy weapons trooper would be smiling. And then, unable to resist the pull any longer, Dak'ir entered the storage room as Ba'ken and the rest of his battle-brothers were lost from sight.

The vast chamber of materiel seemed larger within than it had without. A small army could be outfitted from the ranks of guns, armour and ammunition inside it. As Dak'ir paced slowly down its length, at least a hundred metres from end to end, he noticed racks of heavy weapons stored amongst the bolters: missile launchers sat together in foam-padded crates, their incendiaries snug alongside them in clusters of three; heavy bolters arranged on separate weapons racks looked bulky and full of violent potential, belt-feeds coiled up in drums next to them; rows of flamers, igniter nozzles pristine, rested beside cylinders of volatile promethium. Dak'ir noticed the suits of power armour, too – all dark metal, waiting to be baptised in the colours of the Chapter for whom they were intended, for the artisans and Tech-marines to add insignia and the sigils of honour.

All were as shadows as Dak'ir passed them. They seemed dull and monochrome like a room washed in low light. The keening call, his siren's song, was a buzzing in his ears now, an insistent throb at the base of his skull like a slow-beating heart. Nearing the back of the long chamber, the throb became faster and faster, the noise in his ears more high-pitched. Just when Dak'ir thought he might cry out, the sound stopped. He saw a simple metal chest nestled at the very back of the room, incongruous amongst all the munitions. It was a small thing; Dak'ir could have held it in one hand. Rectangular in shape, it had hard edges that reminded him of the head of an anvil, and something was inscribed on the flat lid.

It was only a chest, an innocuous vessel for some unknown item, yet Dak'ir hesitated as he reached for it. Fear wasn't the emotion that stayed his hand, such things were beneath Astartes; rather it felt like *awe*.

'Dak'ir...'

Dak'ir reacted to the voice behind him, turning quickly then relaxing when he saw Pyriel, but only a fraction. The Librarian was looking at something at waist height on the brother-sergeant.

Dak'ir followed his eye line and saw the chest was cradled in his gauntlets. He hadn't even realised he'd picked it up.

'I found something, Brother-Librarian,' he offered thinly.

'I see that, brother. Though I am amazed you even discovered it.' Pyriel gestured over the other Salamander's shoulder at something behind him.

Dak'ir looked behind him and saw upturned crates, piles of munitions strewn across the floor, weapons racks cast aside in his unremembered fervour to locate the chest.

'You were not quiet in your search,' Pyriel told him.

Dak'ir faced him again, something like disbelief affecting the sergeant's demeanour.

'The ruckus was what alerted me to your presence, brother,' the Librarian continued, and Dak'ir felt that same burning gaze – assessing, gauging, deliberating.

'I...' was all the Salamander sergeant could respond with.

'Let me see it.' Pyriel reached out with an open palm and took up the chest reverently as Dak'ir handed it over.

Now he turned that omniscient scrutiny upon the artefact held in his hand.

'This is Vulkan's mark,' he uttered after a few moments. 'It is his icon, a unique brand borne only by the primarch and his forgefathers.' Pyriel's fingers traced subtle grooves and engravings now suddenly visible on the chest's surface, touching it delicately as if it was fragile porcelain, despite the fact of the chest's hardy metal construction. 'It is sealed,' he went on, although now it appeared he was speaking to himself. 'No skill I possess can open it.' The Librarian paused, as if unlocking some clandestine facet of the chest. 'There is an origin stamp...'

Pyriel looked up, as if struck dumb.

'What is it, brother? Where does it come from?'

Pyriel uttered a single word, as if it were the only sound that could pass his lips at that moment. It was one that Dak'ir knew well, and held the heavy weight of prophecy.

'Isstvan.'

CHAPTER FOUR

I
Unto the Anvil

'Is PYRIEL CERTAIN?' asked Ba'ken as they waited for the cryo-caskets to be secured aboard the *Spear of Prometheus*. The Thunderhawk had been waiting for them upon their return to the fighter bay. So too was the *Fire-wyvern*, together with its capable guardian, Brother Amadeus. The Dreadnought was now secured in his grav-scaffold as the Salamanders made ready to depart the *Archimedes Rex*. They could not linger in-system, especially given Dak'ir's discovery. A beacon had been set on the stricken forge-ship matched to Mechanicus frequencies and numerous astropathic hails sent out in the hope that a Martian carrier or Imperial reclamator crews would hear it. Other than that, there was little else that could be done. The ship might never be found or left to drift for centuries, colliding with other crippled vessels until the conglomeration of ruined metal became a hulk and was inhabited by such creatures who found succour in the cold and dark.

Several kilometres distant, the *Vulkan's Wrath* loitered having laid anchor, small bursts of its hull engines preventing it from drifting in the gulf of space. The materiel cache from the storage room next to the cryo-vault was already aboard and being catalogued by serfs. Though the cryo-caskets and their inert cargo were too precious to risk, the arms and armour were not and so were teleported to the strike cruiser's storage bay in short order.

'Yes, he is certain,' answered Dak'ir, his attention only half on the skeleton crew from the *Spear of Prometheus*. The servitors were part of Brother Argos's retinue and assisted in transporting the suspensor-lofted cryo-caskets up the embarkation ramp into the gunship's otherwise barren hold. The Master of the Forge kept a watchful eye over proceedings. In order to ensure the Chamber Sanctuarine, where the caskets would be housed, was as empty as possible he had shed his servo-harness and wore only a basic Techmarine's rig. He still looked formidable – Argos had lost the left side of his face whilst fighting alongside the 2nd Company on Ymgarl. He had only been a Techmarine then, a mere novice of the Cult Mechanicus and recently returned from a long internship on Mars where he had learned the liturgies of maintenance and engineering, and mastered communion with the machine-spirits.

Fighting side by side with the now Brother-Sergeant Lok of the 3rd Company Devastators, an encounter with a broodlord had robbed him of his face but not his life, Argos severing the creature in half with his plasma-cutter whilst Lok had applied the kill shot to its bulbous cranium with his bolter.

A steel plate concealed his injuries now, augmented by a bionic replacement for the eye that he'd lost. The image of a snarling firedrake was burned into it, tail coiled around the optical implant, as an emblem of honour. The numerous branding marks that swathed his skin in concentric vortices of scarification came much later – proud sigils of his many deeds.

Like many devoted to the Omnissiah, Argos had forked plugs punching from the flesh of his bald head, with a nest of wires and cables that wormed around the back of his neck and into his nose. His armour was old, an artificer suit but not in the same respect as that worn by another veteran of the Chapter. Festooned with mechanical interfaces, tools and power arrays, it was utterly unlike any power armour, relic or otherwise. It carried the cog symbol to show his allegiance to the Mechanicus, but this was married up with the icon of his Chapter displayed proudly on his right pauldron. A device on his gorget translated his hollow, metallic speech into binaric as he directed the servitors.

'The origin stamp was very clear,' stated Dak'ir as the first of the cryo-caskets was brought aboard the *Spear of Prometheus*. 'It came from Isstvan.'

Ba'ken exhaled deeply as if trying to mitigate a heavy burden.

'Now that is an old name, gratefully forgotten.'

Dak'ir said nothing. The fell legend of Isstvan need not be spoken aloud. All of the old XVIII Legion knew of it.

The Isstvan system was notorious in the historical annals of the Astartes. It held perhaps no greater resonance than that felt by the Salamanders Chapter. Though now the substance of myth and ancient remembrance, it was during the Great Betrayal when the Warmaster Horus lured Vulkan and his sons into a terrible trap and almost destroyed them. The Salamanders had been a Legion then, one of the Emperor's original progenitors. Turned upon by those who they thought were their brothers, the Salamanders, together with two other loyal Legions, were devastated on the planet of Isstvan V. In what was later recorded as the Dropsite

Massacre, thousands were slain and the sons of Vulkan pushed almost to extinction.

What miracle transpired, allowing them to avoid that doom, was a mystery some ten thousand years old, as was the fate of their beloved primarch who, some believed, never returned from the battle. Verses were still sung of Vulkan's heroism that day, but they were the stuff of conjecture and halcyon supposition. The truth of what happened during that disaster was lost forever. Yet the pain of it remained, like an old wound that would not heal. Even replenishing fire could not burn it from the Salamanders' hearts.

'So the mission into the Hadron Belt is over?' asked Ba'ken as the last of the caskets was brought aboard the gunship and the Salamanders started making ready for their final departure from the *Archimedes Rex*.

'For now,' Dak'ir replied.

The two Salamanders were apart from the rest of their battle-brothers who stood in discreet groups of two and three, dispersed across the fighter bay, watching proceedings, staying vigilant and awaiting the order to embark.

'And we are going back?'

'Yes, brother. To Nocturne.'

Dak'ir felt ambivalent about a return to their home world. Like all Salamanders, his planet was part of him and to be reunited with it was cause to rejoice, despite its volatile nature. But to come back so soon… it smacked of failure and only made Dak'ir's concerns about Captain N'keln's leadership deepen. 'Pyriel wants to bring the chest before Tu'Shan and have him consult the Tome of Fire.'

'What do you make of it?' asked Ba'ken as Dak'ir's thoughts were steered back towards that moment in the storage room when he'd found the chest with Vulkan's icon upon it.

'The chest? I don't know. Pyriel was certainly unsettled when he ascertained its provenance.'

'It seems strange to have been amongst weapons and armour,' said Ba'ken. 'How did you even find it amidst all of that?'

'I don't know that either.' Dak'ir paused, as if admitting the next part would confirm the reality of it, one that he was unwilling to face. The fact that the two Salamanders were engaged in private conversation and that he trusted Ba'ken like no other was the only reason he spoke up at all. 'I thought the artefact was in plain sight. It was as if I homed in on it, as if a beacon was attached to the chest and I had locked in to its signal.'

Dak'ir looked at Ba'ken for a reaction but the bulky Salamander gave none. He just stared ahead and listened.

'When Pyriel found me, I wasn't even aware I had picked it up. Nor did I remember ransacking the munitions crates to unearth it,' Dak'ir continued.

Ba'ken remained pensive, but his body language suggested he wanted to say something.

'Tell me what you are thinking, brother. In this I am not your commanding officer and you my trooper – we are friends.'

There was no sense of accusation in his posture as Ba'ken faced him, no distrust or even wariness – only a question. 'Are you saying that the chest was *meant* to be found, and by you alone?'

Dak'ir nodded almost imperceptibly. His voice came out as a rasp. 'Am I somehow cursed, brother?'

Ba'ken didn't reply. He merely clasped his battle-brother's pauldron.

IT WOULD BE several days before Tu'Shan and his council emerged from the Pantheon. The chamber was one of few in the Salamanders fortress-monastery on

Prometheus. Though, in truth, the bastion was not much more than a space port linked to an orbital dock where the Chapter's modest armada of vessels could be refitted and repaired. An Apothecarion saw to the outfitting of new recruits and their genetic enhancement as they became battle-brothers. Trial arenas were sunk into the basement level. It was here in these pits that initiate and veteran together could undergo tests of endurance and self-reliance, as was in keeping with the tenets of the Promethean Cult.

Walking across hot coals, lifting massive boiling cauldrons, enduring the searing pain of the Proving Rod or bearing red-hot iron bars were just some of the labours expected of the sons of Vulkan to show their faith and will. There were dormitories and relic halls, too, though again relatively few in number. The most prestigious of these was the Hall of the Firedrakes, a vast and vaulted gallery hung with the pelts of the great salamanders slain by the warriors as a rite of passage, and from which the hall took its name.

The Firedrakes, of which Tu'Shan was captain as well as regent, were barracked on Prometheus along with the Chapter Master himself. These venerable warriors were almost a breed apart; the transition they made to the vaunted ranks of the 1st Company changing them in myriad ways as they embraced the full evolution of their genetic encoding. Unlike their fellow battle-brothers, the Firedrakes were seldom seen on the surface of Nocturne where the other Salamanders would readily cohabit with the human populace, albeit often as part of a solitary lifestyle. Their rites were ancient and clandestine, conducted by the Chapter Master himself. Only those who had undergone the most heinous of trials and endured hardship beyond imagining could ever hope to aspire to become a Firedrake.

Akin to that sacred and revered order, access to the Pantheon was also restricted. Dak'ir for one had never seen it, though he knew it was a small deliberation chamber located at the heart of Prometheus.

Only matters of dire import or of profound spiritual significance were ever discussed in the Pantheon. It had eighteen seats, representing their original Legion number – a fact that remained unchanged during the Second Founding, an act in which, due to their debilitated strength, the Salamanders had been unable to participate.

The head seat was reserved for the Chapter Master, an honour that had been Tu'Shan's these last fifty years or so. Thirteen were for the other masters: six to the captains of the remaining companies; one each for the Apothecarion, Librarius, Chaplaincy and Fleet; with a further three devoted to the Armoury and the Masters of the Forge, an unusual triumvirate but necessary given the Salamanders' predilection for weaponscraft.

Three of the seats were for honoured guests sequestered by the Chapter Master himself and by dint of the rest of the council's assent. Praetor, the Firedrake's most senior sergeant, often assumed one of these seats. Dak'ir knew that Pyriel now occupied another. He wondered if the Librarian would be unflinching before the Chapter's hierarchy, particular under Master Vel'cona's gaze. The last position had remained empty for many years, since before Tu'Shan had even assumed the mantle of Regent of Prometheus. Its incumbent was a figure of much veneration.

Here the Masters of the Salamanders would sit and consult the Tome of Fire. This artefact was written by the hand of the primarch himself in ages past. Though Dak'ir had never seen it, let alone perused its pages, he knew that it was full of riddles and prophecies. Rumours purported that the words themselves were

inked partly in Vulkan's blood and shimmered like captured fire if brought up to the light. It was not merely
one volume, as the name suggested, but rather dozens
arrayed in the stacks around the circular walls of the
Pantheon. Deciphering the script of the Tome of Fire
was not easy. There were secrets within, left by the primarch for his sons to unlock. It foretold of great events
and upheavals for those with the wit to perceive them.
But perhaps most pointedly, it contained the history,
form and location of the nine artefacts Vulkan had hidden throughout the galaxy for the Salamanders to
unearth. Five of these holiest of relics had been discovered over the centuries through the travails of the
Forgefathers; the locations of the remaining four were
embedded cryptically within the tome's arcane pages.

So Chapter Master Tu'Shan and those masters still on
Prometheus had convened and would pore over the
Tome of Fire in the hope of unearthing some inkling
that pertained to the discovery of the chest. The artefact's origin stamp had already ignited something of a
fire within the Chapter. Some proposed that it meant
the return of Vulkan after so many millennia in
unknown isolation; others refuted this, claiming that
the primarch was not lost on Isstvan at all, but had
returned already at the breaking of the Legions and
whatever the chest contained it could not relate to that;
more still remained silent and merely watched and
waited, unwilling to hope, not daring to suggest what
apocalypse might be about to befall the Salamanders if
their progenitor had fated a reunion. Patience, wisdom
and insight were the only true keys to unlocking the
Tome of Fire, and with it the chest's mystery. Like tempering iron or folding steel at the foot of the forge's
anvil, any attempt to try and unravel its enigmas had to
be approached slowly and methodically. It was, after all,
the Salamanders' way.

Dak'ir exercised these credos in the swelter of one of the workshops deep in the undercroft of Hesiod's Chapter Bastion.

The *Vulkan's Wrath* had returned to Nocturne several days earlier. Of the seven Mechanicus adepts in the cryocaskets salvaged from the *Archimedes Rex*, none had survived the journey. Their bodies had been incinerated within the pyreum. It rubbed salt into already bitter wounds as more questions were raised about the viability of the mission into the Hadron Belt and Captain N'keln's decision to undertake it. Such objections were spoken in whispers only, but Dak'ir knew of them all the same. He saw it in the looks of discontent, the agitated postures of sergeants and heard it in the rumours of clandestine meetings to which he was not invited. Ever since 3rd Company had made landfall, Tsu'gan had been waging a campaign of no confidence against N'keln. Or at least, that was how it appeared to Dak'ir.

Promethean lore preached self-sacrifice and loyalty above all else – it seemed that the loyalty felt by some of the sergeants towards their captain was being stretched to its limit.

The only shred of exculpation for N'keln was the chest discovered in the storage room. 3rd Company's strike cruiser had barely landed on Prometheus when Librarian Pyriel stalked down the embarkation ramp, eschewing all docking protocols as he went in search of his Master Vel'cona who could press for an audience with the Chapter Master. The council in the Pantheon had been arraigned in short order. Their verdict and the announcement of it would not be so forthcoming. The rest of the Salamanders aboard the *Vulkan's Wrath* had disbanded, waiting to be recalled by their liege-lords at the appropriate time.

Dak'ir, like many others, had returned to the surface of Nocturne.

Classified a death world by Imperial planetary tax-onomers, Nocturne was a volatile place. Fraught with crags and towering basalt mountains, its harsh environment made life hard for its tribal inhabitants. Burning winds scorched its naked plains, turning them into barren deserts. Rough oceans churned, spitting geysers of scalding steam when they met spilled lava.

Nocturne's settlements were few and transient. Only the seven Sanctuary Cities were strong enough to serve as permanent havens to a dispersed populace eking out an existence amongst rock and ash.

However arduous, it was nothing compared to the Time of Trial. Being one half of a binary planetary system, Nocturne shared an erratic orbit with its oversized moon of Prometheus and great strife befell the planet every fifteen Terran years whenever these two celestial bodies came into proximity. Molten lava would spew from the earth, and entire cities would be swallowed by deep pits of magma; tidal waves, like foaming giants, would smite fishing boats and crush drilling rigs; clouds of ash, belched from the necks of angry mountains, would eclipse the pale sun. Massive earthquakes shook the very bedrock of the world below whilst above, the skies would crack and fire would rain. Yet, in the aftermath rare metals and gems could be reaped from the ash. And it was this which promoted Nocturne's culture of forgesmithing.

After a few short hours since their arrival in-system, Dak'ir alighted from the *Fire-wyvern* on the Cindara Plateau. Several of his brothers went immediately to their training regimen or summoned brander-priests for excoriation in the solitoriums; others made for their respective townships or settlements. Dak'ir chose the workshops and spent his time at the forge. The events aboard the *Archimedes Rex*, in particular his discovery of Vulkan's chest, had disturbed him greatly. Only in solitude and through the purging heat of the forge would he find equilibrium again.

The crafting hammer pounded a steady rhythm that matched the beat of Dak'ir's heart. The Salamander was in total synchronicity with his labours. He wore leather smithing breeches and was naked from the waist up, his branded torso marred by ash and soot. Sweat dappled his ebon body, rivulets following the grooves of his muscles. It came from exertion, not from the heat.

The forges of the undercroft were excavated down to Nocturne's very core and ponds of lava gathered in the cavernous depths providing liquid fire to fuel the foundries and scalding steam to impel bellows. There was a strange anachronism about the sweltering forges, the way they blended the ancient traditions of the first Nocturnean blacksmiths and the technologies of the Imperium.

Adamantium blast doors, strengthened by reinforced ceramite, marked the entrance to the chamber where he toiled. Bulkhead columns, the foundations of the Chapter Bastion, plunged down from a stalactite ceiling and bored deep into the rocky earth below. Mechanised tools – rotary blades, bench-mounted plasma-cutters, belt grinders, radial drill presses – stood side by side with stout anvils and iron-bellied furnaces. Intricate servo-arrays and ballistic components were racked with swages, fullers and other smithing hammers.

The air was filled with heady smoke, turned a deep, warm orange from the lambent glow of the lava pools. Dak'ir drank in the fuliginous atmosphere as if it were a panacea, soaking his every pore with it. And like the metal on the anvil before him, the impurity in his troubled soul was gradually beaten out with each successive hammer blow.

Dak'ir was gasping by the end, a reaction to the purging of emotional trauma rather than physical exertion. As the last ring of the anvil echoed into obscurity, he set down the forging hammer and took up a pair of long-handled tongs instead. He had tempered neither blade nor armour but something different entirely, its glow slowly fading. Gouts of steam rushed off the artefact when it breached the water's surface in the deep vat alongside the anvil. When Dak'ir withdrew it, pinched between the iron fingers of the tongs, it shimmered like molten silver. Captured light from the lava flows blazed over its contours like a fiery sea.

It was a mask – the simulacrum of a human face; his face, or at least half of it. Dak'ir took the newly forged item in his hands. The metal had cooled but it still seared his fingers. He barely felt it as he trod silently to a plane of hammered silver, around a metre wide and three metres high, resting against the wall of the forge. Dak'ir's image was reflected in it. Burning red eyes set into an ebon countenance stared back at him. Only the face was actually half black; the other half was bleached near-white. Its normally black pigmentation, the melanin defect that marked all Salamanders, had been burned away. Apothecary Fugis had told him the scar would not heal, that Dak'ir's deface-ment was damage caused at the cellular level.

Dak'ir touched the burnt skin and the memory of the melta-flare on Stratos rekindled in his mind's eye. Kadai's death pulled at his gut. As he raised the mask to his face, flashes of remembrance like slivers of ice on calm water floated to the surface of his mind: rock harvesting in the depths of Ignea, hunting sauroch over the Scorian Plain, dredging on the Acerbian Sea – all deadly pursuits, but the formative memories of Dak'ir's pre-adolescence. The images faded like smoke before a cool wind, leaving a pang of regret. Some part of Dak'ir felt sorrow the loss of his old life, the death of his former existence before he was 'battle-brother', when he was just Hazon and his father's son.

As the years passed, filled with war and glory in the Emperor's name, with cities burned and enemies slain, the vestiges held by Dak'ir of those old memories eroded replaced by battles, a baptism in blood.

The pull towards his old life – one, in truth, that had scarcely begun – confused him. Was it disloyal, even heretical to have such thoughts? Dak'ir couldn't help wonder why the memories plagued him.

'I am no longer human,' he admitted to his reflection.

'I am more. I am evolved. I am Astartes.'

The mask covered his ebon visage, leaving the burned side of his face, the flesh-pink tissue, exposed. For a moment he tried to imagine himself as human again. The attempt was a failure.

'But if I am not human, am I still capable of humanity?'

The bass retort of the blast doors opening intruded on Dak'ir's reverie. He hastily pulled the mask away and threw it into the open grate of a nearby furnace, immolating it in fire. The silver ran like tears down the half-face of the mask, which held its form only briefly before sagging against the intense heat and becoming little more than molten metal.

'A rejected blade, sergeant?' said Emek, from behind him.

Dak'ir shut the furnace grate and faced his battle-brother. 'No, it was just scrap.'

Emek seemed content to leave it at that. He was fully armoured, the green battle-plate turned a lurid violet in the reflected lustre of the lava ponds. He held his battle-helm in the crook of his arm and his eyes flashed suddenly with zeal and vigour.

'We've been summoned to Prometheus,' Emek said after a few moments. 'Our lords have consulted the Tome of Fire and have divined an answer regarding Vulkan's chest. Your armour is waiting for you in the next chamber, sir.'

Dak'ir wiped his sooty body down with a length of already blackened cloth and began putting away the tools he had been using.

'Where are we to meet?' he asked.

'The Cindara Plateau. Brother Ba'ken will join us there.'

Emek lingered in silence as Dak'ir finished securing his forging equipment.

'There is something else on your mind, brother?' asked the sergeant.

'Yes, but I do not wish to appear insubordinate.'

Dak'ir's tone suggested his impatience. 'Speak, brother.'

Emek waited while he marshalled his thoughts, as if choosing his next words with great care. 'Before we departed for the Hadron Belt, back in the Vault of Remembrance, I overheard Brother-Sergeant Tsu'gan say something about your complicity in Captain Kadai's death.' Emek paused to gauge the reaction of Dak'ir's, who gave none, before continuing. 'Most of us were not present when Kadai was slain. There are... unanswered questions.'

Dak'ir thought about admonishing his battle-brother – to question your superior officer, however delicately couched, was grounds for punishment. But he had asked for honesty from Emek, and that was what he had given. He could hardly take him to task over that.

'The truth is, brother, that we were all culpable when it came to the tragedy of Kadai's death. I, Tsu'gan, all who set foot in Aura Hieron had our parts to play, even the captain himself. There is no mystery, no dark secret. We were outmanoeuvred by a cunning and deadly foe.'

'The Dragon Warriors,' Emek asserted in the following silence.

'Yes,' Dak'ir replied. 'The renegades knew we were coming. They were ready for us, and laid their trap for us to fall into. Theirs is an old creed, Emek – an eye for an eye; a captain for a captain.'

'To plan such a snare... it borders on obsession.'

'Obsessive, paranoid, vindictive – Nihilan is all of these things and worse.'

'Did you know him?'

'No. I met him only at Moribar during my first mission as a scout in 7th Company. Nor did I know his captain, Ushorak, though he schooled his protégé well in the arts of deception and malice.'

'And it was he who died on the sepulchre world.'

'In the crematoria forge at Moribar's heart, yes. Kadai thought Nihilan was dead also, but unless a shade confronted us on Stratos he survived well enough, driven on by hate and the prospect of revenge.'

'And he was once...'

'One of us, yes,' Dak'ir finished for him. 'Even the sons of Vulkan are not without stain. The capacity for betrayal exists in us all, Emek. It is why we must constantly test ourselves and our faith, so that we are girded against temptation and selfish ideals.'

'And Ushorak?'

Dak'ir's face darkened and he lowered his gaze as if in remembrance, though in truth he only knew of the deeds that had led to Ushorak's bloody defection; the act itself was many years old, he had not witnessed it first hand. 'No. He was of another Chapter, though the shame of it is no less galling.'

'Nihilan did all of this just to avenge his lord... He must be very embittered. Is there no way to rehabilitate him and the renegades in his charge? It's not unheard of for forgiveness to be given and penance granted. What about the Executioners?'

Dak'ir shook his head, sadly. 'This is not Badab, Emek. Nihilan and his followers have entered the Eye of Terror, there is no way back from that. His last chance,

Ushorak's last chance, was on Moribar. They didn't take it, and now they are our enemies, no different to the nameless horrors of the warp. But I do not think there was only vengeance on Nihilan's mind when he ambushed us on Stratos. There was something more to his plan.'

'What makes you say that?'

Dak'ir looked his brother in the eye.

'It's just a feeling.'

II
Crossroads

TSU'GAN STAGGERED AS a spike of pain seared up his side, forcing him to reach out with a shaking hand. The black marble of the wall felt cool to the touch as he steadied himself. After a few moments he was able to continue. Through a haze of barely checked agony, Tsu'gan failed to notice the steaming handprint he left in his wake as he toured the Hall of Relics.

Like many of the sergeants, he had stayed on Prometheus to await news from the Pantheon. Speculation was rife as to what the chest discovered on the *Archimedes Rex* might mean. There was a thread of belief that, given the inauspicious times, it might pertain to the location where the primarch had sought solitude following the cessation of the Heresy. Tsu'gan doubted that greatly. He was a pragmatist, certainly too level-headed to indulge in such remote theories. He believed in what he could see, what he could touch. Tsu'gan knew of only one way to resolve a crisis: meet it head on with determination and resolve. With that in mind, while he awaited the Pantheon's findings, he had convened a meeting of his own. Several sergeants had been present, colluded by Iagon,

impelled by Tsu'gan's shining Promethean example
and the respect afforded to him by his contemporaries.
They were there at his request, after all, to address a
'serious concern' within the company. The subject of
the secret assembly, conducted in one of the fortress
monastery's few, and barely used, dormitories, was
N'keln. Tsu'gan recalled it now, the guilt of the union
merging with that he associated with Kadai's death, as
he walked down the black marble corridors of the
gallery.

*Tsu'gan awaited them in the half-dark of the chamber, its
halogen lanterns dulled, with just the ambient light to illuminate the bare room. One by one, they entered: Agatone
and Ek'Bar were the first, dour and long-serving; quiet and
pensive respectively. Both were Tactical squad sergeants like
Tsu'gan. Then there came Vargo from one of the Assault
squads, a campaign veteran. De'mas, Clovius and Typhos
followed a short time after. Last of all was Naveem, who
seemed the most reluctant to have been summoned. These
Astartes, great Salamanders all, encompassed five Tactical
squads and both Assault squads of 3rd Company. Only the
sergeants of the Devastators were not present, those that
had fought alongside N'keln on Stratos. Of course, Dak'ir
was also absent. He had made his feelings very clear on the
subject of the captain's recent ascension.*

*The brother-sergeants present had each removed their
battle-helms – in fact Clovius and Typhos generally did not
wear one – and the lustre of their eyes glowed deeply in the
gloom. Tsu'gan waited until they were all settled, until the
mutual greetings and respectful acknowledgements were
done, before he began.*

*Do not think me disloyal,' Tsu'gan said, 'for I am not.' He
regarded each of the assembled sergeants intently as he
panned his gaze around the room.*

*'Why are we here then, if not to speak of disloyalty, to
renege on the vows we all made before the Chapter Master*

himself?' Naveem's anger was evident in his tone, but he kept his voice down all the same.

Tsu'gan raised a placatory hand, both to mollify Naveem and arrest any reprisals from Brother Iagon, who watched from behind his sergeant in the darkness.

'I seek only what is best for the company and the Chapter, brothers,' he assured them.

'If that is true, Tsu'gan, then why have us skulk in the shadows like conspirators?' asked Agatone, his hard face wrinkled with discontent. 'I came to this meeting to discuss the discord in our ranks, and the way we might mend it. All the talk I have heard prior to this gathering has been of dissension and of N'keln's unsuitability for the role of captain. Tell me now why I shouldn't just turn on my heel and go to Tu'Shan?'

Tsu'gan met his fellow sergeant's intense glare with honest contrition. 'Because you know as well as I that N'keln is not fit for this post.'

Agatone opened his mouth to respond, but clamped it shut in the face of indisputable fact.

Turning his attention back to the assembly as a whole, Tsu'gan spread his arms in a conciliatory gesture.

'N'keln is a fine warrior, one of the best amongst the Inferno Guard, but he is not Kadai and–'

'No one is,' scoffed Sergeant Clovius, shaking his head. His squat body, thick-shouldered and broad of back, made him seem as intractable as an armoured rock. The sergeant continued, 'You cannot hold a man to account by another's memory.'

'I speak only of his legacy,' Tsu'gan returned, 'and of his ability to lead us. N'keln needs a steadying hand, the support of a captain himself. He is like one component of an alloy; strong when bonded with another, but left alone–' Tsu'gan shook his head. 'He will surely break.'

Muttering from around the room intimated his audience was less than convinced. Tsu'gan merely pushed harder.

'N'keln inherits a fractured company, one requiring strength to rebuild. It is strength he does not possess. How *else would you describe the folly of returning to the Hadron Belt?'*

'Had we not, we would never had discovered the chest,' countered Vargo, his deep voice reluctant.

Tsu'gan faced him, his own voice an impassioned rasp.

'A fluke: one that very nearly added to the tally of ignominious dead and indebted us to mercenaries.' He spat the last word as the memory of the Marines Malevolent loomed in his mind. To deal with such honourless curs left a bitter canker in Tsu'gan's mouth.

'Another of N'keln's failings,' Tsu'gan went on, 'allowing Vinyar and his dogs to steal weapons and armour destined for another Chapter. No better than thieves, these Astartes in name only. Yet N'keln lets them go without pursuit or so much as a harsh word.' He paused, letting his damning rhetoric sink in.

'Do not think me disloyal,' he repeated, experiencing no small measure of satisfaction from the realisation dawning on the sergeants' faces. Even Naveem seemed to thaw. 'For I am not. I serve only the will of the Chapter. I always have. I am proud to be Fire-born and I will follow my brothers unto death. But what I will not do is stand idle as a company is brought into ruination. Nor will I participate in baseless missions where a reckless death is the only reward. I cannot do that.'

Agatone articulated what the rest were already thinking.

'So what would you have us do?'

Tsu'gan nodded as if in approval of the decision he had garnered here.

'Ally with me,' he said simply, 'Ally with me in going to the Chapter Master and suing for the removal of N'keln as captain.'

After a few moments, Naveem spoke up.

'This is madness. None of these acts you've mentioned are charges enough for the captain's dismissal. Tu'Shan will punish us all for this conspiracy. We'll be up before Elysius and his chirurgeon-interrogators, our purity in question.'

'It is not conspiracy!' Tsu'gan snapped, then, composing his frustration, lowered his voice. 'I will bring our concerns to the

Chapter Master, as is our right. He is wise. He will see the rifts in this company and have no choice but to act for its betterment.'

'And who will he install as N'keln's successor?' asked Agatone, meeting Tsu'gan's gaze. 'You?'

'If the Chapter Masters sees fit to appoint me, I will not reject the responsibility. But I don't seek to usurp N'keln, I want only what is right for this company.'

Agatone looked around the room, evidently undecided.

'What of Dak'ir and Omkar, Lok and Ul'shan? Why are they not at this meeting to relay their grievances?'

Tsu'gan maintained his imperious air, despite his fellow sergeant's pertinent questioning.

'I did not summon them,' he admitted.

Naveem leapt on the confession.

'Why, because you knew they would never agree to this, that they could not be trusted to keep their silence?' He waved away Tsu'gan's imminent protest. 'Save your answers, brother. I am not interested. Out of loyalty to my fellow sergeants I will keep my silence, but I cannot be a party to this. I know you think you act out of genuine concern for the company, but you are misguided, Tsu'gan,' Naveem added sadly and left the room.

'Nor can I, brother,' said Agatone. 'Don't speak to me of this again, or I will have no choice but to go to Chaplain Elysius.'

In the end, Sergeants Clovius and Ek'Bar went the way of Naveem and Agatone. The others pledged their allegiance to Tsu'gan's cause but without a majority, it stood little chance of succeeding. They left soon after their disgruntled counterparts, leaving Tsu'gan alone with Iagon.

'Why can't they see it, Iagon? Why can't they acknowledge N'keln's weakness?' He slumped down on one of the austere pallet beds that hadn't been used in decades.

Iagon moved slowly from behind Tsu'gan and into his sergeant's eye line.

'I do not think we have failed, sergeant.'

Tsu'gan looked up. His gaze was questioning.

'True, we have only three brother-sergeants allied to our cause, but that is all we really need.'

'Explain yourself.'

Iagon smiled, a thin empty curling of his down-turned mouth bereft of warmth or mirth. Here, in the shadows of the empty dormitory, his true nature could express itself. 'Take your grievance to Elysius. Ensure that N'keln is within earshot when you do, or at least hears of it soon after.' Iagon paused deliberately, inwardly applauding his own cunning. 'N'keln is a warrior of profound conscience. Once he knows about such a vote of no confidence amongst his own sergeants–' his narrow eyes flashed '–he will stand down of his own volition.'

Tsu'gan was suddenly torn. He sighed deeply, trying to exhale his doubts.

'Is this right, Iagon? Am I doing what is best for the company and the Chapter?'

'You are taking the hard road, my lord. The one you must travel if we are ever to be whole again.'

'Even still–'

Iagon stepped forward to emphasise his point.

'If N'keln were worthy, would he not have taken up Kadai's thunder hammer? It gathers dust even now in the Hall of Relics, forgotten and dishonoured by one who is wary of the mantle he assumes by claiming it.'

Tsu'gan shook his head uncertainly. 'No. N'keln rejected it out of respect.' He didn't sound convinced.

Iagon adopted a look of absolute innocent neutrality. 'Did he?'

Tsu'gan had left the dormitory in silence, a slave to his own thoughts. Pain would settle his troubled mind. He had made for the solitoriums at once. And there in the darkness, with the eyes of his secret voyeur looking on, he had indulged in his addiction again and again, hoping, in vain, that with the next strike of the rod his conscience would be eased. It had not, and the guilt gnawed at him still as he trod the long passageways of the Hall of Relics, dressed only in a simple green robe.

Honours and memories of heroes long-past filled the austere gallery of black marble. The hue of the rock, its smoothness and density, promoted a sombre mood, one entirely apt given the reverence felt for this hallowed place. There were shrines to Xavier, Kesare, and even ancient T'kell, chambered in anterooms or deep alcoves regressed into the rock. Artefacts, too precious to be burned, too venerated to be bequeathed, rested within them along with purity seals, medals and other tributes to their legacies. Reliquaries were made of the leg bones Brother Amadeus had lost in the Siege of Cluth'nir. If the mighty warrior should ever fall, they would be burned to ash with what was left animated with his sarcophagus and offered to Mount Deathfire. Tsu'gan passed them all, every step a painful reminder of the damage he had self-inflicted. It paled to the anguish in his mind and failed utterly, despite his sternest efforts, to assuage it. He wondered briefly whether he had urged the brander-priest too far this time. Tsu'gan crushed the thought.

Bowing his head, he stepped into one of the hall's anterooms and was swallowed by darkness. The stygian surroundings lasted only seconds as a votive flame erupted into incandescent life on one of the walls and threw a warm, orange glare across a sombre altar. It was shaped like an anvil, a pall of salamander hide draped across the flat head. Resting on the hide were the shattered remains of an ornate thunder hammer.

Tsu'gan was gripped by a profound sense of loss as he approached the altar and knelt before it in supplication.

'My captain...' The words were barely whispered, but conveyed his longing. He went to speak again, but found he could not, and closed his half-open mouth without further sound. Silence followed, deafening and final. Tsu'gan remembered anew the sight of Kadai's destruction. He recalled gathering up the remains of the beloved captain with N'keln. Warring with a sense of sudden grief and impotent rage, Tsu'gan had looked into the veteran sergeant's eyes and seen clearly what was held there.

What now? Who will lead us? I cannot assume his mantle. Not yet. I'm not ready.

Even then, through a fog of despair, Tsu'gan had witnessed the truth in N'keln's heart. Duty would not allow the veteran sergeant to refuse; prudence should have *made* him refuse. But it had not, and the lingering memory stung like a barb.

The brother-sergeant could bear it no longer and, averting his gaze from the solemn tribute to Ko'tan Kadai, he hurried from the shrine-chamber.

So consumed was Tsu'gan with his own troubled thoughts that he didn't notice Fugis coming the opposite way, and collided with him.

'Apologies, brother,' Tsu'gan rasped, wincing beneath the cowl of his robe as he made to move on.

Fugis held out an arm to stall him. Like the brother-sergeant, the Apothecary wore robes.

'Are you all right, Brother Tsu'gan? You seem… *troubled.*' Fugis's hood was down and his eyes were penetrating as he regarded the sergeant, some of his old sagacity returned.

'It's nothing. I only seek to honour the dead.' Tsu'gan couldn't keep his voice steady enough as the jabs of pain from the branding wracked him. He went to move on again, and this time Fugis stood in his path.

'And yet you sound as if you've recently been in battle.' His thin face accentuated a stern and probing expression.

'Step aside, Apothecary,' Tsu'gan snapped, gasping through his sudden anger. 'You have no cause to detain me.'

Fugis's cold eyes helped formed a scowl.

'I have every cause.' The Apothecary's hand lashed out. Debilitated as he was, Tsu'gan was too slow to stop it. Fugis pulled back the sergeant's robes and cowl to expose the hot, angry scars upon the lower part of his chest.

'Those are fresh,' he said, accusingly. 'You have been having yourself rebranded.'

Tsu'gan was about to protest, but denial by this point was beneath him.

'And what of it?' he snarled, teeth gritted both in anger and to ward off his slowly ebbing agony.

The Apothecary's expression hardened.

'What are you doing, brother?'

'What I must to function!' Tsu'gan's rancour swiftly waned, replaced by resignation. 'He was slain, Fugis. Slain in cold blood, no better than the wretches that lured us to Aura Hieron.'

'We all feel his loss, Tsu'gan.' Now it was Fugis's turn to change, though rather than soften, his eyes seemed to grow cold and faraway as if reliving his own bereavement.

'But you were not there at his end, brother. You did not gather the remains of his body and armour, wasted away and beyond even your skill to revivify in another.' Tsu'gan referred to the destruction of Kadai's progenoid glands. These elements of a Space Marine's physiology existed in the neck and chest. Harvested through the skill only an Apothecary was schooled in, they could be used to create another Salamander. But in the case of Kadai's tragic demise, even that small consolation was denied.

Fugis paused, deciding what to do.

'You must come to the Apothecarion. There I will tend your wounds,' he said. 'I can mend the superficial, brother, but the depth of the hurt you feel is beyond my skill to heal.' For a moment, the Apothecary's eyes softened. 'Your spirit is in turmoil, Tsu'gan. That cannot be allowed to continue.'

Tsu'gan tugged his robe back across his body and exhaled raggedly. A tic of discomfort registered below his left eye as he did it.

'What should I do, brother?' he asked.

Fugis's answer was simple.

'I should go to Chaplain Elysius, make you confess to him what you have been doing, and leave you to await his judgement.'

'I...' began the sergeant then relented. 'Yes, you are right. But let me do it, let me go to him myself.'

The Apothecary seemed uncertain. His searching gaze was back, as his eyes narrowed. 'Very well,' he said at last. 'But do it soon, or you'll give me no choice but to act in your stead.'

'I will, brother.'

Fugis lingered a moment longer, before turning his back and heading towards the anteroom where Kadai awaited him.

Tsu'gan went the other way, unaware of another figure tracking him in the darkened corridors of the Hall of Relics, the very same that had watched him break down at the foot of the anvil shrine and followed him from the isolation chamber.

Pain, grief, shame – they all dulled the brother-sergeant's senses as he came to a fork in the corridor. The light of the brazier-lamps seemed to cast it in an eldritch glow that Tsu'gan failed to notice. East led eventually to the Reclusium, where he would await the Chaplain and purge his heavy soul; west took him back to a small armoury where his battle-plate rested. He was about to turn east when he felt a light touch on his shoulder.

'Where are you going, my lord?' asked the voice of Iagon, 'Your armour is the other way.'

Tsu'gan faced him. Iagon was enrobed too. The hood was pulled far over his face so that only his sharp, angular nose and down-turned mouth were visible. The Salamander's slight form was exaggerated without his armour. It made him look small in comparison to his sergeant.

'I cannot, Iagon,' Tsu'gan told him. 'I must seek Elysius's counsel.' He tried to continue on his way, but Iagon reasserted his grip, stronger this time.

Tsu'gan winced with the pain of his earlier injuries.

'Release me, trooper. I am your sergeant.'

Iagon's face was a dispassionate mask.

'I cannot, my lord,' he said, and increased his grip.

Tsu'gan scowled and seized the trooper's wrist. Despite his wounds, he was still incredibly strong and now it was Iagon's turn to betray his discomfort.

'I am not strong enough to hold you, sergeant, but let me appeal to your better judgement...' Iagon pleaded, letting his brother go.

Tsu'gan released him, the scowl reduced to a displeased frown. It bade Iagon continue.

'Go to Elysius if you must,' he whispered quickly, 'but know that if you do, you will be stripped of rank and made to suffer penitence for what you've done. The chirurgeon-interrogators will probe and incise until they lay you bare. Our Brother-Chaplain will learn of your deceit–'

'I have deceived no one, save myself,' Tsu'gan snapped, about to turn away again, before Iagon stopped him.

'He *will* learn of your deceit,' he pressed, 'and act against all of your brothers who were in that room. Any chance of replacing N'keln will be gone, and the prospect of healing our divided company with it.'

'I don't want to replace him, Iagon,' Tsu'gan insisted. 'That is not my purpose.'

'If not you, then who else will do it?' Iagon implored. 'It is your destiny, brother.'

Tsu'gan was shaking his head. 'I am broken. When battle calls, it is easier. The cry of my bolter, the thunder of war in my heart, it smothers the pain. But when the enemy are dead and the battlefield is silent, it returns to me, Iagon.'

'It is just grief,' the trooper replied, leaning forward. 'It will pass. And what better way to expedite that process than in the crucible of battle, at the head of *your* company?'

Tsu'gan's mind wondered at that. The recently slumbering coals of ambition in his heart started to rekindle. *He* would heal the rift between his brothers, and in so doing make himself whole again.

The words of Nihilan, spoken to him on Stratos before he had leapt down into the temple to witness Kadai's death, came back to him unbidden.

A great destiny awaits you, but another overshadows it.

A traitor's testimony was not to be trusted, but there was a germ of recognition in that statement for Tsu'gan. He told himself that this was his own conclusion, that reasoning would have brought him to a similar epiphany given time. The image of Dak'ir arose in his mind, going to his captain's aid just before the end. The Ignean was something of an outcast, but a strange destiny surrounded him too. Tsu'gan could feel it whenever he was in his presence. The sensation was dulled by his loathing, but it was there. If he did not assume the mantle of captain, then Dak'ir would surely do it. No Ignean was fit to lead an Astartes battle company. Tsu'gan could not allow that to stand.

His eyes and posture hardened as he returned Iagon's attendant gaze.

'Very well,' Tsu'gan growled. 'But what of Fugis? The Apothecary has sworn me to go to Elysius.'

'Forestall him,' Iagon answered simply. 'Our brother is so caught up in his own grief that he will not press this at first. By the time he does, N'keln will step down with respect and *you* will ascend.' Iagon's eyes flashed with unbridled ambition. At Tsu'gan's right hand, as he was, he would cling to the trappings of his lord, a beneficiary of his newfound power and influence, and ascend with him. 'By then, Fugis will not speak out. He will see you are master of your feelings once again.'

Tsu'gan stared at something in the distance: a glorious vision conjured in his mind's eye.

'Yes,' he breathed, though the words did not sound like his own. 'That is what I will do.'

He looked again at Iagon, fresh fire burning in his blood-red eyes. 'Come,' he said, 'I must don my armour.'

Iagon bowed, smiling thinly as his face was eclipsed by shadow.

Together, they took the west corridor. The east remained the path untrodden.

IAGON WAS PLEASED. He had managed to restore his sergeant's mettle and conviction. Ever since they had returned from Stratos, he had been carefully shadowing him. Every dark desire, every tortured secret was his to know and exploit. He came to realise, as he looked on from the darkness, he would eventually need to act. Iagon merely had to wait for the opportune moment. The intervention in the corridor of the Hall of Relics was indeed timely. A moment's hesitation and Tsu'gan would have gone to Elysius, undoing all of Iagon's careful planning and torpedoing any chance he had for borrowed power.

Though still an Astartes, with all the boons and potency that brought, Iagon was not gifted with brawn like Ba'ken. Nor did he possess the psychic might of Pyriel or the religious fervour of Elysius. But cunning, yes, he had that. And determination, the unbendable will that Tsu'gan would be captain and that he, Cerbius Iagon, would bask in the reflected glory of his lord. Nothing must stand in the way of that. Despite his rhetoric to the contrary, Fugis presented a problem.

As Iagon and Tsu'gan arrived at the armoury, a final thought occurred to him.

The threat of the Apothecary must be dealt with.

BA'KEN AND MASTER Argos stood at the foot of the Cindara Plateau, their heavy booted feet sinking slightly into the sands of the Pyre Desert. They were watching a distant procession of Nocturnean civilians making their way to the gates of Hesiod.

Sanctuary City – the name was apt.

During the Time of Trial, the Sanctuary Cities threw open their gates and offered shelter to the people of Nocturne. A primarily nomadic race, much of the planet's populace dwelt in disparate villages or even transient encampments ill-suited to resist the devastation wrought by the earthquakes and volcanoes. Vast pilgrimages were undertaken that trailed the length and breadth of the planet, as Nocturneans travelled great distances seeking succour.

Stout walls and robust gates wrought to be strong and resilient by Nocturne's master artisans were the Sanctuary Cities' bulwark of defence in the earliest years of colonisation. Tribal shamans, latent psykers – before such genetic mutations were demystified and regulated – had been the first to establish the safest locations for these settlements to be founded. They did so via communion with the earth, a bond that the people of Nocturne still recognised and respected. Later, there came the geological pioneers who advised on the construction and development of the nascent townships that would eventually become cities. But as the ages passed so too did these cities evolve. Technologies brought by the Master of Mankind, He who was known only as the *Outlander*, provided stauncher aegis against the capricious will of the earth. Void shields stood in the path of lava flows or pyroclastic clouds; adamantium and reinforced ceramite repelled the seismic tremors or sweeping floods of fire.

These havens and their defences were all that stood between a race and its eradication by the elements.

Ba'ken hailed Dak'ir, his voice deep and strong. 'Brother-sergeant.'

Dak'ir nodded in return as he approached, Emek alongside him.

'The exodus has begun, it seems,' said Brother Emek.

'The Time of Trial is imminent,' Dak'ir replied. He caught Argos surveying the long, trailing lines of pilgrims through a pair of magnoculars.

'Aye,' said Ba'ken, resuming watch with a brief nod to acknowledge Emek. 'The nomadic tribes are gathering in their droves, and the Sanctuary Cities fill, just as they do every long year.'

Emek went unhooded, and appeared wistful as he regarded the long line of refugees.

'There are always so many.'

The civilians came from all across Nocturne: tradesmen, merchants, hunters and families. Some walked, others traversed the sands in stripped-down buggies or fat-wheeled trikes, dragging trailers of belongings or racks of tools. Rock harvesters and drovers wrangled herds of sauroch and other saurian beasts of burden, the cattle-creatures pulling flat-bedded carts and wide-sided wagons. The pilgrims carried what they could, their meagre possessions wrapped in oiled cloth to keep out the dust and grit of the dunes. They wore hardy clothing: smocks, ponchos and sand-cloaks with their hoods drawn up. No one ventured forth without a hat. Some even had thin scarves wound around their heads and faces to ward off the solar glare.

Across the final kilometre approach to the open gates of Hesiod, Dak'ir picked out the green battle-plate of Salamanders dispersed along the snaking line of civilians. It was the task of 5th Company, the only other besides 3rd and 7th still on the planet, to aid the civilians and usher them safely within the city walls.

Bolters trained on the heat-hazed distance, the Salamanders were ever vigilant. They watched for predators like sa'hrk or the winged shadows of dactylids as they circled above in search of easy meat.

'The lines of refugees are thin,' said Argos, mildly refuting Emek in his metallic timbre. Assessing the groups of civilians through the magnoculars, he had extrapolated a brief calculation. 'Many will suffer outside the walls of our Sanctuary Cities.'

Tremors rumbled like thunder in the far distance, coming from the direction of Themis, one of Hesiod's neighbours. There had been minor volcanic eruptions already. En route to Cindara Plateau, Dak'ir had heard that three outlying villages had been destroyed, claimed by earthquakes, vanishing without trace. On the horizon, Mount Deathfire loomed. The great edifice of rock and fury spat gouts of flame and lava in preparation for a much larger and more devastating eruption.

Argos lowered the magnoculars, his face dark.

'Ours is a stubborn race, brother-sergeant,' he said to Dak'ir by way of greeting.

'And proud,' Dak'ir replied. 'It's what makes us who we are.'

'Justly spoken,' said Argos, but his grim expression didn't lift as he went back to looking at the long train of civilians. For most, life expectancy was short on Nocturne. That statistic would only worsen with the coming season of upheaval.

Dak'ir turned to Ba'ken.

'I see you have been busy, brother.' He indicated the heavy flamer rig attached to the bulky Salamander's back.

'To replace the one I lost on Stratos.' Ba'ken's rejoinder came with a feral smile as he showed off the weapon proudly. The flamer's previous incarnation had been destroyed when its promethium fuel supply had reacted with a volatile chemical amalgam released by the cultists on the world of loft-cities. Ba'ken had been injured into the bargain, but the hardy Salamander had brushed it off as a flesh wound. The heavy weapon rig he had so fastidiously constructed did not survive. 'Blessed by Brother Argos himself,' he added, gesturing in the Tech-marine's direction. Argos was walking towards the edge of the circular plateau, outside of the metal disc in its centre.

'Are you not accompanying us, brother?' Dak'ir asked of him.

'I will join you later, after inspection of Hesiod's void shield array is complete.'

Dak'ir looked to the turbulent fiery orange sky and his eyes narrowed, searching. 'Ba'ken, where is the *Firewyvern* to take us up to Prometheus?' he asked, noting that Argos was consulting a small palm-reader.

'Bad news about that, sir,' said the heavy weapons trooper. 'The Thunderhawks are being prepped for imminent departure. We are to be teleported to the fortress-monastery instead.'

Dak'ir recalled his all too recent experience aboard the *Archimedes Rex* and the subsequent translation to the Marines Malevolent ship, *Purgatory*. Inwardly, he groaned at the prospect, realising now that Argos was setting coordinates for a homing beacon.

A huge tremor shook the desert plain, seizing Dak'ir's attention. Pyroclastic thunder boomed in the depths of the earth, deep and resonant. It came from Mount Deathfire. A vast cloud of smoke and ash exuded from the craterous mouth at its tip, boiling down the giant volcano's rocky flanks in a grey-black wave. Civilians were already screaming as a gush of expelled magma plumed into the darkening air. Streams of syrupy lava carrying archipelagos of cinder issued down the mountainside in a sudden flood.

The thunder deepened further as a huge quake rippled across the dunes, setting civilians wailing in terror as they hurried faster in their lines. Draught animals bayed and mewled in despair, struggling against their panicked handlers and added to the chaos. The rising tumult beneath the earth became a cacophony as an immense beam of crimson light tore from the bowels of the mountain. It reached into the heavens, a coruscation of radiant fire, spearing the gathering clouds and tainting them with its passage until it was lost from sight.

The manifestation of natural fury lasted only seconds. In its wake the cries of the populace strung out across the still trembling dunes intensified. The lava flow ebbed and pooled, the clouds of ash rolled away and dissipated into thin veils. The volcano was dormant again, for now.

'Have you ever seen anything like that?' Dak'ir's primary heart was racing as he watched the Salamanders stationed down the line quickly restoring order.

Ba'ken shook his head in awe and wonder.

'An omen,' breathed Emek, 'it has to be. First the chest and now this... It doesn't bode well.'

Dak'ir's face hardened; he was not about to submit to hysteria just yet. 'Brother Argos,' he said. The sergeant's tone invited the Techmarine's opinion.

Argos was using the magnoculars to survey the emergence point of the beam.

'A phenomenon the likes of which I have never seen.'

'What could have caused it?' asked Ba'ken.

'Whatever it was,' offered Emek, 'it portends ill.' He pointed up to the sky. The fiery orange hue had turned the colour of blood, bathing the lightning-wreathed heavens in an ugly red glow.

Despite the apocalyptic respite, the civilians were moving faster. Dumbstruck and gesturing towards the sky in fear, some Nocturneans had to be goaded forwards. The battle-brothers encouraged the line to pick up the pace, their movements urgent but still controlled. The refugees were streaming through the gates of Hesiod now. But many, those whose wagons had floundered during the tremor or who were too afraid to move, were beyond the reach of the Salamanders and at the mercy of the harsh elements.

Moved by the plight of the civilians, Dak'ir stepped out of the portal disc. 'We must help them.'

'Return to the circle, brother-sergeant.' The hollow voice of Argos reined the other Salamander in. 'Your brothers have *their* task, so too do you, sergeant. There is nothing more we can ascertain here. Tu'Shan will have answers.'

Reluctantly, Dak'ir resumed his position within the teleporter.

'Let us hope the news from the Pantheon is good,' he muttered, gritting his teeth as Argos initiated teleport. The metal conductor plate under the Salamanders glowed like magnesium and filled the sergeant's world with light.

TELEPORTATION WAS INSTANTANEOUS, and the confines of the receiver pad resolved around them. It was one of ten such translation points within the teleportarium in the fortress-monastery on Prometheus. Ethereal warp vapours rolled off the hexagonal plate, which was large enough to accommodate an entire squad of Terminators, let alone three battle-brothers in power armour.

Crackling energy sparked then dissipated across three conductor prongs that arched over the pad like crooked
fingers. Warp dampeners, psychic buffers and other safeguards were in place on the remote chance that anything
should go wrong.

Dak'ir adjusted to translation quickly this time. Forewarned, he had steeled himself, and with Nocturne's
stable teleporter array the process was smooth. Automated
servo-gun systems powered down, having not detected a
threat, as he stepped off the teleporter pad and headed for
the docking bay where Salamanders were already assem-
bling.

The docking bay was vast, and accessed through an open
blast door. The Salamanders who had already made the
translation to Prometheus, or perhaps had never left, min-
gled in small groups, discussing the ramifications of what
the Pantheon had uncovered in excited murmurs. Some
readied weapons, checking and loading with methodical
precision. Others knelt in solitude as they took oaths of
moment, an icon of Vulkan's hammer pressed to their lips.
The primarch's name was spoken everywhere.

In a large hangar section, eight Thunderhawks idled
with landing stanchions extended. Directed by
Techmarine overseers, crews of servitors and human
engineers readied them for take-off. Huge pipes that
chugged fuel into the gunships' tanks were trailed across
the deck; operational scenarios were run on the fusion
reactors; tons of munitions were trolleyed on massive
tracked lifters, heavy drum mags slammed into ammo
cavities or the vast power batteries of the nose guns
charged to capacity. Techmarines incanted liturgies to the
machine-spirits, flocks of votive servitors and cyber-skulls
assisting them with their pious labours; troop holds were
cleared and inspected by human deck teams; the
instrumentation panels that ran the cockpits were assessed
and put through exhaustive activation protocols;

turbofans were ignited on low-burn to test performance; and every square centimetre of the gunships' structural integrity was checked and secured.

A strange atmosphere pervaded the docking bay – part parade ground solemnity, part campaign assembly deck resolve. Due to their dispersal across Nocturne, aiding villages and minor townships in preparation for the Time of Trial, the Salamanders did not arrive together. They appeared sporadically, after venturing to whatever sacred teleportation site was nearest. Squads were forming quickly though, filling up the docking bay with their armoured bulk, getting ready to receive their Chapter Master.

Tsu'gan was already present with much of his squad. Others too had started to assemble in ranks.

As he panned his gaze around the room, Dak'ir saw N'keln's Inferno Guard, Kadai's former command squad, waiting for their captain. Fugis stood amongst them, his head low in remembrance. The others fixed their eyes ahead. N'keln had yet to appoint his Company Champion, the role which Dak'ir had rebutted. Nor had he replaced his own vacated post of veteran sergeant – Honoured Brother Shen'kar acted as the captain's second-in-command for now – so the Inferno Guard numbered only three, the last position filled by Banner Bearer Malicant. The Assault squads of Vargo and Naveem assembled on the flanks, strapped up with their bulky jump packs. It could have been Dak'ir's imagination, but he thought he detected some tension between them. Likely, it was just anticipation of whatever was about to be imparted from the Pantheon council. Brother-Sergeants Agatone and Clovius were also present, together with the Devastators of Lok and Omkar.

Watching his fellow sergeants reminded Dak'ir of something he had asked Ba'ken to do before he returned to Nocturne.

'Have you spoken to Agatone and Lok?'

Ba'ken nodded darkly, as if reminded of a bad memory.

'Tsu'gan has approached the sergeants, those of Tactical and Assault at least.'

Dak'ir slowly shook his head in disbelief.

'His arrogance is boundless. I can't believe he still persists with this.'

'Agatone says several of the other sergeants will support him.'

'So, he moves against N'keln blatantly.'

'There is nothing blatant about it, far from it. Iagon's ways are subtle and oblique. There is no actual proof that Tsu'gan wants the captaincy.'

'No, but he *is* pressing for N'keln's dismissal. At best it smacks of misconduct, at worst it is treason.' Dak'ir paused, marshalling his anger. 'However couched, this cannot stand. Something must be done.'

'But what?' Ba'ken asked a fair question. 'Bringing it to the attention of the Chaplain is not an option at this point. Agatone made an oath of silence.'

Dak'ir faced his heavy weapons trooper. His expression was severe.

'I am not Agatone, Ba'ken. Nor am I bound to his oath,' he said sternly. 'This dissension must stop.'

'There is no choice,' Emek decided, entering the exchange for the first time since it had begun. 'Brother Elysius must be told.'

Dak'ir shook his head.

'Discord and division are rife as it is. An investigation by the Chaplain and his interrogators will only exacerbate that. N'keln wants to heal the wounds in this company. He will need our backing, and the backing of others, to do it. Forcing the sergeants to comply, making examples of the disaffected, will only deepen any resentment that already exists. Only by earning the sergeants' respect will N'keln gain their confidence and establish his authority,' reasoned Dak'ir, feeling his desire to act ebbing. 'Though it pains me to admit it, Tsu'gan is not a discontent for the sake of it. I'm not even certain he wants to replace Kadai at all. He wants someone he feels is worthy of Ko'tan's mantle. Once he believes N'keln is that person, he will capitulate.'

'Are you certain of that, brother?' asked Ba'ken.

Dak'ir's answer was frank.

'No. The fires of battle will temper the captain. He will burn or be reborn, that is the Promethean way.'

'Spoken like a true philosopher, brother,' said Emek wryly.

Dak'ir turned to him – a massive gate set into the far end of the docking bay was opening. It led to the inner heart of the fortress-monastery and the Pantheon. Tu'Shan and the council were coming, so Dak'ir kept it brief.

'Spoken like your sergeant,' he corrected. What came next included Ba'ken, too, 'Whose order will be followed.'

Both Salamanders nodded their understanding. The rest of Dak'ir's squad had joined them. The time for talking was at an end. The gate ground open. The Chapter Master entered.

Tu'Shan strode at the head of the Pantheon council, arrayed in his full panoply of war. His voluminous drakescale cloak writhed like a living thing as he walked and his deep eyes burned with all the inner strength of Deathfire's core. 3rd Company was fully assembled. Even Veteran Brothers Amadeus and Ashamon were present amongst their fellow Salamanders. The pair of Dreadnoughts stood stern and unmoving alongside the foremost Tactical squad led by Agatone. Brother Ashamon was an Ironclad. His seismic hammer rippled with electrical discharge, a meltagun appended to its haft, and the igniter flame from the flamer affixed to its claw-like power fist flickered dormantly.

Flanked by a squad of Firedrakes, clanking loudly in Terminator armour, Tu'Shan led the council down a wide aisle. It divided the squads in the company into two equal hemispheres, and was afforded for the ten 1st Company veterans, who were accompanied by Praetor himself. Behind the Chapter Master was Vel'cona, Chief Librarian and Pyriel's direct superior. The Epistolary walked alongside Elysius and N'keln, falling into lock-step with the Firedrakes on either side of them. The other Masters were either occupied on Nocturne's surface or prosecuting missions in distant systems.

Dak'ir's attention was fixed on Elysius in particular as the retinue of warriors past him to alight in front of 3rd Company.

The chest of Vulkan was in the Chaplain's hands.

CHAPTER FIVE

I
Solar Storm

'WELCOME, BROTHERS.' Tu'Shan's voice echoed powerfully around the expansive docking bay, reaching every corner and commanding absolute attention. Even surrounded by the Pantheon council, some of the Chapter's finest warriors, he looked immense and forbidding. The strength and passion of Vulkan blazed in the Chapter Master's eyes, together with the primarch's wisdom and presence.

'The council has consulted the Tome of Fire, and there are tidings from its hallowed pages,' he concluded sombrely. There was no further preamble. Tu'Shan was inclined towards action, not rhetoric, and bade Elysius forward.

The Chaplain bowed curtly and advanced in front of his Chapter Master, so he would be visible to the throng of Salamanders before him.

Elysius appraised them all in silence, allowing the gravitas of the occasion to build, letting his brothers know that he was ever watchful. To show impurity of spirit before the Chaplain was dire folly. He was fond of branding and excoriation to establish a warrior's piety. Chirurgeon-interrogators, servitor drones he had modified himself, assisted him in his *work*. Not all who entered his Reclusium came back. But to endure at the hands of Elysius meant you were above reproach… at least for a time.

He was but one Salamander. Yet without exception, every battle-brother that beheld the Chaplain then felt his presence like a brand of cold steel, just waiting to be ignited.

'*When the sky runs red with blood and the Mountain of the Forge gives up its sons, Vulkan will show us the way,*' Elysius quoted. His voice carried a hard edge like the hot barbs of his confessional tools.

He scoured the faces before him intently.

Purity seals festooned the Chaplain's cobalt-black power armour. Votive chains hung from his pauldrons, plastron and gorget. They were even pinioned to his battle-helm; effigies of hammers, drakes and the Imperial eagle.

'The sky *is* bloody,' he went on, 'Deathfire *has* given up its sons.' He clenched a fist to emphasise his zeal. 'These are the scriptures of the Tome of Fire, as left to us by our primarch. And in this,' he brandished the chest found on the *Archimedes Rex* in the other hand like a holy icon, 'he has shown us *his* way.'

Elysius lowered the chest and unclenched his fist.

'Galactic coordinates, buried within encrypted symbols found in the casket, speak of a stretch of space,' the Chaplain explained, his zeal traded for pragmatism. 'There, at the cusp of the Veiled Region in Segmentum Tempestus, is a system benighted by warp storms, closed off from the Emperor's light for millennia.' His eyes flashed behind his skull-faced visage. '*We* shall shine the torch of enlightenment upon it, brothers. The storms have cleared and the way is open once again. Look to the skies of Nocturne!' The mercurial Chaplain sprang into animation again without warning, thrusting his hands down to indicate the planet below. 'A blood-red haze blots out our baleful sun. It matches a constellation of stars in this very system. At the heart of this celestial arrangement is a single planet, one lost to Imperial record for over ten thousand years – *Scoria*. I need not explain the import of that.'

Murmurs of disbelief rippled around the room. Elysius did nothing to dissuade them. Rather, he seemed to revel in the growing fervour.

Dak'ir was as shocked as his battle-brothers. Had they somehow discovered the fate of Vulkan himself? That was what the Chaplain had implied. It was only supposition, but even still. Tu'Shan's face was unreadable at the potentially monumental revelation. Dak'ir had later learned that the beam of light emitted from the mountain had refracted with the dust particles from the recent eruption, creating the pseudo-celestial representation that Elysius spoke of. Certainly, the phenomenon was unprecedented. It was taken as a sign. Of a great discovery, or an imminent doom, Dak'ir was uncertain. He did know, however, that if there was even the remotest chance of finding Vulkan, or ascertaining his fate, then the Salamanders would take it.

The rest of Elysius's words were brief, and spoke of endurance and the cleansing fire of war. Zealously delivered, Dak'ir knew them all by rote. His mind was reeling with what had transpired and what was to come. When the Chaplain was done and N'keln stepped forward to address them, the brother-sergeant knew exactly what that would be.

The captain's face was stern as rock. '3rd Company, we are going to Scoria to reclaim the progenitor of our Chapter, should that be his whereabouts.' There was intensity in the brother-captain's eyes, as if he realised the import of this undertaking and the opportunity it presented to reunite the company. Dak'ir suspected Tu'Shan knew it too.

'Regardless, we go there with open minds and cautious eyes,' N'keln continued. 'All of us,' he added, nodding sagely. 'Scoria has been out of contact with the Imperium since the 31st millennium. A death world, like our own, it should provide no impediment to our mission. Deep space augurs have revealed the small system it inhabits is a volatile area, wracked by solar storms. This too,' he told them, 'we will overcome. There is no way to tell what we will find when we reach the surface. But enemies or no, we will discover why our primarch sent us there. Nor will we be alone.' N'keln gestured graciously behind him. 'Brother Praetor and his Firedrakes will accompany us.'

The veteran sergeant of 1st Company barely moved as the eyes of 3rd Company alighted upon him. He was an imperious warrior and a peerless tactician, save for the Chapter Master. Like all of the Firedrakes, he was aloof, living and training on Prometheus in the fortress-monastery. A long cape of salamander hide hung from the back of his Terminator armour, his shaven head like a hard, black bolt between the immense pauldrons. Laurels wreathed his doughty form, and a long-hafted thunder hammer was clasped in a gauntleted fist, a circular storm-shield attached to his back.

Praetor's inclusion in the mission raised certain questions. It was a great honour to serve alongside Tu'Shan's company: each one was a warrior-king, an inspiration to their battle-brothers around them. But it also threw N'keln's authority into doubt. Dak'ir was certain it would only add fuel to Tsu'gan's argument. He had lost sight of his fellow sergeant in the muster. It mattered not; Dak'ir would see him soon enough as N'keln brought the assembly to a close.

'No more words then; words will avail us nothing. Fire-born! To your gunships! The *Vulkan's Wrath* waits to take us to Scoria.'

3rd Company donned battle-helms and disbanded at once, sergeants barking orders as they broke up into their squads and marched quickly towards the embarkation ramps of their Thunderhawks. Dak'ir rallied his Salamanders together and made for the *Fire-wyvern*. From the corner of his helmet lens, he noticed the Firedrakes stomping towards *Implacable*, their own gunship. They were travelling with Brother-Captain N'keln and the Inferno Guard. Chaplain Elysius accompanied them. The docking bay was quickly evacuated, leaving Tu'Shan and Vel'cona alone.

To Dak'ir's dismay, Pyriel joined them aboard the *Fire-wyvern*. The Librarian levelled his piercing gaze at the brother-sergeant briefly before assuming his position in a grav-harness in the Chamber Sanctuarine. Tsu'gan acknowledged no one as he led his squad in, consumed with introspection. It seemed many of the Salamanders were lost in thought. The prospect of discovering their primarch, or some clue as to his fate, had silenced them all.

Whining turbofans drowned out the exterior noise as the servitor deck crews retreated. As the *Fire-wyvern* achieved loft, second behind *Implacable*, its landing stanchions retracted. A roar of flame erupted from its fully-ignited engines, and the gunship sped upwards. *Spear of Prometheus* tore right behind it. The gunships *Inferno* and *Hellstorm* followed in the aerial convoy. A trio of Thunderhawk transporters brought up the rear, bearing four Rhino APCs and the Land Raider Redeemer, *Fire Anvil*.

The blast doors in the hangar roof churned open, revealing the gulf of realspace above. Attached to one of the space port's docking claws was the strike cruiser, waiting to take 3rd Company to its destiny.

THE VULKAN'S WRATH was plying its final passage through the empyrean, on its last jump until they translated into the Scorian system. Many of the Salamanders were engaged in battle rituals, in preparation for the coming trials. Some were training fastidiously in the strike cruiser's gymnasia; others spent their time in solitude, reciting the catechisms of Promethean Lore. Tsu'gan, descending into a subdued malaise, had chosen the solitoriums again in a vain attempt to burn away his inner guilt.

Iagon watched Tsu'gan stagger out of the isolation chamber from the shadows.

Steam came off the sergeant's self-tortured body in swathes, ghosting the cooler air around him. Smothering it with a robe, Tsu'gan made for the antechamber where Iagon had left the sergeant's power armour just as commanded.

'Astartes,' a voice emanated from the darkness.

It took Iagon a moment to realise it was directed at him.

The wiry form of Zo'kar, Tsu'gan's brander-priest, shuffled into view. His priest's apparel was limned in the deep red light of fettered lume-lamps as he approached the Salamander.

Iagon's primary heart pulsed like a war drum in his chest. In his sadistic desire to witness Tsu'gan's self-flagellation, albeit via the branding rod of Zo'kar, he hadn't realised he'd leaned forward and revealed his presence. It was fortunate that Tsu'gan was so drunk with pain that *he* didn't notice, otherwise, it could have thrown Iagon's careful machinations into jeopardy. The bond of trust he had cultivated with his sergeant was vital; without it, Iagon had nothing.

'You should not be here,' Zo'kar pressed. He had set his iron rod aside and already banished the votive servitor. 'Lord Tsu'gan is very strict about privacy.'

Iagon's eyes narrowed.

'And has that been impeached, *serf*?'

'My orders were clear, Astartes. I must inform Lord Tsu'gan of this trespass immediately.' Zo'kar made to turn but Iagon reached from the darkness and seized him by the shoulder. He felt bone beneath the brander-priest's robes and through the parchment-thin skin, and exerted a little pressure – just enough to command Zo'kar's attention, but not so excessive that he would cry out.

'Hold…' Iagon used his strength to turn the brander-priest, so he faced him. 'I do not think Brother Tsu'gan is in any condition to hear of this, right now. Allow me to explain it to him.'

Zo'kar shook his head once beneath his cowl.

'I cannot. I obey Lord Tsu'gan. He must be told.'

Iagon fought back a sudden pang of rage, a desire to inflict pain on the insignificant thing in his grasp.

Even as a child, he had been cruel. A dim recollection, obscured further by the fog of his superhuman rebirth, fluttered like a wisp of smoke at the edge of Iagon's consciousness. It was a half-buried memory of staking lacertids on the dunes of the Scorian Plain. In the shadow of a rock, he had waited for the scorching sun to sear the diminutive lizards then watched as the larger draconids came to devour them. Through determination and cunning, Iagon had passed the trials required to become a Space Marine and been inducted as neophyte. The dark urges, which back then he did not fully understand, had been channelled onto the battlefield. With his sharp mind, made sharper by Imperial genetic science, he had advanced, always keeping the blackest recesses hidden away; far from the probing tendrils of Chaplains and Apothecaries. Iagon found through this secrecy that he was adept at subterfuge. He coaxed the black spark within, using his training and his superior intellect to coax it into a flame. It had roared into a dark conflagration of desire, for power and the means to exact it. No screening process, however rigorous and invasive, was perfect. Amongst the untold billions of the Imperium, every populace, every creed harboured the pathological. These aberrations often moved unnoticed, seemingly normal and pious, until the moment came for their deviancy to surface. But by then of course, it was often too late.

Now, Iagon was the draconid and Zo'kar a lizard staked at his mercy. The Salamander drew closer, using all of his height and bulk to cower and intimidate. When Iagon spoke again, it was in the breathy cadence of thinly-veiled threat.

'Are you sure, Zo'kar?'

'MORE WEIGHT.' BA'KEN grunted and relaxed his shoulders. The hefting chains attached to the black exertia-mitts he was wearing went slack. The Salamander's back was like a slab of onyx, hard and unyielding, as he slowly lowered the immense weights being hoisted by the chains. He squatted, the legs in his muscles bunched, sinews like thick cables. Wearing only training fatigues, the musculature of his ebon body was largely exposed.

Dak'ir smiled wryly. 'There is no more, brother,' he said from behind him.

'Then I shall lift you, brother-sergeant. Step upon my shoulders.' Ba'ken's gaze remained fixed, and Dak'ir couldn't be certain that he wasn't actually serious.

'I shall have to decline, Ba'ken,' Dak'ir replied with mock disappointment, checking the chrono mounted on the gymnasia's wall. 'Translation in-system is close. We must prepare for planetfall on Scoria.'

Easing the mitts off his immense hands, Ba'ken set them both down with a *clunk*. 'A pity,' he said, getting to his feet and towelling the sweat off his body. 'I shall have to ask the quartermaster for more weight next time.'

Dak'ir returned the exertia-mitts, akin to massive chunks of smooth-hewn granite, back to the holding station. All around them warriors of 3rd Company were still training hard.

The gymnasia was a vast space. At one end stood ranks of fighting cages, currently at capacity as battle-brothers duelled one another or simply recited their close combat weapon disciplines; others took to the expansive gymnasia floor, which was dark like black granite and filled with all manner of training apparatus. It possessed an ablutions block, and the darker recesses harboured fire pits where Salamanders could build their endurance at the mercy of red-hot coals or burning bars of iron.

Dak'ir's attention was on the ballistica where Ul'shan and Omkar guided their troopers through their targeting rituals. Lok was not present and the two brother-sergeants had divided the veteran's squad members between them for instruction and accuracy assessment. Segregated from the rest of the gymnasia for obvious reasons, the battle-brothers within the ballistica's bullet-chipped confines were still visible through a sheet of transparent armourcrys.

Dak'ir had his back to him when Ba'ken spoke again. 'So, what did you see?'

Prior to his arrival at the gymnasia to guide his squad's battle-training, Dak'ir had spent several hours in the one of the strike cruiser's solitoriums. During meditation, he had experienced another dream. This one was different to the recurring nightmare of Kadai's final moments and Dak'ir's futile efforts to save him. It was not remembrance that he had imagined in his mind's theta state, rather it felt more like a vision or even prophecy. The thought of it chilled him to such an extent that Dak'ir had sought succour from the counsel of the one Salamander he knew the best and trusted the most.

Bak'en's face held no trace of suspicion or agenda as Dak'ir faced him. He merely wanted to know. The bulky Salamander was one of the strongest warriors he knew, but it was his honesty and integrity that Dak'ir valued most.

'I saw a lizard with two heads prowling in the darkness of a barren sand plain,' said Dak'ir. 'It was hunting and found its prey, a smaller lizard, alone on the dunes. It cornered the smaller creature, swallowing it down its gullet. Then it slipped away into shadow, until it too was swallowed, but by darkness.'

Ba'ken shrugged.

'It's just a dream, Dak'ir – nothing more. We all dream.'

'Not like this.'

'You think it portends something deeper?'

'I don't what it means. I am more concerned with why I am dreaming it at all.'

'Have you spoken to Apothecary Fugis?'

'He knows of it, and until Kadai's death, had watched me like a dactylid watches prey. Now, it seems, Pyriel has been appointed my watcher.'

Ba'ken shrugged.

'If it was a concern, Elysius would be your shadow and not our Brother-Librarian, and you'd be having this conversation with the Brother-Chaplain's chirurgeon-interrogators.'

His eyes grew warm and earnest.

'Perhaps it was destiny that you found that chest on the Mechanicus ship, perhaps your vision of the two-headed lizard was for a reason. I know not, for I don't believe in such things myself. I know only this: you are my battle-brother, Dak'ir. Moreover, you are my sergeant. I have fought at your side for four decades and more. That is the only testament I need to your purity and spirit.'

Dak'ir pretended that his mind was eased.

'You are wise, Ba'ken. Certainly wiser than I,' he said with a humourless smile.

The hefty Salamander merely snorted, rotating his shoulder blades to ease out the stiffness. 'No, brother-sergeant, I am just old.'

Dak'ir laughed quietly at that, a sound that smacked of rare, untroubled abandon.

'Gather the troops,' he ordered. 'Armoured and on the assembly deck in two hours.'

Already, the other brother-sergeants were bringing their troops into line. Arming serfs were poised and ready for those who had divested themselves of their battle-plate to train.

'And you will be?' asked Ba'ken.

Dak'ir was pulling on his bodyglove, over which the electrical fibre bundles, interface cables and internal circuitry of his power armour would be placed and conjoined. 'On the bridge.' He ignored Ba'ken's slight impertinence by dint of the respect he afforded the heavy weapons trooper. He knew Ba'ken's inquiry was an honest one, bereft of any insolence. 'I want to speak with the brother-captain before we make planetfall.'

'What happened to the "Promethean way"?'

'Nothing. I want to know what he thinks we'll find down on Scoria and if he believes this mission is the boon we all hope it is.'

Ba'ken seemed satisfied with the answer and saluted, heading off towards the scalding steam jets of the ablutions chamber.

Dak'ir donned the rest of his power armour in silence, staring ahead at nothing. When the arming serf was done, the brother-sergeant thanked him and left the gymnasia. He was determined the long walk to the bridge would clear his head. The memories of the earlier dream gnawed at him parasitically as he tried to discern its meaning.

Any introspection was marred by the sudden appearance of Fugis. He had rounded the corner in the same section of the ship. Dak'ir was reminded again of their exchange outside the Vault of Remembrance in Hesiod. The melancholy shroud had not left the Apothecary then, it had merely spread.

When Fugis looked up, he gazed through Dak'ir at first and even after that recognition was delayed.

'Are you all right, Brother-Apothecary?' asked Dak'ir, his concern genuine.

'Have you seen Brother-Sergeant Tsu'gan?' Fugis snapped. 'He has eluded me since we embarked and I must speak with him at once.'

Dak'ir was taken aback at the curt tone in the Apothecary's voice but answered nonetheless. 'I last saw him headed for the solitoriums, but that was almost six hours ago. It's very unlikely he is still there.'

'I rather think it is highly probable, brother,' Fugis snarled and stalked off, without further word or explanation, towards the solitoriums.

The Apothecary had always been cold; Dak'ir had regularly been on the receiving end of his innate frigidity, but never like this. The darkness had beset him now, strangling hope and smothering optimism. Dak'ir had seen it as they'd surveyed the Pyre Desert. He saw it again as Fugis's diminishing figure was swallowed by the shadows of the long corridor.

Dak'ir gave it no further thought for now. He had business on the bridge that was best unfettered by concern for his grief-stricken Apothecary.

***

THE BLAST DOORS to the bridge parted after a biometric scan ascertained Dak'ir's presence. A diminishing hiss of hydraulic pressure escaped into the air as the brother-sergeant passed through the portal to the command centre of the *Vulkan's Wrath*.

The lume-lamps surrounding the bridge were kept low. The semi-dark promoted an atmosphere of apprehensive silence, in keeping with the gloom. It was always this way when traversing the warp or during battle. The scant, reddish light hugged the outer walls of the hexagonal chamber, bleeding into penumbral darkness. Most of the illumination on the bridge came from strategium tables and overhead pict displays that monitored the ship's multitudinous systems. The raft of icons upon the various screens was green. It meant the Geller fields that proofed the ship against the predators of the warp were holding.

A semi-circle of consoles filled the forward arc of the bridge. Like all Astartes vessels, the crew of the *Vulkan's Wrath* was primarily made up of human serfs, ensigns and shipmasters, servitors and tech-savants, all toiling before the operational controls. Thick shielding had been rolled over the bridge's view-ports to protect them, for even to look upon the warp was to be damned by it.

The warp was an immaterial realm, a layer stretched over the real world, akin to an incorporeal sea. Time moved differently along its waves; portals could be opened in it and routes travelled that allowed ships to move across great distances comparatively quickly. Its dangers were manifold, though. Abyssal horrors and soul-hungering entities plied its depths. The warp was insidious, too; it had a way of creeping into a man's mind and making him do and see things. Many space-faring vessels had been lost this way, not claimed by daemons, just destroyed from within.

Despite his arduous psychological training, his gene-bred mental toughness, Dak'ir had felt a prickle of unease ever since they had entered the immaterium.

He was glad they would be free of it again soon. The warp unsettled him. It tugged at the edge of his awareness, like cold, thin fingers massaging away his resolve. Throbbing insistently, the half-felt presence of the warp was like a lost whisper filled with malicious intent. Dak'ir could ignore it well enough but it briefly cast his thoughts back to the Dragon Warriors, how they had willingly submitted to this *other-reality* of dark dreams and darker promises, even embraced it. As a loyal servant of the Emperor, he could not imagine such a thing, the motivation that had driven them to this desperate act. Nihilan and his renegades were indeed beyond redemption now. His mind drifted to Stratos and the reason the Dragon Warriors were there. Vengeance had always seemed a petty motivation for one such as Nihilan; or, rather, it didn't seem enough of one.

Dak'ir considered it no further. He had reached the rear of the bridge and was standing at the foot of a staired platform where Brother-Captain N'keln sat upon his command throne. N'keln's mood was idle and restive as he watched his Brother-Librarian guide them by the Emperor's Light through the vagaries of the warp. Pyriel was forward of the command throne, on a lower part of the platform. He was encased within a pseudo-pulpit, standing bolt upright. It was not for the purpose of preaching that he was so ensconced, rather his psychic hood was connected integrally to the pulpit's internal circuitry, augmenting his abilities.

A series of tactical plans and schematics, deep-augur maps, blind-sketched by the ship's astropaths, were arranged on a strategio-table to N'keln's right hand. The captain glanced at them absently, while Brother-Sergeant Lok, standing beside the command throne, posited potential landing zones and approaches with a stylus. Evidently, the embarkation plans for Scoria were already in progress. It was all theory until they entered in-system, but Salamanders were nothing if not thorough.

Veteran Sergeant Praetor was nowhere to be seen. Dak'ir assumed that his bulky Terminator suit precluded his presence on the bridge and that he remained with his Firedrakes, locked in whatever clandestine rituals the warriors of 1st Company performed before battle. Perhaps Chaplain Elysius was with them, for he too was absent.

'Brother-sergeant,' N'keln's greeting held a tone of inquiry.

Dak'ir saluted, and took it to mean he was allowed to approach.

'Preparations for our landing are already underway?'

'Since before we left Prometheus, brother.' N'keln's gaze had shifted to the plans that Lok was annotating with arrows and battle-symbols.

Dak'ir noticed the military aspect to the icons the veteran sergeant was scribing.

'Are we expecting trouble, brother-captain?'

'I neither expect nor doubt it, sergeant. I merely wish us to be prepared for whatever is down there.'

N'keln looked up from the strategio-table when Dak'ir fell silent.

'Impatient for answers, Dak'ir?'

'My lord, I–'

N'keln waved away the nascent apology.

'You're the third officer in the last hour who has visited the bridge,' he said. 'I should admonish such restless behaviour, especially for a sergeant who ought to be with his squad, but in this case I shall make dispensations. It is not every day that a Chapter like ours gets the opportunity to discover the fate of its primarch.' It seemed to Dak'ir that N'keln's expression grew slightly wistful. 'I have seen artistic representations, of course,' he said, his voice reverent, 'rendered in stone and metal, but to *see...*' He emphasised the last word with heartfelt vehemence, '...and with my own eyes. Our father, ten thousand years since his fabled disappearance... It would be like myth come alive.'

Dak'ir's mood was less ebullient.

'I hope you are right, brother-captain.'

'You do not think we will find Vulkan on Scoria?' N'keln asked plainly. There was no agenda, no careful probe in his words. Perhaps that was why he struggled at the political side of leadership.

'Truthfully, captain, I don't know what we'll find there or what any of this will amount to.'

N'keln's eyes narrowed and in the pause in conversation, Dak'ir felt the imminence of what was to come like a stone collar around his neck. The captain's gaze was searching.

'It is more pertinent for you than most, isn't it, brother. You found the chest in the *Archimedes Rex*, did you not?'

Dak'ir gave his unneeded confirmation. Even though they faced away from one another, he felt the eyes of the Librarian boring into the back of his skull at the mention of the chest.

'You'll have your answers soon enough, brother-sergeant,' the voice of Pyriel interjected, as if summoned by Dak'ir's thought. 'We are about to emerge from the warp.'

There was a pregnant pause, as all those aboard the bridge waited for translation back into realspace.

'Now...' hissed Pyriel.

A massive shudder wracked the *Vulkan's Wrath*, a sudden shock wave ripping down its spine. The bridge shook. Dak'ir and several others lost their footing. A deep roar filled the hexagonal room. It sounded like fire, but it howled as if truly alive, searching voraciously for air to burn. The human crew, besides the servitors, covered their ears whilst trying to stay upright. The ship was bucking back and forth, tossed like a skiff upon a violent ocean. Consoles exploded, spitting sparks and going dead. Klaxons whined urgently, their warning drowned out by the raging tumult battering the *Vulkan's Wrath* from outside.

'Alert status crimson!' N'keln bellowed into the command throne's vox, gripping the arms tight to stay seated. 'All hands to emergency stations.'

Lok had fallen to one knee, braced against the deck with his power fist whilst his other hand clutched the strategio-table.

'Pyriel...' N'keln's face was slashed by the intermittent strobe of emergency lighting as Dak'ir pushed himself back up from where he had fallen at the base of the stairs. Still groggy, his gaze went to the Librarian. The pulpit was a mess of sparking wires and scorched metal. Pyriel punched his way out of the twisted wreckage, his mood black.

'We must have translated into a solar storm,' he growled loudly, seizing the ragged edge of the shattered pulpit for balance as the ship was smashed again. Helmsmen in front of the Librarian desperately tried to steer the ship, whilst simultaneously fighting to stay on their feet.

The din of churning servos fought against the fiery thunder assailing the vessel, as the blast shields covering the view-points started to retract. It was an automated system that kicked in as soon as the Geller fields powered down and the ship re-entered realspace.

Dak'ir felt the danger before he saw a thin line of ultrabright light creeping into being at the bottom edge of the shielding.

'Shut th–'

Horrified screams smothered the brother-sergeant's warning as multiple shafts of super-heated light reached into the bridge. An ensign nearest the view-point spontaneously combusted as the deadly solar energy washed over him. Others at the consoles suffered a similar fate. A shipmaster spun, crying for the Emperor's mercy, the left side of his face a blackened ruin. A naval armsman, with enough presence of mind to hunker down behind a console, pulled his laspistol and administered a killing shot between the poor bastard's pleading eyes.

Dak'ir felt the heat against his armour tangibly. It was like wading through a wind tunnel as he fought to reach the blast shield's emergency override lever. Not wearing his battle-helm, the view for Dak'ir shimmered through a heat haze. His naked skin was untroubled by it, though he saw a blistering servitor less resilient to the solar flare. It ravaged the inner walls, setting cables aflame and burning out circuitry.

Pyriel threw up a force dome around the crew, who crawled into it on their hands and knees. The blinded and the burned were dragged, mewling, into the psychic sanctuary whilst the dead were left to crisp and blacken, their bodies becoming human torches in the blaze.

The crack in the shielding was only centimetres thick when Dak'ir reached the override panel and threw back the lever. Agonisingly slowly, the armour plates rolled shut again and the hellish light was cut off.

Pyriel ended the force dome and sagged. His face was beaded with sweat, but his eyes conveyed his gratitude as his gaze met Dak'ir's.

The smoking ruins of men lay all about the bridge, their charred corpses like dark shadowy husks on the scorched deck.

'Medical crews onto the bridge now,' Lok spoke into his gorget, linked in with the ship's communication systems. The edges of his pauldrons were black, as if filmed with a layer of thick soot, and heat emanated off his bald pate.

'Master Argos,' N'keln barked into the throne vox. The fiery roar of the storm had not relented, making it difficult to convey orders. 'Damage report.'

Static filled the bridge's vox-emitters. The Techmarine's voice was strained as it fought to be heard through the interference. Background clamour from the Enginarium deck where Argos was situated impeded the clarity further.

'Hull engines are non-functional, aft thruster banks three through eighteen are showing sporadic power emissions. Shields are down and decks thirteen through twenty-six are showing critical damage, possibly an integrity breach.'

It was a grim report.

'What hit us?'

'The port-side of the ship was struck by a light beam from the solar storm. It burned through our outer armour, took out our shields and strafed most of the sun-side decks. Entire sections were ripped out. The worst hit areas were totally burned. Everything there is ash. I've shut them down already.'

'*Vulkan's mercy...*' breathed N'keln.

Somehow, perhaps through his augmetics, Argos heard him.

'Imagine a melta gun at point-blank range against a suit of ceramite.'

Dak'ir found he had no desire to.

'Give me something positive, brother,' said N'keln, interrupting the sergeant's bleak remembrance.

The Techmarine's response was unintentionally dry.

'We are still aloft.'

The captain smiled without mirth. He was distracted for a moment as the blast doors opened and medicae teams spilled through to tend to the injured and remove the dead. Lok directed them for his captain, as N'keln continued to speak with his chief Techmarine.

'How long will that be the case whilst we are breached?'

There was a delay as the crackling retort of the vox-emitters blighted Argos's reply.

'Not long,' he said at last.

N'keln looked Dak'ir in the eye, his face assuming a stern cast. The breached decks would have to be purged and sealed. Hundreds, if not thousands, of human serfs worked in those areas of the ship – N'keln would be condemning them all to death.

'Alone, they cannot survive,' stated Dak'ir, already knowing his captain's mind.

N'keln nodded.

'That's why you're going to gather your squad – Lok, you too–' he added with a side glance, 'and assist in the evacuation. Save as many as you can, brothers. I will order the decks locked down in fifteen minutes.'

Dak'ir rapped his pauldron, and he and Lok ran from the bridge, the din of their armour clanking urgently behind them.

II
Sinner and Saviour

IAGON WAS PITCHED off his feet as a violent tremor rippled across the solitorium. Zo'kar yelped in pain as he was torn from the Salamander's grasp. A low rumble echoed through the chamber, followed by the sound of tearing metal and a crash of steel. Something fell from the ceiling and the brander-priest was lost from Iagon's view. Heaving himself up from his prone position, filtering out the sudden roar invading his senses, Iagon staggered through the half-dark until he came to a pile of wreckage. The ceiling of the solitorium had collapsed. Zo'kar's pitiful face, the hood cast back in the fall, could be seen beneath it. Feeble arms pushed against a thick adamantium rebar crushing the brander-priest's chest. Blood was leaking from a wound concealed by his robes, a dark patch spreading over the fabric as he struggled.

'Lord... Help me...' he gasped, his tone pleading, as he saw Iagon standing over him.

'Rest easy, serf,' said the Salamander. With his Astartes strength, he could lift the rebar and drag Zo'kar out. He wedged his gauntleted hands beneath it, testing his grip. But before Iagon took a proper hold he lifted his head, and his face became an emotionless mask. The Astartes reversed his grip, instead placing his hands on *top* of the rebar, not under it. 'Your pain is at an end,' he concluded and pushed down violently.

Zo'kar spasmed once as the rebar broke his ribs and pulped his chest and internal organs. A gush of blood erupted from his mouth, spattering his face and robe in dark droplets. Then he slumped down, his dead eyes staring glassily.

Something had struck the ship and continued to assail it, that much Iagon knew as he leapt over the wreckage and fought his way into the outer corridor. Alert sirens were blaring and the vessel was plunged into emergency half-light. The upper deck was evidently badly damaged. The destruction had spilled over into its counterpart below, where Iagon was now standing, bringing down struts in sections of the ceiling. He heard N'keln's voice coming over the vox, broken by static interference. All Astartes were being ordered to decks thirteen through twenty-six, whichever was nearest. The ship was breached and needed to be locked down. N'keln was trying to save the crew.

'Noble, but futile,' Iagon muttered, rounding a corner to find a group of human armsmen huddled around a spar of metal piercing the deck grille. As he got closer, Iagon saw a warrior in green battle-plate was pinned by it. He recognised the face of Naveem, one of Tsu'gan's main opposers. He'd torn off his helmet – it lay discarded nearby – likely to aid his breathing, judging by the sergeant's ragged gasps for air. The metal spar had impaled his chest. Going on the sheer size of it, Iagon reasoned that most of Naveem's internal organs were already ruined. The sergeant was hanging on by a sinewy thread.

'Step aside,' Iagon ordered, stalking up to the armsmen. 'You can do nothing for him.'

Buffeted by an unseen blow, the ship bucked again, throwing one of the armsmen to the ground and drawing an agonised moan from Naveem.

Iagon steadied himself against the wall.

'Go to your emergency stations,' he said. 'I will deal with this.'

The armsmen saluted then sped off uncertainly down the corridor.

Iagon loomed over the supine Naveem. The sergeant's mouth was caked with expectorated blood and dark fluid leaked from the copious cracks in his power armour.

'Brother…' he rasped upon seeing Iagon, spitting out a film of bloody vapour.

'Naveem,' Iagon replied. 'You chose the wrong side,' he added darkly.

The sergeant's expression was nonplussed as Iagon leaned in, taking both edges of the metal spar in a firm grip…

'Iagon!'

Whatever Iagon was about to do was arrested by Fugis's voice.

'Over here, Apothecary,' he bellowed with feigned concern, relaxing his grip. 'Brother Naveem is wounded.'

Fugis reached them in moments, narthecium in hand. His attention was fixed on the stricken form of Brother Naveem – he barely acknowledged Iagon at all.

Crouching over the bloodied sergeant, the Apothecary made a quick assessment. His thin face grew grave. Carefully disengaging Naveem's gorget, he took a stimm from his narthecium kit and injected a solution of pain-regressors into Naveem's carotid artery.

'It will ease your suffering, brother,' he said quietly.

Naveem tried to speak, but all that came from his mouth was near-black blood, a certain sign of internal bleeding. His breath became more ragged and his eyes widened.

Fugis pulled his bolt pistol from its holster and pressed the barrel to Naveem's forehead. An execution shot to the frontal lobe, point blank, would kill him instantly but leave both progenoids intact. Since the sergeant's chest was all but destroyed, that only left the one in Naveem's neck.

'Receive the Emperor's Peace…' he whispered. A deafening bang echoed off the corridor walls.

'There was no other choice, brother.' Iagon's tone was consoling.

'I know my duty,' Fugis snapped, going to the reductor mounted on his left gauntlet. The device consisted of a drill and miniature chainblade, designed to chew through flesh and bone to get to the progenoids buried in a Space Marine's body. A syringe, appended to a pre-sterilised capsule, would extract the necessary genetic material once the outer bone wall had been breached.

Fugis moved in, his reductor drill whirring as it bit into Naveem's dead flesh. The *Vulkan's Wrath* was shuddering badly, jolting with severe force every few seconds or so. The Apothecary fought to keep himself steady, knowing that any small mistake would see the gland destroyed and Naveem's legacy ended, just like Kadai's.

Kadai…

The unwanted memory of his captain surfaced in Fugis's mind. Suddenly, the concern he felt at the bucking ship outweighed his caution and he began to rush, fearing a sudden tremor. In his haste, he slipped. The syringe missed the progenoid and the drill sheared the gland in half, spilling it into the dead Salamander's exposed throat.

'No!' Fugis emitted a breathless cry of anguish, thumping the deck heavily with his fist. 'No, not again,' he rasped, and hung his head despairingly.

Iagon leaned in.

'It was an error, brother. No more than that.'

'I don't make errors,' Fugis hissed, his fist clenched. 'My mind is too troubled. I am no longer fit for this,' he confessed.

'You must do your duty,' Iagon urged him. 'You are needed by this company, Brother-Apothecary… as is Brother-Sergeant Tsu'gan,' he added.

Fugis looked up after a few moments when he realised what Iagon was implying. If he would turn a blind eye to Tsu'gan's masochistic affliction, then Iagon would not speak of the Apothecary's apparent frailty. Fugis was caught in a moral web of his own devising, but laid by Iagon.

Anger contorted his features.

'You bastard,' he spat.

'I prefer pragmatist,' Iagon answered smoothly. 'We can ill-afford to lose two officers.'

He offered his hand, but Fugis ignored it.

'How many more will die if you are not there to minister to them, brother?' Iagon asked him. He looked down at his still proffered hand. 'This is what seals our pact.'

'What pact?' Fugis snorted, back on his feet.

'Don't be naïve,' Iagon warned him. 'You know what I mean. Take it, and I will know I have your oath.'

Fugis wavered. There was no time to consider. The ship was being ripped apart.

'Your brothers depend upon you, Apothecary.' Iagon's tone was coaxing. 'Isn't the preservation of life your credo? Ask yourself, Fugis – can you really turn your back on it?'

Fugis scowled.

'Enough!'

He knew he would regret this compact, yet what other choice did he have? Stay silent about Tsu'gan's indiscretion and compromise his ethics, his sense of moral rightness, or speak out and relinquish his position in the company? He could not allow his brothers to go into battle without an Apothecary. How many could die needlessly as a result? Hating himself, he took Iagon's hand.

Why does it feel like I've just made a deal with Horus…?

DAK'IR AND LOK parted company at the first intersection after leaving the bridge. Both sergeants had contacted their squads via the comm-feeds in their battle-helms. Salamanders were rapidly dispersing across the stricken decks, rescuing those who were trapped, quelling panic or opening up escape routes. The *Vulkan's Wrath* was well outfitted with lifters and deck-to-deck conduits, and though the strike cruiser was vast, reaching the crisis areas had been swift.

Reaching deck fifteen, Dak'ir was greeted with a scene of utter carnage. He ranged along darkened corridors lit by fire and filled by the screams of the injured and dying. Twisted metal and collapsed ceiling struts made progress slow and dangerous. Torn deck plates bled away into the darkness of the lower levels, pitch-black pitfalls that he discerned through his battle-helm's infra-red spectra. Leaping across the miniature chasms, Dak'ir tried not to think how many bodies might be lying beneath him in mangled heaps.

Through the gaseous haze of a split coolant pipe, Dak'ir saw Brother Emek crouching by the slumped form of a wounded crewman. Liquid nitrogen was gushing everywhere, freezing whatever it touched. Crushing the pipe either side of the breach and cutting off its supply, Dak'ir effectively sealed the leak. When he reached Emek, his brother was already closing the slumped crewman's eyes for him.

'Dead...' His voice held a trace of sorrow. 'But there are more who still live. In the corridor beyond,' he added. Another survivor was strapped up to his back. The man's legs were a red ruin, crushed to paste by falling wreckage. Clinging on to Emek desperately, he whimpered in pain like an infant.

'Ba'ken is ahead,' he said, and got to his feet.

Dak'ir nodded and moved on, as Emek went in the other direction. Sparking terminals lit the way. They showed hollow-eyed crewmen, those who were still able-bodied rushing from the damaged deck. Continual reports from the Enginarium and Brother Argos issued through Dak'ir's battle-helm. More and more areas of the ship were being sealed off as entire sections of deck fragmented under the solar storm's baleful glare.

The trickle of fleeing crewmen became a surge. Lighting was more sporadic, until it failed completely and even the fires couldn't alleviate the darkness. Dak'ir ushered on the men as he went, telling them to cling to the edges of the corridors and watch their footing. He didn't know if they all heard him. Panic gripped them now. Something approaching that emotion spiked in Dak'ir's mind as he realised that fifteen minutes were up. Thunderous sirens shuddered noisily, communicating the fact that the deck was locking down.

Descending into steadily worse carnage, he started to run. Through his advanced hearing, Dak'ir detected the distant sounds of bulkhead doors slamming shut and zoning off the compromised sections of the ship. He tried not to think about the men that might still be trapped inside them, hammering on the doors with no hope of escape.

Rounding the next corner, barging his way through a flood of crewmen, Dak'ir saw the massive, armoured form of Ba'ken. He was wedged between a bulkhead door and the deck. It pushed down at him from the ceiling as it fought to seal off the section. Swarms of serfs rushed past him as Ba'ken urged them with curt commands. Strong as he was, the Salamander couldn't fight the power of a strike cruiser and hope to prevail. His legs were starting to buckle and his arms to tremble.

Dak'ir went to him at once, getting under the slowly descending door and adding his strength to his brother's.

Barely arching his head to see, Ba'ken caught Dak'ir in the corner of his eye and smiled through a grimace.

'Come to join me, eh, sergeant?'

Dak'ir shook his head. 'No,' he replied. 'I just come to see if this is enough weight for you, brother.'

Ba'ken's booming laughter vied with the lockdown siren for supremacy.

All the while, more and more crewman streamed – limping, running, even carried by their comrades – between the two Space Marines holding the way open for them a little longer.

'There must be thousands on this deck,' Dak'ir growled, already feeling the strain of the pressing bulkhead door. 'We can't hold this open long enough to save them all, Ba'ken.'

'If we only saved ten more, it would be worth it,' snarled the bulky Salamander, as he gritted his teeth.

Dak'ir was about to agree when the comm-feed crackled in his ear and a familiar voice issued through.

'Need assistance on deck seventeen…' Tsu'gan's tone was strained. 'Respond, brothers.'

Static reigned. All the Salamanders dispersed across the decks must either be out of comm-range or they were already engaged in evacuation operations they couldn't leave.

Dak'ir swore under his breath. Ba'ken was the stronger of them. Without him, Dak'ir could not hold the door himself. He would have to be the one to go to his brother's aid.

'Go, sergeant.' Ba'ken spoke through gritted teeth.

'You can't hold it alone,' Dak'ir protested, knowing the decision was already made.

Dak'ir sensed a presence behind him, the clanging retort of heavy footfalls echoing steadily louder as they closed on his position.

'He won't need to,' said a gravel-thick voice.

Dak'ir turned and saw Veteran Sergeant Praetor.

Close up, the Firedrake was even more formidable. In his Terminator armour, Praetor towered over them both. His bulk filled up half the corridor. Dak'ir saw a fire burning in his eyes, unlike that of his brothers. It seemed deeper, somehow remote and unknowable. Three platinum studs ringed Praetor's left eyebrow, attesting to his veteran status, and the immensity of his presence was almost tangible.

Dak'ir stepped aside, allowing the awesome warrior to assume his vacated position. Praetor lumbered beneath the bulkhead door and took the strain with arms bent like a champion weight lifter. The lines of exertion on Ba'ken's face eased at once.

'On your way, sergeant,' grunted the Firedrake. 'Your brother awaits you.'

Dak'ir saluted quickly and chased back the way he had come. Tsu'gan needed him, though he suspected that his fellow brother-sergeant would be less than pleased when he saw the identity of his saviour.

THE IGNEAN... THE thought was a bitter one as Tsu'gan regarded Dak'ir across the gaping chasm of twisted steel and fire. It wasn't enough that he had to capitulate and admit he needed aid; his rescuer was the one Salamander he desired to see the least.

Tsu'gan scowled through the swathes of smoke billowing up from below. He hoped Dak'ir got the message that he was disgruntled. The brother-sergeant was on one side of a huge pitfall some ten metres across. The deck plates had been ripped away as the ship was ravaged by the solar storm. A lifter, torn from its riggings and punched out of its holding shaft, had plummeted through the metal like a hammer dropped through parchment. It had come to rest several decks below, collapsed in a ruined heap, creating a new hollow that was fringed with razor-edged steel and sharpened struts that jutted like spikes.

Fire emanated from where the lifter had crushed an activation console. Sparks flicked from the trashed unit had lit flammable liquids pooling from pipes shorn during the lifter's rapid descent. It was building to a conflagration, the flames so high they licked the edges of the ragged deck plates where Tsu'gan was standing. Smoke coiled upwards in black, ever-expanding blooms.

'Here,' called Tsu'gan, when his fellow sergeant didn't see him straight away. He watched as Dak'ir made his way to the end of the corridor and the junction where Tsu'gan was crouched with fifty crewmen in torn, fire-blackened uniforms.

Dak'ir gave a forced nod of acknowledgement as he reached the other Salamander.

'What do you need, brother?' he asked in a matter-of-fact tone.

'Down there.' Tsu'gan pointed into the fiery shaft.

Dak'ir crouched down with him, peering through the dense smoke.

'You see it?' Tsu'gan asked, impatiently.

'Yes.'

There was a section of the original broken deck plate hanging into the chasm. It was long enough to span the ragged hole but would need to be hoisted up and held in place in order for anyone to cross.

'The bulkheads have not been engaged in this part of the ship, yet,' said Tsu'gan, 'but it's only a matter of time. That way,' – he gestured past the chasm to the darkness on the other side; there was a faint pall of light from still active lume-lamps – 'leads to the lifter and salvation for these men.'

'You want to bridge the gap for them to cross, so they can reach it,' Dak'ir concluded for him.

Tsu'gan nodded. 'One of us has to leap across and take up the other end of the deck section. Then we both hold it in place,' he explained. 'Armsmaster Vaeder will guide his men across.'

One of the deck crew, a man with a gash across his forehead and a makeshift sling supporting his right arm that had been fashioned from part of his uniform, stepped forward and saluted.

Dak'ir acknowledged him with a nod, before turning his attention back to Tsu'gan.

The other brother-sergeant was back on his feet. He held up his hand before Dak'ir could speak.

'If your question is who will make the leap?' he asked without making eye contact. 'I will do it.'

Tsu'gan spread his arms.

'Step back,' he ordered, meaning Salamander and crewman alike. Tsu'gan leant back a little by way of gathering some momentum and then launched himself over the chasm. Fire lapped at his boots and greaves as he flew across the metal-wreathed blackness, before he landed on the opposite side with a heavy *thunk*.

'Now, Ignean,' he said, turning to face Dak'ir, 'take up the fallen deck section and lift it to me.'

'Are your men ready, Armsmaster Vaeder?' Dak'ir asked with a side glance at the crewman.

'Ready to leave this ship, my lord, aye.'

Low rumblings from deep within the vessel gave Dak'ir pause as the corridor shook and creaked ominously.

'We move now, Ignean!' snapped Tsu'gan, seeing no reason to delay. Don't coddle them, he thought. Survival first.

Dak'ir crouched down, once he was certain of his footing, and grasped the hanging deck plate by pushing his fingers through its grilled surface. The metal would normally be latticed with several overlapping layers but those had since fallen away, so only the uppermost level remained, enabling the Space Marine to get his armoured digits through the gaps. Ensuring his grip was firm Dak'ir lifted the ten metres of plate, its twisted metal beams screaming in protest as he bent them back almost straight.

Tsu'gan watched the deck plate rise, frustrated at Dak'ir's slowness. He reached down and took it as soon as he could, hoisting the metal up by the ragged edge that didn't quite meet the end of what he was crouching on.

'Secure,' he growled.

Armsmaster Vaeder had organised his men into ten groups of five. Each 'squad' would take it in turns to cross the makeshift bridge so as not to put too much pressure on the metal or the Salamanders bearing it. Just before the first group was about to muster across, a huge plume of flame erupted from below as some incendiary in the depths ignited and exploded.

Tsu'gan felt the heat of the fire against his exposed face as he was utterly engulfed by it. Smoke billowed up in swathes, obscuring Dak'ir and the crewman from view.

'Send them now,' he bellowed, fighting against the roar of the flames. 'We can afford to wait no longer.'

After a few seconds, the first of several figures started to emerge. Tsu'gan felt the weight of their passage in his arms as he strained to keep the deck plate aloft. One slip and anyone crossing it would fall to their certain deaths. He had no desire to add that to his already troubled conscience.

A thought came unbidden into his mind at that, and he forced it down.

Vulkan's fire beats in my breast, he intoned in his head to steady himself. *With it, I shall smite the foes of the Emperor.* Tsu'gan clung to the mantra like a lifeline, as tenuous and jeopardous as the fragile bridge he clutched between his hands.

The first of the 'squads' made it across without incident, hugging jackets over their heads to ward off the fire and smoke now issuing through the grille plate. A second group wandered through after them, their footing wary because of the poor visibility. All the while, the *Vulkan's Wrath* quaked and trembled as if it was a bird fighting against a tempest.

Too slow, too slow, thought Tsu'gan as the third 'squad' reached the other side, choking back smoke fumes. The ship was tearing itself in half; they had to pick up the pace and get off the deck.

Dak'ir had realised the danger, too, and was ushering the crewmen across in larger and larger groups. He shouted at Armsmaster Vaeder, urging him to take the last of his men across. Screeching and shuddering, the deck plate held just long enough for the last of the crew to reach safety, before buckling and falling into the fiery abyss below.

'Now you,' Tsu'gan bellowed, getting to his feet as Dak'ir nodded in understanding. The Ignean took two steps back and was about to launch himself when a fierce tremor gripped the deck, knocking the humans off their feet. Dak'ir got caught up in it and misstepped, stumbling as he made his jump. He fell agonisingly short. Tsu'gan leant forward and outstretched a hand when he saw what was happening. He grasped Dak'ir's flailing arm and the weight of him dragged Tsu'gan to his knees. He hit the deck with a *thunk* of metal on metal, felt it jar all the way up his spine.

'Hold on,' he growled, fire still lapping around him – the edges of his armour that were exposed to the flames were already scorched black. He grunted and heaved – it was like hauling a dead weight with all that power armour – pulling Dak'ir up so he reached the lip of the jagged deck and dragged himself up.

'Thank you, brother,' he gasped, once he was safely on the semi-stable side and facing his rescuer.

Tsu'gan sneered.

'I do my duty. That's all. I wouldn't let a fellow Salamander die, even one that has not the right to bear the name. And I pay my debts, Ignean.' He turned his back, indicating it was the final word, and focused his attention on the human crew.

'Get them to the lifter, armsmaster,' he said sternly.

Vaeder was on his feet, barking orders, hoisting men up, kicking those who thought to wallow. In a few seconds, all fifty were trudging towards the faint light and the solace represented by the lifter.

Tsu'gan went after them, aware of Dak'ir following behind him. Again, he cursed at being shackled with him of all his battle-brothers. He hated being in the Ignean's presence. It was his fault that Kadai had died at

Aura Hieron. Wasn't it Dak'ir that had sent Tsu'gan after
Nihilan and exposed his captain's flank? Wasn't it Dak'ir
that saw the danger but failed to reach Kadai in time to
save him? Wasn't it Dak'ir that... Or was it? Tsu'gan felt
the weight of guilt upon him like an anvil strapped to
his back whenever he wasn't spilling blood in the Chapter's name; that guilt multiplied tenfold whenever he
saw Dak'ir. It forced him to admit that perhaps the
Ignean wasn't solely responsible, that maybe even he...

Armsmaster Vaeder was raking open the lifter's blast
doors with the assistance of two of the other crewmen.
The raucous screech of metal was welcome distraction.
It didn't last long, as the Ignean spoke again.

'We need to get these men to a flight deck, abandon
ship with as many hands as possible.'

Tsu'gan faced him as the humans were clambering
aboard the lifter. Though large, the lifter reached
capacity quickly and they would need to make several
trips.

'It's too late for that,' he answered flatly. 'We must
have entered Scoria's upper atmosphere by now. The
ship will be at terminal velocity. Any escape would be
suicide. We get them to the upper deck.'

Dak'ir leaned in and lowered his voice.

'The chances of these men surviving a crash are slim
at best.'

Tsu'gan's response was cold and pragmatic.

'That can't be helped.'

The lifter was coming down again, chugging
painfully on overworked cable hoists. Ten metres from
the deck it lurched ungainly, emitting a high-pitched
scream, until finally churning to an uneven stop.

Something approaching despair registered in the
eyes of Vaeder and the ten crewmen yet to ascend.
Compounding their misfortune, an orange glow lit up
the Salamanders' armour from a rolling wave of fire

spilling up from the chasm and over into the deck where the humans cowered.

'Meet it!' roared Tsu'gan, and the two Astartes formed a wall of ceramite between the brittle crew and the raging flames. Heat washed over the Salamanders, but they bore it without flinching.

When the backdraft had died down, sucked into the chasm like liquid escaping through a vent, Dak'ir turned to Tsu'gan again.

'So, what now?'

Tsu'gan eyed the crewmen in their charge. They were huddled together, crouched down against the recently dissipated blaze. Steam was issuing off the Salamander's armour and face, his view filtered through a heat haze.

'We are going to crash in a vessel that is not meant to land, deliberately or otherwise, on solid ground. We shield them,' he said. Wrenching metal resonated loudly in Tsu'gan's ears, as forbidding as a death knell. 'And hang on to something.'

CHAPTER SIX

I
Planetfall

THE CHITIN-CREATURE DIED amidst a welter of exploded bone-plates and shredded mandibles. Grey, sludge-like blood oozed from ragged wounds in its carapace. In its death throes, it flipped onto its armoured back, insectoid legs spasming once and then curled up to remain still.

'Death to the xenos!' spat Brother-Chaplain Elysius, unleashing a storm from his bolt pistol. 'Suffer not the alien to live!'

The *Vulkan's Wrath* had struck the surface of Scoria like a meteorite, its hull still burning from its rapid re-entry into the planet's atmosphere. Impelled by its momentum, the strike cruiser had dug a massive furrow into the earth, hull antennas, towers and engines ripped apart as they met against unyielding bedrock. Hundreds died in the crash, smashed to paste and broken as they were bounced against barrack rooms and hangars in the massive ship. Fires broke out instantly, burning those unlucky enough to be in their path to ash. Some were crushed as the fragile sinews holding up vast sections of damaged upper decks and ceilings capitulated, sending tons of metal debris crashing down onto their heads. Long swathes of armoured shielding had punched inwards, pulping hapless crewmen when the corridor they were clinging to became a single sheet of beaten metal. Others were tossed into chasms of fire and darkness, ripping open like yawning mouths in the deck and swallowing them whole.

In the aftermath, chainswords and cutting tools buzzed into life, the smoke and dust still clinging to the air in a veil, as crewmen sought to cleave escape routes through the bent metal. Hydraulic steam vented in a wave as saviour portals were opened in the hull in a staccato chorus of disengaging locking bars. Survivors spewed out sporadically, some carrying the injured, others forlornly dragging the dead. The Salamanders, who had sustained casualties of their own, organised the evacuation from the worst affected areas and soon a large body of men and servitors had gathered on Scoria's ash-grey soil.

The crash had lasted only minutes, yet they had stretched into hours, even lifetimes, for those aboard praying to the Emperor for deliverance. The furrow ploughed by the strike cruiser's prow ran for almost a kilometre and had disturbed something lurking beneath the ashen surface of Scoria.

The creatures came from the below the earth, whorled emergence holes presaging their arrival. Screams from crewmen dragged under the ash plain were the first indication that they were being attacked. Hordes of the things came on after that, shaking their squat, solid bodies free of clinging ash before wading in with bone-pincers and clicking mandible teeth. Thirty-five crewmen died, swallowed into the earth, before the Salamanders mounted a counter-assault.

Brother-Chaplain Elysius led the Fire-born and he did so with zeal and unrestrained violence.

'Purge them!' he bellowed, his blood-curdling voice amplified by the vox-emitters in his battle-helm, 'With bolt, blade and flame, eradicate the xenos filth!' Barking fire erupted from his pistol, raking a chitin-beast's torso and blasting away one of its mandibles, before the Chaplain advanced and rammed his crackling crozius into its body, gutting it. Grey viscera flecked his skull-face, anointing him in the blood of war.

The bizarre, crustacean-like beasts reminded Dak'ir of the tyranid, as he slew them alongside his Chaplain. He imagined them as the product of some errant spore cluster vented by a stricken hive ship, only to drift into Scoria's orbit and infest the planet. Generations old, they were now an outmoded bio-form that had simply not evolved, but rather stagnated and propagated.

Dak'ir's squad, together with three others, had mustered to their Chaplain's side when Elysius had issued the call to battle. The Salamanders had adopted a wide perimeter, surrounding the horde of chitin-beasts and slowly corralling them with sustained bolter bursts. The creatures were big, almost as large as a Rhino APC, and their bony carapaces were hard, but not impregnable. Their bulk made them awkward, though, and they possessed a limited field of vision. By encircling them, the Salamanders attacked their blind sides and vulnerable flanks. The xenos reacted with confused and impotent aggression as they sought to attack a foe that was everywhere at once.

'Ba'ken,' yelled Dak'ir, as he vaporised a chitin-creature's bone-claw with a bolt of plasma, 'cleanse and burn!'

The hulking Salamander trudged forward as his sergeant retreated and sent a swathe of ignited promethium over the stricken xenos-beast. It keened and clicked in agony as the flames washed over it, the air trapped within its bone-plates escaping in a hissing scream.

Elsewhere, staccato bursts of sustained bolter fire became ever more clipped, indicating that the battle against the chitin-creatures was drawing to its end. The last of them had been enclosed within a circle of green battle-plate that was slowly tightening like a noose. Occasional, desperate assaults from the cornered beasts were met with explosive rounds that punctured alien bodies, rupturing them from within and sending gouts of sludge-viscera spitting from flapping mandible mouths. Flamer bursts harried the wretched creatures further, and they keened and clicked before the hot glare, evidently afraid of fire.

Finally, with only a half dozen remaining, the xenos burrowed back into the earth, away from the armoured giants who brought bellowing thunder and fire from the heavens.

Tsu'gan observed his distant battle-brothers with envious eyes. Behind him, the crash-landed strike cruiser loomed like a canted cityscape, bizarrely off-kilter. Even partially sunk into the ashen ground as it was, the *Vulkan's Wrath* was huge. Its span was the width of several hive blocks and it took several Astartes to guard it at kilometre intervals. The many decks, towers, platforms, superstructures, hangars, bays, even temples and cathedrals stretched like a dull green metropolis slowly smothered by grey falling snow.

As the battle raged, Techmarines, servitors and human labour crews toiled over the ship's storm-lashed surface. The solar flares had scorched fresh battle-scars down the old strike cruiser's flanks, and punctured its armoured skin with fire-fringed, meteor-sized apertures. Aboard grav-sleds, the worker crews made detailed reports of structural damage. Sparks cascaded from the ranks of heavy-duty welding rigs, fusing plates from ancillary sections of the ship over the most heinous of its wounds. A few areas were so bad that the wreckage had to be sheared away with cutting tools and patched over like an amputated limb.

It was demanding work, but Tsu'gan was concerned with other matters as he watched the combat with the chitin-creatures from afar. Blood pulsed in his veins as he lived the battle vicariously. His fists clenched of their own volition. Inwardly, he cursed his fellow sergeants Agatone, Vargo and Dak'ir. Had he not been ordered to remain with the bulk of the company to discuss tactics and set up a command post, he would have rushed joyously into combat. The chitin-beasts presented no challenge, of course, but after months without battle Tsu'gan was eager to shed blood in the Emperor's name.

'The *Vulkan's Wrath* has sustained major damage, my lord.' The metallic voice of Argos brought Tsu'gan back.

He was standing with the Techmarine, Brother-Captain N'keln and several of his fellow sergeants in a makeshift command post, attempting to impose some order and stability after the crash.

The command post itself was a prefabricated structure, little more than four walls, a canted roof and a hololith-projector slab displaying in grainy blue resolution what the sensorium and deep-augur probes had ascertained about the lay of the land. What they knew so far was precious little – Scoria was primarily flat, comprised of ash dunes and some basalt mountain ranges with an indigenous hostile life form akin to a giant Terran crab.

Beyond the command bunker, other prefab structures were being erected. In the main, these were medical tents to which the injured were ferried on stretchers and joined the system of triage set up by Brother Fugis. The Apothecary ministered to both human and Astartes, though the latter were few in number, and was ably assisted by Emek, loaned from Dak'ir's squad as a field surgeon. Human medics, those that had survived the crash, worked diligently alongside the Salamanders, but all had their work cut out for them. Fugis had also tasked rescue teams, comprising Salamanders and able-bodied serfs and servitors, to search the damaged areas of the ship for survivors. Though slow at first, as the ruined decks were gradually re-opened, more and more of the wounded flocked to the medical tents. The dead were also abundant. The pyreum was in constant use, shovel-handed servitors heaping piles of ash into huge storage vats for later interment.

'Can we achieve loft, Master Argos?' asked N'keln, his brow furrowed as the hololith switched to a rolling schematic of the *Vulkan's Wrath*. Red areas made up around sixty per cent of the total image and indicated damaged sections.

'To be brief: no,' the Techmarine replied, using a stylus to zone in on the lower portion of the strike cruiser. The image shifted again, this time incorporating Scoria's geography and the ship's relative position in it. A side view cutaway showed a large area of the *Vulkan's Wrath* below the earth-line, sunk deep into the planet's outer crust. 'As you can see, the ship is partially submerged within the ash plain. Basic geological analysis reveals that Scoria's surface is a mixture of ash and sand. The intense heat of our re-entry reacted with it, resulting in an endothermic metamorphosis. Essentially the ash-sand crystallised and hardened,' he added by way of explanation.

'Surely our engines are strong enough to pull us free,' offered the gravel-voiced Lok.

'Ordinarily, yes,' Argos returned. In addition to the repair crews, the Techmarine had already tasked excavation-servitors and human labour teams with digging out the sections of the ship that were buried deepest. 'But we are down to three banks of ventral engines. An operational minimum of four are needed to achieve loft.'

'What of our thrusters? Can we shake ourselves loose?' asked Brother-Sergeant Clovius, his squat form diminutive compared to the towering Praetor, who observed proceedings in silence.

'Not unless we want to burrow to the planet's core,' replied Argos without sarcasm. 'Our prow is angled downwards. Any thruster burst will simply push us further in that direction. The Adeptus Mechanicus did not build vessels such as this to take off from a grounded position.'

N'keln scowled, displeased at the developments.

'Do what you can, brother,' he said to Argos, switching off the hololith.

'I will, my lord. But without the components I need to repair and rig a fourth ventral engine, we will not be leaving this planet in the *Vulkan's Wrath*.'

'We should reconnoitre,' offered Tsu'gan in a low voice. 'Try to ascertain the technological level of the planet and if it has indigenous human life. It's possible we'll be able to commandeer the materials we need to repair the ship,' he said, to Praetor's nodded approval. Tsu'gan went on, 'The prophecy brought us here for a reason. Securing our method of escape should be our secondary mission. Finding Vulkan or whatever the primarch may have left for us here is of paramount concern right now.'

'I'll warrant our near-destruction to a solar storm wasn't part of Vulkan's vision,' growled Lok. The veteran sergeant had sustained a gash to the forehead during the crash, adding to his numerous scars.

'*And lo, they will be struck down by fire and their eyes opened to the truth.*' The voice of Chaplain Elysius sermonised as he entered the command bunker. Dak'ir and

Agatone were in tow. 'So speaks the Tome of Fire, Brother Lok.'

'This was predestined, Brother-Chaplain?' asked N'keln.

Elysius nodded solemnly.

'A pity then, we could not have been warned,' grumbled Lok.

The Chaplain turned his bone-visage back on to the veteran sergeant.

'Destiny, if forewarned, ceases to be destiny at all,' he chided. 'We were *meant* to crash upon this world. It is merely an element of a much grander design, to which we are not privy. Such things should not be interfered with, lest the balance of destiny itself be thrown out of kilter.'

'And what of the lives of those lost?' Lok countered. 'How are we to *balance* that?'

'Sacrificed in the fires of battle,' Elysius returned. A cold light burned behind the lenses of his battle-helm. The Chaplain did not like to be challenged, especially on matters of spiritual divination.

'It was no battle,' Lok growled, but under his breath. Scowling, he let it go, nodding his assent in spite of his outward disapproval.

'So be it,' said N'keln. 'We will follow whatever path has been laid out for us. Brother Tsu'gan is right. Fate has delivered us, and so we must seek out whatever is hidden on this world. To that end, scouting teams will assemble and conduct a long-range survey of the surrounding area. Population centres, military or industrial installations are our objective.'

Tsu'gan stepped forward. 'My lord, I wish to lead the scouting force.'

'Very well,' N'keln conceded. 'Gather whatever troops you need. The rest will stay here, protect the injured and consolidate our position. Argos,' he met the cold gaze of the Techmarine, 'establish a perimeter around our camp. I want no further surprises from the chitin-creatures. Deep frag mines and photon flares,' he added, glancing outside, where the yellow sun of Scoria was dipping below a grey horizon. 'It'll be dark soon and I want fair warning of any encroachment.'

The Techmarine bowed and went to his duties. The rest of the sergeants were dismissed soon after, saluting as they left the command bunker. Only Praetor and Lok remained, poring over the reactivated hololith and the cold resolution representing the barren plains of Scoria. No matter how hard the captain of the Salamanders stared, he could not discern the mystery beneath them that had brought them here.

'REMINDS ME OF home,' offered Iagon, his gaze on the long dark horizon line. Something was building in the east. A faint glow, not caused by the dipping sun, painted the sky in hazy red. The chains of volcanoes on Nocturne exuded a similar patina across the heavens when they were about to erupt. Tiny tremors registered below the earth, too. They were deep, so deep as to emanate from the core of the planet and represented a fundamental shift in its tectonic integrity. Even as the seconds ticked by, Scoria was changing. Iagon felt it as surely as the bolter hung loosely in his grasp.

The Salamander had regrouped with his brother-sergeant after leaving Fugis following the crash, confident that the Apothecary would not speak of either his or Tsu'gan's indiscretion. He didn't mention this to his sergeant, who assumed that Fugis had taken him at his word and would say nothing more of it.

The scouts had left the camp behind an hour ago. Argos's bomb-laying servitors established a perimeter of sunken fragmentation grenades in their wake that was patrolled in turn by a pair of Thunderfire cannons the

Techmarine had liberated from the hold of the *Vulkan's Wrath*. The tracked war machines, not unlike the mobile weapon platform that the Marines Malevolent had employed on the *Archimedes Rex*, were ideally suited to dissuading further assaults from the indigenous chitin-creatures.

Combat awareness filled Tsu'gan's mind now, as he crouched on one knee and allowed the dark Scorian ash to filter through the gaps in his half-clenched fist. He cast about, but all he saw were grey dunes stretching in every direction.

'It is more like Moribar,' he countered, scowling as he stood up and reached out a hand to Brother Tiberon, saying: 'Scopes.'

Tiberon handed a pair of magnoculars to his sergeant, who took them without looking.

Tsu'gan brought the magnoculars up to his eyes and swept them around in a wide arc.

'De'mas, Typhos – report,' he ordered through the comm-feed. It was no great surprise that Tsu'gan had selected two sergeants who had previously sworn fealty to him in the event of a leadership challenge to N'keln.

Both came back curtly with negative contacts. Tsu'gan lowered the magnoculars and exhaled his frustration.

Night was drawing in, just as N'keln had predicted. Chill winds were skirling across the ashen desert in low, scudding waves, kicking up swirls of ash that rattled noiselessly against the Salamanders' greaves. Besides the evening zephyr, the plain was deathly quiet and still.

'Yes,' Tsu'gan muttered grimly, 'just like Moribar.'

'There,' Tsu'gan hissed. 'You see it?'

Iagon peered through the magnoculars. 'Yes...'

A fine smirr of grainy dark smudged the horizon, barely visible over a high dune. The two Salamanders were lying flat on an ash ridge. Brothers S'tang and

Tiberon were either side of them, while the rest of the squad acted as sentry below.

'What is it?' asked Iagon, handing the magnoculars back to Tiberon.

'Smoke.' Tsu'gan's tone suggested a predatory grin behind his battle-helm.

It was the first sign of life they'd seen for several hours. On route to the ridge, they'd passed structures that might once have been the edges of cities. Whether ruined by war or merely dilapidation, it was impossible to tell under the ash fall that furred the buildings in grey.

In his marrow, Tsu'gan felt the sign spotted above the dune was significant. Through the rebreather mounted in his helmet, he detected trace amounts of carbon, hydrogen and the acrid stench of sulphur dioxide, carried towards them on the breeze – in other words, oil. It meant several things: that the chitin-beasts were not the only creatures on Scoria, and that these cohabitants had the technological ability to both mine and refine oil; not only that, but use it in a manufacturing process.

Tsu'gan opened up the comm-feed with De'mas and Typhos.

'Converge on my position,' he ordered, then switched the link to his own squad. 'Battle-speed to the edge of that dune, dispersed approach.'

Pushing himself to his feet, Tsu'gan jogged down the ridge and then headed towards the next dune, his battle-brothers behind him in an expansive formation. He drove on hard, eating up the metres despite having to slog through the shifting ash underfoot. Widening his stride when he got to the base of the next incline, Tsu'gan powered up the dune until he had almost crested the rise, then slowed. Battle-signing, the sergeant instructed his brothers to match him. Together, they reached the edge of the second ash ridge and peered over it into a deep basin below.

Tsu'gan's breath caught in his throat when he realised what sat in the basin. He felt his anger rise.

'Abomination...' he growled, taking a firm grip on his bolter.

II
Ash and Iron

THE PLAINTIVE CRIES of the wounded bled into one doleful dirge as Dak'ir toured the medical tents, looking for Fugis.

So great was the toll of dead and injured that the tents were arranged in ranks, patrolled by a combat squad of Salamanders to ensure the safety of the wounded. The stench of blood was strong beneath the sodium-lit canvases, pallet-beds stacked side to side and end to end. Medics swathed in ruddied smocks, mouths shrouded by masks, busied themselves between the slim conduits that linked the beds in a lattice. Through a plastek sheet, steam-bolted to one of the larger tents' struts, was a makeshift operating room, a rudimentary Apothecarion. It made sense that it was here Dak'ir found Fugis.

The half-naked body of Brother Vah'lek lay on a slab before the Apothecary. Blood, still dark and wet, shimmered on Vah'lek's black flesh. It was exposed where the front of his plastron had been torn away and the body-glove beneath sheared with a sharp blade. From there his tough skin had been cut open, his ribplate cracked and levered wide to allow access to his internal organs. All effort had been made to save him; but all, sadly, in vain.

Fugis sagged over the cooling corpse of Brother Vah'lek, his head bowed. His gauntleted hands were covered with Astartes blood, and his armour was spattered in it. Medical tools lay about the Apothecary on metal trays. A small canister like a capsule that could be inserted into a centrifuge sat alone from the rest. Fugis's reductor lay next to it. Dak'ir knew that his dead battle-brother's progenoids nestled safely within the canister. At least his legacy was assured.

'He was one of Agatone's,' said the Apothecary wearily, dismissing the serfs who had been assisting in the surgery.

'How many of our brothers have we lost, Fugis?' Dak'ir asked.

The Apothecary straightened, finding resolve from somewhere, and started to unclasp his blood-caked gauntlets.

'Six, so far,' he replied, left gauntlet hitting one of metal trays with a resounding *clang* as he let it drop. 'Only one sergeant: Naveem. All killed in the crash.' Fugis looked up at the other Salamander. 'It is no way for an Astartes to die, Dak'ir.'

'They all served the Emperor with honour,' Dak'ir countered, but his words sounded hollow even to himself.

Fugis gestured to something behind him, and Dak'ir made way as two bulky mortis-servitors lumbered into the room.

'Another for the caskets,' intoned the Apothecary. 'Take our brother reverently, and await me at the pyreum.'

The hulking servitors, bent-backed and all black metal and cowled faces, nodded solemnly before hauling the slab, and Brother Vah'lek, away.

'Now what is it, brother?' Fugis asked impatiently, attempting to clean his gauntlets in a burning brazier. 'There are others who require my ministrations – the human dead and injured number in the hundreds.'

Dak'ir stepped farther into the tent and lowered his voice.

'Before the crash, when I met you in the corridor, you said you were looking for Brother Tsu'gan. Did you find him?'

'No, I didn't,' Fugis answered absently.

'Why were you looking for him?'

The Apothecary looked up again, his expression stern.

'What concern is it of yours, sergeant?'

Dak'ir showed his palms plaintively.

'You appeared to be troubled, that is all.'

Fugis seemed about to say something when he looked down at his gauntlets again. 'A mistake, nothing more.'

Dak'ir came forward again.

'You don't make mistakes,' he pressed.

Fugis replied in a small voice, little more than a whisper. 'No one is infallible, Dak'ir.' The Apothecary pulled his gauntlets back on and the coldness returned. 'Is that all?'

'No,' said Dak'ir flatly, impeding Fugis as he tried to leave. 'I'm worried about you, brother.'

'Are you at the beck and call of Elysius then? Has our beneficent Chaplain sent you to gauge my state of mind? Strange, isn't it, how our roles have reversed.'

'I come alone, of my own volition, brother,' said Dak'ir. 'You are not yourself.'

'For the last five hours, I have been elbow-deep in the blood of the wounded and dying. Our brothers search in vain amongst the ruins of our ship for survivors. We are Space Marines, Dak'ir! Meant for battle, not this.' Fugis made an expansive gesture that compassed the gory surroundings. 'And where is N'keln?' he continued, gripped by a sudden fervour. 'Poring over hololiths in his command bunker, with Lok and Praetor, that is where he is.' Fugis paused, before his anger overtook his good sense again. 'A captain must be seen! It is his duty to his company to inspire. N'keln cannot do that locked away behind plans and strategium displays.'

Dak'ir's face became stern, and he adopted a warning tone to his voice.

'Consider your words, Fugis. Remember, you are one of the Inferno Guard.'

'There is no Inferno Guard,' he countered belligerently, though his ire had ebbed. 'Shen'kar is little more than an adjutant, Vek'shen is long dead and N'keln has yet to appoint a successor to his own vacated post. That leaves only Malicant, and our banner bearer has had precious little reason to unfurl our company colours of late. You yourself refused the mantle of Company Champion.'

'I had my reasons, brother.'

Fugis scowled, as if the fact meant little to him.

'This mission was supposed to heal the rift in our company, a righteous cause for us to rally around and draw strength from. I see only the dead and more laurels for the memoria wall.'

'What has happened to you?' Dak'ir let his anger be known. 'Where is your faith, Fugis?' he snapped.

The Apothecary's face grew dark as all the life that was left there seemed to leave it.

'I was forced to kill Naveem today.'

'It's not the first time you've administered the Emperor's Peace,' countered Dak'ir, uncertain where this was going.

'When I went to extract his progenoid gland, I made a mistake and it was lost. Naveem was lost – forever.'

A brief, mournful silence descended before Fugis went on.

'And as for my faith… It died, Dak'ir. It was slain along with Kadai.'

Dak'ir was about to speak when he found he had nothing further to say. Wounds ran deep; some deeper than others. Tsu'gan had chosen rage, whereas Fugis had actually given in to despair. No words could counsel him now. Only war and the fires of battle would

cleanse the Apothecary's spirit. As he stepped aside to
let his brother pass, Dak'ir hoped they would come
soon. But as Fugis left without word, the brother-
sergeant feared that the Apothecary might be consumed
by them.

Leaving the medical tent shortly after, Dak'ir caught
up to Ba'ken who he had asked to meet him outside.

'You look weary, brother,' observed the giant Salamander as his sergeant approached.

Ba'ken was standing alone, bereft of his heavy flamer
rig. He had left it in one of the prefabricated armoriums, guarded by Brother-Sergeant Omkar and his
squad. Duty rotation meant that the Salamanders
moved between the search and rescue teams, digging
crews and sentry. Ba'ken was preparing to join the crews
trying to excavate the *Vulkan's Wrath*. He was looking
forward to the labour, as the plains were quiet and sentry duty was beginning to numb his mind. He had
purposely met Sergeant Agatone on the way.

'Not as weary as some,' Dak'ir replied, the truth of the
remark hidden.

Ba'ken decided not to press.

'The sergeants are restless,' he said, instead. 'Those not
involved in sentry duty are digging out the *Vulkan's
Wrath* or tearing apart its corridors only to find the
dead. We are at company strength, but kicking our heels
with no enemy to fight.' He shook his head ruefully, 'It
is not work for Space Marines.'

Dak'ir smiled emptily.

'Fugis said much the same thing.'

'I see.' Ba'ken was wise enough to realise that it was
the Apothecary that his sergeant had been referring to
with his earlier remark. He remembered watching him
on the gunship platform outside the Vault of Remembrance at Hesiod. In the entire time he'd waited for
Dak'ir, Fugis had neither moved nor spoken a word.

With characteristic pragmatism, Ba'ken put the thought aside and focused on the matter at hand.

'Agatone is one of the most loyal Astartes I have ever known,' he said, changing tack. 'Besides Lok, he is the longest serving sergeant left in the company. But he lost one of his squad tonight.'

'Brother Vah'lek, I saw him,' said Dak'ir. 'Fugis just sent the body for interment.'

'*So unto the fire do we return…*' intoned Ba'ken. 'If this mission comes to nothing, Vah'lek's death will be meaningless,' he added, and lightly shook his head. 'Agatone won't stand for that.'

Dak'ir's voice was far away as he looked out in the endless grey plains.

'Then we had best hope for better news soon.'

It was then that N'keln appeared, striding meaningfully with Lok and Praetor in tow. The brother-captain and his entourage strode right past them.

'Lok, what is happening?' Dak'ir called out.

The Devastator sergeant turned briefly.

'We are preparing for battle,' he said. 'Brother-Sergeant Tsu'gan has found the enemy.'

A LONG WALL of grey, rusted iron stretched along the nadir of the ash basin. It was festooned with spikes, and grisly totems hung on black chains from battlements crested with spirals of razor wire. Sentry towers punctuated the high, sheer wall that was shored up by angular buttresses. The abutments were fashioned of steel, but torn and jagged-edged to dissuade climbing. Static gun emplacements, tarantula-mounted heavy bolters trailing feeds of ammunition like brass tongues, sat menacingly behind the tower walls. Fat plumes of dense, black smoke coiled from chimney stacks behind these outer defences, hinting at a core of industrial structures within the fortress itself.

Sigils bedecked the walls, too – graven images that made Tsu'gan's eyes hurt just to look at them. They were icons of the Ruinous Powers, hammered like a penitent spike in the forehead of an unbeliever. Streaked rust eked from where the icon had been pressure-bolted and it made the Salamander think of sacrificial blood. For all Tsu'gan knew, it was.

At the gate – a slab of reinforced iron and adamantium, crossed by interlocking chains, that looked solid enough to withstand a direct hit from a defence laser – was stamped the most prominent of the idolatrous symbols. It boasted the fealty of their Legion and left the identity of the warriors inside the fortress in no doubt.

It was a single armoured skull with the eight-pointed star of Chaos behind it.

'Iron Warriors, sons of Perturabo,' hissed Brother-Sergeant De'mas, with obvious rancour.

'Traitors,' seethed Typhos, clutching his thunder hammer.

Upon sighting the fortress and contacting his fellow sergeants on the scouting mission, Tsu'gan had then immediately raised N'keln on the comm-feed. Distance and ash-storm interference gave rise to rampant static, but the message was relayed clearly enough.

Enemy sighted. Traitors of the Iron Warriors Legion. Awaiting reinforcements before engaging.

Tsu'gan had wanted to charge down into the basin there and then, to unleash his bolter in a righteous fury. Sound judgement had tempered his zeal. The Iron Warriors were no xenos-breed, ill-equipped to face the might of the Emperor's holy angels. No: they were once angels themselves, albeit now fallen from a millennia-old betrayal. Peerless siege-masters and fortress-builders, except perhaps for the loyal sons of Rogal Dorn, the Imperial Fists, the Iron Warriors were also fierce fighters who possessed devastating ability at long-range or protracted warfare. An all-out assault into their jaws, without numbers or heavy artillery, would have ended bloodily for the Salamanders. Instead, Tsu'gan chose that most Nocturnean of traits: he chose to wait.

'The Iron Warriors were at Isstvan, where Vulkan fell,' added Typhos, with a sudden fervour. 'It cannot be coincidence. This must be part of the prophecy.'

The three sergeants were atop the ridge, looking down on to the traitors' territory below. Their squads were nearby, hunkered in groups, surveying the surrounding area for enemy scouts or merely guarding the flanks of their leaders.

De'mas was about to answer, when Tsu'gan cut him off.

'Settle down, brothers,' he growled, gauging the fortress defences through a pair of magnoculars. 'We can assume nothing at this stage.' Tsu'gan observed the Iron Warrior's bastion carefully, but didn't linger too long on any one structure so as to mitigate his discomfort. The gate was the only way in. Perimeter guards patrolled the walled battlements, though the muster was curiously thin. Sentries stood stock-still in the towers, almost like statues, presiding over autocannon emplacements. In one of the towers, a searchlight strafed the ash dunes in lazy sweeps. Moving his gaze farther back, Tsu'gan counted the roofed redoubts that filled the no-man's land in front of the wall. Again, they seemed quiet and he could detect no movement from within. The fortress itself was angular, but its ambit was bizarrely shaped. Tsu'gan tried but couldn't seem to pin down how many sides it possessed, the number of defensible walls. He cursed, recognising the warping effects of Chaos. Averting his gaze, he handed the magnoculars back to Tiberon and muttered a quick litany of cleansing.

'Nothing is certain,' he asserted to the other two sergeants, when he was done warding himself. 'Vulkan's fall, or otherwise, at Isstvan is immaterial.'

'It is significant,' argued Typhos, a truculent tone entering his voice.

'You expect the primarch to come striding out of the dunes, thunder hammer in hand? It is a ten thousand year old myth, brother, and I will hear no more of it,' Tsu'gan warned.

'Tu'Shan believes in it,' pressed the other sergeant. 'Why else send an entire company on such a spurious mission, if it were not in fact a *holy quest*!'

'The Chapter Master does what he must,' Tsu'gan replied, his temper fraying. 'He cannot ignore the possibility of the primarch's return, or even the chance to unearth the facts of his demise. *We*, brother, are not so shackled that we must believe what our eyes cannot see. *This*,' he said, brandishing his bolter, 'and *this*,' he slapped the pauldron of his armour, 'even *this*,' Tsu'gan took up a fistful of ash, 'are real. *That* is what I know. Allow blind zeal to guide your path and it will end up leading you to your doom, Typhos,' he added in a derisive tone.

'Afford me some respect,' the other sergeant hissed through gritted teeth. 'We are of equal rank.'

'Out here on these dunes,' Tsu'gan told him, 'I outstrip your "equal rank".'

A brief, charged silence descended, but in the end Typhos was brow-beaten into submission.

Perhaps, Tsu'gan considered, it was not wise to aggravate another sergeant when he desired to impeach the captain of the company, especially one that had previously sworn his support. But I need to demonstrate strength, thought Tsu'gan, and knew by asserting his will he had only cemented Typhos's allegiance.

'For siege-specialists, it is a poor location to build a bastion,' remarked De'mas, ignoring the slight altercation. 'Within the basin, the view it commands is restricted.'

During the Heresy, Tsu'gan knew the Iron Warriors had fortresses across all the segmentums of the galaxy. Often these bastions were isolated, single-squad outposts. Despite the paucity of troops, he also knew these bastions were almost impregnable. This supreme defensibility was a result of Iron Warrior tenacity, but it also depended on where the Legion chose to raise its walls. De'mas was right – the fortress before them had no vantage, no high ground to observe the approach of an enemy. It was counter-intuitive towards siege strategy. But then perhaps holding ground was not the traitors' main concern.

'They built it here to hide it,' Tsu'gan realised, a thin smile splitting his face at his deduction. 'Anywhere else would be too conspicuous.'

'To what end?' asked Typhos. 'What could the traitors have to hide here, on this backwater?'

Tsu'gan's expression hardened, as he looped his bolter around his pauldron on its strap.

'I intend to find out,' he said, and made his way back down to the base of the ridge.

Tsu'gan's battle-brothers surrounded him as he outlined his plan. With a combat knife, he drew a rough sketch of the fortress in the hardened ash.

'That looks like an assault strategy,' muttered De'mas, standing at Tsu'gan's shoulder.

'It is,' said Tsu'gan curtly.

'I assume I don't need to remind you, brother, that the Iron Warriors are siege-experts in both attack and *defence*?'

'You do not.'

Typhos scoffed. 'Then you'll also know that such an assault with thirty men and negligible heavy guns is–'

'Suicide,' Tsu'gan concluded for him, as he looked Typhos in the eye. 'Yes, I am aware of that too, which is why we are attacking the redoubts and not the walls, brother-sergeant.'

'Explain.' Brother-Sergeant De'mas's interest was apparently piqued.

'Four combat squads,' Tsu'gan began, sketching arrows of approach in the dust, 'one per redoubt. Blades and hammers only, flamers standing by as backup. Tactic is silent and stealthy. We enter the redoubts undetected, kill any sentries we find and then occupy their positions. There we will wait until Brother N'keln arrives and then launch a surprise attack, storming the gate and rigging diversionary charges.'

'You mentioned four combat squads?' voiced Typhos.

Tsu'gan nodded, fixing the sergeant with a stony glare.

'I did. You will stay behind in command of our rear-guard. You are tasked with apprising the brother-captain of the situation upon his arrival.' Tsu'gan moved his gaze to encompass the entire force, 'All long-range heavy weapons will report to Brother-Sergeant Typhos. You will be our support in the unlikely event of our discovery. De'mas,' he added, switching his attention to the other sergeant. 'Gather the ten best stealthers from yours and Typhos's squads then join me and the rest of my men at the eastern side of the ridge-base.'

Tsu'gan marched away, leaving Typhos no time to protest and only Brother M'lek with his multi-melta in the brother-sergeant's charge. The rest of his squad followed him.

De'mas made his acquisitions quickly and quietly. The rearguard, then, would be an amalgam of the three squads. It was unconventional, but it also demonstrated the strategic flexibility of Tactical squads and the reason why the Astartes were warriors supreme.

The Salamander assault force divided into four five-man squads wordlessly. Battle-sign between each of the squad-leaders ensured total clarity and efficiency as the

Astartes made their way around the lip of the vast dune and approached the enemy bastion from an oblique angle. Rubbing ash onto their battle-plate, even smothering their blades so a glint of light would not betray them, the Salamanders moved like invisible phantoms across the dark plain. Even the burning fire in their eyes was extinguished, hidden by battle-helm lenses set to maximum opacity like one-way glass in an interrogation chamber.

Traversing the open dunes in a crouching run, his widely-dispersed squad slowly converging, Tsu'gan reached the edge of the first redoubt. Even in the dark, his keen eyes picked out the silhouettes of sentries lurking within. The sergeant took care to remain out of their direct eye line, his movements low and fluid so as not to arouse suspicion. The Iron Warriors had, up to that point, not moved, so he assumed his advance had gone undetected.

Creeping around the edge of the redoubt, using its bulk to hide his position from the lofty walls of the fortress several hundred metres back, he listened intently.

Only the wind and the faint *clank* of booted feet on the battlements above came back at him.

Tsu'gan edged further, sliding the tarnished blade of his close combat weapon from its sheath in preparation for the kill. The redoubt wasn't gated at the back and could be accessed freely through an open doorway in its rear wall.

That was good. It would make creeping behind the sentry that much easier. He considered briefly how it might affront the martial pride of some Chapters to sneak up on an enemy in this way. The Salamanders, though, had always been pragmatic in the ways of war. They believed its fires could cleanse the soul and purify the spirit, but they also adhered to the end justifying the means, and victory at all costs.

Out of the corner of his eye, Tsu'gan saw more dark phantoms sweeping silently through the night as the other combat squads moved into position. His own cadre of warriors arrived at his back. Brother Lazarus was foremost amongst them and nodded to indicate his readiness. S'tang was right behind him. His battle-helm, like his brothers', was swathed in camouflaging ash. Honorious and Tiberon guarded the entrance, ensuring no enemy escaped. Silently, the other three Salamanders entered the redoubt.

Two sentries waited within, Iron Warriors both, with their backs to them. S'tang would hold back, only intervening if needed. The traitors were standing stock-still, surveying the dark dunes beyond the redoubt.

Death is upon you, brothers, Tsu'gan thought bitterly, noticing a battered but razor-edged storm shield leaning against the wall inside. His sheathed his blade silently, deciding not to sully the weapon with traitor's blood, and took up the shield.

Lazarus was poised to strike, his jagged spatha held in a reverse grip so he could strike downwards, aiming for the slim gap between gorget and cuirass.

Tsu'gan was ready too, and battle-signed the order to attack.

He leapt forwards, resisting the urge to roar a battle cry, and battered the Iron Warrior to the ground with a fierce, two-handed smash from the shield. The momentum of the strike carried Tsu'gan forwards. He dived on the prone traitor, pinning his arms with his knees and ramming the razor-edge of the shield into the Iron Warrior's neck, cutting off his head.

He turned to Lazarus. The Salamander was withdrawing his blade and wiping off the blood, which seemed oddly sparse. Tsu'gan put it down to the low light impeding his vision, but when he looked at his dead sentry he knew that something wasn't right.

There was almost no blood.

He had severed the bastard's neck; there should be blood – lots of it. Yet, there was almost none. Tsu'gan tossed the shield aside and lifted up the sentry's decapitated head, inspecting the wound. It was dark and viscous, but didn't flow. The blood was clotted. The Iron Warriors had been dead before they'd even entered the redoubt.

'The guards were already dead,' he hissed into the comm-feed, patching in all combat squads and breaking vox silence.

A slew of similar reports came from the other four assault groups. Each had entered their respective redoubt undetected and killed the sentries inside, only to discover the enemy was deceased.

Tsu'gan rasped a reply.

'Go to bolters.' The brother-sergeant scanned the dark through the redoubt's firing slit and then the open doorway. Inwardly, he cursed. The Iron Warriors had drawn them in like neophytes, exposed their position. Racking his bolter's slide, preparing to unleash death if he was to meet his end, he crouched down so he presented a smaller target. Then he waited.

Several minutes passed in the silent blackness. No assassins came creeping from the dark; no kill-teams closed the elaborate trap they had set.

The expected counter-attack did not materialise, was not going to materialise. For some unknown reason, the Iron Warriors had manned their redoubts with the dead.

'They weren't trying to lure us,' Tsu'gan realised, keeping his voice low. 'They were deterrents.'

'Sergeant?' Brother Lazarus hissed.

Tsu'gan waved away the question. He had no answer to it. Yet.

'We hold here,' he said. 'We wait.'

CHAPTER SEVEN

I
Besieged

BILLOWING ASH CLOUDS were dissipating slowly on the grey horizon. It was the last evidence of N'keln's muster from the Salamanders' encampment. Brother Argos had managed to release the land vehicles from the hold of the *Vulkan's Wrath*. N'keln had taken the Land Raider, *Fire Anvil*, with the Firedrakes, his Inferno Guard and Chaplain Elysius aboard. Even Fugis made the journey. The Apothecary had considered staying behind to tend the wounded, but his place was by N'keln's side and his brothers would likely need him in the coming battle against the Iron Warriors, so he had ventured back to the front line for the first time since Stratos.

The rest of the Salamanders' vehicles comprised four Rhino APCs that conveyed all three squads of Devastators and Brother-Sergeant Clovius's Tactical squad. The captain had selected his task force according to firepower. He intended to breach the fortress walls at distance, rather than storm them. Devastators were well

suited to that task, and since Clovius boasted both missile launcher and plasma gun in his ranks, he was an
ideal fourth squad choice and occupied the remaining
Rhino.

Vargo and his Assault squad were the final element to
the task force. His troops would make their way on foot,
using bursts from their jump packs to keep pace. Once
the walls were breached, Brother-Sergeant Vargo and his
troops could quickly exploit the gap.

Dak'ir was left back to maintain vigil over the encampment. Though he would rather have joined the task
force, he knew his duty and respected the will of his
captain. The other squads continued with their rota-
tional duties of excavating the *Vulkan's Wrath*, guarding
the medical tents and searching for survivors. Naveem's
old squad spent most of its time within the battered
confines of the ship, opening up sealed areas and
exhuming the dead from their metal, airlocked tombs.
Brother Gannon had taken temporary charge, though he
was untested as a sergeant. Agatone was content to
remain behind. There were the observances of ritual cremation to be conducted for Vah'lek, and he was keen to
be present for them.

These thoughts tumbled through Dak'ir's mind like
flakes of ash drifting from the far off peaks of Scoria's
volcanoes. As he stared into the grey void, the vista
before him seemed to blend and shift…

*…once distant mountains loomed suddenly large and
immediate, arching over Dak'ir's head like crooked fingers
until they touched and formed a canopy of rock. Ash, so ubiquitous before, drained away as if escaping through the cracks
of the world to flee certain doom, and left solid rock beneath
Dak'ir's feet. He was in a cave. It reminded him of Ignea. A
tunnel led down, down into the heart of Scoria where
promised fire lurked, flickering against the walls like dancing,
red spectres. They took him deep, these imagined apparitions,*

to the nadir of the earth where lava ran thick in streams and shimmered with lustrous heat. Pools of liquid fire threw murky, joyless light that seemed to cling and conspire instead of illuminate. And there, dwelling within a vast cavern and surrounded by pits of flame like balefires, the dragon uncoiled. Scales shimmered like spilled blood in the lava-light, its sulphurous breath overwhelming the reek of the mountain.

Dak'ir was standing across from it. A tall pike was gripped in his gauntlet, and the lake of fire separated them. Hunter and beast eyed each other across the flaming gulf that ignited in empathy for their mutual anger.

'You are my captain's slayer.' The voice sounded distant and strange to him, but Dak'ir knew it as his own. It was a much a promise as an accusation.

Rage lent strength to his body that he didn't know he possessed, as Dak'ir leapt across the massive lake of fire to land crouched on the other side.

Challenge given and accepted, the dragon came at him, a bestial roar ripping from a fanged mouth wreathed in black fire.

Dak'ir cried out for Vulkan, and the primarch's vigour steeled him. As the beast came on, its footfalls shedding rock and cracking stone, Dak'ir took the pike and drove it like a lance into the dragon's belly. It screeched and the cave shook. It was a cry so full of wrath and agony that it levelled mountains and opened up the roof to a grey sky that was steadily turning red.

Clawing, rending deep grooves into the stone, the dragon struggled. Dak'ir pushed. He drove it to the lake of fire, heaved it flailing over the edge and let it burn as the heat rose up to consume it.

The dragon died, and in the haze and smoke of its conflagration it changed to become a man. His armour was red like scale, his mouth was fanged like a maw and he wore the defiled livery of a former angel who had turned his back on duty and loyalty, to embrace corruption. The body broke away, naught but bones and ash, a frugal meal for the lake of fire. Then the world broke away with it. A great tremor wracked the earth and Scoria split. Columns of fire erupted like bursts of incendiary exploding from under the ash, and the mountain was swallowed beneath the earth. Dak'ir witnessed a world die, consumed by itself. Then the fire came to him, and he was burning too…

'I sense doubt in you.'

Arrested suddenly from the dream, Dak'ir flinched. He kept the reaction small, though, and barely noticeable. Until that moment, he had thought he was alone.

'It's not doubt, Brother-Librarian,' he replied coolly, shrugging off the remnants of his vision as Pyriel came to stand beside him.

They were a hundred metres or so from the edge of the encampment, looking out across the dunes past the relentlessly pacing Thunderfire cannons and the hidden grenade belt beyond them. 'More a lack of resolution. Something I can sense, but beyond my reach.'

It wasn't a lie. The instinct had been there throughout the dream, just subdued by his subconscious mind.

'That there is something here, beneath the ash, that we are just not seeing,' stated the Librarian.

'Yes,' said Dak'ir, looking for him to extrapolate, uncertain why he himself was so surprised at Pyriel's prescience. The Librarian kept his gaze on the horizon, inscrutable as rock.

In the absence of further explanation, Dak'ir decided to go on.

'Ever since we made landfall, after the crash, I felt as if I was… being *watched*.'

Now Pyriel turned to regard him. 'Go on,' he said.

'Not the ash creatures that attacked us,' Dak'ir explained. 'Not even an enemy as such, just something… *else*.'

'I have felt it, too,' admitted the Librarian, 'A glimpse of a consciousness unknown to me. It is not the mind of a xenos that I feel. Nor is it the taint of Chaos exhibited by the traitors Brother Tsu'gan has found. It is, as you say, "else".'

The Librarian stared at Dak'ir a little longer, before turning back. 'Look out there,' he said, gesturing to the grey horizon. Dak'ir did as he was told. 'What do you see?'

Dak'ir opened his mouth to speak, when Pyriel raised a hand to stop him.

'Think carefully,' he advised. 'Not what there *is*, but what you *see*.'

Dak'ir readjusted and looked hard. All he saw was ash and spires of distant rock crested by dark clouds, and a grey horizon smudged with umber and red where the volcanoes vented.

'I see…' he began, but stopped himself to truly open his eyes. 'I see Nocturne.'

Pyriel nodded. It was a small movement, near undetectable, but expressed his satisfaction elegantly.

'*That* is what I see also. Beneath the layers of ash there is rock. The volcanoes have been venting for so long and so continuously that the grey flakes have made this place a grey world, with darkling skies, bereft of life. The oceans, for I believe the deep basins in the ash deserts were once large water masses, dried up long ago. Underground tributaries might still exist, but I doubt they're enough to support significant life. Scoria, I suspect, was once much like Nocturne, only more advanced in its geological cycle.' Pyriel stooped and placed a hand against the ground. He beckoned Dak'ir to do the same.

'You feel that?' the Librarian asked, closing his eyes, shutting out smell and sound, focusing purely on touch.

Dak'ir nodded, though he had no way of knowing if the Librarian had seen or realised his affirmation. There was a tremor running through the earth, faint but insistent like a pulsing vein.

'Those are the last heartbeats of a dying world, brother.'

Dak'ir's eyes snapped open and he stood. The recent vision came back at him, and he wondered briefly if somehow Pyriel had seen it, had looked into his mind and perceived his very dreams.

'What are you saying, Librarian, that Nocturne will suffer the same fate?' The question came across more petulantly than he would have wanted.

'All worlds end, Dak'ir,' Pyriel answered pragmatically. 'Nocturne's demise might be millennia from now, it might only be a matter of centuries. I wonder if our progenitor brought us here to *see* something of our home world's fate.' His eyes flashed with cerulean fire. 'Is that what you've seen, brother?'

Seismic thunder erupted from the crash site before Dak'ir had to answer. Both Space Marines, even several hundred metres from the quake, were staggered by it. Then they were running, heading for the swathes of ash pluming into the air as the *Vulkan's Wrath* shifted and sank. A hundred metres from the ship and the Salamanders were engulfed by a grey cloud that struck their power armour in a gritty wave.

Dak'ir had rammed on his battle-helm, snapping on his luminator as he cycled through the optical spectra to best penetrate the murky explosion of ash. Pyriel needed no such augmentation. His eyes blazed like blue beacons in the darkness, more piercing that any lume-lamp.

'There,' he said, barely raising his voice and pointing towards the dark shape of the strike cruiser's hull. Dak'ir heard him perfectly, and saw vague silhouettes through the ash storm. Some were moving about, others lay huddled with their heads down.

'Ba'ken, report,' the sergeant shouted into the commfeed.

Crackling static returned for a time, but as the billowing grey wave began to disperse, the bulky trooper's voice came back.

'A seismic shift, brother-sergeant. The entire ship moved with it.'

'Casualties?'

'Just minor injuries. I pulled back the excavation crews when I felt the vessel beginning to move.' There was a pause, as if Ba'ken was gauging what he should say next. 'You're not going to believe what it's shaken loose.'

The grey dust had all but cleared, settling as a veneer across the plains as if it had never been disturbed, though the serfs bore the evidence of it on their overalls as did the Salamanders on their armour. The silhouettes through the ash proved to be Ba'ken and one of the excavation crews. Coughing and spluttering, the humans lay on their backs and gasped for air. Servitors stood alongside them, impassive and untroubled. Ba'ken left them and went to meet Dak'ir and Pyriel as they approached him.

He was stripped out of his armour and wearing labour fatigues. Sweat-dappled muscles were still bunched from his efforts, and he carried a flat-bladed shovel in one hand.

'Brothers,' he said, snapping a quick salute across his broad, black chest.

'Just like being back home, eh, Ba'ken?' said Dak'ir.

'Aye, sir. It puts me in mind of the rock harvest after the Time of Trial. Though it's usually snow and ice, not ash, that I'm digging through.'

'Show me what you've found,' ordered the sergeant.

Ba'ken led them to where the *Vulkan's Wrath* had clearly shifted during the geological event. A deep, seemingly fathomless chasm had formed between the edge of the strike cruiser's hull and the surface of the ash plain. Languid drifts, motes of grey, trickled into it and were quickly lost from sight in the darkness. The chasm was narrow, but not so acute that a warrior in power armour couldn't squeeze down it.

'I can feel heat,' said Pyriel, peering over the edge into the darkness. 'And the consciousness I experienced earlier, it is stronger here.'

'You think there is something down there, brother?' asked Dak'ir, moving to stand alongside him.

'Besides the chitin-beasts? Yes, I'm certain of it.'

'How deep do you think it is?' Ba'ken leaned over to get a better look but the chasm was only lit by the ambient light for about fifty metres before the blackness claimed it. Even Astartes eyesight couldn't penetrate much further. If Pyriel had any better knowledge, he was keeping it to himself.

'It could run to the core of Scoria for all we know,' Dak'ir replied. 'Whatever the case, I mean to find out.' He turned to Ba'ken. 'Don your armour, brother, and meet us back here. I want to know what lurks in the darkness beneath our feet. Perhaps it will provide some answers as to why we are here.'

THE LUMBERING FORMS of a vehicle convoy ground to a halt at the peak of the ridge. Exhaust fumes pluming smoke, their engines growled like war-hounds straining at the leash. N'keln and his warriors had arrived.

Tsu'gan watched them from the redoubt, his view enhanced through the magnoculars. The sergeant had switched to night-vision, rendering the image before him into a series of lurid, hazy greens. Embarkation ramps in the Land Raider and Rhinos slammed down in unison, the squads within debussing as one coherent unit. Tsu'gan watched the Salamanders deploy in a firing line along the ridge, and cursed.

'Close up,' he hissed, inwardly bemoaning N'keln's apparent over-caution. 'Your guns are outside effective range.'

A few seconds lapsed before the firing began. Iridescent beams from the multi-meltas stabbed into the
gloom in lances of red-hot fury. Missiles spiralled from
the ridge, buoyed along on twisting contrails of grey
smoke. Gun chatter erupted from the heavy bolters, pin-
tle mounts and secondary arms. The heavy *chug-chank*,
chug-chank of the *Fire Anvil*'s forward-mounted assault
cannon joined it, building to a high-pitched whirr as it
achieved maximum fire-rate. Blistering and bright, the
storm of shells and lashing beams torn apart the darkness like a host of flares.

Throughout the fusillade, the Iron Warriors hunkered
down. Unwilling to commit themselves, they stayed out
of sight, content to let the fortress walls weather the
assault.

The barrage persisted for almost three minutes before
N'keln, a distant figure in the lee of the Land Raider's
rear access hatch, ordered a halt to allow the firing
smoke to clear. It revealed little: just patches of scorched
metal and the odd ineffectual impact crater. No
breaches, no dead. The gate was still intact – the assault
had failed.

'Vulkan's teeth, bring them forward!' snarled Tsu'gan,
unwilling to vox in case the Iron Warriors were monitoring transmissions, overheard him and discovered his
guerrilla force staked out in the redoubts.

Even in the lull, the traitors didn't act. Only when
N'keln gave the order to withdraw and re-advance did
the Iron Warriors show their strategy.

Seemingly innocuous at first, a single hunter-killer
missile emerged from behind the battlements on an
automated weapons platform. Escaping incendiary
choomed loudly as the missile's booster ignited and
coiled off towards its intended target at speed. It fell
short of the reforming Salamanders by several metres
and for a moment Tsu'gan thought its homing beacon

must be out. That was until a chain of explosions tore across the ash ridge from a field of hidden incendiaries.

Grimacing at the sudden burst of fire, Tsu'gan turned away. He adjusted quickly and when he looked back he saw the ridge collapsing under its own weight, the foundations pulverised in a single blast of explosives. Cries echoed from the gloom as the Salamanders foundered in it. The ground was disintegrating beneath them and their bulky power armour was dragging Tsu'gan's battle-brothers along with it. Flailing and cursing, they tumbled down the diminishing ridge, barely coming to rest before a raft of tracer lights knifed into the dark and illuminated the fallen Salamanders. Sporadic bolter fire replied but it merely *pranged* off the armoured carapace of automated defence guns churning into position across the length of the wall. Chugging thunder erupted from above Tsu'gan as heavy bolter and autocannon emplacements started to eat through their ammunition belts.

Crying out in rage and anguish, Tsu'gan saw three of his battle-brothers threaded by munitions fire. Power armour was tough; tough enough to withstand such weapons as these, but the sheer rate of shells increased their potency threefold.

Unfortunately, in Tsu'gan's eyes at least, N'keln had not been one of those caught in the ash slide. Barking swift commands from what was left of the ridge peak, he attempted to restore some coherency to his forces. Pinned down in the basin, though, the stricken Salamanders were getting slaughtered.

'Use the transports as armoured cover,' Tsu'gan implored. 'Bring them down into the basin. Our brothers are dying, damn you!'

Igniting columns of smoke spilled out across the ridge as Vargo's Assault squad took to the air. It was an act of desperation, an attempt to alleviate the relentless volley targeting the warriors in the basin and force the enemy to split its fire.

Vargo landed a few metres short of the wall, ahead of the redoubts, just as Tsu'gan knew he would. Chainswords whirring, primed melt bombs winking in their mag-locks, the Assault squad made ready to jump again.

Chained detonations erupted down the length of the wall, engulfing Vargo and his squad in exploding frag. It was a first-strike deterrent, designed to stun and weaken an impatient attacker who sought to sack the bastion in his first foray. Smoke and flame died away to reveal the casualties of that ill-conceived strategy. Brother-Sergeant Vargo was on his feet but dazed, his armour blackened and cracked at the edges. Three of the Assault squad were down, unmoving. Four more carried obvious injuries, limping and cradling arms as they tried to drag their prone brothers next to the wall and outside the firing arcs of the sentry guns stitching lines of ammunition into the area where they had faltered. Jump packs looked shot to pieces, their turbines shredded or full of frag.

Tsu'gan was ready to abandon his post, when at last the vehicles came roaring down the half-flattened slope.

'*Hellfire,*' he snarled into the comm-feed, the order reaching all four combat squads. 'Execute!'

Brother S'tang hammered the switch on a palm-sized detonator taken from his combat-rig and flung himself to the ground along with his squad.

Explosions rippled across the edge of the redoubts, sending thick clods of dirt spitting high into the air amidst clouds of smoke and flame.

The Salamander assault force had been prepared for this, thanks to the careful instruction of Brother-Sergeant Typhos. Using it as a distraction, the beleaguered Space Marines managed to regroup.

Tsu'gan was first out of the redoubt. Debris from his grenade line was still falling as he raced towards the wall, bolter blazing. Behind him, the mobile armour of the vehicles had slewed into position and was taking fire. Another missile-launcher *choomed* overhead and one of the Rhinos went up in a ball of flame, flipped onto its back and burning. Astartes crawled out of the wreckage, using what was left of the hull for cover as the inevitable shots rained down at them from the walls.

'Combine fire!' Tsu'gan cried, skidding to a halt and dropping to one knee to steady his aim. Through his bolter sight he found an autocannon sentry gun, its muzzle lit by barking munitions. It jolted and collapsed as Tsu'gan brought his wrath to bear, Brothers Lazarus and S'tang adding to the fusillade that destroyed it.

Once the killing was done, Tsu'gan ordered the squad to move on, making it as hard as possible for the automated guns to track them. 'Advance!' he yelled. 'We have their attention now.'

Tiberon was picked off by an accurate bolter shot. It took him through the joint at his knee, crippling the Salamander instantly.

'S'tang,' said Tsu'gan as he saw Tiberon fall, 'to your brother.'

S'tang obeyed at once, jinking as he doubled back the short distance to Tiberon and dragged him into the cover of a crater cut by the grenade line.

Whickering fire came down at Tsu'gan and the other combat squads in earnest, as the Iron Warriors realised the more immediate threat in their midst. Tsu'gan didn't have time to take out another sentry gun before he was forced to move on lest the remote weapons platforms draw a bead and shred him and his squad.

The sound of rumbling adamantium offered a solution as the *Fire Anvil*, using the momentum from the ridge ramp, bulldozed through the recently vacated redoubts, smashing them into rubble and slewing to a stop in front of the brother-sergeant.

The other combat squads took the initiative and rallied to the formidable assault tank. A missile *whooshed* overhead and struck the Land Raider's roof, spilling fire and shell debris like rain. Smoke dispersed quickly. The *Fire Anvil* was left unscathed and started to rotate on its tracks, one side locked whilst the other churned it into position.

'Flamers!' yelled Tsu'gan as he realised what was coming next.

Brother Honorious and the other special weapons troopers came forwards, bodies pressed against the Land Raider's rear armour.

'Cleanse and burn!' Tsu'gan roared as the *Fire Anvil's* flamestorm cannons erupted gloriously. At the same time, Honorious and his brothers stepped from behind the Redeemer-pattern battle tank and added their own fire to the conflagration.

Roaring promethium scathed the walls, spilling through murder holes and firing slits, invasive and consuming. Muffled cries rewarded the blitz attack, and Tsu'gan smiled. The traitors were burning.

The rear embarkation ramp of the Land Raider slammed down and out stomped Veteran Sergeant Praetor and his Firedrakes in full Terminator armour, wielding crackling thunder hammers and storm shields.

All around them, the Salamander heavy weapons had been revivified. Heavy bolters raked the ramparts, splitting sentry guns apart in showers of metal; multi-meltas drawn up to lethal range burned into the walls, stripping away ceramite; missiles zoned in on the towers themselves, blasting the stoic bodies within to fragments.

'Concentrate fire on the wall guards,' bellowed Tsu'gan into the comm-feed, tactical-band, so it reached all fighting forces. Advancing upon the fortress, the brother-sergeant had realised something that had been staring him in the face since the redoubts.

'My lords,' he said, turning to acknowledge the Firedrakes.

'I am at your disposal, brother-sergeant,' boomed Praetor, his squad behind him like silent green sentinels.

'Break the gate and we break this siege,' Tsu'gan told him. He released a melta-bomb where he'd mag-locked it to his battle harness. Sergeant De'mas did the same, whilst some of their battle-brothers palmed krak grenades. 'There's enough explosive here to rip down three gates,' Tsu'gan boasted, eyeing the stretch of open ground between the Land Raider and the wall. 'I just need you to get me there and finish the job.'

Praetor nodded, though whether he saw Tsu'gan's plan or simply trusted him implicitly, the brother-sergeant didn't know.

Another missile strike lit up the flank of *Fire Anvil* this time, even as the flamestorm cannons continued to spew burning death from their battle-scorched maws.

'We advance under the blaze.' Tsu'gan had to bellow to be heard.

'Into the fires of battle then, brother...' The voice came from the shadowy confines of the Land Raider. It was harsh and filled with steel. Chaplain Elysius emerged into the half-light, though it was as if the gloom of the tank's hold clung to him like a shroud. The grinning skull mask of his battle-helm made him macabrely jocund.

'Unto the anvil of war,' Tsu'gan concluded. 'I am honoured, Brother-Chaplain.'

Elysius swung his crozius arcanum loose from its strap and impelled its power field into a vivid coruscation. He bade Tsu'gan go on.

The brother-sergeant turned back to Praetor. 'Can you make a mobile shield wall, brother?'

Praetor's loud laughter sounded like thunder. With well-executed precision, he and the Firedrakes formed a barrier wall with their storm shields, warding the front and flanks of Tsu'gan, De'mas and seven other battle-brothers. Elysius stepped outside of the protective cordon.

'Shoulder them, brothers,' Elysius bellowed with stentorian conviction. 'The Emperor and the will of Vulkan is *my* shield.'

Praetor wasted no further time. 'Forward, assault pattern *Aegis*,' he boomed, and the Firedrakes began to move.

Heavy weapons fire hammered against the Terminators and their upraised storm shields, but fell away harmlessly against their locked defence. Elysius strode alongside them, matching their ponderous pace, hurling canticles of faith and the litanies of the forge at the traitors like barbed spears.

'*…and lo, upon the anvil did Vulkan smash the heretics, his hammer like a comet that falleth from heaven. Into the blood of Mount Deathfire are they consumed…*'

Rosarius field flickering with every blow, the Chaplain did not once relent.

'*…quail, base traitors, and receive the promised price of your perfidy. Burn, malfeasants, burn! Flayed in fire before the Emperor's glory!*'

A rattling chorus of staccato gunfire joined Elysius's diatribes and was heard by Tsu'gan from within the protective shell of the Firedrakes' storm shields. Four Terminators formed the brunt of the armoured wall, shields locked in a seamless barrier. The energy fields generated by the shields crackled and spat with their joining, throwing off azure sparks and the reek of ozone. Two further Firedrakes guarded each flank, their shields held up and combined to configure a makeshift roof with the storm shields of two of their brothers that bisected the front line of four and acted as the spine of the formation.

The power-armoured Salamanders, crouched low and clutching their grenades, were interspersed between them, five Space Marines either side of the 'spine', each led by a sergeant with a Terminator at both flanks.

Tsu'gan counted fifteen steps, the weapons fire intensifying with every one. Outside his mobile redoubt of reinforced ceramite, he heard the shuddering reports of the Salamanders' guns and felt the heat from the venting flamers blazing overhead.

'*...and slay the enemies of the Imperium with bolt and blade...*' Elysius continued. His voice, normally cold like iron, burned with a zealot's passion now. The caustic rhetoric was amplified by the vox-emitters in his battle-helm, and his fiery sermons rang with the clarity and force of a loud hailer.

'*...commit their vile forms to the flames of purgation...*'

Ten more steps.

'*...hurl the wretched into the abyss to be torn asunder by claws of iniquity...*'

Five more.

'*...and the tainted shall burn within the pit, smote from the earth...*'

Three.

'*Heed me traitors and tremble!*'

The gate was before them.

Praetor's shield wall broke. An aperture in the barrier of ceramite was forged to allow Tsu'gan and his commandoes through. The line divided into two, storm shields facing outwards, the Terminators drawing as much fire as they could from the remote guns.

Hunter-killers emerged from concealed firing slits, triggered by proximity. De'mas took out one, the incendiary in the rocket exploding in the wall, spitting out debris like iron hail. The other released; its target, the

Chaplain who had stalked forwards to join his brothers at the gate.

Elysius disappeared amidst a cloud of fire and shrapnel. Tsu'gan fully expected him to be dead but when the dust cleared the Chaplain was down on his knee but very much alive, his Rosarius field flickering intermittently around him. The hunter-killer had retracted, only to return seconds later with a fresh payload.

'Dare bend me to my knee, craven tool of heresy,' spat Elysius, standing straight. 'With the fury of Prometheus, I smite thee!' His bolt pistol roared with the voice of damnation and the hunter-killer was no more.

Returning to the squad outside the gates, the Chaplain unlocked his own melta-bomb from his belt.

'Let the tainted be purged,' he intoned, tendrils of smoke rising off his armour from where the missile blast had breached his shield of faith.

Standing before the gate, Tsu'gan felt the baleful influence exuding from its central icon as tangible as heat. It was raw defiance and aggression, promised destruction and bloody threats. Brother-Chaplain Elysius smothered it with his mere presence, though it was an act of will to defy the malignity imbued within the symbol of iron. Tsu'gan and his brothers were emboldened by the Chaplain's example, drawing on their own inner belief to overcome the terrible gate. One conviction was left in their minds: the fortress *must* fall.

Together, the Salamanders attached their grenades and bombs, priming the charges for a three-second delay before retreating back behind the Terminators and their storm shields as they closed around them again.

The blast wave was like a baptism. Tsu'gan revelled in it washing over him and began to laugh, deep-bellied and loud.

'What is so amusing, brother?' asked Sergeant De'mas, the incendiary vapours dissipating from around the gate.

Tsu'gan's eyes burned like hellfires behind his battle-helm, aglow despite the darkness of his lenses.

'War at last, brother,' he intoned. 'Only war.'

Though, incredibly, the gate still stood, it was bent and crippled. Tsu'gan could see the inner fortress beyond it through fist-wide cracks as the Terminators parted slightly.

'Are you ready to face the traitor garrison, brother?' bellowed Praetor, the wild glint of anticipation in his eyes.

Tsu'gan matched it, grinning ferally behind his battle-helm. 'It's a small matter. But let us see, lord Firedrake.'

Praetor smiled, a thin fissure cracking the hard stone of his countenance, and brandished his thunder hammer.

'Bring it down!' he roared, and the Terminators before the gate struck as one.

II

Prisoners

'I WILL LEAD,' asserted Dak'ir as he tested the weight of the steel cable spooling from the winch-rig. One of the Salamanders Techmarines had set up the climbing device and each of the six Fire-born standing at the threshold of the chasm that had opened next to the *Vulkan's Wrath* was hooked to it. Threading the thick cable through loops on their battle harnesses, each Salamander made ready for a descent into the unknown.

Ba'ken had returned quickly after his sergeant had dismissed him to re-armour. He carried the weighty rig of his heavy flamer upon his back, insisting that the bulky weapon would fit through the narrow crevice that led into the depths of Scoria. Brother Emek joined him, having left the remaining medical operations to the human chirurgeons of the strike cruiser. His surgeon-craft was limited to field wounds; he didn't possess the necessary skill to conduct complex procedures. In any case, a Space Marine's time was better spent than languishing amidst the injured and dying.

Brothers Apion and Romulus were also from Dak'ir's squad, and hand-picked by the sergeant for their battle experience. The final place in the small expeditionary team went to Pyriel. The Librarian would follow after Dak'ir, tracking the psychic thread he had discerned emanating from below like a bloodhound.

'Luminators on. Vox-silence until we reach the bottom and know what we're dealing with,' Dak'ir ordered, the lume-lamp attached to his battle-helm stabbing into the blackness of the chasm below. Taking the strain of the cable, he plunged into stygian darkness.

Sensors in his battle-helm attenuated to the planet's atmospheric conditions registered a slight increase in temperature as Dak'ir descended. The reading glowed coldly on the inside of his lens display. Deafening silence filled the narrow space, only broken by the dull drone of the spooling winch-rig above. Sharp crags from the chasm's internal wall scraped against Dak'ir's armour. Gusts of steam, vented from the strike cruiser's partially submerged lower decks, passed over him and filmed his battle-plate with condensation. Soon, the solid adamantium of the ship's outer armour gave way to abject darkness. It was like delving into the bowels of an *other*world, one that fell away endlessly.

After an hour of painstakingly slow descent, Dak'ir's lume-lamp threw an oval of light that touched solid ground. Alighting at the bottom of the chasm at last, the brother-sergeant voxed his discovery through the comm-feed. Disengaging the cable from his battle-harness, Dak'ir stepped aside to allow space for his battle-brothers and drew weapons as he surveyed the pervading dark around them. The luminators on his battle-helm revealed a corridor of bare rock, terminating at the edge of the lume-lamp's effective range where the light was swallowed by blackness.

'THE TUNNEL APPEARS to be manufactured,' Emek reported down the comm-feed in a subdued voice. He drew his gauntlet lightly across the wall, interrogating its surface under the glow of his luminator.

Ba'ken had been the last to reach the bottom of the chasm. Determined to get through with his heavy flamer rig still attached, he had damaged his battle-helm on a jutting spike of rock. The sporadic interference plaguing his lens display as a direct result of the collision had driven him to distraction. When he reached the ground he removed the helmet, hooking it to his belt. The hulking trooper had acknowledged Dak'ir's look of reproach with a grunt, adjusting the promethium tanks on his back.

After exploring a few hundred metres, Brother Emek leading with flamer readied, the squad of Salamanders had stopped to surround him when he'd discerned a variation in the tunnel's structure.

'It's cambered and smooth, as if ground by tools or digging equipment,' he added.

'Must be quite some rig to cut an opening this large,' replied Ba'ken, his back to Emek as he guarded the way they had come. Brothers Apion and Romulus trained their bolters forwards, moving to the head of the Salamanders' formation whilst Emek examined the wall.

Dak'ir agreed with Ba'ken. The tunnel was easily wide enough to accommodate all six Astartes abreast and so high that even Venerable Brother Amadeus could have marched along it without needing to stoop.

'Definitely machine-hewn,' Emek concluded, reassuming his position at point.

Pyriel said nothing. His eyes were shut, and his expression was focused.

'Brother-Librarian?' Dak'ir asked.

Pyriel opened his eyes and the cerulean glow faded.

'Not the chitin-beasts,' he whispered, still surfacing from the psychic trance. 'Something else...' he added.

When it was clear the Librarian wasn't about to elaborate, Dak'ir ordered them on.

SPLIT DOWN THE middle by a thick blade, the Iron Warrior's battle-helm broke apart as Tsu'gan nudged it with his armoured boot. The face beneath was contorted in its final death throes, a dark and ragged wound bisecting it. Nose shattered beyond recognition, puckered flesh – festooned with chains and graven sigils – semi-parted to reveal yellowed bone; whatever had killed the traitor had done so long ago.

'This one is no different,' said Tsu'gan, letting the body loll back into a prone position.

The Firedrakes had brought the gate down with successive blows from their thunder hammers, its structural integrity weakened by the grenade blasts. Within was not the traitor garrison that Praetor had predicted. Instead, the Salamanders found corpses, arranged in positions that parodied the Iron Warriors' former duties. Those traitors not pitched off their feet during the assault remained at sentry, or crouched by now silent gun emplacements. It was exactly how the warriors in the redoubts had been set up: dead, but maintaining the illusion of numbers and protection. Only five of the slain Iron Warriors had been fresh: the rest were necrotic husks, decaying in their armour.

Five Chaos Space Marines and an array of automated defence guns had kept out a force of over eighty. Three of the Salamanders had been slain during the ill-conceived assault; two of those had come from Vargo's squad. The third was the driver from the destroyed Rhino. Space Marines were not easy to kill: the Assault squad troopers had been almost rent apart, taking the brunt of the heavy explosion, whereas the APC driver was shredded by shrapnel and shot through the skull as he tried to stagger from the vehicle wreck. Their progenoids had been secured by Fugis whilst under fire, and were safe within his reductor's storage casket. Several more were injured, and the Apothecary was tending to them as the rest of the task force secured the fortress.

'Dead before we even attacked...' N'keln's voice held a trace of annoyance to it as it came from behind Tsu'gan.

'They were dead a lot longer than that, my lord.' The brother-sergeant's diction was clipped. He blamed the needless deaths of his battle-brothers on his captain for his trepidation and unwillingness to commit their forces properly when the Salamanders had initiated assault.

'Five Astartes to man an entire fortress,' N'keln thought aloud. 'What were they doing here, brother-sergeant?'

'Annals recount that during the Great Crusade, the sons of Perturabo occupied many frontier bastions such as this,' said Praetor, his mighty physical presence moving implacably into Tsu'gan's eye line. 'Squad-strength garrisons were not unusual, but for them to still exist over ten thousand years later...' The Firedrake's voice trailed off. His fiery gaze went to the fortress of iron's inner keep, a squat structure of broad bulwarks and grey metal. Chimneys, venting smoke, sprouted from its flat, crenulated roof. Another gate barred entrance to the inner keep. Sergeant De'mas and his squad were rigging charges to blast it in.

Tsu'gan felt a keen sense of apprehension as he regarded the secondary gate. Even just standing within the expansive inner courtyard, surrounded by Iron Warrior bodies, a pall of unease seemed to wax and wane as if already probing his defences.

A flame burst seen from the corner of his helmet lens arrested his attention. Brother-Chaplain Elysius was ordering the corpses rounded up and burned. Flamer teams, sequestered from the Tactical squads, doused the mangled pyre in liquid promethium.

'Whatever killed them, did so with brute force and outside these walls,' Praetor's voice interrupted Tsu'gan's thoughts, the veteran sergeant of the Firedrakes having followed his gaze.

'So they dragged the bodies back inside after a much earlier battle?' offered N'keln. 'They must have been victorious, though I can see no evidence of enemy dead.'

'The Iron Warriors burn their foes too, brother-captain,' said Praetor, 'An anachronism of old Legion custom that some warbands still adhere to.'

'They are ash,' spat Tsu'gan, struggling to rein in his anger, 'as our slain brothers soon will be.'

If N'keln felt the barb, he didn't show it. Nor did Praetor seem about to reprimand.

'Victory is correct, brother-captain,' said the Firedrake, 'but at what cost, and against whom?'

'Those xenos we encountered at the crash site are not foe enough to trouble Astartes,' Tsu'gan asserted. 'I have seen no other encampments, no evidence of vessels or an army's movements.' He eyed the burning pile of corpses again: some fifty or so Iron Warriors. Renegades, yes, but still Astartes once fashioned by the Emperor; still formidable warriors slain up-close and brutally. An enemy like that didn't simply disappear. It didn't lie down and die, either.

Tsu'gan's voice was low and forbidding. 'I think something other than the chitin lurks in the earth beneath us. It brought death to these traitors.'

THREE HUNDRED METRES farther into the darkness and the tunnel became a labyrinth. Several corridors branched off from the main passage like a lattice within a giant hive. It put Dak'ir in mind of the chitin, but throughout their exploration of the underground network they had yet to encounter the creatures.

Ba'ken scoured each and every opening, the igniter from his heavy flamer casting a weak glow into the shadows. The Salamanders kept to the central tunnel, Dak'ir reasoning that it must lead to some nexus or confluence.

Ba'ken moved to the next junction. Panning his heavy flamer slowly and steadily, he started when an object skipped out of the darkness and rolled towards him.

'Contact!' he snapped smartly, preparing to douse what he thought could be a grenade in roaring promethium. The appearance of a diminutive figure scurrying into his firing arc stopped him.

It was a boy, and the 'grenade' was a rubber ball.

Ba'ken lifted his finger off the release bar of his weapon just in time. A tiny spurt of flame spilled from the nozzle like a belch, but didn't ignite fully.

Grinding to an abrupt halt, the boy stared at the green-armoured hulk that brandished fire in his hands. In the ephemeral spit of flame, Ba'ken saw that the dark-skinned youngster was dressed in coarse grey fatigues. The clothing was patched, as if amalgamated from several different sources, and the boots strapped to his feet looked a few sizes too big for him. Terrified, the boy's eyes widened as Ba'ken came forward, lowering his heavy flamer.

'Have no fear,' he intoned, his voice deep and resonant in the narrow side-tunnel. Stepping into the darkness as he extended an open hand, the burning red blaze in the Salamander's eyes flashed casting his onyx-black skin in a diabolic lustre.

A whimper escaped from the trembling boy's mouth and he fled, leaving the ball behind.

Ba'ken's hand dropped and a tic of consternation afflicted his face.

'A child...' he said, acutely aware of Dak'ir arriving behind him. Ba'ken turned to face the sergeant. The rest of the squad had gathered at his sudden warning. Emek stood next to Dak'ir, whilst Apion and Romulus surveyed the shadows behind them. Librarian Pyriel stood a few steps back from the rest, his eyes smouldering with power.

'Human.' It was a statement not a question, but Ba'ken answered anyway.

'Yes, a boy.'

'Follow,' ordered Dak'ir in a low voice. 'Eyes open,' he warned, remembering the last time they'd encountered a human child in similar circumstances. It was back on Stratos, and the boy had led them into a trap. Dak'ir still recalled the *crump* of detonation and the skeins of shrapnel slewing across his visor.

He hoped this would not end the same way.

A VAST IRON hall was the first room the Salamanders encountered upon demolishing the inner keep's gate. It was bare, but much deeper and wider than the outer structure had suggested. Doorway yawning open, reinforced plasteel slabs hanging off their hinges, a pall of displaced dust rolled across the plated floor as Praetor entered. The other Firedrakes followed closely behind their sergeant, storm shields raised, a poised electrical charge rippling across their thunder hammers.

Recently reformed, the three Tactical squads followed in the wake of the Terminators. Issuing clipped orders, the sergeants dispersed their squads swiftly to reconnoitre. Negative contacts came back from De'mas and Typhos, who had been tasked to clear the alcoves and immediate anterooms. Brother-Captain N'keln and the Inferno Guard joined the rest of the Salamanders in the hallway soon after.

Lok's Devastators maintained guard at the inner keep's broken gate, whilst Brother-Sergeants Omkar and Ul'shan patrolled the battlements. *Fire Anvil* and one of the Rhino APCs blocked the main fortress gate. The dead from Vargo's squad and the slain driver were laid reverently in a second personnel carrier, parked further back in the courtyard. The third Rhino was kept idling. As soon as the Salamanders had ascertained what the Iron Warriors had been doing, it would go back to collect Argos or one of his Techmarines in the hope they'd be able to plunder and sanctify some of the traitors' technology.

'This room is secure, brother-captain,' said Praetor as N'keln entered the hall to stand alongside him, 'but there are further chambers that should be scoured leading off from this main hall–'

Praetor was interrupted by the sudden reappearance of Tsu'gan, back from reconnoitring. 'There is more than that, my lords,' he said, stalking towards them. Tsu'gan's tone was laced with animus. It suggested the Iron Warriors burning in the courtyard were not the only ones garrisoning the fortress.

N'keln's jaw hardened as old enmity surfaced. The Iron Warriors had been at Isstvan. 'Show me.'

KEEPING PACE WITH the fleeing boy wasn't easy. He moved nimbly and took the Salamanders on a winding path through darkened tunnels strafed by their luminators. Grainy white beams criss-crossed, cutting frantic sweeps through the gloom with the urgent movements of Dak'ir and his squad.

'Stay vigilant,' he warned, voice low over the commfeed.

Pyriel was on the sergeant's heels. Emek followed closely with Apion and Romulus keeping a few paces distant deliberately, in case of an ambush.

Despite his prodigious strength, hefting the heavy flamer rig was slowing Ba'ken down, especially in the close confines of the tunnel complex. The hulking Salamander brought up Dak'ir's rearguard.

Dak'ir lost the boy from sight as he emerged from around a tight corner into a much wider cavern. He slowed to a cautious tread, checking out the debris left either side of a steadily narrowing channel. Piled rocks, steel-bucketed mining carts, metal crates, discarded lume-lamps and other detritus flanked the Salamanders as they formed a single file.

Detecting movement to his right, Dak'ir was about to order his squad to repel ambushers, when Pyriel stopped him.

Let them come, he warned his brothers psychically, *and keep your weapons low.*

Dak'ir wanted to protest, but this was not the time. He had to trust his squad to the Librarian's instincts and hope they weren't flawed.

'Follow Brother Pyriel's lead,' he ordered quietly over the comm-feed.

Emek's voice replied in a whisper.

'Five targets to the left, tracking us.'

Apion chimed in after him...

'Four more, static, in my fire arc.'

...then Romulus...

'I detect another six slowing to envelop.'

...and finally Ba'ken.

'Threats spotted, ten of them to our rear.'

Dak'ir knew there were five more up ahead, lying in wait at the tunnel's junction. The Salamanders could have neutralised them in seconds.

Within fifty more metres, the watchers lurking in the shadows sprang their 'trap'. Concealed light rigs blazed into life around the tunnel, throwing off a harsh sodium glare. Groups of men, armed with archaic-looking lasguns and solid shot rifles, emerged from hiding places behind crates and under dusty tarpaulins. Each of the Salamanders covered an enemy squad, though the humans' formation was anything but uniform. They were organised, their ambush-craft rudimentary though not beneath a well-drilled PDF regiment, but their movements suggested well-trained amateurs not soldiers. Dressed in coarse grey fatigues that were patched and worn like the boy's had been, they were hard-looking men with dark skin, who lived even harder lives if Scoria's harsh environs were anything to go by. Some carried anachronistic armour plates over the rough material: dull steel pauldrons and plastrons. Every man wore a pair of photo-flash goggles, evidently hoping to disadvantage their opponents by blinding them with the sudden light glare. They had not reckoned on facing Space Marines, whose occulobes reacted instantly to the shift in conditions.

A pair of what appeared to be mining engines rumbled into position on thick track-beds either side of the tunnel, effectively blocking it. Tripled-headed drilling apparatus comprised much of the front facing of the machines, with thick armour-plates and plastek glacis shielding the operators from view.

'Stand down and relinquish your weapons,' a stern voice echoed. 'You are surrounded and outnumbered fivefold.'

Dak'ir followed the source and saw a figure step forward out of the group of men in front of him. The human was attired like the rest, but he also wore a short, ragged cloak that felt oddly familiar to the Salamander. Thick, ribbed boots almost went up to knees that sported rounded metal plates. He carried a lasgun low-slung with the ease of a man who knows his troops are watching his back for him. When he lifted the goggles from his face, Dak'ir saw the man was in his middling years. Wrinkles eked from his eyes and gave him a perpetual frown. Rock dust smothered his close-cropped hair, but much of the grey patina was his own. Despite his age, the human leader possessed undeniable presence and his muscles were still taut, his body and jaw solid.

'Remove your battle-helms, too,' he added. 'I want to see if you all look like this one.' The human leader gestured towards Ba'ken, who glowered at him.

We could disarm them with minimal casualties, thought Dak'ir, hesitating to consider the next course of action.

Pyriel intruded on his musings.

Do as he asks, brother-sergeant. Stand down your squad.

Dak'ir heard the grip of his chainsword tighten as he squeezed it impotently.

'You can't be seriously suggesting we yield to this rabble?' he hissed through the comm-feed.

'That is precisely what I'm suggesting. Do it now, before they start to twitch.' The Librarian turned his head slightly to regard the brother-sergeant. 'We must earn their trust.'

It went against his instincts and his training, but in the end Dak'ir gave the order to stow weapons.

The Salamanders obeyed instantly, despite their obvious misgivings, following suit as their brother-sergeant removed his battle-helm.

'I am Brother-Sergeant Hazon Dak'ir of the Salamanders Chapter, 3rd Company,' Dak'ir told the human leader, who smiled without it reaching his eyes.

'Sonnar Illiad,' he replied, gesturing to another of his group, a tall man with a blunt-looking head, facial scars and a pepper-wash of stubble colonising his broad jaw and pate. 'Overseer Akuma and his men will take possession of your weapons.' The tall man and four others came forwards warily.

Ba'ken bristled behind his sergeant.

'No Astartes relinquishes his weapon unless it is prised from his cold, dead hand,' he snarled through gritted teeth.

From the demeanour of his battle-brothers, it was clear that they agreed with him. Throne, Dak'ir agreed too. Pyriel had insisted they stand down, and stand down they had. This he would not accede to.

'You may take my blade and pistol, as a gesture of good faith,' Dak'ir told the one called Illiad. The overseer stopped at once, looking back to his leader for guidance. A battle of wills was begun, between Dak'ir and the human. It played across Sonnar Illiad's face as clear as a plasma flare.

'Very well,' he conceded at last, before motioning to the one called Akuma. 'Take them.'

Dak'ir unsheathed and unholstered his weapons, proffering them to the overseer.

'Treat them reverently,' he warned, 'For I will be taking them back very soon.'

Akuma tried not to let his fear show, but was obviously intimated by the red-eyed Salamander and was swift to back away once he had his weapons.

The brother-sergeant then faced the man who called himself Illiad.

'We surrender,' he said. 'What now?'

Tsu'gan battle-signed for his squad to surround the trapdoor concealed at the back of the giant hall. Forged in thick iron, the gate looked sturdy, unashamedly designed to keep things out… or in. Dust-clogged and veneered in rust, it was invisible to a cursory examination of the area. Empty ammo crates and munitions tubes had been piled on top of it, draped over with a ragged tarpaulin. The fact that the stores of ammunition were exhausted revealed much about the Iron Warriors' desperate defence. They had used up almost everything they'd had to repel the attackers. Tsu'gan didn't doubt that the belt feeds and drum mags wedged in the sentry guns were their last.

He held up a fist, ordering his squad to wait.

Praetor and Brother-Captain N'keln were close by with weapons drawn.

Auspex was wretched with interference, bio-signatures seemingly appearing and disappearing like smoke on a stiff breeze, so Tsu'gan had ordered Iagon to shut the device off for now. Instead, he used his own senses to discern the presence of his enemies and found them when he detected the faintest *clank* of metal on metal through the iron door.

Pointing to his ear, Tsu'gan indicated that very fact to the others. He made a chop and pull motion with one hand – the other gripped his bolter. Brothers S'tang and Nor'gan heaved the gate open, its locks sheared by a plasma-torch from one of the Rhinos' equipment bays. Scraping back the entrance to the lower level as silently as possible, the two Salamanders moved aside quickly to allow Tsu'gan and the flamer-wielding Brother Honori-ous to cover the now gaping portal.

The din of striking metal grew louder but there were no enemies lurking in the shadows, only a steel-runged ladder extending into blackened depths.

Tsu'gan made his hand into a flat blade, giving the all-clear, then splayed his fingers and made another fist. Half of his squad would accompany him into the dark-ness; the rest would remain on the surface and protect the exit. Praetor and N'keln would remain too; the Ter-minator too bulky and cumbersome to fit into the tight confines suggested below, the captain too valuable to risk on a scouting mission into the unknown.

Extending two fingers, Tsu'gan chopped down twice in rapid succession. Tiberon and Lazarus, waiting at the periphery, took the ladder one-by-one and plunged below. Once the two Salamanders were down, he raised one finger, made a fist, and then raised two and chopped down twice again. Tsu'gan descended next, knowing that Honorious and Iagon would follow as rearguard.

Keeping luminators snuffed, the Salamander combat squad moved slowly down a tight corridor that reeked of dank and copper. A strange pall pervaded the air: invisible but tangible, as if a second skin was forming over their battle-plate.

Tsu'gan followed the clamour of metal, still persisting, but seemingly farther away than when he'd first heard it in the hall above. Though his optical spectra were set to night-vision and then infra-red, the dark was oddly impenetrable as if subsuming any and all ambient light. Only sound guided him and his squad as they ranged cautiously through cloying shadows.

'Sire,' hissed Honorious.

Tsu'gan whirled around to face him, incensed that he had broken vox-silence.

The flamer trooper had stopped dead and was aiming his weapon down a sub-corridor branching off from the one the combat squad was traversing.

'You break vox-silence at my command only, trooper,' Tsu'gan snarled in a low voice.

Honorious turned, nonplussed.

'I didn't speak, sergeant.'

'Sire,' rasped Tiberon.

The battle-brother was at point, intent on the way ahead and seemingly oblivious to the fact that a large gap was developing between him and the rest of the squad.

A reprimand formed on Tsu'gan's lips, but he didn't give it voice.

'Squad halt,' he said into the comm-feed, instead.

Iagon's auspex blazed into life, multiple signatures plaguing the hazy screen at once.

'Contacts!' he snapped, swinging his bolter around to aim at shadows.

'I have movement,' hissed Lazarus.

'Over here…' whispered a voice that Tsu'gan didn't recognise. He trained his combi-bolter in its direction, finger poised over the jet-release for the weapon's flamer.

'Sire,' Honorious's voice came again, far away this time, but the battle-brother was crouched right next to him in a ready-position. There was no way he could have actually spoken and it sound that distant.

'Sir, multiple contacts closing…' said Iagon, jerking his bolter back and forth as he sought targets.

The reek of dank and copper grew stronger.

Tiberon was still going. He was almost lost from Tsu'gan's sight altogether. For a moment the brother-sergeant gave in to something approaching fear, filled with a deep knowing that if Tiberon was swallowed by the darkness, he would never come back and they would never be able to find him.

'Hold, brother. Hold!' Tsu'gan cried, but his shout was smothered by the maddening din of hammered metal and the warnings of his squad.

'Over here…'

Clank!

That voice again; the one Tsu'gan didn't know…

'Enemy movement! Engaging!'

Clank!

Tiberon fading into the darkness ahead…

'Contacts closing, no target!'

Clank!

His mind spinning…

'Sire…'

Clank!

The sudden compulsion to make it stop…

'Sire, help us…'

Clank!

The bolter in his hands, pressed against his temple, tool of his salvation…

Clank!

The only way to end it…

'Please, make it stop,' Tsu'gan gasped. The muzzle felt cold against his sweat-drenched forehead. The sound of the slowly squeezing trigger was as deafening as thunder.

'*Vulkan's fire burns in my breast,*' a powerful voice intoned, eclipsing the beat of hammered metal. '*With it I shall smite the foes of the Emperor!*'

Sensation, vague and indistinct at first, returned to Tsu'gan. He was faintly aware of a reassuring presence nearby, a lodestone to which he could anchor himself.

'*For we are the Angels of the Emperor, servants of the Golden Throne, and we shall know no fear.*'

Tsu'gan caught hold of the voice, stentorian and commanding, grasping it like a rope of salvation. A refulgent figure stood beside him, a crackling stave held in his outstretched hand.

'*From the fires of battle are we born.*'

No, not a stave – the warrior, sable-armoured with a face of death, held a hammer.

'*Upon the anvil of war are we tempered.*'

A blazing aura roiled from it like a fiery wave, chasing down the darkness and burning back the apparitions that tried to clench to them like parasites.

'Speak the words!' Brother-Chaplain Elysius snapped. 'Speak them and find your courage, Salamanders!'

Tsu'gan and his squad uttered the words as one, and the fog of insanity lifted.

The Chaplain smacked a reassuring hand against Tsu'gan's pauldron.

'Good enough, brother-sergeant,' he said. 'I will take the lead from here. Restore your battle-helm and follow me.'

Tsu'gan looked down at the battle-helm cradled in his grasp, agog. He hadn't even realised he'd removed it. Wiping away the sweat that was very real, he set his helmet back on and obeyed. The rest of his brothers had come to their senses as well, and followed with weapons ready. Even Tiberon had stopped. He let the Chaplain catch up to him before falling in behind.

Elysius had secured Vulkan's Sigil to his belt, though the artefact still glowed faintly with remembered power. Undoubtedly, the Chaplain had saved their lives. Whatever malfeasance preyed upon these lower catacombs had very nearly forced Tsu'gan and his squad to turn their guns on themselves. A few moments more and they would have done.

'Heretics are close,' Elysius rasped, his crozius arcanum igniting like a flaming torch in his mailed fist.

Tsu'gan realised that the heavy metal *clank* had returned to normal. It was still loud, and emanated from a sealed hatch ahead of them.

A few steps from the hatch, the Chaplain brought up his bolt pistol.

'Steel yourselves,' he warned.

The strange malaise affecting the tunnel returned but lingered at the periphery of Tsu'gan's thoughts as if unwilling to press further. The brother-sergeant gripped his bolter for reassurance, running a gauntleted finger over the flame icon embossed on the stock. Muttering a litany of warding, Tsu'gan opened his eyes and saw that the Chaplain had stepped aside from the hatch.

The entrance was locked and barred.

Tsu'gan beckoned Tiberon and Lazarus, who came to the front of the squad with krak grenades primed. After affixing the explosives with a dull, metallic *thunk*, the two Salamanders fell back. Honorious moved ahead of them, but kept low and at a safe distance. Tsu'gan pressed his body against the wall. He noted the

Chaplain did the same on the opposite side, trusting to solid steel rather than his rosarius this time.

Squad in position, spread either side of the tunnel and outside the blast funnel, Tsu'gan drew his hand across his gorget in a slashing motion.

Aiming down his bolter's targeter, Iagon fired a single shot into one of the mag-locked krak grenades. A second later the hatch exploded.

Smoke and fire surged down the corridor in a plume, sending pieces of shrapnel brushing against the Salamanders' armour.

Stalking through the dirt cloud, Chaplain Elysius was the first to enter the room beyond the hatch, Tsu'gan close behind him. They emerged into a metal-bound vault, dimly lit and filled with the stink of copper and iron. Rust streaked the walls like blood. Barbed hooks embedded in the metal resonated with remembered agony. Pitted manacles dangled slackly like hanged men.

This was a place of death and horror.

Crunching servos heralded a sudden attack by a quartet of ghoulish drones. Grey-faced, skin webbed by livid red veins, the automatons were an analogous but twisted variant on the servitors from the *Archimedes Rex*. The wretched parodies screamed in agony as they came at the interlopers, as if their bodies were still in pain from the invasive techno-surgeries employed to fashion them. Pain synapses flared with every motion, fuelling a terrible rage, only leavened by the shedding of blood and the rending of flesh.

Swollen with grotesque musculature, the monstrous ghoul-drones were the size of ogryn. They barrelled for the black-armoured warrior suddenly in their midst. Elysius ignored them, bent on an ironclad figure toiling over some device at the back of the chamber, apparently oblivious to the fight.

Tsu'gan only caught flashes of the mysterious artificer between the gaps in the Chaplain's body as he moved: a servo-arm attached to the generator on the figure's back; the colour of the dirty steel; yellow and black chevrons framing the armour; gilded greave plates fringed with rust around the bolts; pipes and cables, serpentine and alive; hydraulic gases venting and spitting like a curse.

Evil emanated from this being. Every blow from its incessant hammering was like the beat of a fell heart. Even as he closed, Tsu'gan couldn't tell what the War-smith laboured at so furiously, smothered as it was by thick shadows and an even thicker sheet of coal-black plastek.

A bolter flare lit up Tsu'gan's left flank as a ghoul-drone was torn apart in a welter of oil and viscera. His battle-brothers were covering him as the sergeant shadowed his Chaplain, knowing that he couldn't leave Elysius to face the Warsmith alone.

Another ghoul-drone was destroyed, engulfed by Honorious's flamer. Its biologically unstable frame collapsed hideously in the intense heat. It muscles cooked and burst in blood-red torrents. A third beast dragged lengths of saw-toothed chain from the stump of its arm. Hot bile rose in his throat as Tsu'gan realised the chains were actually part flesh, part sinew and that some of the teeth were human bone. Boltgun roaring, he sundered the abomination and stamped over the remains. Punching a fourth, he knocked the creature aside to try and stay in the Chaplain's wake. Gore and charred meat peppered Tsu'gan's armour in a grisly spray. Maintaining momentum, Iagon had punctured the ghoul-drone's cranium with a bolt round that exploded it from within and obliterated the eight-pointed star branded onto its face.

The ghouls were all dead, but their hellish master endured still.

At last, the Warsmith seemed to realise his peril and reached for a combination melta-bolter on a work-slab alongside him. Lightning arcing from his crozius arcanum, Elysius severed the clutch of cables linking the weapon to the Iron Warrior's fusion generator. Undeterred, the Warsmith spun about, revealing a reaper cannon morphing from the constituent parts of his right arm. It glowered evilly as the long-gun corporealised, a hot yellow line searing from the vision slit in the angular battle-helm encasing his head.

Elysius swung again, but the Warsmith swatted the blow away with his left arm, a bionic limb like one of its legs – this thing was more machine than man. Pistons heaved, spewing gaseously as power was fed to the augmetic. The arm ended in a razor-edged claw that the Iron Warrior used to split the Chaplain's battle-plate.

Gasping in pain, Elysius brought up his bolt pistol only for the servo-arm, curled over the Warsmith's right pauldron, to snap down viperously. The Chaplain screamed as his wrist was seized and slowly crushed. All the while, the reaper cannon was slowly resolving. Coagulated flesh and iron blended into solid, dull metal. Inner mechanisms were forming, the hellish strain of the obliterator virus rapid and pervasive. If fully forged and allowed to fire, that weapon could shred the Salamanders into flesh and chips of battle-plate.

Determined that wouldn't happen, Tsu'gan reached Elysius and waded into the melee with a roar.

Unloading a full clip into the Warsmith's body, he watched between the sporadic *flash-bang* of explosive rounds as the Iron Warrior bucked and jerked against the fusillade. The transmutation halted, the need for self-preservation briefly outweighing the desire to kill.

Elysius staggered, dropping his pistol as his wrist was released. Battered, the Iron Warrior fell back, howling in pain and fury. The sound resonated metallically around the vault. There was something ancient and hollow about it, images of jagged metal and age-old rust surfacing in Tsu'gan's mind. The brother-sergeant followed up, ramming in a fresh clip as he moved, and was about to issue a lethal head shot when Elysius stopped him.

'Hold!'

Tsu'gan's blood was up; he wasn't about to relent. 'The traitor must be executed.'

'Hold, I will not be merciful if you disobey,' the Chaplain retorted. Dark fluids were running down a gash in his plastron, flowing more vigorously as he staggered forwards, and his wrist hung limply at his side. 'Lower your weapon, brother-sergeant.' Though laboured and rasping, Elysius's tone made it clear this was an order as he approached the supine Warsmith. The Iron Warrior's breastplate was wretched with holes and scorch marks. Inert and unconscious, he was barely alive. 'I want to interrogate him first,' the Chaplain added, 'To find out what he knows about this bastion, its purpose and what happened to the garrison.'

Tsu'gan stood down, aware that behind him his squad had the room secured.

Elysius spoke into the comm-feed.

'Brother-captain, have flamers brought down to the vault. We need to scour the taint from its walls,' he said, spitting the last remark. 'And I need my tools,' he added. 'The prisoner and I have much to discuss.'

CHAPTER EIGHT

I
Those Who Lived…

THERE WAS SOMETHING strangely familiar about the human settlement under the earth. It was based on a series of honeycombed chambers of varying height and depth, resembling a shantytown in part, replete with hab-shacks, corrugated work sheds and lived-in tubular pipes appended to some of the larger chambers, the makeshift structures layered upon each other like the strata of some half-developed world. Exposed metal and plastek peeked out from beneath calcified layers of rock and decades, perhaps centuries, of ingrained grit. This melding was incongruous, much like the attire of the humans that led Dak'ir and his brothers through the settlement's main thoroughfare.

Staring at the green-armoured giants from the shadows of humble dwellings, behind the corners of bucket-carts and atop sturdy-looking towers were men, woman and children. Like Sonnar Illiad's ambushers, they were dressed in coarse grey fatigues, patched and shabby from the rigours of daily use. Some, the bold or stupid, stood in open defiance of the newcomers, challenging with their upright postures. Dak'ir noticed they stood in large groups, these men, and that the boldness did not extend to their eyes where fear dwelt instead; and that they took an involuntary half-step back as the Salamanders passed them.

Flanked by Illiad's troops, Dak'ir wondered again at how easy it would be to subdue these humans and take the settlement in a single attack. Lesser Chapters, those with a bloodletting bent and a shallow disregard for innocent life, might have slaughtered them. Salamanders were forged from different stock. Vulkan had taught them to be stern and unyielding in the face of the enemy, but he had also encouraged compassion and the duty in all Fire-born to protect those weaker than themselves.

Only now, watching the scared faces flit by as he considered that calling, did Dak'ir start to understand Pyriel's rationale in surrendering. By capitulation, the Salamanders had showed they were not a threat, or at least that they did not intend to pose one. Proud and possibly noble, Illiad's people might hold the key to the fate of Vulkan and the significance of Scoria to the primarch. The Salamanders would not discover that through intimidation and duress, they would only learn of it if given willingly.

Sadly, not all his brothers shared in Dak'ir's epiphany.

'To give up without a shot fired, it is not the way of Promethean lore,' Ba'ken growled. He kept his voice low over the comm-feed, now coming to Dak'ir through his gorget since he had removed his battle-helm, but made his discontent obvious by his body language.

'This isn't Nocturne, brother.' As he gave voice to the rebuke, Dak'ir paused to acknowledge the truth of his remark, conceding that Scoria was actually extremely cognate with their home world. Even the settlement, bunker-like and rendered in stone and metal, contained an almost atavistic resonance. 'Nor will we learn what we need to from these people with fiery retribution.' He looked to Pyriel for support, but the Librarian appeared oblivious, locked in some half-trance as he trod automatically through the numerous dwellings and holdings.

'But to be cowed like this...' muttered Ba'ken.

'I believe our brother's warrior spirit is offended, sir,' offered Emek, who seemed intrigued by the presence of the humans, scrutinising every structure as the Salamanders passed it, and analysing the subterranean populous that lived in them.

Dak'ir smiled thinly to himself. Ba'ken was wise, but was warrior-born, a native of Themis, whose tribes valued strength and battle prowess above all else. For all his great wisdom, once Ba'ken was affronted his view became myopic and intractable. It was a useful trait in combat, one Dak'ir likened to attempting to shift a mountain with one's hands, but at peace it bordered on cantankerous.

Romulus and Apion held their tongues. Their silence suggested an accord with Ba'ken.

'Show humility, brothers. This is not the time to act,' Dak'ir warned. He turned to Emek, then gestured to the Salamanders' human escort. 'What do you make of them?'

'Brave,' he said. 'And afraid.'

'Of us?'

'Of something like us,' Emek replied. 'These people fled into the darkness for a reason and have stayed here for many years.' His eyes narrowed, as the tone of his voice changed to become more speculative. 'When we removed our battle-helms, they didn't seem shocked or even perturbed by our appearance.'

The domestic dwellings, the pseudo-caves of rock and metal, started to thin and fade away as Illiad then led them to another structure that loomed large ahead. A pair of grand blast doors, at least they might once have been grand, framed by ornate designs but buried under caked dirt and encrusted grime, stood before them like weary bronze sentinels.

'They may have seen Salamanders before,' Dak'ir ventured, unable to suppress a tremor of anticipation. If they had, it could mean…

Pyriel's voice intruded on his thoughts.

'I suspect the answers lie within.' He was indicating the bronze blast doors.

A few metres from the entrance, Illiad stopped the column with a gesture and went the rest of the way alone. All the while, the one called Akuma watched the Salamanders vigilantly, readjusting his grip on his lasgun every few seconds.

Rapping on the blast doors three times with his gun stock, Illiad then stepped back. Grinding gears broke the silence moments later as an ancient mechanism was engaged. Dust poured from the inner workings, dislodged with their sudden activation. The blast doors parted shudderingly and within yawned a barren chamber, more metal and calcified rock, but with thick buttressed walls and no exits.

'You mean to incarcerate us, Sonnar Illiad?' asked Dak'ir as he was confronted by the hangar-like dungeon.

'Until I can decide whether you are friend or foe, yes.'

Ba'ken stepped forward upon hearing this, the muscles in his neck bunched, fists clenched.

'This, I cannot abide.' His tone was threateningly level.

Apion backed him up.

'Nor I, sir.'

Dak'ir turned to regard Romulus.

'Are you of the same opinion?'

The Salamander nodded, slow and evenly.

Glaring down at Illiad, Dak'ir knew the time for indulging the humans was at an end. To his credit, the old man didn't flinch. He kept his warm, dark eyes on

Dak'ir, staring up to him as a child might an adult. Yet, he did not appear diminutive. Rather, it only enhanced his stature.

'I am in agreement with my battle-brothers,' Dak'ir concurred.

Illiad matched his gaze, perhaps uncertain what to do next.

'How many are in your colony, Illiad?' the brother-sergeant asked him.

Akuma came forwards quickly, his mood agitated.

'Don't tell them, Sonnar,' he warned. 'They seek to gauge our strength and return with numbers. We should seal them in the vault now.'

Illiad looked at his second-in-command, as if considering his advice.

Ba'ken turned on Akuma, who retreated before the Salamander's bulk.

'How though, little man, will you do that?' he growled.

Akuma raised his lasgun protectively, but Ba'ken snatched it from his grasp. It was met by a frantic bout of lasguns priming as the human guards prepared for a fight. None of the Salamanders reacted, not without word from their sergeant.

Illiad raised his hand for calm, though Dak'ir could detect the increase in his heart rate and see the lines of perspiration beading the side of his head.

'Just over a thousand,' Illiad replied. 'Men, women and children.'

'This settlement you have fashioned for yourselves, it was once a ship, wasn't it?' said Dak'ir, the pieces falling into place as he spoke.

A Space Marine's memory was eidetic. It was a useful trait when reviewing battle plans or on long-range reconnoitre to ascertain the lay of the land or an enemy's strategic positions. Dak'ir used that flawless recall now to form accurate pictographic memories of some of the human dwellings they had passed, those where the extruding rock had crept over metal to obscure it. Examining details in his mind, cycling through images in milliseconds, interpreting and cross-analysing, Dak'ir stripped away the calcified rock. Clods of dust fell away in his mind's eye to reveal metal corridors, barrack rooms, minor strategiums, deck plating, defunct lifters, extinct consoles and other structures. Broken apart, forcibly disassembled, it was a ship nonetheless.

'One that crashed long ago,' said Illiad. 'Its reactor still functions and we use its power to generate heat, purify the air and water. The sodium light rigs are kept burning through the conversion of fusion energy.'

'And this, a sparring hall?' Dak'ir had stepped out of the column to approach the frame around the blast door. It had sunk into the rock; or rather the cave had grown around it. He tore at a section of it, gauntleted fingers prising off a layer. Grit and dust came with it and an origin stamp became visible beneath, fusion-pressed in blocky Imperial script.

154TH EXPEDITIONARY

Dak'ir shared a meaningful glance with Pyriel. The shattered remnants in which the human colony had made its home had once been a vessel of the Great Crusade fleet. He tried not to consider the ramifications of that discovery.

'I cannot say for certain,' Illiad replied. 'All we really know are legends, passed down by our ancestors.'

'Sonnar, don't–' Akuma began, but Illiad scowled and cut him off with a sharp gesture.

'They could have killed us in the tunnel, or at any point from there to here,' he snapped, ire fading into resignation as he turned back to Dak'ir.

The sound of a commotion echoing from the tunnels behind them interrupted Illiad. A young boy, Dak'ir recognised him as the one who had fled from Ba'ken earlier, ran into view. He balked a little at the sight of the armoured giants again – Ba'ken's posture seemed to relax upon seeing him – and was panting for breath.

'Chitin,' he rasped, forcing out the words between gulps for air, hands pushed down on his thighs as he fought to compose himself.

'Where, Val'in?' asked Illiad, concern creasing his features.

The boy, Val'in, looked back nervously.

'In the settlement.' Va'lin's eyes were wide with terror and filling with tears. 'My papa…'

Las-fire echoed down the corridor in sharp cracks of noise.

Screaming followed it.

'They don't stand a chance,' said Emek, his voice low.

Dak'ir's expression hardened as he looked behind them into the half-light.

'Then by Vulkan, we'll even the odds.'

'WE HAVE FOUGHT the chitin-beasts for generations,' growled Akuma, with a half-glance at the green-armoured warriors running alongside them. 'What do we need *them* for?'

'I doubt we could stop them even if we wanted to, Akuma,' answered Illiad.

Dak'ir saw that the old man's face was grave at the sounds of carnage just ahead of them. The Salamander felt the human's pain, and his anger boiled at the thought of the settlers' suffering.

The weak will always be preyed upon by the strong. He remembered the words of Fugis many months before, outside the Vault of Remembrance at Hesiod. The words of his reply then came swiftly to his lips now, like a catechism.

'Unless those with strength intercede on behalf of the weak, and protect them.'

Emek turned to the sergeant as they were nearing the invisible boundary line of the settlement. The crack of las-fire and the flat bangs of solid-shot rifles were like a discordant chorus to the shrill of terror, ever rising in pitch and urgency.

'What did you say, sir?'

Dak'ir kept his gaze ahead as he answered.

'We must save these people, brother. We must save them.'

Akuma's voice intruded suddenly as they ate up the last few metres. He was addressing his men.

'Once we reach the settlement, break into squads. Surround them and aim for the eyes, between the plates. No chitin will ever...' The words died on Akuma's lips as they emerged into the open and saw their home.

Chitin swarmed from emergence holes, dragging screaming settlers to their deaths. Bloodied bodies, mangled by bone-claws or rent with razor-sharp mandibles, were strung out over the ground, or slumped in the archways of once peaceful dwellings like butcher's meat. There were women and children amongst the dead, as well as armed men. Some were so badly mutilated that it was impossible to tell either way.

A sudden tremor wracked the ground, pitching a man sniping off the roof of a hab-shack. He screamed as a chitin scuttled over his prone form with surprising speed. It severed his torso with a snip of its claws and the screams were abruptly silenced. In his wake came a woman carrying a shotgun who'd managed to hold on. Scurrying into his place, she started firing.

Two men and a lean-faced youth fended off a chitin with long, spiked poles. Screeching, the xenos creature rolled back onto its hind legs as its soft belly was pierced and its blood spilled out in a grey morass. The victory for the humans was short-lived as two more chitin took its place, one smothering a pole-wielder with its bulk, before the second gouged another with a snapping bone-claw. The youth fled in terror only to be lost from view in the desperate battle.

A woman brandished a flare like a spear, thrusting it towards the eye of a chitin intent on devouring her and the two children she protected. The flare, like the life of her and her children, was slowly fading.

Everywhere, the humans fought. Some only had spears or crude ineffectual rifles, and they were badly outnumbered, but these were their homes and families, so they battled on regardless.

'I have never seen so many…' breathed Illiad. He staggered as another tremor rippled through the cavern, sending chunks of rock and dust spiralling from the roof. Each time, the chitin hordes increased, pouring from their emergence holes like vermin. 'The quakes must have disturbed them.'

'That or they were driven here,' Dak'ir muttered darkly. 'I'll take my weapons back now, Illiad.'

The old man gestured to Akuma who had the chainsword and pistol in a heavy pack on his back. He unveiled them swiftly and returned them begrudgingly.

Dak'ir nodded grimly to him, testing his grip on pistol and blade before turning to his brothers.

'The preservation of human life is priority. Do all that you must to protect the colonists. In Vulkan's name.'

Dak'ir raised his chainsword, the dim light reflected off its ancient teeth as if relishing the blooding to come.

'Into the fires of battle!' he roared, leading the charge.

'Unto the anvil of war!' his brothers replied as one.

'THIS PLACE REEKS of death,' snarled Tiberon, sifting through the wreckage of the Warsmith's tools.

The captive Iron Warrior was gone. The ghoul-drones had been removed too, and burned upon the same smouldering pyres as the slain Iron Warrior garrison.

Chaplain Elysius had already left, going to his duties. Tsu'gan and his squad had remained behind.

Another flamer burst lit up the outer corridor as Honorious and his brothers continued to purge the walls and alcoves where Tsu'gan and his warriors had almost met their demise. Cleansing by fire had quietened the voices, but not engulfed them completely. The brother-sergeant was grateful this would be a short stay. Their mission was to search amongst the wreckage for anything that might shed light on the Iron Warriors' presence on Scoria and stand guard over Techmarine Draedius.

The Mechanicus adept had been sent from the *Vulkan's Wrath*, at N'keln's behest and Master Argos's concession, to examine the device the Warsmith had laboured over so manically. It was a cannon: forged of dark metal with a long, telescopic barrel and angled towards a blast door mounted in the ceiling. Though hidden in the metal floor plating, the weapon was obviously elevated into position via a pneumatic lifter. Its intended target, however, remained a mystery.

Tsu'gan knew artillery and he likened this one to the Earthshaker cannon most commonly employed by regiments of the Imperial Guard. Few Astartes Chapters had need for such a static bombardment weapon. Strike cruisers and Thunderhawk gunships provided all the long-range support a Space Marine army needed. Surgical strikes, swift and deadly, that was the Astartes' way of war. Patient, grinding shelling went against the Codex, but then the Iron Warriors followed no such tome. Tsu'gan knew enough of the Traitor Legion to be acquainted with their use of long-range artillery. Siege-specialists as they were, the sons of Perturabo preferred to employ such weapons to crush their foes from distance, before closing in to apply the killing stroke.

Only cowards feared to attack and finish an enemy before it was already beaten. Tsu'gan felt his rancour for the Iron Warriors deepen further.

'It is more than just death that pervades the air in here,' replied Brother Lazarus with obvious distaste.

Tsu'gan scowled.

'I smell cordite and sulphur.' It was more than that. The stench was redolent of a memory, an old place just beyond reach that Tsu'gan would rather not revisit.

'Here, my lord,' called Iagon from across the chamber. 'I may have something.'

Tsu'gan went over to him and knelt down next to the crouching trooper who gestured to a dark stain seared onto the floor.

'The metal is fused,' said Iagon as his brother-sergeant traced the edge of the stain with his finger. 'It would take a great amount of heat to do that.'

'Looks old,' Tsu'gan wondered aloud, 'and shaped like a boot print. What's this?' he added, smearing a fleck of something with his finger. He tasted it and grimaced. 'Cinder.'

The grimace became a scowl.

'The Iron Warriors are not the only traitors on Scoria.'

The voice of Techmarine Draedius intruded on Tsu'gan's thoughts.

'There are no shells, no ammunition of any kind for this cannon,' he said, almost to himself. 'It is powered by a small fusion reactor.'

'Nuclear?' asked Tiberon, who was closest.

Draedius shook his head.

'No. More like energy conversion. I've found several receptacles containing trace elements of a fine powder I have no records of.'

Tsu'gan looked up. The sense of unease that permeated the lower deep of the fortress had still not abated.

'Retain a sample but hurry with your work, brother.' A blast of fire from the purging that continued outside threw haunting shadows over the side of the sergeant's face. 'I don't wish to linger here any longer than is necessary.'

CORUSCATING FIRE RIPPED from Pyriel's fingertips in blazing arcs. It lit the cavern in smoky shadows and burned a ragged hole through an advancing chitin. The xenos swarming the human settlement reacted to the sudden threat in their midst. They faltered, losing purpose in the face of such fury. In contrast, the settlers were galvanised, redoubling their efforts as the spark of hope became a flame.

Dak'ir took the blow from a chitin's bone-claw on his pauldron, where it dug a jagged groove in the ceramite. He lunged with his chainsword, forcing it into the creature's abyssal-black eye up to the hilt. As he wrenched the weapon free, the chitin-beast screeched. Fluid spurted from its ruined eye socket, painting Dak'ir's armour in watery grey. The Salamander moved inside its death arc, weaving around retaliatory strikes, before severing a champing mandible and burying his blood-slick chainblade into the chitin's tiny brain. Shuddering, the creature shrank back and died. Dak'ir sprang off its hardened carapace as he vaulted over the chitin, its insectile limbs spasming still, and flung himself towards another enemy.

The boy, Val'in, was running again.

He'd followed Illiad and his warriors after the Salamanders had charged, and now found himself in the midst of the fighting. Clutching a shovel in trembling hands, he came face-to-face with a chitin. The creature's blood-slick mandibles chattered expectantly as it scuttled towards him. Val'in backed away but with a hab-shack suddenly at his back, could retreat no further. Tears were streaming down the boy's face but he held his shovel up defiantly. Rearing back, the chitin chittered in what might have been pleasure before an armoured hulk intervened between the creature and its kill.

'Stay behind me!' Ba'ken yelled, grunting as he held back the chitin's bone-claws that it had thrashed down upon him. He couldn't risk the heavy flamer – the blast would have torched the boy too. Instead, he had stowed the weapon in its harness on his back and went hand-to-hand instead. Back braced, his legs arched in a weight lifter's stance, the Salamander heaved. Furrows appeared in the dirt as the creature was forced back, scrabbling ineffectually with its hind legs as it tried to regain balance.

Hot saliva dripped from the creature's mandibles as they snapped for Ba'ken's face. Finding purchase, the chitin dug in and pushed. Its body closed with the Salamander. Ba'ken scowled as the stench of dank and old earth washed over him in a fetid wave. The chitin was about to bite again, aiming to take off the Salamander's face, before Ba'ken spat a stream of acid and seared the creature. Squealing, the chitin's mandibles folded in on each other and retracted into its scalded maw.

The beast was tough, with the bulk and heft of a tank. Ba'ken felt his strength yielding to it and roared to draw on his inner reserves. His secondary heart pumped blood frantically, his body adopting a heightened battle-state, impelling a sudden surge from the Astartes's muscles.

'Xenos scum,' he spat, using hate to fuel his efforts.

A second chitin, just finished gnawing on a settler, emerged on Ba'ken's left flank. The Salamander saw it scuttle into his eye line.

Unarmed, there was no way he could fight them both.

The ragged corpse of the half-devoured settler slumped from the second chitin's maw. Stepping over it, bones crunching under the chitin's weight, the creature advanced upon Ba'ken.

Rushing into its path was Val'in. He swung his shovel madly from left to right in a vain effort to slow the beast.

Ba'ken's face contorted with horror.

'Flee!' he urged. 'Hide, boy!'

Val'in wasn't listening. He stood before the massive chitin bravely, trying to defend his saviour as he had defended him.

'No!' cried Ba'ken, distraught as the chitin loomed.

Explosive impacts rippled down the creature's flank, tearing up chips of carapace and punching holes through flesh. The chitin was spun about from the force of the bolter fire thundering against it. Screeching, grey sludge drooling from its shattered maw, it slumped and was still.

Apion drew close and fired an execution burst into the creature's shrivelled head.

Emek appeared alongside him, smoke drooling from his flamer. 'Cleanse and burn!' he bellowed, then, 'Down, brother!'

With a supreme effort, Ba'ken shoved the creature he was wrestling with. It rolled back onto its haunches as the Salamander dropped into a crouch and fiery prome-thium spewed overhead. Ba'ken felt its heat against his neck, and couldn't resist looking up into the flames that consumed the chitin. His eyes blazed vengefully as the creature was incinerated, its death screams smothered by the weapon's roar.

Ba'ken scowled at the beast, unhitching his heavy flamer before turning and unleashing a torrent of fire into a shambling chitin. Stomping over to a hab-shack, he checked inside and saw several settlers cowering within. They shrank back at the Salamander's sudden appearance.

Ba'ken showed them his palm, his deep voice resonating around the metal dwelling.

'Have no fear,' he told the settlers, before turning to address Val'in. 'In here. Come now,' he said and the boy obeyed, clutching the shovel to his chest as he scampered inside. Ba'ken closed the tin door after him, hoping it would be enough to keep them safe.

In the distance, war was calling. Ba'ken's warrior spirit answered and he hurled himself, flamer blazing, into the fight.

All across the settlement, the Salamanders were gaining the upper hand. The heavy *thunk-thud* of bolters filled the air. The chitin were blasted apart in the storm, chased down by rampant settlers descending murderously on their stricken and wounded attackers.

Illiad was fearless as he led a group of men, Akuma at his side, driving back the creatures with determined lassalvos. Though not as deadly or decisive as the Astartes, they accounted an impressive tally.

Against the combined might of the Astartes and Illiad's well-drilled troops, the chitin did not last long. Unprepared to face such an implacable foe as the Salamanders, what was left of the horde fled into their emergence holes bloodied and battered.

Dak'ir was wiping grey chitin blood from his powered-down chainsword when he saw Akuma spit down one of the emergence holes. Anger was written indelibly on the overseer's face. It turned to despair when he surveyed the destruction around him.

Blood soaked the thoroughfare now and hab-stacks lay crushed or torn open. As Illiad gathered teams to begin collapsing the emergence holes using explosives, a mournful dirge was struck up by the wounded and the grievers for the dead. Wailing infants, some of them now orphans, added their own sorrowful chorus.

One hundred and fifty-four had died in the chitin attack; not all men, not all armed. Another thirty-eight would not live out their injuries. Almost a fifth of the entire human population killed in a single blow.

Silently, the Salamanders helped retrieve the dead.

At one point, Dak'ir saw Brother Apion looking down emptily at a woman clinging to her slain husband. She was unwilling to let go of him as the Salamander tried to take the body and set it upon the growing pyres. In the end she had relinquished him, sobbing deeply.

Illiad lit a flare and ignited the pyres as the last of the dead were accounted for and set to rest. Dak'ir found the custom familiar as he watched the bodies burning and the smoke curling away forlornly through a natural chimney in the cavern roof. The cremation chamber was already blackened and soot gathered in the corners.

Val'in was at the ceremony too, and approached Ba'ken who watched solemnly alongside his brothers.

'Are you a Fire Angel?' asked Val'in, reaching out towards the massive warrior.

Ba'ken, almost three times the boy's height and towering over him, was surprised at the sudden upswell of emotion as Val'in's hand pressed against his greave. Perhaps the boy wanted to make sure he was real.

A part of Ba'ken was deeply saddened at the thought of this innocent knowing something of the terrors of the galaxy, but he was also moved. Val'in was not Astartes: he did not wear power armour or wield a holy bolter; he didn't even carry a lasgun or rifle. He'd had a shovel, and yet he was brave enough to stand in the path of the chitin and not run.

Ba'ken found an answer hard to come by.

'I...'

Dak'ir spoke for him, but to Illiad and not the boy.

'What does the boy mean when he says "Fire Angel"?' he asked.

Illiad's face was set in a look of resignation. The flames from the pyres seemed to deepen the lines on his brow and throw haunting shadows into his eyes. He looked suddenly older.

'I must show you something, Hazon Dak'ir,' he said. 'Will you follow me?'

After a moment, Dak'ir nodded. Perhaps it was at last time for the truth of why the Salamanders had been sent here.

Pyriel stepped forwards, indicating that he would accompany them.

'Ba'ken,' said Dak'ir, facing the massive warrior who still found himself daunted before the boy but managed to look up.

'Brother-sergeant?'

'You have command in my absence. Try to establish contact with the *Vulkan's Wrath* and Sergeant Agatone if you can, though I doubt you'll get a signal through all of this rock.'

'Don't think we need your protection,' snapped Akuma, having overheard the conversation.

Ba'ken turned on him.

'You are stubborn, human,' he growled, though his eyes betrayed his admiration for Akuma's pride and die-hard spirit. 'But the choice isn't yours to make.'

Akuma grumbled something and backed off.

After he'd checked the load of his plasma pistol and secured his chainsword, Dak'ir rested his hand on Ba'ken's pauldron and leaned in to speak into his ear.

'Guard them for me,' he said in a low voice.

'Yes, sergeant,' Bak'en answered, eyes locked with the recalcitrant overseer. 'In Vulkan's name.'

'In Vulkan's name,' Dak'ir echoed, before departing with Pyriel and following Illiad as he led them away from fire and grief.

II
Angels and Monsters

ILLIAD TOOK THEM back down the winding tunnel road to the blast doors of the massive chamber they'd visited before. The bronzed portal was closed again now, its ancient mechanism engaged as soon as they'd left to join the battle.

Dak'ir recalled Pyriel's words as he stared silently at the gate again. The Librarian, standing alongside him, was characteristically inscrutable.

Answers lie within.

Illiad opened the gates once more and this time stepped inside, without waiting to see if the Salamanders followed.

Dak'ir passed through the threshold first, slightly tentative. But all he saw on the other side was a vast, barren room. He watched Illiad approach one of the walls and wipe away the layers of dust and grit that swathed it. Slowly, images were revealed, not unlike cave paintings but inscribed upon bare metal. The renderings were crude, but as Dak'ir approached, drawn inexorably to them, he discerned familiar shapes. He saw stars and metal giants, clad in green armour. Humans were depicted too, emerging from a crashed ship the size of a city. Flames were captured in vivid oranges and reds. In each subsequent interpretation, the ship was slowly being swallowed up by the earth as ash and rock buried it. Beasts came next, the visual history of the colony spreading down the massive walls. First were the chitin, easy to discern with their bulky carapace bodies and claws; then came something else – brutish, broad-backed figures, with dark skins and tusks. The humans were depicted fleeing from them as the metal giants protected them.

'How did you survive down here for so long, Illiad?' Dak'ir's voice echoed, breaking the silence.

Illiad paused in his unearthing of the colony's ancient lore.

'Scoria has deep veins of ore. Fyron, it is called.' He wiped the sweat of his labours from his brow. 'We are miners, generations old. Our ancestors, in their wisdom, realised the ore was combustible. It could be used to keep the reactor running, to charge our weapons and maintain our way of life, such as it is.' His face darkened. 'It was this way for many centuries, so our legends tell us.'

Dak'ir indicated the wall paintings.

'And these are your legends?'

'At first,' Illiad conceded, changing tack. 'Scoria is a hostile place. Our colony is few. One in a generation has the duty to record that generation's history in a log, though much of its formative years are drawn upon these walls. Long ago that task fell to my grandfather, who then passed it on to me after his son, my father, was killed in a cave-in.'

Illiad paused, as if weighing up what to say next.

'Millennia ago, my ancestors came to Scoria, crash landed in a ship that had come from the stars,' he said. 'We were not alone. Giants, armoured in green plate, came with us. Most who now live don't remember who they were. They call them the Fire Angels, for it was said that they were born from the heart of the mountain. This is why Val'in addressed your warrior in this way.'

Dak'ir exchanged a look with Pyriel and the Librarian responded with a slight widening of his eyes.

Fire-born, he thought.

Illiad went on.

'After my ancestors crashed, the Fire Angels tried to return to the stars. Our history does not say why. But their ship was destroyed and terrible storms engulfed the planet. Those that ventured into it, taking the ship's smaller vessels, did not return. The rest remained with us.'

'What happened to these other Fire Angels?' asked Dak'ir.

Illiad's face became grave.

'They were our protectors,' he began simply. 'Until the black rock came, and everything changed. It was thousands of years before I was born. Brutish creatures, like tusked swine and who revelled in war, descended upon Scoria in ramshackle vessels, expelled from the black rock. It eclipsed our sun and in the darkness that followed, the swine made landfall. The stories hold that the Fire Angels fought them off, but at a cost. Every few years, the swine would come back but with greater and greater hordes. Each time the Fire Angels would march out to meet them, and each time they were victorious but less and less of them returned. Inevitably, they dwindled, falling one by one until the last of them retreated underground with my ancestors and sealed themselves in. The last Fire Angel took an oath, to protect my ancestors and pass on the tale of him and his warriors if others like them ever returned to Scoria.

'The years passed and the fate of that last Fire Angel was lost to history, the warriors from beyond the stars committed to mere memory… until now.

'We didn't venture above the earth after that, and the surface of Scoria became lifeless, inhabited only by ghosts. The swine did not return. Some reckon it was because there was no further sport to be had.'

Dak'ir's brow furrowed as he listened intently to Illiad's story.

'You stayed like this… for millennia then?'

'Until several years ago, yes,' Illiad replied. 'The storms that blighted our planet lifted for no reason other than they had run their course. Soon after, the Iron Men came.' Illiad's expression darkened at this memory.

'"Iron Men"?' asked Dak'ir, though he thought he already knew to whom Illiad referred.

'They came from the stars, like you. Thinking they were akin to the Fire Angels, I led a delegation to meet them.' Illiad paused to take a steadying breath and marshal his thoughts. 'Sadly, I was wrong. They laughed at our entreaties, turning their guns upon us. Akuma's wife and son were slain in the massacre. That is why he is so distrustful of you. He cannot see the difference.'

'You say you led the delegation, Illiad. How did you escape from the Iron Men?' asked Dak'ir, keen to learn all that Illiad knew of the Iron Warriors and their forces, for there could be no doubt that it was the sons of Perturabo who had perpetrated the massacre.

Illiad bowed his head. 'I am shamed to say that I fled, just like the rest. They didn't give chase and those who eluded their guns stayed alive. We watched them after that from hidden scopes bored deep beneath the earth.'

Dak'ir remembered the sense of being watched he'd felt outside the wreck of the *Vulkan's Wrath*, and assumed this must have been Illiad or one of his men.

'They built a fortress,' Illiad continued.

'Our brothers have seen it,' Dak'ir told him, 'out in the ash dunes.'

Illiad licked his lips, as if slicking them so the words wouldn't stick in his throat.

'We kept a vigil on it at first, as the walls and towers went up,' he said. 'But the men keeping watch began to act erratically. Two of them committed suicide, so I put a stop to it after that.'

'Your men succumbed to the taint of Chaos,' said Pyriel sternly.

Illiad seemed nonplussed.

'Do you know what the Iron Men are doing in the fortress?' Dak'ir asked in the lull.

'No,' Illiad answered flatly. 'But we encountered them again, this time at the mine where we used to extract the fyron ore. We never got further than their sentries and though they must have known we were there, they seemed disinterested in slaying us.'

Pyriel's silken voice interrupted.

'They come for the ore, and are drilling deep to get it,' he said. The Librarian turned his cold gaze onto the human. Illiad, despite his obvious presence and courage, shrank back before it.

'Where is this mine?' Pyriel asked. 'Our brothers must be told.'

'I can take you there,' Illiad answered, 'but that is not why I brought you here. The legends of the Fire Angels are just tales to protect our young and placate the ignorant. I alone, know the truth.' Illiad turned to Dak'ir. 'You are not the first Fire Angel I have seen. There is another living among us.'

That got the Salamanders' attention. All thoughts of the mine and the Iron Warriors faded into sudden insignificance.

'The duty of recording our history was not the only thing my grandfather passed on to me,' Illiad told them. He moved to the back of the chamber. Dak'ir glanced over at Pyriel but the Librarian's gaze was fixed on the human. 'Wait there,' Illiad called back to them, working at a dust-clogged panel in the far wall.

Dak'ir saw the faint glow of illuminated icons as Illiad pushed them in sequence. A deep rumbling gripped the chamber, and for a moment the Salamander sergeant thought it was another tremor. It was, but not one caused by Scoria's fragile core; instead, it came from the flanking wall.

Stepping back, the Salamanders saw a recessed line emerge in the encrusted metal, spilling out tracts of dirt as a portal formed within it and opened with a hiss of pressure. Old, stale air gusted out from a darkened chamber beyond.

'Until my grandfather showed me this place, I thought the Fire Angels were just a myth. I know now they are very real and lived by a different name,' said Illiad upon reaching them. 'Now, I am the old man and I'm passing on the legacy of my ancestors to you, Salamanders of Vulkan.'

CHAPLAIN ELYSIUS NEVER got his gauntlets dirty during an interrogation. He was fastidious about this, to the point of obsession. This was an Astartes who knew how to inflict pain; agony so invasive and consuming so as to leave no mark, save the one in the victim's psyche.

Watching the partly dismantled Warsmith in the flickering half-light of the cell, Tsu'gan fancied that Elysius could even wrest a confession from one of the tainted.

After the brief battle in the torture chamber-cum-workshop – for Tsu'gan was convinced it was a union of both – the half-conscious Warsmith had been dragged above ground and taken to an abandoned cell in the upper level. There he lay now, as Tsu'gan watched, chained to an iron bench and bleeding from the wounds the Salamander sergeant had given him.

The tools the Chaplain had requested included a pair of chirurgeon-interrogators that he'd had stored in the *Fire Anvil*'s equipment lockers. The creatures, servitor-torturers, had unfolded from their metal slumber like the jagged blades of knives extending. Wiry and grotesque, the interrogators' mechadendrites were fashioned into an array of unpleasant devices, excruciators, designed to inflict maximum pain. Elysius had constructed the servitors in part himself – at least, he had taken the Mechanicus stock and modified them for his own purposes.

'Is this butchery strictly necessary?' asked N'keln, look-ing on from the shadows.

Since the battle to take the fortress and Tsu'gan's squad's near miss in the catacombs, the brother-captain's stock had depleted further. Though no one spoke of it openly, his disastrous command at the gates of the iron fortress was viewed with ever more critical eyes. Tsu'gan could feel the discontent building like a wave, whilst his own standing had been greatly increased, especially in the eyes of Veteran Sergeant Prae-tor. The Firedrake had commended the brother-sergeant several times for his valour and strategy. Undoubtedly, it was Tsu'gan that had prevented further deaths and restored parity in the battle.

'I can break him, brother-captain,' Elysius replied. The Chaplain stood back, directing his chirurgeon-interrogators expertly.

'Have you even asked him anything yet, Brother-Chaplain?' said N'keln.

The Warsmith's bionic arm had been removed and dismantled, bloodily. His right arm had been severed and the wound cauterised so that he wouldn't fall unconscious from blood loss. Nor would he be able to morph a weapon from his flesh. Stripped of his body armour, the injuries Tsu'gan had dealt him were visible as a dense patch of welts and purple bruises. Elysius had allowed the Iron Warrior to keep his battle-helm on, for it was his belief that none should look upon the face of a traitor. Let him hide it in shame.

'I am about to,' the Chaplain hissed, a little strained under his captain's scrutiny. After Elysius had issued a sub-vocal command, the chirurgeon-interrogators retreated, taking their blades, their wires and their torches with them. The stench of burned flesh and old copper wafted over to Tsu'gan and the other onlookers, which included Captain N'keln and Brother Iagon.

Tsu'gan's second had requested he be allowed to observe the Chaplain's techniques. Most within the company, like N'keln for instance, found Elysius's methods distasteful, at the same time acknowledging their necessity. Iagon, it seemed, did not, and since Tsu'gan saw no reason to prevent him, he allowed the battle-brother to bear audience with him.

The shadow of Chaplain Elysius fell across the traitor like a deathly veil.

'What precisely were you constructing in the vault?' he asked simply.

Burned copiously, the vault had been resealed again following Techmarine Draedius's analysis. He had yet to ascertain the exact nature of the weapon.

Something fell and evil lurked in the darkness below their feet. Tsu'gan had felt it all the while he was down there and had no desire to reacquaint himself with it. More than once, he had fought the urge to take out his combat knife and press it against his flesh. He knew whatever malign presence lurked in the fortress's lower levels was just preying on his inner guilt and the manifestation of that guilt in his addictive masochism.

The Iron Warrior laughed, breaking Tsu'gan's reverie. It was a hollow, metallic sound that echoed around the small cell like a discordant bell chime.

'What did it look like to you, lapdog of the False Emperor?'

It was a small gesture – like the twitch of one of Elysius's fingers – that brought one of the chirugeon-interrogators forward. Something happened, hidden by the servitor's body, and the Iron Warrior shuddered and grunted.

'Again,' ordered the Chaplain in a low voice. There was a pause and the Iron Warrior shuddered for a second time. Smoke issued from his flesh, though Tsu'gan couldn't see its source. The Iron Warrior laughed again.

But it was pained laughter this time and when he spoke, his voice was cracked and hissing.

'A weapon…' The breath wheezed in and out of his lungs.

'We know that.' Elysius went to order the chirurgeon-interrogator for a third time.

'A seismic cannon…' gasped the Iron Warrior.

Tsu'gan knew of no such weapon. Had this warband somehow acquired knowledge of an undiscovered standard template construct? It seemed impossible. Still thinking on it, the brother-sergeant detected the faintest tremor of movement in the Chaplain. The chirurgeon-interrogator retreated.

'How long have you been on this world?' Elysius asked, deliberately altering the course of his questioning to try and disorientate the prisoner.

'Almost a decade,' the Iron Warrior rasped, as if his breath were raking against his throat.

'Why are your brothers dead?'

'Killed in battle, of course!' Sudden rage gave the Iron Warrior strength and for the first time he struggled against his chains.

Bonds of loyalty and brotherhood were still strong, Tsu'gan considered, even in traitors.

Elysius struck the Iron Warrior's ruined chest with the flat of his palm. It was a hard blow that pushed the air from the traitor's lungs and smashed him against the bench.

'By what or whom?' demanded the Chaplain, patience thinning.

The Iron Warrior took a few seconds to catch a ragged breath.

'They will come again, the ones that bested my brothers,' he said, his yellow lenses flashing maliciously. 'Very soon, much too soon for you to save yourselves…' A clicking sound scraped from his mouth, growing steadily faster and louder. The Iron Warrior was laughing again.

Elysius was about to send the chirurgeon-interrogators forwards when Sergeant Lok interrupted them. The veteran was in command of the outer defences and the wall, and had rushed in from outside.

'Captain,' he uttered sternly, his face grave.

N'keln gestured for him to give his report.

'It is the sun, my lord,' Lok began.

'What of it, sergeant?'

'It has been partially eclipsed.'

N'keln was taken aback.

'By what?' he asked.

Tsu'gan felt fresh tension suddenly enter the cell. Lok's tone suggested he had seen something that troubled him. For a veteran of Ymgarl, such a reaction was not to be treated lightly.

'A black rock, as large as the sun,' he said. 'Parts of it are breaking off. Many parts.'

'Explain yourself, Lok,' demanded N'keln. 'Are they meteors?'

'They are moving erratically, and at different speeds. More and more fragment each minute.'

N'keln scowled, reaching for his bolter instinctively. They all knew what was coming next.

'Whatever they are,' said Lok, 'they're headed for Scoria.'

'*And with the dark comes a swarm of war, and beneath it the sun shall die,*' Elysius intoned, now facing Lok.

Grating laughter issued from behind him.

'You're too late,' croaked the Iron Warrior. 'Your doom has come…'

ILLIAD STEPPED AWAY from the recently opened portal, bowing his head in reverence.

It was difficult to see within; the gloom was thick and a pall of disturbed dust hung in the air like a grey veil. Dak'ir was aware of his primary heart thundering in his chest. It was not because he was about to go into battle; it was excitement and something approaching fear that gripped him as he stood before the threshold to the room. He turned to look at Pyriel.

'Your lead, brother-sergeant,' he said, a faint cerulean glow limning his eyes as he used his witch-sight to better penetrate the half-dark.

Dak'ir muttered a litany to Vulkan and stepped forwards. A few metres into the chamber and he saw musty-looking consoles, veneered by dirt. Cables hung down from the ceiling like the tendrils of some unseen sea plant. Brushing them aside with careful sweeps of his hand, Dak'ir half expected to be stung. His entire body seemed numb, yet electrified at the same time. The pounding cadence of his heart smothered the echoing report of his boot steps against the metal floor. He was only dimly aware of the presence of Pyriel behind him. The Librarian kept at around a metre's distance, surveying the murky surroundings slowly and cautiously.

It was like descending into a dream.

At last, the hanging cables gave way to a metal esplanade. Dak'ir recognised the symbol embossed in its centre. Though weathered and evidently damaged during the crash, the icon of the Firedrakes was discernible.

A set of stairs led off from the esplanade. Dak'ir followed their trajectory with his gaze. There, at the summit, his eye alighted on a command throne and the figure sitting in it.

Half-shrouded in shadows, details were hard to see, but the armour the figure wore looked old and massive.

Dak'ir reached out a hand without realising. His heart had actually stopped beating for a second of time that felt like minutes. When he spoke, his voice was little more than an awe-struck whisper and he felt an overwhelming compulsion to sink to knees.

'Primarch…'

CHAPTER NINE

I

Black Rock, Green Tide

Tsu'gan joined Lok and the others on the wall. N'keln was handed a pair of magnoculars by the veteran sergeant and he peered up at the dark shape blighting the sky.

An almost penumbral cast had engulfed Scoria, the ash deserts made supernatural in its eerie lustre. The sun was all but gone, little more than a dwindling sickle of yellow light swallowed in the maw of something black and massive. An odd sense of stillness had fallen and Tsu'gan felt that niggle at the back of his mind again, as if he was down in the lower levels once more.

He detected the same tremor of unease in his brothers standing alongside him on the wall. Only Chaplain Elysius had stayed in the cell, intent on his prisoner. The rest had followed Lok outside to bear witness to the coming of something terrible.

Tsu'gan's eyes narrowed.

'What is it?' he asked.

Dark slivers were peeling off the black object steadily blotting out the sun, gradually forming a cloud that arrowed towards the planet.

N'keln handed the sergeant the magnoculars.

'See for yourself,' he replied grimly.

Though the magnoculars didn't have the range to penetrate beyond the planet's outer atmosphere, they did
reveal the black shape to be a massive asteroid. The dark
slivers, like fragments of its body, were in fact ships.
Details were hard to discern but Tsu'gan managed to
make out the ramshackle design of the nearest vessels.
They moved at speed, spilling plumes of black smoke,
engines roaring fire. There could be no mistaking the
nature of the enemy closing on them.

Tsu'gan scowled as he lowered the magnoculars.

'Orks.'

A RUSH OF activity greeted Tsu'gan's revelation. Extrapo-
lating the sheer numbers of greenskins heading towards
them from the ships breaking off from the black rock,
N'keln had ordered the fortress to be re-fortified at once.

Techmarine Draedius set about constructing a
makeshift gate that would be further reinforced by the
Land Raider and one of the company's Rhinos. All Salamanders were mustered at once and squad sergeants
barked clipped orders to their troopers, who assumed
defensive positions along the wall. Some undertook
their oaths of moment, swearing muttered litanies as
icons of the hammer and the flame were pressed to lips.

Though the ramparts were chipped and in varying
stages of ruination from the Salamanders' earlier battery,
they were still defensible. The automated guns had all
been destroyed. It mattered little. Despite their
pragmatism, no Salamander would ever turn to the
weapons of the Traitor Legions for deliverance. Instead,
N'keln ordered the three Devastator squads to occupy
the chewed-up gun towers. With four towers in total, the
last post went to Clovius and his Tactical squad due to
the nature of their weaponry. The towers provided a

serviceable vantage point, even though a long-range view was impossible due to how the fortress was situated in the ash basin.

Sergeant Vargo's depleted Assault squad and Veteran Sergeant Praetor's Firedrakes were kept in the outer courtyard just beyond the gate as reserves. The Terminators were too bulky to climb the shallow stairways leading up to the wall, so had to content themselves as guardians of the inner keep. That left two Tactical squads, those of Sergeants De'mas and Typhos, strung out across the wall with Captain N'keln and two of his Inferno Guard, Shen'kar and Malicant. The company standard bearer unfurled his banner proudly and it snapped in the growing wind. It seemed a long time since it had last been upraised, but it instantly lifted the spirits of all who saw it. The last of the troops on the wall were a combat squad, led by Battle-Brother S'tang. The other half of the combat squad were operating outside of the fortress, climbing the ridge that would allow them to see much farther across the ash plain and report the enemy's movements back to their brother-captain.

An arid wind was blowing off the ash desert, kicking up gritty drifts that painted the Salamanders' armour a dull grey. The view through Brother Tiberon's magnoculars was grainy in the building storm, but Tsu'gan could see the approach of vehicles by their spewed smoke and the displaced ash gusting away from them. The cloud was massive, hugging the horizon in a dense, black pall. The air that came with it was redolent of oil, dung and beast-sweat.

'Must be hundreds of vehicles amidst all of that,' offered Lazarus, lying flat on his stomach on his sergeant's right.

'More like thousands,' Tsu'gan corrected, muttering. He handed the magnoculars back to Tiberon on the opposite side of him.

'Anything yet?' Tsu'gan asked Iagon, who was in a slightly more advanced position scrutinising his auspex. He had set it to its maximum wave band and the widest possible area array. The signals coming back were intermittent and hazy.

'No accurate readings,' he reported through the commfeed in a clipped voice. 'Could be environmental interference, or there could simply be too many for the device to calculate.'

'There's a sobering thought,' replied Honorious, crouching just behind his sergeant and trying to keep the grit out of his flamer's igniter nozzle.

Tsu'gan ignored him and looked back over his shoulder. It had taken around half an hour to cover the distance from the fortress gate to the summit of the ridge, over uneven ground and on foot. Encumbered in power armour and fully armed, Tsu'gan reckoned they needed to leave at least twenty minutes for a return trip. He planned to mine part of the ridge, using all of the frag grenades he had left. It might not slow the greenskins to any great degree, but it would give them a sting they weren't expecting.

Above them the yellow sun had become a pale, convex line. In the conditions of the partial solar eclipse, it was difficult to pinpoint the exact time of day. Tsu'gan's rough calculation put it at around late afternoon. Judging by the speed of the approaching dust cloud, he reckoned the orks would reach them in less than an hour. Around an hour later and the sun would have set and total darkness would engulf the desert. He resolved to wire some photon flares and blind grenades amongst the redoubts before they returned behind the fortress walls.

'No way through that,' said Tiberon, interrupting Tsu'gan's thoughts, peering through the magnoculars. 'I hope to Vulkan that Agatone isn't facing a similar horde.'

The troops left guarding the *Vulkan's Wrath* were neither as numerous nor as well-defended as those at the fortress. They were also hindered by masses of injured crewmen. It left them and the strike cruiser vulnerable to attack. Tsu'gan had wanted to lead a band of reinforcements to bolster his brothers, but N'keln had forbidden it. All they could do was warn them to expect the enemy. It was scant consolation.

'Whatever augurs the orks use will draw them to the crashed ship,' Tsu'gan answered Tiberon. 'But they'll be scavenger warbands, hoping for easy pickings. The bigger bastards will be coming here. Orks go where the best fight is. They'll remember the bloody nose given to them at the fortress and will return to it, eager to settle the score. Even if it's against us and not the traitors.' He turned to look straight at Tiberon. 'Don't worry, brother,' Tsu'gan added in a feral tone. 'There'll be plenty for us to kill.

IT WASN'T VULKAN who sat upon the throne before him.

Dak'ir realised this as he approached the recumbent Salamander, having climbed halfway up the stairs. But the Fire-born sitting there *was* old, ancient in fact. His armour harked back to the halcyon era of the Great Crusade, when all Space Marines had been brothers in arms and a new age of prosperity and oneness was in prospect for the galaxy. Those dreams were as dust now, just like the ashen patina that veiled the old Salamander in front of Dak'ir.

The venerable warrior bore the Legion markings of a trooper. His antiquated power armour was a deeper green than that of Dak'ir's. It had a Mark V Heresy-pattern design with its studded pauldron and greaves. The helmet was similarly attired and sat next to the Salamander's boot where he had set it down but never reclaimed it.

A glow behind Dak'ir, emitted psychically from Pyriel's hand, revealed the old Salamander's leathery skin, his battle-weathered face and thinly cropped hair the colour of silver wire. His eyes, where once a fire had burned with the fury of war, were dulled but not without life. He faced away from both Dak'ir and Pyriel, visible in side profile. He also appeared to be staring at something concealed from their view by the bulkhead columns of the dilapidated bridge, for there could be no doubt that this was the part of the ship where they now found themselves.

Dak'ir wondered briefly how long the Salamander had been sitting like that. It seemed to him a desolate charge that the ancient had undertaken.

Reaching the top of the stairs, Dak'ir followed the seated warrior's eye line and felt a slight tremor of shock.

The wall of the bridge had broken away, presumably destroyed when the ship had crash-landed, to reveal another chamber through the ragged tear in the metal. Though it was dark inside, Dak'ir's occulobe implant utilised all of the ambient light to discern a natural cavern. Within he saw row upon row of Astartes battle-plate. Salamanders all, these husks of former Fireborn were arranged in serried ranks. There were fifty in total, ten files and five Space Marines deep. The armour was empty and supported by metal frames so that the warriors stood to attention proudly in parade formation. Each one matched the style and age of the old Salamander's battle-plate and was gouged and battered.

Dak'ir noticed that one or two of the suits had toppled over, due to the rigours of time or the capriciousness of nature. He saw a helmet landed on its side, resting near the boot of its owner. Here and there a bullet-holed pauldron had slipped, to sag forlornly near a suit's elbow joint.

Looking back at the old Salamander, Dak'ir was filled with a tremendous sense of sadness. He had watched his brothers stoically for millennia, keeping vigil until such a time as someone else took up his mantle or he could perform his duty no more.

'How is this possible?' hissed Dak'ir, unsure if the old Salamander was even still cognisant enough to be aware of their presence. 'If his ship is indeed from Isstvan, he must be thousands of years old.'

'A fact we cannot be certain of,' Pyriel replied. 'Obviously, he has been here for some time. Whether that period extends to millennia we cannot know. The armour is old, but still worn by some in the Chapter today. The ship itself could simply be a reclaimed Expeditionary vessel, re-fitted and re-appropriated by the Adeptus Mechanicus.'

Dak'ir faced the Librarian.

'Is that what you believe, Pyriel?'

Pyriel returned a side glance at the sergeant.

'I don't know what I believe at this point,' he admitted. 'The warp storms could have affected the passage of time. But it's also entirely possible that this Salamander is simply many years old, longevity being a benefit of our slow metabolic rate. Such a thing has never been tested, given that most of our number invariably meet their end in war or, if death is not forthcoming and age arrives first, by wandering out into the Scorian Plain or setting sail on the Acerbian Sea to find peace. It is the way of the Promethean Creed.'

Pyriel shone the corona of psychic fire around his hand a little closer so they could get a better look at the old Salamander. The light reflected off the warrior's eyes, turning them a cerulean blue.

The old Salamander blinked.

Dak'ir almost took an involuntary step back, but marshalled his sudden shock as the old Salamander spoke.

'Brothers...' he croaked in a voice like cracking leather that suggested he hadn't spoken in some time.

Dak'ir approached the old Salamander.

'I am Brother-Sergeant Hazon Dak'ir of the Salamanders' 3rd Company,' he said, before introducing the Librarian. 'You have been on watch duty for a long time, brother.'

Dak'ir knew he needed to be careful. If this ancient warrior before them really did hark back to a time before the Heresy, if he was a survivor of the Dropsite Massacre, then much had changed that he would be unaware of. They needed answers but any unnecessary information might only serve to confuse him at this point.

'Brother Gravius...' The ancient Salamander tailed off, his precise disposition within the old Legion deserting him. 'And yes,' he started anew, seeming to recall that he had been asked a question. 'I have been sitting here for many years.'

'How did you come to be here on Scoria, Brother Gravius?'

The venerable Salamander paused, frowning as he dredged through old memories. 'A storm...' he began, the words starting to come easier as he remembered how to articulate himself. 'We... withdrew from battle, our enemies in pursuit...' Gravius's face hardened and drew back into an angry snarl. 'Betrayers...' he spat, before lucidity failed him again and his features slackened.

'Was it Isstvan V, brother?' said Pyriel. 'Is that where you journeyed from?'

Gravius screwed up his face again, trying to remember.

'I... see fragments,' he said. 'Impressions only... disjointed in my mind.' He seemed to look past the two Salamanders in front of him.

Dak'ir thought Gravius was gazing into space, when the old Salamander slowly raised his arm from the side of the throne and pointed a finger. Dak'ir turned to see what Gravius was gesturing at. It looked like an old pict-viewer, some kind of ancient data-recording device half smothered by millennia of dirt.

Exchanging a glance with Pyriel, the brother-sergeant descended the stairs and went over to the pict-viewer. Dak'ir knew that many ships kept visual logs as the basis for battle simulations or to chart the progress of a campaign for future reference. Gravius had indicated that this device might contain the log of his ship and with it some clue as to its provenance.

Though it had been broken apart, Illiad and his men had fed power to some areas of the vessel. Dak'ir hoped that this was one of them. Even so, he expected nothing as he activated the pict-viewer and lines of snowdrift interference appeared on the dust-swathed screen.

Using his gauntlet, Dak'ir smeared the worst of the grime away just as an image was resolving in the small square frame. There was no sound; perhaps the vox-emitters no longer functioned, or perhaps the audio was not recorded along with the visuals. The point was moot.

Though the image was grainy and badly marred by constant static, Dak'ir recognised the bridge, as it must have been before the crash. The scene was frantic. Fire had taken hold of some of the operational consoles – Dak'ir looked over to them as they were now and saw a hint of heat-blackening underneath their grey veneer – and several crewmen were lying on the deck, presumably dead. They wore grey uniforms that bore an uncanny resemblance to the attire of Illiad and the settlers. Most were shouting – their voiceless panic, the half-realised terror in their faces, was disturbing.

Dak'ir saw Salamanders, too. The throne was shrouded in shadows, but the bulk of the armour was clear, the flash of fire and warning lights illuminating it just long enough for the brother-sergeant to make the connection. Several of the Astartes were injured too. The image was shaking badly, as if the bridge itself was being subjected to a fierce ordeal. No one addressed the recording, and Dak'ir assumed, with a fist of lead in his stomach, that the captain of the ship had ordered it switched on to capture the last moments of him and his crew. He had not expected to survive the crash.

There was a particularly violent tremor and the screen went blank. Dak'ir waited to see if there was any more, but there the recording ended.

A grim mood had settled over the ruined bridge, quashing the earlier excitement and optimism that Dak'ir had felt. Another tremor rocked the chamber, sending a pauldron crashing nosily to the ground and shaking the brother-sergeant out of his dark introspection.

He exchanged a look with Pyriel.

If the quakes did indeed presage a cataclysm that threatened the planet itself, as the Librarian had predicted, then Brother Gravius and the battle-suits needed to be moved, and quickly. Perhaps, upon returning to Nocturne and under the Chapter Master's guidance on Prometheus, the secrets within Gravius's shattered mind could be unlocked. If this was what the Salamanders had been sent to find – their prize – then all efforts must be made to recover them intact. Not only that, but Illiad and his settlers would need to be rescued too. The pict-recording of the ship's final log had cemented in Dak'ir's mind that the ancestors Illiad had spoken of were in fact the ship's original crew and he and his people their descendants.

The revelation was remarkable. Against all the odds, they had endured, creating for themselves a microcosm of Nocturnean society here on ill-fated Scoria.

The visions Dak'ir had experienced earlier, just before the tectonic shift had revealed the chasm into the subterranean realm, came back to him. On a strange, almost instinctual level, it confirmed to Dak'ir that Scoria was doomed and that its demise was soon to be at hand.

Yes, all would need to be delivered from the fires of the planet's inevitable destruction. There was just the small matter of the *Vulkan's Wrath* half-buried in the ash desert, and without the means to break free of it. If this was the primarch's will, a part of his prophecy etched in the Tome of Fire, then Dak'ir hoped that salvation would present itself soon.

The brother-sergeant's gaze flicked over to Gravius.

'Can you arise, brother?' Are you able to walk?' he asked.

'I cannot,' Gravius answered with regret.

Pyriel touched a hand to the venerable brother's greave and shut his eyes. He opened them a moment later, the cerulean glow still fading.

'His armour is completely seized,' said the Librarian. 'Fused to the throne. His muscles have likely atrophied by now, too.'

'Can we move him?'

'Not unless you want his limbs to break off as we attempt it,' Pyriel replied grimly.

'This is my post,' Gravius rasped. His breath reeked of slow decay and stale air. 'My duty. I should have died long ago, brothers. If Scoria is to expire, become dust in the vastness of the universe, then so must I.'

Dak'ir paused, as he tried in vain to think of some other solution. In the end he clenched his fist in frustration, Pyriel looking on patiently. His tone betrayed his anger and frustration to the Librarian.

'We return for the armour, and report back our findings to Brother-Sergeant Agatone. We must be ready when we have a way to leave this accursed rock.'

Tsu'gan returned to the battlements of the iron fortress just in time to see the first explosions tear into the orks.

A series of fiery, grey blooms rippled in a line before the greenskins' advance, chewing up footsoldiers and wrecking their ramshackle vehicles. Implacably, the orks marched over the debris of bodies and twisted metal, the carnage only seeming to increase their lust for battle.

Through the magnoculars, Tsu'gan saw several of the greenskins pause to kill off their wounded brethren and remove their tusks or strip them of wargear or boots. 'Filthy scavengers,' he snarled, regarding the massive horde of green.

Inwardly, he cursed the fact their forces were divided before such a massive host. Consolidation was needed now, not division. Yet, they could not simply abandon the *Vulkan's Wrath*, nor her crew. At any account, there could be no envoys sent to the rest of their brothers – nothing could get through the green tide arrayed against them and live.

The creatures mobbed in indistinct groups that the brother-sergeant likened to rough approximations of battalions or platoons. Each mob was led by a massive chieftain, usually riding a battered wagon, buggy or truck; all bolted metal, hammered plate and the bastardised components of enemy vehicle salvage. Tsu'gan assumed the beasts' ships, the ones that had brought them to the surface, had landed farther off in the ash dunes and were beyond the reach of the magnoculars.

At least the falling slivers, peeling off the black rock like bullet-nosed hail, had abated.

Fights broke out intermittently amongst the orks. Their diminutive cousins – cruel, rangy creatures known as gretchin – lingered at the periphery of such brawls, hoping for scraps, an opportunity to defile the loser or simply to hoot and bray for more carnage. Often these lesser greenskins would be seized during the indiscriminate and seemingly random affrays and used in lieu of a club to bludgeon an opponent with bloody consequences for both.

Orks were a breed of xenos that lived solely to fight. Their behaviour was largely inscrutable to the Imperium, for the creatures possessed no discernible method that any tacticus logi or adeptus strategio had ever qualified. The aliens' predisposition towards battle was obvious in their musculature and build, however. Trunk-necked, their skin as tough as a flak jacket, they were hard beasts to kill. Broad shouldered with thick bones and still thicker craniums, they stood as tall as an Astartes in power armour and were also his match in strength and raw aggression. The ork's only real weakness was in discipline, but nothing focused a greenskin's mind like the prospect of a fight against a hardy foe like the Space Marines.

Judging by the sheer mass of green approaching them, Tsu'gan knew this would be one battle not easily won.

Discipline and loyalty, Tsu'gan reconsidered. *The greenskins have no loyalty to speak of; they possess no sense of duty to guide them.* Yes, 'loyalty' – *that is our strength, that is our...* His thoughts tailed off.

'How many?' asked Brother Tiberon.

Ever since they had fallen back in good order from the advancing greenskins, the horde's numbers had increased. Tsu'gan had related his best estimates to the forces in the iron fortress, but suspected they were now wildly conservative.

Brother-sergeant and combat squad had rejoined the rest of their battle-brothers on the wall, two sections down from where N'keln and his entourage were positioned. Iagon caught Tsu'gan's errant gaze as he looked away from the magnoculars to regard his brother-captain.

This battle will either forge or break him, was the unspoken exchange between them.

Brother Lazarus seemed to pick up on the vibrations between Iagon and his brother-sergeant. All in Tsu'gan's

squad shared their leader's desire to see N'keln no longer
at the head of 3rd Company.

That is not disloyalty, Tsu'gan told himself, still unsettled by his previous thoughts, It is duty – for the good of
the company and the Chapter.

'If he falters,' said Lazarus in a low voice, 'then Praetor
will step in. You can be sure of that.'

Then the way will be clear for another...

It was almost as if Tsu'gan could read the thoughts in
Iagon's earlier expression.

Tsu'gan had his battle-helm mag-locked to his harness, preferring to feel the growing wind on his face and
hear the bestial roars of the greenskins without them
being distorted through the resonance of his armour. He
narrowed his eyes as if trying to fathom his captain's
demeanour.

'Let the fires of war judge him,' he said in the end.
'That is the Promethean way.'

Tsu'gan turned to Tiberon, the deep-throated bellows
of the greenskins growing louder by the second.

'There are thousands, now, brother,' he uttered in
answer to Tiberon's earlier question. 'More than my eye
could see.'

In the wake of the dissipating smoke from the hidden
grenade line, the orks stopped. Night was falling across
the ash desert, just as Tsu'gan had predicted. The infighting amongst the greenskins ceased abruptly. They were
intent on the killing now, on the destruction of the Salamanders.

In the fading light, the orks began to posture, slowly
stirring themselves up into a war frenzy.

Chieftains jutted out their chins, like slabs of greenish
rock. Their skin was darker than the rest and swathed in
scars like that of their minders, who roamed protectively
around them. The darker an ork's skin, the bigger it usually was and the older and more dominant. Irrespective

of their brutish hierarchy, the orks began to beat their armoured chests, clashing fat-bladed cleavers and axes against scale, chain and flak. They hollered and roared, discharging their noisy guns into the air, creating a pall of rancid smoke from the cheap powder.

Tsu'gan could feel the energy within the creatures building. He was no psyker like Pyriel, but he still recognised the resonance of its effects. Orks generated this energy when in large groups and it was magnified when they fought. It prickled at the Salamander's skin, made his teeth itch and his head throb. Tsu'gan put on his battle-helm. The time for soaking in the coming battle's atmosphere was over.

The orks began to roar in unison, and Tsu'gan sensed an end to the savage ritual was near. Though their brutish tongue was virtually unintelligible, the brother-sergeant could still discern the meaning in their crude, bellowed words.

'DA BOSS! DA BOSS! DA BOSS!'

Flurries of ash came spilling down the ridge as if fleeing, disturbed by the passage of something large and indomitable.

Through the ranks of green, a huge ork emerged. It battered its way to the front of the horde, clubbing any greenskin that dared get in its way with a clenched power fist that rippled with black lightning. Unlike the Astartes' power fists, this orkish device was akin to a massive, plated claw and bore talons instead of fingers. Not only was it a deadly weapon that left any greenskins it struck bludgeoned to death, it was also a sign of prestige, as limpid as any rank insignia or Chapter honour a Space Marine might carry.

The beast wore a horned helmet with a curtain of chainmail hanging from the back and sides. Its armour looked to be some form of mesh-carapace amalgam, daubed with glyphs and tribal tattoos, though Tsu'gan thought he caught the glint of power servos in the ork's protective panoply. Its boots were thick and black, dusted by ash that collected in the armoured ribs of metal greaves. Grisly trophies dangled from its neck like macabre jewellery: bleached skulls, gnawed-upon bones and the chewed-out husks of helmets. Dark, iron torques banded its bulging wrist and arm; the other was taken up with the power claw. A thick belt girdled the ork's even broader girth and was heavy with a bulky pistol and chained-toothed axe.

Miniscule eyes, pitiless and red, held only menace and the promise of violence.

Tsu'gan felt his face tighten into a scowl. He would only be too happy to oblige the beast in that regard.

Satisfied that its presence had been properly noted, the giant ork threw back its head and roared.

'*WAAARRRGH BOSS!*'

'The beast establishes its dominance.' Brother Lazarus's voice had a sneering tone to it as he watched the display.

'No,' Tsu'gan corrected him, 'it is a call to war and blood.'

II
The Last Redoubt

PHOTON FLARES BLAZED into the steadily thickening night like forlorn beacons in a black sea. They threw a red cast over the slow march of the orks that tinted them the colour of blood. Magnesium bursts followed as the blind grenades Tsu'gan and his combat squad had set up went off. The orks howled and bellowed in pain as their eyes were flooded with harsh, angry light. Those who were closest stumbled into their brethren – some were slain by their belligerent cousins, others struck out and killed the greenskins in their path, swiping in wild agony.

The disruption was minimal. Many orks, upon witnessing the effects of the blind grenades, drew down bug-eyed goggles or simply shaded their eyes with a meaty hand.

Confusion wasn't the only purpose for the bank of flares; the Salamanders used the percussive glow like a search light. Ork clan leaders were identified in the pellucid bursts and executed with accurate bolter shots. Brief internecine skirmishes broke out until another ork established its dominance, but it gave more time for the heavy bolters to reap a bloodier toll. Lead vehicles were pinpointed and destroyed by multi-meltas or missile launchers, causing fiery pileups in those following in column behind them. Trucks and buggies mangled together in a twisted metal embrace, as their dazed crews were shot dead crawling from the wrecks.

The greenskins responded in kind. Random fire came from their long range weapons but to no effect, save chipping rockcrete or kicking up clods of ash. Orks were not built for shooting, their efforts were half-hearted at best. They did it more to hear the guns go off, the *thud-bang* and the stink of expelled smoke, than to actually kill anything. Orks preferred to fight close up, where they could smell the blood and fear.

The beasts will find little of the first and none of the second from us, Tsu'gan thought.

The orks were close now and the brother-sergeant knew the order to unleash a firestorm was close too. Crackling static in his ear over the comm-feed gave way to Captain N'keln's voice, and Tsu'gan realised that order was at hand.

Salamanders were pragmatic, not as given to lofty speeches and rousing rhetoric as some of their distant cousins, such as the Ultramarines. The fact made N'keln's speech comparatively epic.

'Sons of Vulkan, Fire-born all, this is our last redoubt. There is no line beyond this wall, no further gate to defend or keep to garrison. This is it. I have but one edict: None shall pass.' He punctuated each and every word. 'Into the fires of battle!' cried N'keln, as his voice became many. 'Unto the anvil of war!' the Salamanders chorused.

'Let them close,' uttered Tsu'gan to his squad. Across the battlements, sergeants were priming their troops in the wake of the captain's speech.

Sighting down his bolter's targeter, Tsu'gan felt a presence behind him and turned to see Elysius appearing on their section of the wall.

'You have missed the start of the battle, brother,' Tsu'gan offered wryly.

The Chaplain snorted with derision.

'I have missed the parlay, you mean, brother-sergeant.' By his tone, it was difficult to tell whether or not Elysius was serious. Tsu'gan would find out later if his idle remark had been taken in jest.

'*The xenos are a stain upon the galaxy,*' the Chaplain intoned, zealotry affecting his timbre as he lowered his voice. '*Let them burn in the fires of retribution.*'

Eyes flashing with hate, Elysius ignited his crozius and pointed it in the direction of the onrushing horde.

Tsu'gan sighted down the targeter again. 'Unleash hell!'

It was as if all the sergeants were somehow synchronised or linked by empathy as weapons fire erupted across the wall in unison. Muzzle flashes ripped down the battlements of the iron fortress in a fiery wave, the resultant din like thunder. Greenskins were torn apart in the brutal bolter salvo, the explosive shells wreaking terrible havoc even amongst creatures as tough as orks. Exhorted by threats and the bellows of their captains, the beasts weathered it, trudging over the chewed-up remains of their kin implacably and without remorse. Some fled – those whose nerve had broken, or who'd lost their captains to enemy fire or infighting – they were met mercilessly with a cleaver or axe upon reaching the line of green still poised at the apex of the ridge. For this was just a first wave.

'Bolter fodder,' growled Tiberon, over the comm-feed. It was difficult to be heard above the roar of gunfire, though Chaplain Elysius managed it with his scathing diatribes and xenophobic tirades. Pistols and flamers were still out of range, as the orks had yet to close, so he directed each caustic utterance like a bullet aimed to kill.

The side of Tsu'gan's battle helm lit up as Brother M'lek fired his multi-melta. The hungry beam burned a hole through an advancing ork truck, cooking its engine and turning it into a white fireball that engulfed several foot sloggers rushing alongside it.

The brother-sergeant paused to commend M'lek's fine shooting, before addressing Tiberon.

'That is why we must break them, brother, and maintain our strength for the real fight to come.'

Tsu'gan gunned down a chieftain's armoured bodyguard, turning its skull into bone fragments and red vapour as the bolter round entered its eye and exploded outwards. He saw only one ork battle leader in the midst of the fighting, and judging from the clan markings of the greenskins barrelling towards them, this was its tribe. Perhaps the claw-armed warboss on the ridge was letting his subordinates take turns at trying to crack open the iron fortress.

'Let them come,' Tsu'gan hissed belligerently. He took aim again and executed the chieftain itself, who had strayed too close to the fight. 'They'll die by my hand,' he concluded grimly.

With the death of their tribal leader, the orks faltered. A bloody killing field had materialised in the no-man's-land before the wall; the greenskins in the first wave, despite their efforts, having been unable to get close enough to launch a meaningful assault upon it.

Seeing this, up on the ridge, the warboss bellowed his anger. Sweeps of his brawny arm sent the other tribes forwards, one after the other. Orks in their thousands charged at the Salamanders. Their tribal chieftains hooted and roared, eager for their clans to be the first to reach the enemy. The swell of the greenskins' brutish voices rose into a clamour.

Tsu'gan felt the dull nagging at the back of his head again, the sensation of being in the tunnel below the iron hall. The feeling of cold metal against his forehead where he'd pressed the bolter's mouth returned. Nascent psychic energy from the orks was building. Perhaps it was somehow fuelling whatever lurked in the darkness beneath the fortress.

Elysius's voice responded to it, became the anchor once more to keep the Salamanders grounded. In their multitudes, the orks had got beyond the killing field and were readying for a first assault against the wall. The Chaplain used the bark of his bolt pistol to punctuate his spite-filled sermons, whilst all across the battlements flamers spewed with promethium fury.

'Cleanse and burn!' roared Honorious, as his faceplate was lit by his weapon's fiery glow.

Despite the Space Marines' strategic acquisition of targets, and their spoiling tactics, the sheer mass of greenskins meant a close-up battle was inevitable. That suited the Salamanders well.

'Here is where your mettle shall be tested,' cried N'keln, his voice clear as a silver spear thrown in sunlight, resonating through the comm-feed. 'Be the anvil, become the hammer!'

The effect was galvanising.

'Judged in the fires of battle…' remarked Lazarus with genuine admiration.

Iagon stayed silent, focused on slaying the approaching orks with angry bursts of his bolter.

'Hold them here,' snarled Tsu'gan, steeling his squad as he knew his brother-sergeants would be too. 'We knew this was coming,' he added, as the first of the ork grapnels *clanged* and found purchase against the battlements. He blasted apart the thick chain dangling off it, waiting for the line to become taut before he fired. Muffled screams from the unseen greenskins once climbing up the severed chain, now falling to their deaths, made Tsu'gan smile beneath his battle-helm.

Three more grapnels followed it. Brother S'tang took out one, before another five rattled onto the battlements, biting deep.

Brother Catus mistakenly hacked at a chain with his combat blade before leaning over to strafe the orks below with his bolter. He lurched back with a cleaver lodged between his neck and clavicle, spurting blood. S'tang dragged him aside, putting a bolt through the cranium of the ork that dared be the first to poke its head up over the rockcrete lip of the wall.

Ugly greenskin faces emerged en masse after that. They were attached to brutish bodies carrying cleavers and saw-toothed blades.

Chaplain Elysius brained one of the orks with his crozius, electricity still coursing through its shattered frame as it fell back in the morass of warriors below, before jamming his bolt pistol into the maw of a second and reducing its head to shredded meat. A red haze spattered his skull-faced visage, anointing him in blood. Yet as deadly as he was, Elysius could not kill them all.

'Honorious!' yelled Tsu'gan.

The battle-brother swept his flamer around from pouring gouts of promethium down the wall and sent a searing blaze over the greenskins trying to outflank the Chaplain.

'Burn in the fires of perdition, xenos!' spat Elysius, as the orks were consumed and plunged, flailing, into the mobs amassing at the foot of the wall.

Tsu'gan wiped a swathe of blood from his visor and took a moment to look around the battle site. Sporadic skirmishes had erupted all across the wall. The Tactical squads bore the brunt of the attacks, allowing the Devastators in the higher, less accessible towers to continue wreaking carnage amongst the greater horde that swelled beyond in the ash basin like a green slough.

Many sergeants had broken their warriors up into combat squads; those that fought hand-to-hand or to disengage the grapnels, and those that maintained a ranged fusillade.

In the brief seconds of assessment he allowed himself, Tsu'gan also noticed ork vehicles prosecuting suicide runs against the walls. He saw a bulky wagon, festooned with plates and brimming with orks, rammed headlong in the wall. Shot apart by heavy bolters and multi-meltas, the wagon was a wreck, but now the greenskins were climbing up its tower-like pulpit and using the debris to gain the battlements. Missiles *choomed* overhead, super-heated beams crosshatched the night obliterating the ork suicide runners before they could close, but couldn't stop them all.

An impact against the lower part of his section almost knocked Tsu'gan off his feet. The tremor rippled up through the metal and rockcrete. A blast wave of heat washed over the sergeant and his squad, as the vehicle that had collided into the wall ignited and exploded. A few seconds later, scrapes and clanks could be heard as the orks scrambled up the makeshift siege tower.

'Grenades!' ordered Tsu'gan, knowing that he was out, but that half of his squad could oblige him. Frag grenades bounded down the wrecked carcass of the vehicle, pulped and burning against the wall, and exploded in a series of dull percussions. The scraping and clanking ceased.

'Glory to Prometheus!' he yelled, exultant in this small victory.

Then he saw the force approaching the Techmarine Draedius's gate.

A mob of heavily armoured orks advanced under fire towards the fortress's only ingress.

Something moved amongst the larger ork bodies. Tsu'-gan caught the glint of metal, a spherical object daubed in jagged iconography, akin to a mine...

'Concentrate fi–'

A concussive blast erupted from the gate below, cutting the sergeant off before he could issue the order to try and stop it. The Salamanders occupying the section of wall directly above it were thrown off their feet. Out the corner of his eye, Tsu'gan thought he saw Shen'kar pitched off the battlements. His vision was marred by coiling smoke and exploding debris, so he couldn't be certain. Brother Malicant stumbled and the company banner fell. Only Captain N'keln kept his footing, snatching the banner in defiance of the fire crawling rapidly up the wall, lashing tongues of flame devouring everything they touched.

'Tank bombers,' said Tiberon, groggily. The squad had felt the blast wave like the full force of a hammer blow. 'Must've cracked open the gate...'

Greenskins swarming into the dust cloud billowing from the gate confirmed Tiberon's theory. The Salamanders still standing aimed through the murk, trying to

take out the ork assault force that had seemingly
appeared from nowhere. Ork commandos returned fire,
and Tsu'gan saw another of his brothers fall; a lucky shot
through his gorget disabling him.

The heavy-armoured brutes also returned, obscured
by the grey fug of smoke and churned ash now swathing
the battlefield. The throaty rumble of revving chainblades could be heard through it, anonymous and
forbidding.

The orks converged on the gate and the brother-
sergeant was powerless to stop it. He cursed his position
on the wall, wanting desperately to be where the fighting was fiercest. A bright plume of fire, its roar so loud
it eclipsed the chugging chorus of mechanised blades,
tore through the smoke and murk below, devouring the
assaulting horde with voracious hunger.

Fire Anvil had unleashed its flamestorm cannons and
the orks tasted the Land Raider Redeemer's fury. Howling in rage and pain, the greenskins fell back. Enflamed
bodies stumbled from the ruined gate, before sinking to
their knees and collapsing in charred heaps upon the
ground. No Salamander put them down; they just let
them burn.

Three consecutive bursts and the conflagration ebbed,
leaving scorched earth, edged by fire, in its wake.

'*In Vulkan's name and for the glory of the Chapter!*'

Praetor's stentorian timbre thundered across the
comm-feed like a rallying bow wave. The Firedrakes had
filled the breach.

'In Vulkan's name!' echoed N'keln, standing tall
amidst the dying flames wreathing the battlements
before him. Brother Malicant was down, but the captain
held aloft the company banner in his stead. The coiling
drake depicted on the sacred cloth snapped and snarled
in the wind as if alive within the fabric. The edges of it
were burned and blackened, but that only added to its

belligerent allure. N'keln became a beacon, forged as steel upon the anvil of war at last.

'None shall pass,' he roared, and the firedrake upon the banner seemed to roar with him.

Tsu'gan found a smile was curling his lip.

The orks were doomed.

In desperation, the last of the tribal chieftains had assaulted the wall up one of the wrecked wagon towers. It gained the battlements, bloodied but unbowed.

Elysius, just finished dispensing with one of its lessers at the end of his bolt pistol, rammed his crozius through the foul beast's chest as it appeared. It snarled, only for the Chaplain to head-butt it with his battle-helm, shattering a tusk and then snapping off the other with a savage pistol-whip from his still-smoking sidearm. He tossed the weapon aside, seizing the dying chieftain in his gauntlet, the other hand gripped tightly around the haft of the crackling crozius, and lifted the ork into the air.

In a stunning feat of strength, or faith, Elysius raised the flailing ork above his head and flung it, screaming, onto the ground far below.

'I cast thee out, abomination!'

Coupled with the *Fire Anvil's* fury and the wrath of Praetor's Terminators, it proved a decisive blow.

The orks fled en masse, back across the killing field and up to the ridge.

Their warboss took their capitulation badly. Every one of the fleeing greenskins was slaughtered by the hordes that still remained.

A strange lull descended. It was punctuated by a deep throbbing in the back of Tsu'gan's skull, like the Salamander could feel the ork warboss's rage. So potent was the beast's fury that it had manifested physically, a distinctive pulse in the greenskins' natural psychic overspill.

In the absence of battle, the sense of despair from earlier returned. Tsu'gan lurched forward to grip the lip of the battlement for support.

'Sire?' hissed Iagon, leaning conspiratorially towards his sergeant.

Tsu'gan held up his hand to show he was all right. He gripped his bolter for reassurance. Guilt flooded his body pervasively like a cancer, and he longed for the brander-priest's rod and the pain that dulled the ache inside him.

'There is evil here...' he heard himself slurring, as low as a whisper.

It was eking out of the stones. In his delirium, Tsu'gan almost imagined he could see it: a thin, trailing mist of utter black.

'Hold together, brothers,' Elysius girded him, 'and we shall smite the alien.'

The baleful effects of the iron fortress ebbed. It was not yet strong enough to overcome the Chaplain's fervour. Tsu'gan straightened again, gritting his teeth.

'Let's finish this.'

The warboss bellowed, reasserting his dominance. The orks charged again.

DAK'IR EMERGED FROM the chasm to a different world than the one which he'd left previously. An eldritch darkness blanketed the ash dunes now. A black shape, like a moon or planetoid, smothered whatever celestial body of Scoria should have held prominence in the night sky. This then was the black rock of which Illiad had spoken; the carrier for the orks. Its orbit had brought it close enough to the ashen world for the greenskins to launch an assault. As time passed, Dak'ir knew it would only bring them closer.

The strange milieu brought other sensations with it, too – the sounds and smells of battle. The bulk of the

Vulkan's Wrath, still high as an Imperial bastion's defence tower even though it was partly sunken into the desert, obscured Dak'ir's view but he could still see a warm orange glow tinting the darkling sky. There was something serene and beautiful about it, despite the distant *crump* of explosions and the whiff of smoke and promethium wafted on a hot breeze.

The comm-feed in his battle-helm crackled, like life breathed back into a corpse, and he heard the voice of Brother-Sergeant Agatone.

'Marshal your forces, brother,' he snapped, clearly perturbed that they'd been out of vox contact for so long. The inquest would come later. 'We are about to be under attack.'

Dak'ir didn't question it. Instead, he ran around the half-submerged prow of the *Vulkan's Wrath* and climbed up to the summit of a small dune. What he saw there quickened his heart to a state of combat readiness.

'Pyriel,' said Dak'ir. The Librarian had been right behind the sergeant and followed him up the shallow dune. 'When you said there were no oceans on Scoria…'

Before their eyes, still distant but closing, there boiled a belligerent green sea.

'I was wrong,' Pyriel replied simply.

The voice of Illiad intruded.

'Swine-tusks…' he uttered, hoarsely.

The rest of the combat squad had positioned themselves around him in battle formation. They'd all heard Agatone over the comm-feed.

'The swine-tusks have returned,' rasped Illiad, gaping in terrified awe at the grotesque spectacle swarming the dunes. 'The slayers of your brothers are back to kill us all.' Dak'ir hadn't heard fear in the human before… until now.

The main swell of the greenskin horde was far off at the iron fortress, yet still their masses could be seen by the defenders of the *Vulkan's Wrath*, spreading across the land like a dark stain. A tributary had peeled off from the major force and was surging towards the stricken strike cruiser.

Do you feel them, Dak'ir? Pyriel asked psychically.

Dak'ir nodded slowly. Yes, he felt it.

'Such rage…' he muttered.

The orks were not that far away now. Dak'ir could make out the crude and jagged forms of their vehicles and see their brutish weapons as they discharged them into the air. He discerned the snarled visage of the barbarous greenskin and his fist clenched. These were the spore of those beasts that virtually wiped out his ancient brothers. Here, upon the same ashen fields, the battle would be refought – Salamander versus greenskins. Dak'ir was adamant that this time, the orks would not be back.

The comm-feed spat static for a few seconds and then cleared again.

'Sergeant,' growled the voice of Agatone. 'I need your forces now.'

'On our way,' Dak'ir returned and cut the feed. He ordered his combat squad to move out. They left the dune swiftly, Illiad in tow, and went to liaise with Agatone and the others.

Rounding the vast bulk of the *Vulkan's Wrath*, Dak'ir saw that the medical tents were already emptying. The injured that could walk or be moved safely were trailing out in ragged groups.

Battle-Brother Zo'tan – from the other half of Dak'ir's squad – had taken charge of the armsmen and able-bodied human crew, forming them into auxiliaries. A quick head count revealed almost three hundred troops, divided into six fifty-man battalions, assigned squad leaders and commanders. The auxiliary had started to assume strategic positions around the medical tents.

They were the last line of defence, there to protect those still festering in their pallet-beds. Even though the badly wounded probably wouldn't survive, the Salamanders would not leave them to be butchered.

Brother-Sergeant Agatone was stalking towards them. Sergeant Ek'Bar remained behind where they had been discussing a holo-chart, and waited patiently.

Agatone dispensed with any preamble.

'We have three Tactical and one depleted Assault squad,' he began. 'Venerable Brothers Ashamon and Amadeus have also been roused from slumber by Master Argos.' The doughty forms of the Dreadnoughts loomed in the distance, prowling the extremity of the defensive cordon designated by Agatone.

As he looked, Dak'ir noticed acting Sergeant Gannon also up ahead. He was kneeling upon a high dune, his Assault squad gathered around him, surveying the orks through a pair of magnoculars.

Agatone was interrupted abruptly by the comm-feed. The sergeant pressed a gauntleted finger to his gorget, as his battle-helm was mag-locked to his belt.

'Go ahead,' he instructed.

Gannon's voice came through.

'I estimate four thousand enemy,' reported the acting sergeant, 'with assorted vehicles and bikes. Armament is mainly automatic chain-gun and solid shot rifles and pistols.'

'Good work, sergeant. To your positions. In Vulkan's name.'

'In Vulkan's name.'

Gannon secured the magnoculars and stood up. A second later he and his squad took to the air, jump pack engines screaming as they ignited, and trailing smoke and fire.

Agatone gestured to the middle distance, where the Thunderfire cannons had patrolled earlier. There was no sign of the tracked heavy guns now, or their Techmarine operators.

'The grenade line is still untouched,' he told them, 'and we've added additional explosive payloads. Our stratagem is to funnel the orks into it, launching a full assault into their vanguard when they're scattered, hurting and confused.'

Dak'ir regarded the greenskin splinter force as Agatone relayed his plan. The xenos had forged some distance between themselves and the parent horde; the latter was just a dense black line cresting a far-off high dune now. He also noticed that the splinter force had become stretched in its eagerness for a fight. A vanguard of bikers, trucks and the faster orkoid elements ranged ahead of a much larger body of greenskins comprising foot soldiers and rumbling half-tracks.

'See how they are spread?' said Agatone. It was wide, widening all the time as the speed-obsessed orks raced and tried to out do each other. Dak'ir was put in mind of a giant maw slowly opening as it prepared for its first bite. 'We need them to become a dense column.'

'Corral them,' said Dak'ir, seeing the potential at once to manoeuvre the fast, but brittle greenskin advance forces.

Agatone nodded, a slight hint of irritation in his manner. 'It is already in place.' He pointed to distant flanks, just beyond the Dreadnoughts. Dak'ir saw something moving there, obscured by the eerie half-darkness.

'Thunderfire cannons,' he thought aloud.

'Just so,' Agatone replied. 'Subterranean blast shelling will commence as soon as we've got the orks' attention. The tremors will force them into line. Any that don't will be dealt with by the Dreadnoughts.'

Dak'ir's eyes narrowed as he pictured abstractly the full realisation of Agatone's plan.

'We need bait to draw them in.'

The other sergeant nodded.

Dak'ir checked the load of his plasma pistol, then secured it in its holster again.

'I'll take a combat squad only,' he said. 'Where should we deploy?'

'Five Astartes is all I can spare, Dak'ir,' Agatone replied. He gestured to a patch of rocky ground about two hundred metres shy of the grenade line. 'That's your squad's position.'

It was as good a staging point as any. The rocks provided some cover and the ground was set into a small depression the Salamanders could use like a crater to hunker down in if necessary.

'Five Fire-born to engage a horde of about five hundred,' said Ba'ken, his tone sardonic. 'Good odds.'

'And the rest of the force – what will you do about the ork reserves?' asked Dak'ir.

'Argos is working on something,' Agatone replied looking slightly uncomfortable for the first time during the impromptu briefing, 'We just need to give him some time. Stall the greenskins.'

'How much time?' Dak'ir asked levelly.

Agatone's expression was stony.

'As much as we can.'

It didn't take an anthro-linguistic servitor to realise that Agatone's obvious misgivings were grave. The sergeant went on.

'Once the vanguard is eliminated, fall back to the second line. You'll see it because I'll be stood at it with the rest of our forces.'

'And after that, if the orks get through?'

Agatone snorted in mock derision. There was a sense of pathos to the gesture.

'After that it won't matter.'

CHAPTER TEN

I

Into the Dragon's Mouth

DAK'IR CRADLED THE bolter in his gauntleted hands, feeling its heft and running his fingers down its stock. He muttered litanies of accuracy under his breath as he familiarised himself with the holy weapon.

The *Vulkan's Wrath* carried several additional Astartes armoriums aboard. It was well stocked with surplus bolters, ammunition and other materiel in the event that the company should require it. During his scout training, when he was just a neophyte and not part of the 7th Company, Dak'ir had been instructed in the use of the bolter by the stern-faced Master of Recruits. Old Zen'de was dead now but the lessons he had imparted upon Dak'ir lived on.

All of the Salamanders crouched in the shallow depression, the rocky outcrop to their fore, advancing orks glimpsed over the jagged tips of these crags, had a bolter slung to their sides. Bursts of sporadic fire, at range, were intended to attract the attention of the onrushing greenskin vanguard. The squad would then stay visible but hunkered down so as not to present an easy target. Only Ba'ken and Emek, bearing their flamers, wouldn't be so armed.

Dak'ir's five had also become six with the addition of Pyriel. He too hefted a bolter, his force sword and pistol remaining sheathed for now. The Librarian had not been swayed by Sergeant Agatone's arguments when he had insisted he stay with the main force. His talents, he surmised with a tone that brooked no further discussion, would be best served aiding Dak'ir.

Illiad was another matter, of course. With no time to explain what had occurred beneath the surface right now, Dak'ir had merely expressed how important the human was to them and that if they survived the fight with the greenskins, Illiad would need to be brought before N'keln immediately. As it was, the leader of the settlers was determined he would stand with his distant Nocturnean kin and so joined one of the battalions. The human could fight and had his own lasgun, so Agatone saw no reason to oppose him. Dak'ir would see him protected, of course, but supposed that standing shoulder-to-shoulder with fifty other armed men was about as safe as it got right now.

'A thousand metres,' Apion reported, keeping sentry on the orks' approach with a pair of magnoculars.

'Weapons ready,' snapped Dak'ir. His tone was clipped and precise as he brought up his bolter. Each Salamander occupied a section of the outcrop, snug in makeshift firing lips rendered by the natural permutations in the rocks. A staccato of arming sounds disturbed the heavy silence before the air was still again.

'Eight hundred…'

Dak'ir sighted down the bolter's targeter.

'Seven hundred…'

Dull percussions from the Thunderfire cannon salvo were rippling across the dunes. Clustered explosions plumed in fiery grey, slowly pushing the greenskin vanguard together.

'Six hundred…'

'In Vulkan's name!' Dak'ir roared and the bolters roared with him.

Muzzle flares ripped into the darkness followed by the flash of explosive rounds tearing up the leaders of the motorised ork vanguard. Bikes spun front over end, chewed up by the brutal fusillade coming from the Space Marines. Trucks flipped as their fuel tanks ignited, turning them into rolling fireballs. Spitting shrapnel shredded those outside the heart of the bolter storm, forcing bikes to slew into others and trucks to veer widely and crash as their drivers were cut to pieces.

The frenzied ork advance slowed momentarily as the ones that followed on picked their way through flaming wreckage, and as the greenskins at the periphery were forced into a cordon by the distant bombardment of the Thunderfire cannons.

Bellowing curses like wielded blades, the orks regrouped and found a focus for their anger – the six Salamanders blazing away at them from an outcrop of rocks. Like a hot spear-tip the orks came together. In truth, the bolter fire had barely scratched them, but the bloody nose they'd received was stinging.

Errant bullets from the greenskins' chainguns and solid-shot cannons chipped at the rock wall. A shard *spanged* against Dak'ir's pauldron but he barely felt it. The spatial display on his right helmet lens told him the orks were just three hundred and sixty-five point three metres away.

In less than a minute they'd be hitting the grenade line. Then there would be two hundred metres between them and the horde.

'Reloading,' shouted Dak'ir, ducking back behind the rocks to expel the partially spent magazine and ram home another one. The process took less than three seconds. As he returned to the firing lip to resume the fusillade, Brother Apion ducked back in his sergeant's stead, cycling through the ammo replenishment strategy Dak'ir had devised. This way, the Salamanders could maintain a barrage of uninterrupted bolter fire with little deterioration in intensity between reloads.

At the head of the greenskin pack, a howling ork biker was suddenly kicked up into the air, riding a blossoming fireball. It tore out the vehicle's undercarriage, blasting off its rugged wheels, as well as shredding the ork's legs and abdomen. The beast was still raging until it struck the ground with a wet crunch. Others followed it, shooting up into the air in a macabre, pseudo-pyrotechnic display. Explosions from the grenade line churned up ash in a dense cloud, causing further carnage and confusion. Riderless bikes trundled through the fog aflame, slowly succumbing to inertia without their throttles opened up. A truck barrel rolled out of the murk, its hapless passengers battered to death as they thrashed continuously against the ground. It settled into a mangled heap, a pair of ork bikers blinded by their ash-smeared goggles, colliding into it and exploding after the impact.

The damage was horrendous, the densely-packed greenskins, precisely corralled by the Thunderfire cannons and impelled by Dak'ir's 'bait' squad, suffering badly in the grenade field. Momentum carried the greenskins behind into deadly debris and the remnants of the sunken grenades yet to be disturbed. They couldn't stop; their maddened fervour, coupled with the undeniable instinct to go faster, wouldn't let them. The orks piled on through and kept on dying.

Two hundred metres became a hundred and fifty in Dak'ir's helmet lens. With so many orks in the vanguard, it was inevitable that some would make it through. But the brother-sergeant had made contingency for that too.

Raking a slide of his bolter, he switched the gun to rapid fire. They'd burn through ammunition much faster this way, but the punishing effects of such a salvo would be irresistible. Loosing his fury, Dak'ir saw the muzzle flare at the end of the bolter expand into a knife-edged star of fire. The oncoming orks became a haze before it, rendered into steaming flesh and bent metal.

The orks, more tenacious than a plague, rolled on into the firing line, scarcely fifty left in the vanguard from the five hundred who had broken off from the slower element of the splinter horde.

Solid shot struck his elbow, finding a spot between the plates, and bit. Dak'ir grimaced, another deflecting off his left pauldron as the orks got close enough to be partially accurate with their return fire.

Ignoring the bullets skimming off his power armour, some punching small holes but stopping at the layered ceramite, Dak'ir rose to his feet. His brothers followed him.

'Purify!' roared the sergeant and the flamers opened up at last.

A curtain of fire swept over the last of the orks. Super-heated promethium cooked engines and melted tyres to rubberised slag. The greenskins bayed as they burned, crumpling down as they were engulfed by the intense wave.

Caught between the twin storms of bolters and flamers, barely a score of orks remained. Roughly half staggered, bereft of their vehicles, dazed and enraged to within a few metres of the outcrop when Dak'ir let his bolter hang lose on its strap and unsheathed his chainsword. His voice buzzed like the sound of the blades churning with their sudden activation.

'Charge!'

Dak'ir led, bounding over the rocks with his brothers on his heels. A flash of cerulean blue in his limited peripheral vision told him that Pyriel had drawn his force sword.

The Salamanders descended on the battered remnants of the ork vanguard.

And tore them apart.

It was over in seconds, and as the dust finally cleared the greenskin dead were revealed, littering the ground. Orks possessed strong constitutions; they were hard beasts to kill. Amongst the carnage there'd be those that still lived, but none posed a threat to the Salamanders at this point. Beyond the dissipating smoke and ash, the rest of the splinter horde was closing. It was a sobering sight that dispelled the heady battle-euphoria of their recent victory.

Over a thousand orks: more heavily armed, more resolute, more wrathful.

Whatever Argos was planning, Dak'ir hoped it would be ready soon and powerful enough to level a small army.

'Fall back,' he ordered, 'and recover any partially spent clips. We're going to need every single round.'

THEY ARRIVED AT the main Salamander deployment almost at the same time as the Thunderfire cannons and Dreadnoughts.

Agatone had ordered the withdrawal of the heavy guns as soon as the ork vanguard was in the 'dragon's mouth', as he would later refer to it. Dak'ir's troops had fallen back a short time after that, but the better foot speed of the battle-brothers had averaged out the head start fairly equally.

The brother-sergeant seemed distracted. As Dak'ir approached him, he realised it was because Agatone was listening intently to the comm-feed in his ear. He nodded curtly, his face grim.

'A much larger horde of greenskins has amassed against the iron fortress. Captain N'keln is currently under siege,' he announced.

'How large a force are we talking about, here?' asked Dak'ir, aware that the main horde they would soon face numbered in the thousands.

'Estimations are hazy,' Agatone replied. 'They reckon tens of thousands.'

Dak'ir shook his head ruefully, before pointing to the lunar eclipse. 'The black rock up there orbits this planet, and when it closes the orks will increase in number again.'

Agatone looked up to the ghastly planetoid, like a baleful black orb, and frowned darkly.

'We must reunite our forces,' he decided. 'Find a way to get to Captain N'keln and our brothers before they're worn down by the siege.'

'We are in no position to lift it, Sergeant Agatone,' Pyriel interceded, displaying a cold pragmatism normally associated with their Chaplain. 'Our brothers will be measured against the anvil, as will we all.'

Agatone nodded at the Librarian's wisdom, but said in a low voice:

'Let us hope it doesn't break them.'

After that he summarised the troop dispositions one final time and went to rejoin his squad, leaving Dak'ir to do the same. With Zo'tan leading the human auxiliaries a few hundred metres back from the line of Salamanders, Dak'ir would have been a trooper down if not for Pyriel appending himself to his squad.

The Librarian had taken a keen interest in Dak'ir; for good or ill, the brother-sergeant did not know. The only certainty was that Pyriel would not let him out of his sight.

A rugged defensive line of metal storage crates, partially broken down prefab bunkers and empty ammo drums was strung out for the Salamanders to take cover behind. Battle-Brother G'heb raised his fist to indicate to his sergeant where they would be stationed. Dak'ir could

feel the questions in his burning gaze, reflected in the
eyes of all the Salamanders, of what happened below the
earth and who this human was in their midst. Discipline
let them compartmentalise the desire for veracity; survival and the protection of innocent human life
overrode it for now.

Answers would come if they lived out this next battle.

Dak'ir was reticent to leave the armour suits, the settlers and especially ancient Brother Gravius behind, but
was afforded little other choice. He reasoned that they
had survived this long without intervention, and so they
were as safe as anywhere could be on Scoria. At least
while the orks' attention was fixed on their foes on the
surface, they would not decide to probe any deeper.

A rhythmic chant pervaded on the breeze, interrupting
Dak'ir's thoughts. The orks were marching in time to
beaten drums. They saw an outnumbered foe, out of
tricks, who had shown their hand and was now in the
open. It galvanised them. Dak'ir felt their belligerent
confidence as an intense pressure at the front of his
skull. He put a hand to his forehead in a vain effort to
ward off the discomfort. The others seemed affected to,
but not nearly as badly.

Stand straight, sergeant, Pyriel's voice was little more
than a whisper in Dak'ir's mind. *It is the subconscious psychic emanation of the greenskins that you can feel.*

It was crippling. Dak'ir felt like his head was about to
explode with it. He gritted his teeth, unaware that he'd
stooped, and straightened up.

'Dak'ir...' Ba'ken, on the other side of his sergeant to
Pyriel, reached out to him.

'I'm all right, brother,' he lied. The noise in his head
was deafening and blood tanged his mouth.

Ba'ken edged closer to his sergeant; the Salamander
lines were packed so tightly they were almost shoulder-
to-shoulder anyway.

'Lean on me until the fighting begins,' he breathed, lowering his heavy flamer slightly and using his free hand to support Dak'ir surreptitiously beneath the elbow.

Dak'ir found he had no voice to respond. Was this another vision, but manifesting in some physically debilitating way? The approaching ork horde blended into a single note of raucous white noise that eclipsed everything else. Hot, angry green light burned like sunspots before Dak'ir's eyes and he lost focus. Rage: gratuitous, boiling rage filled his mind, and he felt his fists clench in defiance of it. Something primal within him was waking, and Dak'ir fought the urge to cry out and hurl himself at the orks. He wanted to tear into them with his bare hands, to rip their flesh apart with his teeth, to beat upon their bodies until there was nothing left but bone splinters and viscera.

Through the haze of mindless anger that descended, the world was tinted an ugly green.

Listen to my voice, Dak'ir. It was Pyriel again. *Remember what you are.*

He clenched his fists tighter. Blood flowed into his mouth as Dak'ir bit into his lip.

Fire-born, said Pyriel.

Fury like chained lightning wracked his body and it began to tremble against the strain. Synaptic warning icons behind his helmet lens that were slaved to his body's biorhythms started spiking. Heart rate was nearing cardio infarction levels, Dak'ir felt it like a frag grenade going off continuously in his chest; breathing intensified; red, flashing icons warned of imminent anaphylactic circulatory collapse; blood pressure was rising, bordering on extreme hypertension.

Fire-born, Pyriel repeated.

Dak'ir felt again the heat of Mount Deathfire. He recalled ranging through the caves of Ignea, plying the

Acerbian Sea and the long climb to the summit of the Cindara Plateau.

The green haze filtered away until his vision was red-rimed once more.

'Fire-born,' uttered Dak'ir. His voice was in unison with the Librarian's psychic casting inside his head.

Dak'ir moved away from Ba'ken to show he no longer needed his brother's support. The unspoken exchange between them said more than any words of gratitude ever could. The bulky Salamander merely nodded his understanding and reaffirmed his grip on the heavy flamer.

The Thunderfire cannons were booming at either end of the defensive line. Unseen, they pummelled patches of advancing greenskins with clusters of surface detonations. It was like dropping a bullet into an ocean. The orks parted briefly before the explosions then closed up again, the ripples short-lived and ineffectual, the slain crushed underfoot and forgotten.

'Merciful Vulkan…'

Dak'ir heard Emek over the comm-feed.

'Never despair,' said Dak'ir to bolster his troops. The blood caked against his teeth tasted like copper. 'Never give in. Salamanders only go forward.'

Bolter fire erupted down the line as the orks came into range. The greenskins weathered it as before, but no longer marched; they had broken into a run.

'This is it. For Tu'Shan and the Emperor,' declared Dak'ir. 'For Vulkan and the glory of Prometheus!'

Forty against three thousand.

Dak'ir had looked into the primitive psyche of the orks. He knew, on an almost cellular level, their fury and aggression. Unless something changed to even the balance, many Fire-born would not live out this fight. Dak'ir vowed that he would not submit to the pyreum easily.

A dense throb built at the back of his skull. For a moment, Dak'ir thought it was the ork rage returned, but as the sound started to resonate across the ash plain he realised it was from a different source.

The massive capacitors in the *Vulkan's Wrath*'s guns were charging. Huge upper-deck turrets swivelled into position with the churning retort of metal. The air crackled with slow actinic discharge, magnetising the metallic elements in the ash and grit particles, statically adhering them to the Salamanders' boots and leg greaves. The throb built to a high-pitched whine and Dak'ir saw a nimbus of electrical energy spark and fork around the mouth of the guns.

An instant later and they were unleashed.

A blast wave, so heavy and powerful it put the Salamanders on their knees, rippled across the ash plain. Concave slashes of grey scudded in the wake of the turret guns' lethal discharge, swirling mini-vortices of displaced ash and dirt.

The barrage lasted a few seconds but the greenskin horde was left devastated by it. Strike cruiser guns were intended to be fired at extreme ranges in the depths of space against massive, heavily-armoured and void-shielded targets. The firepower they could bring to bear was insanely destructive. Argos, in his genius, had only activated a small portion of the guns. The laser battery was enough to atomise vast chunks of the greenskin army, slaying hundreds in a deadly las-cluster. Several thousand super-powerful blasts had emitted from the guns, but at such frequency and velocity that they appeared as one continuous beam. Those not caught directly in the beam were burned by it. Several hundred greenskins were already ablaze; some wandered about aimlessly amongst the scorched earth, others were just charred husks. The rest were crippled by shock and disorientation, blinded and deafened by the terrible assault.

Dak'ir was getting to his feet when Agatone, his voice cold and menacing, came over the comm-feed.

'The greenskins are down. Close in and finish them. Salamanders attack!'

A roar of thrusters ripped into the air as Acting-Sergeant Gannon and his Assault squad surged upwards on contrails of smoke and fire. Their blades were drawn, eager to taste ork blood.

The foot troops barged over the makeshift barricade together, bolters flaring. Flamers tramped alongside them, whilst the heavy static guns stayed behind and pummelled the decimated greenskin horde from distance.

From the flanks, the Dreadnoughts closed the deadly trap and in the resulting carnage the ork splinter force was destroyed utterly.

GREENSKIN BLOOD SWATHED Dak'ir's faceplate and he removed his battle-helm so he could better see. Execution teams roamed through the smoke coiling across the dunes. Anonymous bursts, sharp and sporadic, occasionally broke the eerie quiet of post-battle as greenskin wounded were finished off.

Looking above the carnage, Dak'ir saw the horizon and imagined the greater horde still out there laying siege to the iron fortress. He also wondered how they could hope to break such a massive force with the troops at their disposal. Defenders would have to remain with the *Vulkan's Wrath*. It was their only way off a planet that was slowly breaking apart. The tremors were almost constant now, the distant volcanoes erupting with ominous regularity. Even without the eclipse, Dak'ir reckoned the skies would still be grey with falling ash.

'Like Moribar,' he muttered to himself, unaware that he'd just echoed the earlier words of his rival, Tsu'gan. At the back of his mind, Dak'ir felt that the dark legacy of the Dragon Warriors was interwoven with the fate of 3rd Company somehow, particularly that of him and Tsu'gan. He even sensed their clawed caress on this distant world.

Agatone emerged through the murk into Dak'ir's eye line. He was wiping greenskin blood from his power sword as he approached.

'The orks are slain,' he said with finality.

'If they return, we'll have Master Argos engage the *Vulkan's Wrath*'s guns again.'

Agatone shook his head.

'No we won't. Argos has told me he can only fire them once. The recoil might collapse the bedrock holding up the ship and bury it for good. He won't risk it.'

'Then our reprieve is short-lived,' said Dak'ir.

'Precisely.'

'Any word from Captain N'keln?'

'We're trying to raise him now, but there are other matters I wish to attend to first.' Agatone's cadence was leading.

'The human settler?' Dak'ir asked, already knowing the answer.

'Precisely,' Agatone repeated. 'What did you find below the earth?'

Dak'ir kept his tone level, so his brother-sergeant would be sure of his sincerity.

'We found Nocturne.'

Agatone's face betrayed his incredulity.

'Let me introduce you to Sonnar Illiad,' said Dak'ir. 'There is much you should know, brother.'

II
Death by Guilt

THE DULL REPORT of explosions rumbled through the walls of the keep, manifesting physically as dust motes spilling from the ceiling. The siege was in its second phase as the greenskin warboss threw his seemingly inexhaustible forces against the Salamander-held wall. Thus far, the casualties had been few. Brother Catus had needed his neck patching up before he could return to battle and Shen'kar had received several broken bones from his fall, but those had been swiftly righted and the Inferno Guard was back at his captain's side.

There were more severe cases. Two Salamanders were currently laid out, supine, their sus-an membranes having shut their bodies down in response to the grievous wounds they'd received during the first ork assault.

Other more minor injuries – severed hands, gouged eyes, punctured lungs – appeared more frequently. Gauntlets drenched in blood, Fugis was glad of the work, but he was also glad of the solitude of the keep. Ever since Naveem and his much-maligned pact with Iagon, the Apothecary had begun to doubt himself. An excuse to stay behind the lines, away from the thunder of battle, was ready-made with the need for him to monitor the two comatose Astartes.

It was anathema for a Salamander, for any Space Marine, to shirk away from combat like this. Fugis knew it, and it preyed upon his thoughts destructively.

He allowed his gaze to wander out of the open-doored cell, one of many in the keep – this one had been cleansed by Chaplain Elysius and a flamer team, and reappropriated for use as an Apothecarion, though Fugis doubted the Iron Warriors had used it for such a curative purpose – and alight upon the shadowed confines of the torture chamber. It was close by, and the doorway to the cell was concealed by a black curtain of plastek. The traitor prisoner was inside, secured upon one of the Chaplain's devices, his chirurgeon-interrogators acting as dutiful but deadly lapdogs outside.

It felt odd to Fugis; a place of torture and a place of healing in such close proximity. On reflection, though, perhaps the two were not so disparate.

An internal chrono-icon flashed up on the Apothecary's medi-gauntlet display, reminding him that the monitoring cycle for the stricken warriors in his care was due. Fugis gripped the edges of a mortuary slab and bowed his head.

'Vulkan's fire beats in my breast…' he began, in an effort to steel himself.

Footsteps approaching before him arrested what was next in the catechism. Fugis started to look up slowly and saw first the green of a Salamander's battle-plate.

'Brother…' he started to say, when he noticed the ragged hole in the Salamander's plastron and found the dead eyes of Naveem glaring back at him.

'Brother.' Naveem's words were slurred, but as if there were a second voice laid over the first. His breath was rank with decay and a strong stench of old blood wafted from his wound, as stinging as the irony in Naveem's tone.

His face was set in a rictus sneer.

'You're dead,' Fugis asserted ludicrously. He reached for his bolt pistol, recognising an emanation of the warp. It seemed the Chaplain's blessing had not been stringent enough and the flamers had failed to purify completely.

'Thanks to you,' replied Naveem, in that same dual voice. He didn't move, but just stood there, radiating malice and accusation. 'You killed my legacy and me, *brother*.'

Fugis's anger swelled at the apparition's mockery. He felt the reassuring solidity of the bolt pistol in his grasp.

'You cannot kill me twice, *brother*,' said Naveem.

'You are not my brother, denizen of the warp,' Fugis countered and levelled the pistol.

'I am your guilt and your doubt, Fugis,' it said.

The Apothecary faltered. What good would a bolt pistol do against a figment of his mind? The weapon wavered in his grasp.

'Now,' it said. 'Put the gun to your forehead.'

Fugis's face creased defiantly, but he found himself slowly turning the pistol around. He *did* feel guilty for what had happened to Naveem. It gnawed at his soul, and weighed down his spirit. Fugis wanted to succumb to it, to be drawn down into the darkness there and to never resurface.

He closed his eyes.

The bolt pistol's muzzle was hard pressed against his skull. He hadn't even realised it had got that far.

'Do it now,' the apparition's voice insisted. 'Pull the trigger and sink down, down to where the darkness calls, down to silence and peace.'

Fugis's grip was tightening. He thought of Naveem and the ignominious end he'd condemned him to, and Kadai – he had failed him, too.

A sudden pressure exerted itself on the bolt pistol's barrel, slowly but firmly easing it away from the Apothecary's forehead.

…with it I shall smite the foes of the Emperor… a familiar voice echoed in Fugis's mind.

'Ko'tan…' he rasped, opening his eyes again.

Naveem, or the thing that wore his image like a ragged cloak, was gone. The sense of something at the very edge of Fugis's vision was dissipating too. He didn't try to find it, for he knew it could not be seen. The remnant of green gauntlets, of a thunder hammer reforged and a captain reborn, stayed with him, though. It was there just long enough for Fugis to activate the comm-feed.

'Brother Praetor,' he said, knowing the 1st Company sergeant was held in reserve at the broken gate. 'I am evacuating the keep at once. All injuries will be treated at the battle front from this point.'

'THEY'RE EVACUATING THE keep,' stated Tiberon.

Iagon nodded absently as he saw Apothecary Fugis emerge through the doors. A pack of servitors followed with a pair of collapsible medi-sleds for the two unconscious battle-brothers.

The chirurgeon-interrogators of Elysius came a few moments later, the captive Iron Warrior in tow. The Chaplain was on hand in the courtyard to survey proceedings keenly. The prisoner would be moved and secured within one of the Rhinos until such a time as Elysius was done with him. Judging by the Chaplain's demeanour, Iagon thought that might be soon.

Techmarine Draedius sealed the doors behind them with his plasma-torch.

Iagon cared little for the others. His attention was on Fugis alone. Though some fire had been undeniably restored in him, the Apothecary was still an ersatz version of his former self. Iagon saw these things; he saw weakness as clearly as a clenched fist or a drawn blade. His compact, the one he had sworn to protect Tsu'gan, was still intact.

A lull had fallen over the almost constant fighting with the Salamanders' defeat of the ork warboss's second assault. The Fire-born were tenacious, it was just their nature; Nocturneans had to be in order to survive a death world. Though perhaps ill-suited to a static defence, much preferring to engage the foe at close quarters and burn them aggressively from the face of the earth, they gritted their teeth, dug in and made every ork assault a suicidal charge into death and fire. Yes, they were winning the war of attrition it seemed. Though the orks spread out into the distance, the lapping green tide was slowly being dragged in and smashed against the

Astartes' breakers. The warboss had even pulled his forces back, out of the range of the Salamanders' long guns. Orks were stubborn creatures, but even they would stop smashing their skulls against a wall if it showed no sign of capitulation. At least those with rudimentary intellect would.

Iagon imagined the beasts on the summit of the ridge conversing in low cunning, trying to devise a strategy to open up the fortress. Or perhaps they were simply waiting, waiting for the black rock to weep its dark splinters again and replenish the orks' dwindling hordes. Too many to engage in the open, not enough to force a breach in the fortress and exploit it – the two old foes found themselves at an impasse.

The recently risen sun was a shallow ring of broken yellow behind the ominous black rock. In the few hours since the last assault, it had grown larger. Whatever this thing was that had brought the greenskins to Scoria, it was closing.

'It'll be the walls next,' grumbled Sergeant Tsu'gan, appearing alongside them. He'd removed his battle-helm again and his face was grim. It was like he wore a perpetual grimace, as if a heavy weight dragged down on his features invisibly.

'Sergeant?' asked Tiberon.

Tsu'gan's attention was caught for a moment as he saw the keep being shut up for good, when he turned and peered out idly into the orks amassed at the ridgeline.

'Can't you feel it, Tiberon?' he asked. Ever since the break in the fighting, Tsu'gan had slumped gradually into a miserable stupor. They all felt it, and he guarded it keenly, but Iagon saw the effects of it in his would-be patron more severely than anyone else.

'We all do, sire,' Iagon responded. The Salamander's tone was carefully measured as he recognised the hint of mania that had entered the sergeant's voice. Tsu'gan was

Iagon's route to power and influence. He must not falter, not now. A glance over to the gatehouse revealed N'keln deep in concert with Shen'kar as they sought to stymie potential breaches and reinforce. Eventually, it would not matter. Iagon knew they couldn't stay here. They all felt the baleful effects exuding from the Chaos-tainted stone and metal of the iron fortress. No fire could burn that away, no voice of faith, however ardent, could quash it. No, sooner or later they would have to abandon this strange haven, or be consumed by it.

For now, Iagon needed to bolster his sergeant. Support for Captain N'keln was growing by the hour. He had endured the fires of war and so far emerged unscathed, even re-forged.

The troops were spread thinly across the walls, and large gaps had to be tolerated by virtue of the fact that there simply weren't enough Salamanders to defend every inch of it. Iagon carefully manoeuvred Tsu'gan away from Tiberon, so that they might gain a modicum of privacy. If the other Salamander thought anything of the clandestine exchange, he didn't show it. Instead, he peered through the magnoculars at the massing ork horde readying to attack again.

'Sire, you must stand firm,' Iagon hissed.

Tsu'gan had a feral look in his eyes as he stared down at the ruddy plated-iron of the parapet. The metal looked darker, as if stained with blood. He shut his eyes to block it out and thought again of the knife and the need to use pain as a way to escape his feelings.

'This fell place is affecting us all,' Iagon pressed, desperate for some acknowledgement from his sergeant. He gripped Tsu'gan's pauldron tightly. 'But we cannot let it deter us from securing the future of the company, brother.'

Tsu'gan looked up at that. His gaze was hard.

'What are you insinuating, Iagon?'

Iagon was taken aback by Tsu'gan's sudden harshness and couldn't hide the fact.

'Why, your leadership and petition to be captain,' he answered, easing back a little as if stung.

Tsu'gan's face formed an incredulous frown.

'It is over, Iagon,' he said flatly. 'N'keln has been judged in the fires of war and found worthy. *I* have found him worthy.'

For a moment, Iagon was lost for words.

'Sire? I don't understand. You still have supporters in the squads. We can rally them round. If enough dissenting voices speak out–'

'No.' Tsu'gan shook his head. 'I was wrong, Iagon. My loyalty was always to the company and my battle-brothers. I will not contest N'keln, and nor should you. Now to your post,' he added, his resolve and purpose returning. 'In Vulkan's name.'

Tsu'gan turned away, and Iagon's hand fell from his pauldron. A great void had opened up within him, and all of Iagon's desires and machinations were plunging into it.

'Yes, sire...' he answered, almost without knowing he had spoken. His gaze went to N'keln at the gatehouse, the captain reborn who had somehow torn Iagon's plans from beneath him. 'In Vulkan's name.'

BROTHER-SERGEANT AGATONE LISTENED to Sonnar Illiad's story, his expression impassive. Dak'ir and Pyriel flanked the diminutive human in the gloomy confines of a pre-fabricated command bunker.

Following the victory over the ork splinter force, the Salamanders had returned to their previous duties: searching the ship for survivors, excavating the worst buried areas of the hull and defending the perimeter from further attack. In the wake of the battle, the medi-tents were re-established and surgeons told to put down their borrowed lasguns and get back to work. Several of the critically wounded were found dead in their cots upon the return of the medical staff. Either shock or simply inevitable death had claimed them in the absence of continued care. They would be burned with the rest and interred later.

Though the Salamanders went to their duties earnestly, each and every one was ready to muster out at Agatone's order. They all knew he intended to lead an assault to liberate their embattled brothers at the iron fortress and lift the siege; they merely needed to means and the stratagem to do it. Reports had filtered in sporadically over the last few minutes of urgent need for the besieged Salamanders to quit the fortress. It seemed there was something unholy about it, a malicious presence that had already tried to claim some of the Astartes, a presence that was growing in strength with every moment. This imperative was part of the reason Dak'ir had insisted Agatone have an audience with Illiad, so that he could learn what the leader of the human settlers knew.

Agatone took it all in, processing the information without emotion. Immediately afterwards, Dak'ir had divulged what he and Pyriel had seen on the former bridge of the old Expeditionary ship that the settlers were partly living in. He spoke of the antique power armour suits, the pict recording and of the ancient Salamander, Gravius.

Agatone nodded as he listened, but it was as if Dak'ir had told him he was about to conduct a weapons drill, rather than the fact that possibly the oldest living Salamander in the Chapter resided beneath their feet, a potential link to Isstvan and their lost primarch.

'I'll send word to Argos, have him requisition servitors and a Techmarine to secure the armour,' Agatone replied with almost tangible pragmatism. He didn't need to see the chamber and the stony-seated Brother Gravius. He had other matters to attend to, like the rescue of Captain N'keln, and took his brothers at their word. 'We'll need Apothecary Fugis to move our ancient brother, and we cannot have him until the siege has been broken at the iron fortress,' he added, moving the conversation swiftly on to matters of strategy.

'We cannot breach the orks' lines with the forces we have,' said Dak'ir.

Immediately after the battle, Agatone had sent out scouting forces beyond the perimeter of the encampment to spy on the greenskins, to ascertain numerical strength and forewarn of any further incursions. For now, the orks were focused on N'keln only but their forces were vast. The reports that came back from the reconnoitring troops were bleak.

Agatone considered a hololith projector that showed as accurately as the Salamanders knew the greenskins' dispositions and numbers. It looked like a grainy, dark sea lapping against a tiny bulwark on the strategic imager.

'A lightning attack would be our best option,' he said. 'If we could get amongst the orks before they knew of our presence, kill their leaders and power base, it might be enough to overcome them.'

'The dunes are mainly flat on our approach,' returned Pyriel, 'and offer a clear vantage point to the ork sentries and pickets. I doubt we would get close enough to launch a surprise attack before even the dull-witted greenskins spotted us.'

Agatone scowled, continuing to scrutinise the hololith as if an answer might present itself miraculously.

It did, but not through the means the brother-sergeant had expected.

'Use the tunnels,' a voice said behind them.

The three Salamanders turned to see Illiad, who had yet to take his leave.

'Go on,' coaxed Agatone.

Illiad cleared his throat and took a step forward.

'Throughout this region, there are subterranean tunnels. Some are manmade. We dug them to expand our settlement or seek new veins of ore. It's perilous on account of the chitin and the fact that the Iron Men took up residence in our mine. Some are hewn by the chitin themselves, often deep and wide for their burrows or whilst hunting for food. All the tunnels are linked and they go as far as the iron fortress.'

'To the surface?' asked Dak'ir, pointing upwards as he said it. 'Have you mapped them, Illiad?'

Illiad licked his lips. 'Some do breach the surface, but they are not mapped. Please understand, we have lived in these tunnels for many years, generations even, and all the cartography we will need is up here.' He put a finger to his forehead. 'And not just me,' Illiad added. 'Akuma and several others know the routes intimately too.'

Agatone nodded, his mood improving.

'We can utilise the tunnels to attack the orks directly, even in their midst.' His approving gaze fell upon Illiad. 'Your men can lead us?'

The human nodded. 'I ask only one thing,' he said.

Agatone's silence bade him to continue.

'That you let us fight.'

Dak'ir was about to protest, when Illiad raised his hand.

'Please hear me out,' he said. 'I know this world faces its last days. I have seen it in your faces and heard it in the tone of your voices. Even without that evidence, I have known it for some time. The tremors worsen, and they are not because of the chitin or the overmining. It is because Scoria is slowly breaking apart. Its end nears and I would have my people die fighting for it, rather than huddled in the darkness, waiting for the lava or the earth to claim them.'

Agatone came forwards – his shadow engulfed the human before him – and laid his massive hand on Illiad's shoulder.

'You are noble, Sonnar Illiad, and you will have your wish.' Agatone held out his other hand, offering it to the human settler. 'The Salamanders would be proud to have you at our side.'

Illiad took Agatone's hand, though it almost swallowed his, and sealed the pact of honour that was offered.

'If we can save your people and leave this planet, we will,' said Agatone. 'You shall not be abandoned, left to an ignominious death. We, human and Salamander both, will live or die together. On that you have my word.'

The moment passed and Agatone released the human from his grasp and was all business again.

'How many flamers do we have in the armorium?' he asked Dak'ir.

'Enough for two per squad.'

'Take them all, arm those who are trained to use them,' said Agatone. 'All static heavy weapons are to be stowed. We will burn these greenskin down,' he asserted. 'Then gather the squads together. We'll need every one, even the sentries.'

'Are we leaving the *Vulkan's Wrath* undefended?' asked Dak'ir.

Agatone's face had never been more serious.

'Every one, brother-sergeant. If we fail here, there'll be nothing for the *Vulkan's Wrath* anyway. We'll set up the auxiliaries again and have Argos command them. Our Master of the Forge will not leave his ship, so he can watch over it instead.'

'We will still need a distraction,' suggested Pyriel. 'Something to occupy the greenskins before we launch our assault.'

'Vox Captain N'keln,' Agatone told Dak'ir. 'Tell him of our plan and ensure that he is ready for it. Our brothers in the iron fortress will have to be our distraction.'

Illiad's voice invaded the war council for a second time.

'There may be another way.'

Agatone looked down at him.

'You are full of surprises, Sonnar Illiad,' he said, hinted humour breaking his stoic resolve. 'We are listening...'

CHAPTER ELEVEN

I
The Beast Comes…

WAR DRUMS POUNDED on an arid breeze, increasing in intensity as they signalled another ork assault. The warboss thumped its muscle-slabbed chest with a drawn chainblade, bellowing and roaring its warriors into frenzy. The greenskins' chants built with a rhythmic cadence, reaching a natural peak when they charged again. This time the warboss entered the fray itself and committed all of its tribes to the attack. Like a dark green tsunami, the greenskins rolled off the ridgeline and down into the ash basin. As they hit the bottom, the orks overcame inertia and barrelled headlong towards the wall at speed. They moved as one, the faster trucks and wagons slowing to the pace of the greenskin foot sloggers, denying their urge to go faster in favour of shielding their brethren behind the mobile barricades offered by the vehicles. Even the reckless bikers held their nerve, impelled by the warboss who rode amongst them on a massive, smoke-spewing trike.

Bolter fire barked from the walls, lighting up the gloom of the unnatural eclipse. Missiles sped outwards on streamers of white smoke, whilst the incandescent beams of multi-meltas speared the darkness and caused blossoms of fire to erupt in the shadows. The orks absorbed the terrible punishment and just kept going. Hundreds died in the punitive barrage, but thousands struck the wall and the iron fortress seemed to groan with their sudden weight.

Captain N'keln raised his gore-drenched power sword for all to see. It was a weapon wielded by a hero and a rallying symbol. N'keln understood that now and had accepted his heavy mantle, just as Tu'Shan knew he would.

'Fire-born,' he called across the comm-feed, a few minutes before the orks struck. 'Stand ready. The beast comes. Now we shall remove its head!'

Cheers echoed into the courtyard below, where Tsu'gan waited impatiently at the gate. Techmarine Draedius had repaired it from the orks' earlier assault and a cohort of almost forty Salamanders clustered behind it.

Tsu'gan was on one flank of the *Fire Anvil*, just behind the Land Raider's deadly side sponson. Though he couldn't see them with the massive assault tank in the way, he knew Praetor and the Firedrakes waited on the opposite side. Tsu'gan could feel the electricity of their thunder hammers charging the air. The scent of ozone prickled his nostrils and he focused on it in order to clear his thoughts. Soon they would be free; free of the traitor bastion's malign influence. For Tsu'gan and his squad, it couldn't come soon enough. Each was as eager as their sergeant to leave its confines and embrace true battle on the field. Only Iagon appeared subdued.

Upon ending contact with Agatone at the *Vulkan's Wrath*, Captain N'keln had thinned down the troops on the walls.

Tsu'gan's and Typhos's squads were redeployed with the other reserves in the courtyard. Though any details of the plan with Agatone were kept to N'keln himself, it was obvious to Tsu'gan that they would soon be sallying out.

Chaplain Elysius thought so too. He was standing next to Tsu'gan, having joined his squad, and ignited the crozius arcanum clenched in his black, gauntleted fist.

'This day we anoint the ash with greenskin blood,' he snarled, 'and scourge the taint of xenos from Scoria.'

The sounds of close combat filtered down to them from above. The orks had met the wall and were assaulting. Nothing came from the gate, save for the muffled din of explosions and battle cries. *Fire Anvil's* flamestorm cannons rotated meaningfully before it. Tsu'gan guessed this was the reason for the greenskins eschewing the main route into the fortress.

'You'll still burn,' he hissed beneath his breath, and listened to the static crackle down the comm-feed.

N'keln's order would unleash them into the enemy.

'Come on...' Tsu'gan muttered, gripping his bolter as if it was an ork's neck.

DAK'IR CROUCHED IN the darkness of the tunnels. Ahead of him came the echoing screech of the chitin-beasts, followed by the roar of Ba'ken's heavy flamer. The flare of fire lit the Salamander's imposing silhouette, roughly fifty metres in front, as he corralled the creatures with careful bursts.

Illiad hunkered down beside Dak'ir with fifty of his men. He huddled a lasgun close to his chest and watched the driven chitin intently as they became lost in the darkness.

The scent of something sharp and acerbic bit at Dak'ir's enhanced senses. It was pungent, sulphurous and held the trace of a lingering memory. It put him in mind of smoke and cinder...

'How close are we to the mines from here?' he asked Illiad.

Illiad shook his head. 'Not very,' he said. 'The mines are much closer to the core and several kilometres distant.'

'Distant enough so as not to hear the battles above us?'

'Definitely. The rock face is shored up by reinforced struts and metal plating to keep out the chitin. It also insulates the mining chamber against ambient sound. In any case, they are far from here.'

Yet the acerbic tang remained.

Illiad's expression suggested he craved an answer.

Dak'ir wasn't about to give it to him. Instead, he signalled the advance.

The Salamanders at the *Vulkan's Wrath* only had four squads at their disposal. The Thunderfire cannons were ill-suited to close assault warfare and so stayed behind in a small concession by Agatone to help protect the crash site. The rest were divided up into combat squads; with injuries some were only four men strong. Settlers accompanied them, both as guides and reinforcements. With their help, the Salamanders had found the chitin burrows swiftly and set about stirring their nests.

As Dak'ir moved, he heard the ruckus of battle above them like muted thunder. It was getting closer all the time.

THE WALL WAS in danger of being overrun. Even the Devastators, aloft in the high towers, were coming under pressure. They targeted the orks assailing the fortress directly now, going to their bolters and ignoring the distant wagons and trucks that jostled their way from the back of the horde. Desultory cannon fire from the far off vehicles carrying most of the greenskins' heavy guns occasionally raked the parapet but was mercifully ineffective.

A rocket exploded overhead, showering Tsu'gan's armour with debris. He half-glimpsed snarling ork faces through the tiny fissures in the makeshift gate. Still they refused to assault it. All their efforts were bent against the wall. The pressure there was building to breaking point. Tsu'gan's battle-brothers were holding on tenaciously, heaving orks bodily into the green surf pounding against the foot of the wall below. The bite of chainswords ringed the air in a churning chorus. On the opposite side, the wrecked corpse of a Salamander crashed down into the courtyard. It was Brother Va'tok, his power armour cloven, battle-helm staved in by an ork mace. The dead Salamander's fingers were still twitching in his gauntlets when Fugis rushed forwards to extract Va'tok's geneseed.

Tsu'gan raged at the death. It took all of his willpower not to turn around and climb up to wall to vent his fury.

'Vulkan's blood!' he snarled, forcing as much venom as he could into the invective.

Elysius felt it too, rotating his crozius in small arcs to keep his wrist loose and muttering spleenful litanies under his breath. The Chaplain would wait for the opportune moment to give his canticles of hate full voice.

'Raise shields!' Tsu'gan heard Praetor cry out to the Firedrakes from the other side of the Land Raider. The *clank* of metal resounded in the courtyard as the Terminators' storm shields met their pauldrons and locked in place.

The order from N'keln was imminent.

Crackling static in Tsu'gan's battle-helm gave way to the captain's steely voice.

'Unto the anvil, brothers!'

The gate came down. A long burst from the *Fire Anvil's* flamestorm cannons burned clear the immediate area beyond it.

Led by Praetor, the Firedrakes were the first out, tramping onto scorched earth, smoking husks of orks crushed in their sudden charge. Thunder hammers filled the air with flashing discharge from their power generators. Trying to respond, the greenskins hurled themselves at the Terminators but found an unyielding rock against which they were smashed.

The Firedrakes were devastating, and Tsu'gan almost found himself agape at their fury. They moved amidst the greenskin horde, pummelling with their shields, crushing skulls with their hammers. Praetor extolled the glories of the vaunted 1st Company as they killed, his sheer presence impelling his warriors to even greater efforts. Tsu'gan saw the veteran sergeant's plan at once. He had his sights set on the ork warboss.

'To the fires of war!' roared Elysius, once the Terminators had cleared the threshold.

Tsu'gan ran with him, closing the gap behind their 1st Company brothers swiftly. Close-ranged bolter fire tore into the orks, as Tsu'gan ordered 'weapons free', and blasted the greenskins apart.

Expulsed promethium merged with the stink of burning ork flesh as Honorious unleashed his flamer. To the rear of the assault group a combat squad made a staggered advance, allowing M'lek to loose his multi-melta. A brutish greenskin, two heads taller than Tsu'gan, its body an armoured shell of plates and whining servos, had its torso liquidised to visceral slag by the multi-melta's beam. It fell back into a steaming heap, crushing two of its smaller brethren.

Tsu'gan heard the bass tones of Sergeant Typhos as he sang a Promethean battle anthem, describing bloody arcs with the rise and fall of his thunder hammer.

As the three squads slowly converged, forming into a spear shape with Praetor and the Firedrakes as its burning tip, the ork attack on the wall was stymied. Without constant reinforcements, the greenskins already contesting the fortress were left isolated. It allowed the defenders to cleanse the parapets.

Overhead, the warriors of Vargo's Assault squad soared on wings of fire. Plunging down amidst the greenskins, they released bolt and blade with a zealot's fervour, small bursts from the squad's flamer adding to the carnage. They were the last element of the Salamander assault force, and in their wake the *Fire Anvil* rolled into the breach left behind by the fallen gate. The tank's bulk easily filled the blackened arch. Sporadic spears of flame from its sponson guns kept the orks at bay. When the initial shock of the Salamanders' attack had waned, they found themselves locked in a deadly melee. Ork bodies pressed on every side, raw aggression lending the beasts the impetus they needed to get back on an even footing. Only now, wading in the belligerent sea of green, did Tsu'gan fully appreciate what they were up against. Between bolter bursts, he heard a muffled cry and saw what he thought was one of Vargo's brothers falling into the morass of orks. The Salamander didn't resurface. Another, Typhos's special weapons trooper Urion, took a chainblade to the forehead. The exultant ork was shredded by return fire from the dead Salamander's battle-brothers, and the body was left quivering with the still churning blade that the greenskin had lost its grip on wedged in the wound. Soon Urion was swallowed up by the ork horde too.

They gained about three hundred metres from the gate when the *Fire Anvil*'s engines stirred into life. The assault tank barrelled into the killing field, barging greenskins aside with its hull or mulching them beneath its grinding tracks.

This was 'hammer', the second phase of N'keln's assault stratagem. The captain was embarked in the Land Raider with the Inferno Guard and the Tactical squad of

Sergeant De'mas. Filling the void left behind by the tank was Clovius and his squad. They would hold the gate, whilst the Devastators, utilising the respite bought by Praetor's and the assault force's bravura, would abandon the towers and defend the walls in the absence of the Tactical squads. Lok assumed command position over the gatehouse and was charged to hold the iron fortress in case N'keln needed to order a retreat.

Even as ork blood spat across his visor, Tsu'gan knew there would no such retreat. The Salamanders were committed now. It was a simple matter of do or die.

A cleaver rang against his pauldron, spitting sparks, and he staggered. The ork assailing him lunged forward, strings of spittle punched from its maw on stinking breath. Tsu'gan rammed his bolter's muzzle into the beast's mouth and pulled the trigger. Blood and brain matter burst out the back of the ork's head, mixing with skull fragments.

Tiberon came in from the left and smashed the greenskin corpse aside, allowing Tsu'gan to drive forward. Iagon and Lazarus followed, maintaining pace with the implacable Firedrakes.

Praetor was battering his way to the ork warboss. Seeing prey and the prospect of a good fight, the immense leader of the greenskins spurred its biker-mounted entourage forwards. A thickening horde of orks still lay between it and the Terminators.

Assault cannon whining, the *Fire Anvil* scythed down a first rank of orks spilling from the throng with blades raised. More greenskins came in their stead and Tsu'gan met them with a bolter storm from his troopers.

Praetor exploited the slight gap, crushing the dead and wounded underfoot, as something huge lumbered into view. Orks scattered before it, bellowing and roaring for more carnage. A steel-plated machinery loomed. Trunk-bellied, resembling a can festooned with weapons and two razor-edged power claws, the greenskin war machine thundered forward on piston legs. One of the Firedrakes charged into its path, hammer aloft and crackling lightning. The machinery punched the warrior aside. Swinging its power claw, the crude creation clove a storm shield in two, overloading its force field and smashing its bearer to the ground. Buoyed by its own infernal momentum, the machine, with the band of orks following, drove a wedge into the Salamanders' spear formation. The Firedrakes' tip fragmented apart. Praetor, desperate to close with the war machine, was engulfed by greenskins. Capering gretchin, heedless of death, clung madly to his arms and legs in an effort to slow the hero of Prometheus.

Honorious bathed the sergeant of the Firedrakes with his flamer, burning the diminutive greenskins off him like they were an infestation.

The ork war engine was rampaging still. Its pilot was obviously deranged, so fuelled by the psychic energy of the orks that the machine was almost unstoppable. It turned and fought in every direction, battering at the Firedrakes who surrounded it, but couldn't close.

Tsu'gan went to Praetor's aid, rushing on even as the flames from Honorious were still dying, and forging a bloody path with the rest of his squad. The pressure on the Firedrake sergeant lessened and he broke free, ramming an ork aside with his storm shield as he approached the ork machine that had scattered them.

In the distance, something was happening. A thick cloud of dust spewed into the air and Tsu'gan swore he saw a cluster of orks disappear below the earth. Bestial screams followed swiftly as the greenskins reacted to something in their midst. On the opposite side of the battlefield, another dust plume spiralled upwards, then another and another. Grey columns of ash were erupting all across the dunes and orks were sinking down into an unseen mire.

Behind him, the *clang* of the *Fire Anvil*'s frontal ramp announced N'keln's arrival on the battlefield. Tsu'gan turned briefly to witness the company banner unfurled by Malicant and his captain leading a fresh charge into the enemy with the rest of the Inferno Guard and Brother-Sergeant De'mas.

Turning his attention back on the greenskin machinery, Tsu'gan went in support of Praetor. The Firedrake sergeant faced off against the manic war engine, rebounding a blow from one its power claws with his storm shield. The ork pilot had overreached itself and was off balance. Praetor shattered the claw arm with a blow from his thunder hammer, before stepping in heavily to shoulder barge it. The ork pilot flailed at its controls, emulated by the machine itself. Tsu'gan, blindsiding it, ducked beneath a madly swiping claw and attached a melta-bomb to the war engine's body. Throwing himself backwards, Tsu'gan felt the heat of the explosion wash over his armour as the machine burst apart. Chips of debris fell like steel rain, a steaming pair of ruined legs holding up an abdomen of sloughed metal all that remained of the machinery, collapsing onto the ash.

Praetor had withstood the blast and drove on almost instantly, whilst Tsu'gan was still getting to his feet. The intensity of the ork assault was lessening. The guttural cries from those greenskins seemingly swallowed by the dunes were much closer now. At last he saw the cause.

Swarms of enraged chitin were rampaging amongst the horde. The orks hacked away at the carapace bodies of the subterranean creatures, their silt-blood mingling with the ash dunes in a grey soup. Sink holes devoured greenskins by the score, the soft earth, churned up by the chitin, no longer supporting the weight of the orks.

Familiar forms followed in the ash clouds, surging from the emergence holes bolters flaring. Agatone and the Salamanders from the *Vulkan's Wrath* had joined up with them, driving the chitin before them like cattle to dig their assault tunnels.

Flame bursts spat through the murk, burning down orks in a fire-tinged haze of grey.

Through the dissipating ash cloud and the rampant pull and thrust of warring bodies, Tsu'gan saw an Assault squad crest the edge of a fresh emergence hole. They took to the air immediately, jump packs screaming. Orks were set ablaze in the violent discharge; one stumbled blindly into the gaping chasm made by the chitin and was lost from view.

Then he saw Dak'ir amongst the reinforcements. The Ignean came out fighting, gutting an ork on his chainsword whilst vaporising the snarling head of another with a shot from his plasma pistol. Tsu'gan felt his jaw harden. He was determined not to be outdone. He caught sight of Chaplain Elysius going after Praetor and the Firedrakes. They were headed towards an inexorable confrontation with the ork warboss. Smiling darkly, Tsu'gan followed.

II
Be the Anvil. Become the Hammer

ISLANDS OF OPEN ground were appearing in the green sea as Dak'ir led his combat squad up to the surface. Orks still thronged the ash dunes, just as Agatone's scouts had reported, but a single mass had become isolated knots. The coherency alloying the greenskins together was breaking. Survival instincts were overthrowing the desire for conquest, and tribal rivalries, once quashed by their overlord's brute menace, had begun to surface. Infighting ravaged groups of orks at the fringes of the battle, sensing the turn in fortunes and staking early claims of leadership.

'Stay with me, Illiad,' shouted Dak'ir, the flare of his plasma pistol dying down as a headless ork crumpled away from him and the humans reached the surface.

Sonnar Illiad merely nodded. His rugged face was pale, his muscles bunched tight as he gripped his lasgun harder than he needed to. The other settlers were the same. To their credit, they were organised and steadfast, but they had obviously never fought in such a conflict before. For a moment, Dak'ir regretted not opposing their role in the battle in front of Agatone. When a lasgun salvo shredded a mob of onrushing orks, he changed his mind. A man fighting for his home will do so to the death and with all of his resolve. Dak'ir wouldn't deny the settlers that.

Even as the orks broke, Dak'ir saw N'keln bringing the disparate forces of the Salamanders together.

Be the anvil. Become the hammer.

The captain's words returned to him.

'Cleanse and burn,' Dak'ir barked into the comm-feed.

Ba'ken was the first forward from his sergeant's right shoulder, spewing a carpet of fire into the greenskins.

A second burst erupted from the heavy flamer of Venerable Brother Amadeus, who had lumbered from the chitin emergence hole behind them.

'*Cleanse and burn,*' echoed the Salamander Dreadnought. The tinny resonance of its vox-emitter boomed above the roar of the conflagration engulfing the orks.

Scorched earth was all that stood between Dak'ir and the Inferno Guard once the flames had died. Ashen husks broke apart under booted feet as the brother-sergeant sought his captain's side. N'keln was cutting his way through the greenskins with his power sword. Behind him, the company banner was providing a glorious backdrop upheld by Malicant behind him. *Fire Anvil* ground slowly after them, spitting out plumes of fire and stitching orks with explosive rounds from its assault cannon.

Reunited with his captain again, Dak'ir levelled his chainsword as more orks came at them.

'Forward!'

As more Salamanders fought their way to N'keln, a nexus of strength started to gather.

The anvil was slowly forming. Next would be the hammer.

Dak'ir saw its target through a fiery heat haze.

THE GREENSKIN WARBOSS ignored the bickering hordes, intent on the 'tin men' who had just destroyed its orkoid war machine.

Slewing to a halt, barely a hundred metres away from the advancing Salamanders, the beast bellowed out a challenge. Sitting up in the bucket-seat of its wartrike, the warboss thrust its chin at Praetor.

Tsu'gan reached the veteran sergeant's side in time to hear his order to the Firedrakes.

'Kill it,' he growled.

Praetor was a hero, a veteran of countless battles and campaigns. His personal roll of honour in the Firedrakes was long and distinguished with many kill markings. But he was also a pragmatist and not given to grand gestures. Vainglory simply didn't appeal to him. Let the scribes and remembrancers write what they would. Praetor just wanted the green bastard dead. So, he'd level everything he had at it.

The Firedrakes came forward as one, an imposing wall of armour.

Annoyed that the tin man wasn't responding to its goading, the warboss sent its biker squadrons ahead of it. A mob of its own clan orks followed, more heavily armoured and better disciplined that the other tribes.

Tsu'gan's world shrank to a single combat – his squad with Elysius and the Firedrakes versus the warboss and his brood.

'Take them down!' he roared. The onrushing bikers were engulfed in a bolter storm.

JAGGED WHITE DAGGERS seared behind Dak'ir's eyes and he felt blood on the side of his head. He'd lost his battle-helm. Maybe he'd wrenched it loose, he couldn't remember. The ork swung at him again. He could smell the stink of blood on its cleaver as it missed his face by centimetres. Swiping low, Dak'ir chewed up the beast's leg with his chainsword. Brother Zo'tan put a bolt through its brain before it struck the ground.

Three more greenskins came howling at them from the side. A wave of heat rippled there for a few seconds as Ba'ken torched them with his heavy flamer. Dak'ir gave a curt nod of thanks and drove on.

The battle was far from over.

Orks were everywhere, and though many had died in the shock assault or were fleeing, fighting amongst themselves or finishing off the chitin, there were hundreds of others still intent on killing the Salamanders.

Illiad's settlers had taken the worst of it so far. Easy meat, the orks must have decided. Of the fifty that had joined Dak'ir's squad, only twenty-three remained. The Salamanders had tried to shield them, but with foes coming at them from every direction it was an impossible task.

Blood and death were ubiquitous on the killing field. As a Space Marine, Dak'ir was able to assess and regulate every combat, carefully compartmentalise it and, in his enhanced battle state, prosecute the Emperor's justice with efficiency and focused fury. The humans had no such resource and simply fought what they could and tried to stay alive.

'Stay with the captain!' Robbed of the comm-feed in his battle-helm, Dak'ir was forced to shout the order to his combat squad.

N'keln was several paces ahead of them, long strides taking him into the thick of the greenskins where his power sword flashed like an angel of judgement. The lead only increased as he killed, slaying the orks with utter impunity. The spirit of Vulkan was with him now, the indomitable will and matchless strength of the primarch. Even the Inferno Guard, his retinue, were struggling to keep up.

Dak'ir saw Fugis lagged the farthest behind. He was cradling Brother L'sen, one of Dak'ir's troopers, part of the second combat squad – he hadn't even witnessed him fall. Badly wounded, his chest opened up by an ork cleaver, but still alive, L'sen fired his bolter one-handed and shot the legs out from under a charging greenskin, whilst Fugis, bolt pistol bucking violently in his grasp, destroyed the face of another.

Illiad and the humans stayed with them as Dak'ir's group caught up. They adopted a circle formation and issued a standing fusillade of las-fire into the approaching orks.

Dak'ir couldn't protect them any longer. He saw the warboss looming in the distance. The Firedrakes were about to engage it.

N'keln would reach the warboss after them. Dak'ir upped his pace, determined he would face the beast at his captain's side.

TORQUING THE THROTTLE of his wartrike, the ork warboss tore across the dunes and straight at the Firedrakes.

The spoiling force the ork had sent ahead was all but destroyed. Bikers lay in mangled heaps, entwined with the wreckage of their mechanical steeds. The Terminators had hit them like a battering ram. Any orks that survived the suicidal run, through either fluke or cowardice, were cut up by Tsu'gan's and his squad's bolters.

Chaplain Elysius took great pleasure in despatching the riders, scything them down as they sped past, screams of glee turning to horror and ultimately agony as he shattered bones and severed heads with his crozius. Every ork death was punctuated with a different tirade. The clan orks still endured though and they barrelled after their leader in a raging mob as the warboss surged ahead of them.

Meaty fists clenched around the fat triggers of the trike's chainguns, the warboss cackled, the throaty sound emulating the cracking report of the frontmounts. White muzzle flashes lit up the beast's snarling visage as the cannons barked loudly.

A hail of slugs rattled against the armour of the Terminators ineffectually, little more deterrent than an insect swarm. Hastily, Praetor ordered them to form a shield wall to block the ork's charge. The Firedrakes locked together and presented a stout barrier of ceramite.

This only seemed to drive the beast into a greater frenzy, hooting and bellowing as the hot air rushed past it, spittle drooling from the corner of its mouth in a long stream.

Tsu'gan smiled grimly when he saw the warboss commit to the charge.

It'll be smashed into oblivion.

Then he noticed the mass of incendiaries packed around the trike. His smile turned into a horrified grimace. Sticks of dynamite were strapped around the frame, other more volatile explosives piled up in lashed-together canisters and dull grey packets.

The wartrike was a giant, moving bomb.

Insane chuckling from the warboss preceded a gout of fire erupting from hidden boosters below. As the beast was launched into the air, Tsu'gan noticed the crude endeavours of orkish science; the warboss's legs were largely mechanical and a single-shot rocket burst was fashioned into them that lifted it free of the trike, igniting the incendiaries at the same time.

The sergeant didn't even have time to shout a warning as the explosives went up in a huge mushroom cloud, tearing the trike apart in a maelstrom of fire and frag. The blast wave alone smashed Tsu'gan off his feet. He and his squad were flattened by it. Pain, like white fire, engulfed them.

Even the hardy Terminators staggered, appearing as vague silhouettes through the dirty cloud that expanded outwards voraciously.

Several orks died in the blast, those at the head of the charging mob. They were spun into the air like sticks and landed gracelessly in broken heaps. Amidst this orkoid rain, the warboss came down too. It landed heavily, a tremor rippling outwards from its impact on the densely-packed ash dunes, as the rocket fuel in its boosters bled away to extinction.

Though still groggy from the explosion, Brother Namor of the Firedrakes came at the landed warboss, thunder hammer swinging. He'd lost his storm shield, severed in two halves by the destroyed ork war engine. The warboss laughed, and smacked Namor's blow aside, before tearing a hole through his Terminator armour with its power claw. Despite all its proofs, the venerable suit was badly rent, and Namor with it. The Firedrake was spilling blood and intestine as he fell forwards into the ash and lay still.

Brother Clyten charged in from the opposite flank, hoping to catch the beast off-guard. Reacting to the destruction at different speeds, the Firedrakes were attacking piecemeal. The oath of vengeance on Clyten's lips died abruptly when the warboss lunged forward and head-butted him. The blow was so powerful it cracked open the Firedrake's helmet and he too fell.

A cry of anguish ripped from Praetor's mouth when he saw his brothers falling. He tried to marshal his remaining warriors and close with the beast but by now the ork mob had caught up. Greenskin bodies swamped them, a multitude of crude blades, cudgels and chains flashing out at the Firedrakes. It was like using a rubber hammer to bring down a bastion wall. But then the orks were not necessarily intending to kill, only to delay.

All the while, the warboss laughed loudly, revelling in the carnage it was wreaking.

Brother Elysius aimed to sour the beast's ebullient mood. Stepping into a void in the aftermath of the explosion, he brandished his crozius. Lightning crackled over the surface of the weapon, emulating the Chaplain's hatred. The bile-filled litany was already half-formed as it passed his lips.

'*...and the perfidy of the alien shall be met with cleansing fire and burning blade. Its form, reviled and repugnant, shall be cast down into the pit of damnation.*'

Elysius swung his crozius in a short arc, making a jagged trail of sparking energy that hung for a few seconds in the air. It was meant as a goad.

'Face *me*, xenos filth,' he snarled.

Recognising another challenger, the warboss beat its chest in anticipation of a good fight.

Tsu'gan was still getting to his feet when he saw Elysius facing off against the beast. The Chaplain, ordinarily imposing, looked small against the sheer bulk of the massive ork. It was easily several heads taller, and almost twice as wide. Tsu'gan felt dazed; his ears were still ringing from the blast and black clouds circled menacingly at the periphery of his vision. He shook them away through force of will.

He must have been thrown from the blast. A skid furrow in the ash in the shape of his body, several metres long, bore testament to the sergeant's supposition.

Putting his foot forward, Tsu'gan realised he was bleeding. He felt it, wet heat behind his battle-plate, and bit back a rush of agony.

'To the Chaplain,' he croaked, tasting copper in his mouth and forged towards where man and beast faced off in uneven contest.

N'KELN WAS BECOMING a distant figure. Dak'ir slew a greenskin at almost every stroke, his chainsword clogged with churned flesh, but still the captain bested him. A bloody path, ragged and limb-strewn, described his passage through the orks. It made following him easier, and as the carnage wore on, fewer and fewer greenskins filled the void left in N'keln's wake.

The Inferno Guard were closest, Shen'kar cutting down swathes of orks with his flamer, whilst Malicant held the company banner aloft. Fugis, Dak'ir had lost from sight. He had been left behind, ministering to the fallen even as he killed the enemy, the ultimate dichotomy of life and death expressed through an individual.

Dak'ir judged he was roughly four paces behind the Inferno Guard, and they four paces behind N'keln. The brother-sergeant had Emek at his side with Apion and Romulus. Ba'ken had opted to lag back and try to protect the settlers. Dak'ir lauded his heroism, but wished the bulky trooper was with him now.

Shattering an orkoid clavicle with a blow from his chainsword before burning a hole through its torso with his plasma pistol, Dak'ir saw the black armour of Chaplain Elysius in the gap left by the greenskin's falling body.

He faced off against the ork warboss. The shadow of its horrifying stature eclipsed him. Others were rushing in support; Dak'ir saw Praetor and two of his Firedrakes free themselves from a swarm of greenskins. Tsu'gan, too, was staggering towards him, his squad belatedly in tow.

Even from distance, Dak'ir could tell they would not reach Elysius in time. The Chaplain would have to fight the beast alone.

AN ORK TRUCK exploded somewhere off to Tsu'gan's right, a roiling smoke cloud obscuring his vision as he lost Elysius from view.

By the time it cleared, he saw the Chaplain was bent down to one knee. The beast loomed above him, pressing Elysius down into the ash by grinding his chainblade against the Chaplain's upraised crozius. There was a dark welt above the ork's left eye and an angry black scorch mark where the crozius had stung him.

Elysius was buckling.

Tsu'gan struggled to reach him, pain anchoring his legs and weighing them down. He watched, almost transfixed, as the Chaplain aimed his bolt pistol through a gap in the crackling arcs thrown off by the crozius, only for the warboss to lash down with its power claw.

The ground trembled as another tremor wracked Scoria. Elysius screamed in unison with it, and his anguish seemed to shake the world. His arm was severed at the elbow. Blood was gushing from the wound, creating an ugly red mire around the Chaplain's feet and bended knee. Elysius seemed to sink into it, the beast pressing down relentlessly as it stepped forward to crush the severed forearm into paste in a wanton act of mutilation.

He was only a few metres away, but Tsu'gan could taste the death blow coming, feel it like a change in the wind or a lurch in his stomach.

The Chaplain was about to die, and there was nothing Tsu'gan could do to prevent it. Another hero of the company slain, just like–

Then N'keln was there, drakescale cloak billowing with the rush of his charge, twin-bladed power sword gleaming, and fate was reversed. Bellowing Vulkan's name, he rammed the master-crafted sword into the ork's neck and drew it out in a welter of dark blood. The beast roared; a ragged cry emitted from its ruined throat where the gore was pumping readily. Elysius was forgotten and the Chaplain collapsed from shock and blood loss. N'keln took a blow from the ork's power claw against the flat of his blade and the air around them became electrified.

Tsu'gan tasted the ozone. It numbed his lips and tanged his tongue as if it were on fire. Despite the pain, he was running. His bolter was out, the promethium canister for the flamer attachment long spent too, so he drew his spatha.

The earth shook again, in eerie synergy with the titanic battle unfolding upon it. The ork warboss rained down blows upon the Salamander captain like an angry giant. Each was like a comet, skull-bound and destined to kill before N'keln's sword skill diffused or deflected it. A dark and viscous tabard of blood coated the ork's chest now, a second mouth cut by N'keln's power sword in its neck frothing crimson. Digging furrows in the ground, the Salamander captain was pushed back by the ork's fury, finding no purchase in ash.

Slow exsanguination was making the warboss sluggish. Its movements were heavier; its prodigious strength fading. The more it exerted itself, the faster its blood spilled from its body. N'keln knew it and based his combat strategy on attrition – it was a gloriously Promethean way to slay an enemy. None could match a Salamander for sheer tenacity. Fire-born never knew when they were beaten.

The warboss slipped, its intended death blow failing to connect, and N'keln took his chance. Having dodged the downward swipe of the ork's power claw, he stepped into its fighting arc and cut off the wrist holding the chainblade. N'keln then reversed the cut and brought it up into the beast's exposed flank. The mono-molecular edge of the power-charged blades melted metal and overloaded the narrow-field force generator rippling energy across the greenskin's armour. It howled as the sword bit into hide then flesh and finally bone.

The stink of cooking meat assailed Tsu'gan's nostrils as he came at the ork from its blind side, ramming his spatha into an exposed patch of green skin between the plates and the chain links.

N'keln drove his sword deeper, searching for organs and grisly ways to ruin this monster from within. The beast lifted its power claw, a heavy burden, in attempted retaliation. Praetor smashed it down again with a blow from his thunder hammer, the sergeant and his warriors having joined the battle at last. One of his Firedrakes, Brother Ma'nubian, rammed the edge of his storm shield into the ork's screaming maw.

Still it refused to die, its tiny eyes like malevolent red suns making false promises of retribution. The warboss bowed, the weight of its body dragging it downwards. A plasma blast seared its shoulder, Dak'ir shooting through a gap in the melee.

A dark figure loomed before the near-dead ork.

It was Elysius. He was bent-backed too, agony creasing his features behind the skull-faced grimace of his battle-helm. The cleaved forearm had clotted almost, the Larraman cells working hard to staunch the wound. A fine drizzle of blood issued from the ragged stump where at first there had been a torrent, and the Chaplain cradled it close to his body protectively. Despite his passing out, he had maintained his grip on his crozius arcanum.

'Death to the ork!' he rasped, bringing the crackling mace down and staving in the beast's skull.

It was to prove the final blow in the greenskins' defeat. Without their warboss to unify them, the clans broke apart fully. Ill-disciplined, fighting amongst themselves, the orks were soon destroyed. Many fled across the dunes into oblivion in the face of the Salamanders' victory.

The beast's own clan fought to the end, but the Fire-drakes and the newly arrived squads of Dak'ir and Tsu'gan, together with other reinforcements, quickly vanquished them. The Inferno Guard went to their lord's side. Brother Malicant passed the company banner to N'keln who thrust it into the gloaming sky and roared.

'Glory to Prometheus! Glory to Vulkan and the Emperor!'

The Salamanders cheered, as did the human settlers, though they didn't know what they were cheering about, only that they were alive and the swine-tusks were dead.

Ba'ken caught up to Dak'ir and the rest, the slumped carcass of the ork warboss cooling slowly in front of them.

'The greenskins have broken,' he announced.

Dak'ir saw Illiad following behind him and was glad the human had survived. Seventeen other settlers accompanied him.

'They gave their lives for their home,' said Illiad as he approached, guessing the Salamander sergeant's thoughts. 'It is what they and their families would have wanted.' His mood was defiant, but sombre and grim too. The grief would come later.

'Akuma?' Dak'ir asked of the only other settler he knew the name of that had fought in the battle.

'He died with honour,' Ba'ken told him, and was struck by the sadness in his voice. 'He is resting now, before I take him to the pyreum to join the other heroes who fell today.'

A sombre quietude followed, broken by the arrival of the captain.

'Well met, brothers,' said N'keln, handing the banner back to Malicant and going to stand amongst them.

The assembled Salamanders bowed slightly, humbled by their captain's courage and prowess.

Dak'ir felt emboldened by it and was gladdened that N'keln had found his strength through the fires of battle. The anvil had tested him and he had emerged reforged. His optimism was abruptly crushed when he caught the baleful gaze of Tsu'gan regarding him. The glow in the brother-sergeant's eyes was dimmed as he moved awkwardly. Fresh scars crosshatched his face, the honour markings of a battle well fought. Others would be added in recognition of this day by the brander-priests. Tsu'gan's look of ire was fleeting as he passed from Dak'ir to N'keln. Dak'ir was heartened to see respect there and surprised to admit to himself that perhaps Tsu'gan's concerns were legitimate at first, that he desired what was best for the company and not some grab for glory. If his brother-sergeant could acknowledge his mistake in hasty judgement, then perhaps Dak'ir should do so also concerning Tsu'gan's motives. It didn't mean the enmity between them had lessened, though.

'Apothecary Fugis will tend to that,' N'keln told Elysius, his tone brooking no argument from the Chaplain.

Dak'ir was astounded the Chaplain was still standing given the severity of the wound, even for one as robust as an Astartes.

Elysius merely nodded. The adrenaline was leaving his body now, and he had to focus all of his efforts on staying on his feet and conscious.

'What now, my lord?' asked Praetor, carrying scars of his own. His gaze flicked briefly to the distance where Namor and Clyten had fallen. Two of their battle-brothers had dragged them together in readiness for Fugis's reductor. Sadness shadowed Praetor's face for a moment before the sternness returned. 'The orks are defeated, but the *Vulkan's Wrath* is grounded still and we are no closer to discovering why the Tome of Fire led us here.'

'And the tremors worsen by the hour,' said Tsu'gan, his voice a strained rasp. 'How much longer before this world cracks apart and is sundered to galactic dust?'

A nerve trembled in Illiad's cheek, just below his left eye, at Tsu'gan's callous remark. The brother-sergeant neither appreciated or noticed the effect his referral to the imminent demise of Scoria had upon the human native.

Dak'ir stepped forward humbly, bowing his head in respect to Praetor and N'keln.

'I may have an answer to the second question,' he said.

'For now, it must wait,' Elysius interrupted. Fugis was now at his side and attending to the Chaplain's severed arm.

With his other hand, Elysius gestured to the sky.

The Salamanders around N'keln followed his gaze to where the black rock throbbed like a malignant tumour. It seemed larger than before. The sun was now totally engulfed by it. Not even a ring of light remained, just blackness, empty and consumptive. Splinters were breaking off from it, like jagged, purposeful hail homing in on the planet.

Ork ships. Many more than before.

Despite the victory, the Salamanders were weakened. Though united, they had fought and paid much to defeat the greenskins. There were no further reinforcements, no way to replenish their numbers. All that they had was there before them, tired and battered upon the bloodied ash dunes.

'How long?' asked N'keln, his voice was deep and forbidding.

'A few hours,' answered Elysius. 'That is all the time we have left.'

CHAPTER TWELVE

Decisions

CHAPTER TWELVE

I
Doomed

'BRING HIM OUT.'

The Chaplain's severed arm was swathed in a bloody sling, and he hugged it close to his body subconsciously as he issued the curt order.

The chirurgeon-interrogators responded dutifully. The excrutiator frame and its incarcerated Iron Warrior War-smith were dragged into the eldritch day.

The prisoner had been secured within the hold of one of the company's Rhinos. The idea was to keep him away from the Salamanders on the walls and prevent him spewing any Chaotic dogma in an effort to dissuade them from their purpose.

A small group looked on in the courtyard of the iron fortress as the traitor was wheeled into view. Dak'ir was amongst the party that also included N'keln, Praetor and Pyriel. True to recent form, the Librarian was never far away from him now and glanced at the brother-sergeant studiously from time to time. Dak'ir did not know what was happening to him, nor what Pyriel made of it. If

Scoria was to prove the 3rd Company's final battlefield, he might never find out. He knew it was getting stronger however, and despite all of his experience, training and hypno-conditioning, he was afraid of it.

Elysius was leading the interrogation, refusing any further medical assistance besides the bandaged layer of gauze beneath the sling used to bind his grievous wound.

Fugis had expected nothing less. There was little love lost between them, operating as they did at opposite ends of the war spectrum. Dak'ir assumed the Apothecary was busied elsewhere, tending to the injured, extracting the geneseed of the dead. The brother-sergeant guessed that Fugis did so in the troop compartment of *Fire Anvil*. N'keln had declared that the keep of the iron fortress remain sealed. True, the intensity of the ill-feeling and baleful emanations coming from the very stone and metal it was forged of, had, in the absence of the orks' natural psychic effusion, ebbed, but whatever lurked in the bowels of that place, corporeal or not, needed to stay there, locked away.

The Land Raider was a good enough substitute in lieu of a more expansive makeshift Apothecarion. Many injured Salamanders, even human settlers, gathered around the periphery of the assault tank awaiting an Apothecary's ministrations.

Dak'ir had seen Tsu'gan enter a half hour ago, annoyed that he would not bear witness to the interrogation but ordered by N'keln to be assessed and made ready for battle again as soon as possible. In the light of his apparent reneging over contesting the captaincy of 3rd Company, Dak'ir resolved to meet with him and settle a few things before the orks came.

The rest of the Salamanders, those whose wounds were not severe or requiring Fugis's attention, were arrayed around the battlements in front of the gate.

Together, they watched the skies and dunes. Overhead, the black rock loomed like a curse. A few hours were all that remained before the greenskins made landfall, the sky blotted with the orks' raking ships.

'Speak, traitor, and your death will be swift,' declared Elysius, summoning up his hatred despite his pain and discomfort.

The Iron Warrior failed to speak out loud, but there was a muttered sound emanating from his covered mouth.

'Louder, craven worshipper of the false gods,' spat Elysius. 'True servants of the Emperor do not cower behind whispers.'

Dak'ir caught the susurrus of words as the Iron Warrior turned to face the Chaplain and raised his voice.

'Iron Within. Iron Without,' he chanted, like a mantra.

A lightning flash pre-empted Elysius's cudgelling of the traitor across the chest with his crozius. The weapon was at low power, so it didn't kill the prisoner. The scar of scorched flesh was visible on his body, though, and infected the breeze with its noisome odour.

Dak'ir noticed that the Chaplain wasn't using his chirurgeon-interrogators to question the Iron Warrior, preferring, uncharacteristically, to do the work himself. He was obviously angry at the ork's mauling of him and levelled that anger at the traitor.

'No riddles,' he snarled, stowing his crozius to draw out his bolt pistol. He pressed the cold muzzle against the Iron Warrior's forehead. 'Speak.'

'Iron Within. Iron Without,' replied the prisoner, continuing to be uncooperative.

'I will not ask a third time,' Elysius promised, pressing the bolt pistol hard against the Iron Warrior's head. 'Tell me now how you defeated the greenskins. How were you able to survive? Is the cannon in the bowels of your foetid bastion something to do with it? What is its purpose? Speak quickly!'

'Iron Wi–' the traitor began, before stopping abruptly. The shadow of the falling splinters from the black rock had shrouded the courtyard. 'Doomed,' he rasped.

Elysius followed his gaze, along with Dak'ir and the others. They all knew what was coming.

Earlier, on the return journey from the killing fields beyond the fortress, Dak'ir had described to N'keln the nature of the black rock as told to him by the human settler, Illiad. It was akin to a planetoid, rotating on a horseshoe orbit around Scoria; a planetoid inhabited solely by orks. Every few years it would come close enough to Scoria for the orks to launch their crude atmospheric craft to make war on those that inhabited the planet – for orks love war. Prior to the Salamanders' arrival that war had been waged against the Iron Warriors, constructing their fortress and seismic cannon for some unknown purpose. Dak'ir suspected he knew part of the reason, but the rest of it was shrouded from him.

'Doomed,' the Warsmith repeated. 'Our numbers were vastly in excess of yours, Emperor's lapdogs, and still the greenskin fought us to near oblivion. You cannot prevail.'

'Is that why you were building the weapon?' Elysius asked, pressing his bolt pistol harder against the Iron Warrior's temple. 'You were planning to use it against the orks, tip the balance back into your favour.'

An amused, metallic rasp issued from behind the closed helm of the traitor.

'You cannot see,' he snorted. 'It will save you. It is your destruction that we wrought here. The doom of the sons of Vulkan is at hand! Your doo–'

The wash of blood and matter against Elysius's black armour was an epilogue to the barking retort of his bolt pistol as he shot the Iron Warrior through the head.

A slight tremor registered on Captain N'keln's face, the only clue to his shock or displeasure at the suddenness of the execution.

'He was an empty vessel, devoid of further use,' explained the Chaplain. 'Let him rot in the fires of the warp. The pit will claim him.'

'The traitor was right, though,' said Pyriel.

Elysius whirled to confront him. The body language of the Chaplain suggested he had just cast aspersions on his loyalty and faith, such was the fervour in it.

'We cannot prevail against the orks,' Pyriel affirmed. Elysius backed down before his cerulean glare. The Librarian turned his attentions to N'keln. 'The black rock draws closer. Soon it will be at its optimum range. The skies are already thronged with greenskins. A planetoid of orks, my lord,' he said, 'possibly in their *millions*. Even with the greatest strategy, perhaps even with the entire Chapter and Lord Tu'Shan at our side, we would likely lose such a fight.'

'I'm not sure I like where this line of reasoning leads us, Brother-Librarian,' said N'keln.

'I have spoken to Techmarine Draedius–' this Dak'ir was surprised to learn, he had been with Pyriel almost all of the time prior to and before the battle '–and he believes the weapon forged by our traitorous brothers is functional.'

Elysius exploded at this remark.

'You cannot suggest we employ the tools of the enemy!' he raged. 'Heresy lurks down that path, Librarian. I would gladly choose death before compromising my purity with the taint of Perturabo's spawn.'

'You may get your wish, yet,' Pyriel returned, his voice measured. 'But I would not willingly offer my life, or the lives of my brothers or the people of this world, upon the anvil of war for futile pride. Trust in faith and the fortitude of Nocturne bred into us from our very birth and rebirth,' he implored. 'We can activate the cannon, use it to destroy the black rock and the greenskin hordes upon it.'

'And to what end?' the Chaplain countered. 'We risk compromising our purity in the eyes of the Immortal Emperor, and suppose we do so untainted and our enemies are vanquished. What then? Our ship is still mired in the ash, bereft of the engine power to free itself, as this planet is disintegrating from within.'

As if on cue, a tremor rumbled deeply below the earth and fire from the raging volcanoes turned the darkling sky red.

'To abandon a chance for victory here is to abandon hope,' said Pyriel. 'I refuse to believe that Vulkan, through the Tome of Fire, would have sent us to Scoria without reason and to our inevitable destruction. You said yourself, brother, that it was our destiny to be struck from the sky, our eyes opened to the truth.'

Elysius heard his words replayed back to him and found he had no answer. Instead, he looked to N'keln. It was for the captain to decide.

N'keln stood in silence for what seemed a long time before he eventually spoke.

'Though it offends me to my core to dirty my hands with the weapons of traitors, I see no other choice. We cannot use the *Vulkan's Wrath* to destroy the black rock, nor is any weapon we possess here capable of such a feat – the Iron Warriors' seismic cannon is our choice. Practicality must outweigh false glory. My decision is made.'

Pyriel nodded. Elysius echoed him a few moments later, reluctant but relenting to his captain's will and counsel.

'What would you have me do, my lord?' asked the Chaplain.

'After unsealing the keep, Brother Draedius will accompany you to the catacombs where the weapon is kept. Take flamers, take whatever you need and cleanse it, sanctify the cannon and allow our Techmarine to marshal its tainted machine-spirits. Then we bring it into the light of day and remove the dark stain that has so blighted this world's sky.'

'The weapon still requires an amount of fyron, the ore mined by the settlers here, for it to fire,' cautioned Pyriel.

N'keln turned his hard gaze upon the Librarian. To Dak'ir, it seemed the captain was growing in stature with every passing moment.

'You know where this mine is to be found, brother?'

'A guide can be seconded from the human survivors,' he said flatly. Dak'ir thought at once of Illiad, only to realise that he hadn't seen the leader of the settlers since they'd returned to the iron fortress. He also now noticed the fact that a Rhino APC was missing, too.

'Then do so,' N'keln's stern reply interrupted Dak'ir's thoughts. 'Brother-sergeant,' he added, catching Dak'ir's direct attention. 'Gather a combat squad to accompany you and Brother Pyriel. It is paramount you return with enough fyron ore to power at least one blast of the cannon.'

'Yes, my lord.' Dak'ir saluted.

'To your tasks then, brothers,' said N'keln. Brother Shen'kar was waiting patiently at the periphery with schematics and potential combat scenarios for the captain to assess. Even if they were successful in destroying the black rock, a great many orks were already on their way and would soon land upon Scorian soil. Battle with them was inevitable and the rest of the Salamanders would need to be ready.

There was little else to be done for Master Argos and the *Vulkan's Wrath*. N'keln had denied all requests to go and reinforce the ship. Their position was strong at the fortress and the orks would come to them again. If any did find their way to the crash site, the auxiliaries would have to handle them. But N'keln did not think that likely. The Salamanders would not seek shelter behind tainted walls this time. Its effects were too dangerous

and unpredictable with the psychic backwash from the
greenskins. No, they would face the hordes out in the
open and meet them at close arms where the sons of
Vulkan excelled. If defeated, then N'keln deemed they
were unworthy of the primarch's love anyway and
deserved no better a fate. He chose to trust in faith and
that salvation for the company would present itself
through the fires of war.

Dak'ir wanted to speak with N'keln personally, to discuss the fate of Gravius and the armour suits of the old
Legion in more detail, but by now the captain was intent
on his battle plans. So far, all he had delivered was a suc-
cinct appraisal of the facts: of his and Pyriel's discovery
of the ancient Salamander and that the power armour
suits were being secured aboard the *Vulkan's Wrath*, in
one of the ship's many armoriums.

The captain had taken all of this in with silent
inscrutability and not indicated to Dak'ir what his plan
might be concerning it.

Destroy the black rock, salvage what they could from
the world and hope for a means of escape – those were
the Salamanders' priorities now, and in that order.
Everything the else was of secondary concern.

'Gather your warriors back here,' said Pyriel once both
N'keln and Elysius, gone to find Draedius and his
flamers, had departed. 'I will find us some guides.'

Dak'ir nodded, his mind suddenly on other things as
he regarded the open embarkation hatch of the *Fire
Anvil*. Ba'ken was waiting for him as he approached the
Land Raider.

Clutching the hulking warrior's pauldron, Dak'ir
leaned in and said: 'We are bound for the mines. I need
four battle-brothers, yourself included.'

Ba'ken nodded and went off to gather the troops.

Dak'ir continued on his way and soon found himself
at the *Fire Anvil*'s embarkation ramp. The internal

lighting was kept low but he still made out injured battle-brothers hunched upon the assault bunks, awaiting treatment. Dak'ir also noticed two medi-caskets where comatose Salamanders reclined, preserved by the action of their sus-an membranes, in response to the grievous harm they'd suffered in battle against the orks.

He'd seen other caskets too: these contained the bodies of slain heroes, destined for the pyreum, their progenoids removed to cultivate later generations of Salamanders. The dead amongst the settlers, almost half of those who had gone bravely into battle with the Astartes, would join them as a mark of honour and respect for their sacrifice.

Dak'ir entered and he saw what at first he thought was Fugis tending to a wounded Salamander at the rear of the hold, his back to him. When he saw the green, not white, battle-helm resting on a medi-slab alongside him, Dak'ir realised it was not the Apothecary at all.

'Where is Fugis?' he asked curtly, annoyed at the perceived deception.

Brother Emek turned to face him, but his patient spoke for him.

'N'keln sent him on another mission, as soon as we returned to the iron fortress,' Tsu'gan told him, his spike of beard jutting out like a static, red flame. The sergeant's plastron and a detachable portion of his torso under-mesh had been removed. Emek had just finished bandaging Tsu'gan's chest. The bindings were tight and muddied dark pink with his diffuse blood beneath them. Salves and unguents had been applied to his body to speed up the recovery process. They smelled of ash and burning rock. Dak'ir also saw the many branding scars visited upon the sergeant's skin. They were deep and wide, and he wondered how Tsu'gan's brander-priest could've been so crude in his honour marking.

'I'll leave you, brothers,' said Emek, ever the diplomat, and moved to the other side of the hold where another patient awaited him. Dak'ir nodded as he passed, but his attention was upon Tsu'gan who had got up and was replacing his plastron.

'What about his duties here?' Dak'ir asked. 'And what mission?'

'There was little for him to do, save the removal of the progenoids from our fallen brothers. That was done upon the field of battle, the rest are patch-ups that your trooper, Emek, seems more than capable of performing.' Tsu'gan fitted the armour in place and clasped the front and back, betraying a wince of pain for his efforts. 'Perhaps Fugis is grooming him for a role in the Apothecarion.'

Dak'ir clenched a fist at the brother-sergeant's deliberate goading.

'Where is Fugis?' he asked again.

'Gone,' Tsu'gan answered simply, flexing his left arm and rotating his shoulder blade within his pauldron. 'Stiff,' he said, partly to himself.

'Tsu'gan…' Dak'ir warned. In their time apart, he'd almost forgotten how much he despised the other sergeant.

'Calm yourself, Ignean. N'keln sent him to the chamber where you found the ancient. He's going to extract his geneseed.'

'And Illiad would be leading him there,' Dak'ir muttered, but not so quietly that Tsu'gan couldn't hear him. It also explained the missing Rhino APC.

'The human you arrived with, yes.'

Dak'ir felt a pang of regret. It was only right that Gravius's geneseed be preserved, but there was so much that the ancient Salamander knew that given time they could have unearthed. Instead, now, it would be forever condemned to oblivion, the same fate as Gravius's body.

Dak'ir had hoped they could restore him somehow, at least return him to Prometheus and the Chapter. It saddened him to think that this was the old hero's end. It didn't seem fitting.

'Is that why you came, to speak to Fugis?' asked Tsu'gan, interrupting Dak'ir's reverie. 'He is unlikely to return here and we'll be neck-deep in orks before you have another chance.' A mirthless grin passed over his features, and Dak'ir was reminded of a sa'hrk, one of the predator lizards of the Scorian Plain back on Nocturne.

Dak'ir moved a step closer, so the two of them were just under a metre apart, and lowered his voice.

'I came to speak with you,' he admitted. 'I saw the way you looked at N'keln after he slew the beast. Am I to believe your opinion has changed?'

'The fires of war have made their judgement,' was Tsu'gan's only reply, before he double-checked the pressure seals on his power armour.

'An end to clandestine meetings then and your ambition to lead the company?' Dak'ir's tone was leading.

Tsu'gan looked up sharply. There was anger, even violence, in his fiery gaze.

'Petty threats are beneath even you, Ignean,' he said, misunderstanding. 'Don't test me,' he warned.

Dak'ir matched his defiance with steel of his own.

'Nor you me,' he said. 'And I make no threats. I merely seek to know where we stand on this.'

'On even ground,' Tsu'gan snarled through clenched teeth. 'Do not think this accord has anything to do with you, Ignean. It does not. We still have unfinished business, you and I.'

'Oh yes?' Dak'ir invited.

Tsu'gan leaned in close. The scent of acerbic oils on his skin was pungent and put Dak'ir in mind of sulphur.

'Your dreams and portents, Ignean – they are not natural.'

Dak'ir's expression gave away his inner fear that this could be true.

Tsu'gan continued unabated.

'I see how the Librarian watches you. I don't know what it is you are hiding, but I will discover it...' Tsu'gan moved so close he was eye-to-eye with the other sergeant, '...and know this: I will not hesitate to strike you down should it mean you veer from the righteous path.'

Dak'ir took a step back, but his posture was defiant.

'You sound like Elysius,' he snarled. 'This is not about me, Tsu'gan. It is about Kadai and Stratos.'

The certainty in Tsu'gan's face flickered for a moment.

You fear everything...

Nihilan's words had a habit of returning when he least wanted them to.

'I fear nothing,' he muttered, too quiet for Dak'ir to hear.

The other sergeant went on.

'Let your guilt go, brother,' he said, shaking his head sadly. 'It will only destroy you in the end.'

Tsu'gan's knuckles cracked and for a moment Dak'ir thought he would strike him, but he reined in his anger at the last moment and bit it back.

'I have nothing to be guilty for.' It sounded hollow, Dak'ir suspected, even to Tsu'gan's ears. 'Are we done here?' he added after a charged pause.

'I go to the mines,' said Dak'ir, not certain why he was telling Tsu'gan. Perhaps it was because of what he suspected he might find down there and that it connected them both somehow.

Tsu'gan merely nodded.

'They intend to fire the cannon to destroy the black rock,' he guessed.

Now it was Dak'ir's turn to nod.

With nothing else to say, unsure why he had really come to speak with Tsu'gan, Dak'ir turned away. He was approaching the ramp when he heard the other sergeant's voice after him.

'Dak'ir…'

He seldom called him that; usually it was 'Ignean'. Dak'ir stopped and looked back.

Tsu'gan's face was grave.

'In the chamber where we discovered the cannon,' he said. 'I found burned metal and cinder.'

Dak'ir knew what that meant. Tsu'gan's gaze would have clinched it for him, even had he not understood the import of his words. For Dak'ir had sensed them too. In the few days since they had crashed upon Scoria, the feeling had been there. It was merely bubbling under the surface like the magma lifeblood of the world, readying to burst forth and change Scoria forever.

'In Vulkan's name,' uttered Dak'ir. His tone was solemn.

'Aye,' Tsu'gan answered, before turning away to pick up his bolter.

When he looked back to embarkation ramp, Dak'ir was already gone.

II
Old Foes

EXPERIENCE IS BUT a series of moments strung together across the web of time. Most go by unheeded, barely noticeable tremors through the lattice of personal chronology, but some, the truly momentous, are felt as wracking shudders that threaten all other moments. Such things can often be felt before they occur, a low tremble in the spine, a shift in the wind, a *feeling*. They are presaged, these moments; their coming is palpable.

As Dak'ir travelled through the darkened hollows of the subterranean world beneath Scoria, he felt such a moment was in the making.

'All clear ahead,' Apion's voice returned through the comm-feed. A half minute later, the Salamander reappeared in the gloom of the tunnel having finished his initial recon.

There were seven of them in their party – a combat squad of five Astartes, and a guide as selected by Pyriel. The Librarian kept to the shadows, a silent, brooding figure as he reached out with his psychic senses to try and touch what might lurk ahead of them in the mines.

The boy Va'lin had brought the Salamanders this far. Dak'ir had at first objected to the use of such a young adolescent but Pyriel had reasoned Val'in knew the tunnels better than any other settler, and was likely to be far safer below the surface with them than above against the greenskin onslaught.

It had been almost an hour since they'd entered the emergence hole left by the chitin just outside the fortress confines, and found the trail that would lead them to the mines. Their pace was slow and cautious. Dak'ir thought it prudent.

Burned metal and cinder.

It could mean only one thing. Dak'ir's thoughts went to his brothers above him, drawn in battle lines upon the surface of a dying world. By now, the first of the ork ships would have made landfall and the hordes would be converging on N'keln's last stand.

Dak'ir resisted the feeling of despair that gnawed at him. Even if they managed to secure the fyron needed to fire the cannon and used it to destroy the black rock, there was still no guarantee they would be able to overcome the orks that had already landed. If such a victory should prove possible, the Salamanders still had no means of leaving Scoria, a planet that was slowly tearing itself apart with steadily greater vigour. They might defeat their foes only to be consumed by a rising ocean of lava or swallowed down into the deep pits of the earth as the world's crust cracked open. Dak'ir supposed it would be a fitting epitaph for a company of Fire-born.

'Your orders, brother-sergeant,' whispered Ba'ken, who was standing alongside Dak'ir with his heavy flamer readied.

Dak'ir suddenly became aware that Apion was awaiting instruction. Brothers Romulus and Te'kulcar, too, taking up rearguard positions, appeared anticipatory.

The sergeant swung his attention around to Va'lin. Dak'ir recalled the bravery the boy had shown during the chitin attack on his settlement. He seemed equally stalwart now, watching the shadows, listening and assessing the sounds emanating from the rock.

'How far, Va'lin?' Dak'ir asked, crouching slightly so as not to intimidate him.

The boy kept his gaze on the tunnel darkness ahead, regarding the curvature of the earth, the shapes – though largely indistinct to Dak'ir and the other Salamanders – that were as clear as a road sign to him. After a moment's cogitation, he spoke.

'Another kilometre, maybe a half more.'

Another kilometre deeper into the earth, where the air grew hotter by the metre and the glow of lava could be seen flickering against the black walls of rock. Descending into the dark was like crossing the gateway to another world, one of fire and ash. For the Salamanders it felt more than ever like home.

Dak'ir remembered the scent of smoke and cinder that he had experienced in the tunnels just before they'd clashed with the orks and been reunited with their battle-brothers. It came again to him now, only this wasn't just a sense memory, it was real. A draft was stirred up from somewhere, channelled up to them as an acrid breeze that held the reek of burning and the faintest trace of sulphur.

Dak'ir thought of red scales, of a serpentine body uncurling amidst a pall of cloying smoke. It was as if the thing in his mind's eye had emerged from a fell pit of fire, hell-spawned and terrible.

'They are close,' the voice of Pyriel intruded upon the gloom. His eyes were blazing cerulean orbs when Dak'ir turned towards him.

'Who are close?' asked Te'kulcar. He was not with the squad when they had fought on Stratos. Brother Te'kulcar had been a replacement for the slain Ak'sor, recruited from a different company altogether.

Dak'ir's voice was grim.

'The Dragon Warriors.'.

RAKING THE SLIDE of his combi-bolter, Tsu'gan felt a slight twinge in his chest. The explosion from the dead ork warboss's wartrike had cracked his ribplate and punctured a lung. Enhanced Astartes biology was healing him quickly, but the ache still remained. Tsu'gan ignored it. Pain of the body was easily mastered. He thought again of Dak'ir's words about guilt and its consumptive nature. How many deeds of heroism would it take to wipe away the stain of conscience he felt at Kadai's death? He hated to admit, but the Ignean was right. It wasn't the presence in the walls of the iron fortress speaking this time, either.

The Salamanders had quit the confines of the traitor bastion. Tsu'gan was glad of it – the protection it offered was no sanctuary and they were better off without. The Fire-born were arrayed in front of the wall in stout, green-armoured battle lines, the stone and metal of its construction several metres behind them, bulwarking their backs. They were so advanced in order to cover and protect the emergence hole that Pyriel and the Ignean had taken to the mines. Should they prove successful and retrieve the fyron ore, they would need a clear run to the fortress and the catacombs of the inner keep where Elysius and Draedius awaited them.

Casting his eye across the army, Tsu'gan saw Captain N'keln in a position of prominence at the front, the Inferno Guard arrayed around him. The banner of Malicant hung low but stalwart on a weak breeze.

Fire Anvil and the other vehicles, barring the Rhino APC Fugis had taken to the *Vulkan's Wrath*, punctuated the line at strategic anchor points. The transport tanks had little in the way of meaningful firepower but the mobile protection they provided was useful.

Venerable Brothers Ashamon and Amadeus stood stoic but ready. The unyielding forms of the Dreadnoughts were like armoured pillars amidst the field of Salamander green. As their weapon mounts cycled through preparation routines, the occasional flicker of electricity across their close combat armaments was the only betrayal of impatience for battle.

A churning ash cloud, building on the horizon, grasped Tsu'gan's attention. The orks were making their approach, as they'd done before. More were coming this time. Their ships hung like a shroud overhead, blighting the sky in a swarm.

THE PRIMARY ENGINARIUM deck of the *Vulkan's Wrath* was hot like a steaming caldera. Haze made the air throb and flicker as if only partially real, as if it were overlaid by a mirage. Gouts of expelled gas plumed the air, thick and white, whilst dulled hazard lighting illuminated sections of machinery, hard-edged bulkheads and sweating deck serfs.

Fugis found Master Argos amongst the throng, a pair of Techmarines assisting him as he toiled at the ventral engines. Lume-lamps attached to his servo-rig bored lances into the gloom of the sunken chamber where he worked, large enough to accommodate twenty Astartes shoulder-to-shoulder. The Apothecary discerned the reek of unguents and oils designed to placate the out-of-kilter machine-spirits. Doleful chanting emanated from the attendant Techmarines on a recycled breeze, thick with carbon dioxide. There was the hint of engine parts, of blackened metal and disparate components revealed in the half-light.

'You've come from the Apothecarion, brother,' the voice of Argos echoed metallically from the darkened recess where he was working. The whirring action of unseen mechadendrites and servo-tools provided a high-pitched refrain to the Master of the Forge's automated diction.

Fugis noted it was not framed as a question. Even if Argos hadn't known the Apothecary was returning to the *Vulkan's Wrath*, he knew every square metre of his ship intimately. He felt its every move subconsciously, as certain as if it were one made by his own body.

The Master of the Forge continued, 'The power armour suits have been secured in the aft armorium of deck twenty. You've come to ask if our efforts in retrieving them and the geneseed of the ancient are in vain.'

Fugis gave a small, mirthless laugh.

'You demonstrate as much prescience as Brother-Librarian Pyriel, Master Argos.'

The Master of the Forge's head appeared out of the gloom for the first time. He went unhooded and Fugis saw the bionic eye he wore retracting as it readjusted to observe him from whatever detailed work it had been analysing.

'It is merely logic, brother.' He went on. 'The *Vulkan's Wrath* is repaired as best as I am able without a Mechanicus workyard at my disposal. Nothing has changed – we still require four functional banks of ventral engines. Three are primed and ready, the fourth – the access conduit to which you see me in here – is not. Crucial parts, damaged in the crash, and not salvageable from other areas of the ship, are needed for its operation. It is a relatively quick and rudimentary procedure to effect, the correct rituals are short and simple to perform but the machine-spirit will not be coaxed into life half-formed, Brother Apothecary.'

Fugis looked impassive at the Techmarine's clipped and precise reply.

'Then let us hope something *does* change so we might avert our fate,' he said.

Fugis was not certain he believed in fate or destiny. As an Apothecary he was practical, putting his faith in his hands and what he saw with his eyes. These few days upon the doomed world of Scoria had changed that. He had felt it most strongly in the ruined bridge of the old Expeditionary ship, where Gravius had sat like a recumbent corpse. By the laws of nature, the ancient Salamander should not still be alive. As Fugis had approached him, a sense of awe and reverence slowing his steps, Gravius was nearing the end of his endurance. It seemed he had held on for millennia, waiting for the return of his brothers.

Fugis didn't know what the significance of this discovery was. He was following the orders of his captain, but experienced a peculiar sense of woe and gravitas as he'd administered the Emperor's Peace through a nerve-serum injection. It was almost like defilement as he cracked open the ancient armour and retrieved the ancient's progenoids. In them was the genetic coding of the Legion, undistilled by time or generations of forebears. The experience was genuinely humbling and called to his fractured spirit.

'Brother Agatone and I are returning to the iron fortress,' he told Argos. The sergeant and his combat squad had accompanied Illiad in the Rhino APC. Agatone had waited outside the bridge when Fugis had gone to meet Gravius. Right now, he and his troopers were directing the evacuation of the settlers, those who had fought against the orks included – N'keln had decided no more human life would be lost to the greenskins if it could be avoided. All would return to the *Vulkan's Wrath* in the hope that the ship be made void-worthy again and deliver them to salvation.

Fugis and Agatone, leaving the combat squad to protect the settlers and escort them to the ship, would head back and support their battle-brothers if they could. For the moment, the orks had not attacked the crash-site, nor showed any signs of interest in it. That was just was well – there were only auxiliaries to defend it now.

'Sensors indicate the greenskins have already made landfall, brother. You will arrive too late to reach the battle lines, unless you plan on killing your way through a sea of orks,' Argos replied. Remarkably, there was no sarcasm in his tone.

'We'll take the tunnels, track our route through them to emerge next to the fortress walls.'

'Then you had best be going,' said Argos, before returning to the gloom of the conduit. 'Time is short for all of us now, brother.'

Fugis turned his back on him as he left the enginarium. The Apothecary wondered if it would be the last time.

THE SOUNDS OF the battle above drifted down to the catacombs of the inner keep like muffled thunder. The orks had brought their war host and were now fighting the Salamanders tooth and claw across the blood-strewn ash dunes.

Chaplain Elysius had dismissed the flamer bearers, though the acrid reek of spent promethium still remained. The troopers would be better employed above against the greenskin horde than here amongst the dark and the whispers.

An itch was developing at the back of the Chaplain's skull. He felt it lightly at first, muttering litanies under his breath as he watched Draedius go to work on the seismic cannon, trying to cleanse and purify its machine-spirits – the Techmarine would need to visit the reclusium after this duty, so that Elysius could appraise his sprit and ensure it wasn't tainted. The itch had grown to a nagging insistence, a raft of sibilant whispers, drifting in and out of focus, pitched just at the edge of his mind. The Chaplain was steeled against it. The dark forces slaved to the iron fortress's walls, were trying to breach his defences but the purifying fire had weakened them for now and his sermons were keeping them in check.

Draedius, standing before the cannon, performed his own rituals. Restoration of the weapon's machine-spirit would not be easy, though it was a necessary task. Without it the cannon would not fire; it might even malfunction with dire consequences. The only small mercy was that the weapon was not already daemon-possessed.

It rankled with Elysius that they had been forced into employing the weapons of the enemy. It smacked of compromise and deviancy. Though devout, the Chaplain was no fool either. The cannon was the only means of destroying the black rock and halting the near-endless orkish tide. The rational part of his brain did wonder why the Iron Warriors would construct such a weapon. Its purpose here on Scoria seemed narrow and limited. He felt as if he were looking at it through a muddied lens, the edges caked in grime. His view was myopic, but instinct had taught Elysius to perceive with more than just his eyes. There was something lurking within that grimy frame, just beyond sight; only by seeing that would the full truth of the Iron Warriors' machinations be revealed. It bothered him that he could not.

'Vulkan's fire beats in my breast,' he intoned as the presence in the catacombs detected his doubts and sought to feed upon them, using them to widen the tiny cracks in the armour of his faith, 'with it I shall smite the foes of the Emperor,' the Chaplain concluded, gripping the haft of Vulkan's Sigil and drawing strength from the hammer-icon's proximity.

No matter how hard he stared at the cannon, the obscurity around the 'lens' remained.

THE DIN OF clunking machinery filtered up to them in the tunnel. The sounds were coming from a glowing opening below. Lava stench and the prickle of heat came with it. The mines were just ahead.

'Stay back, Val'in,' Dak'ir warned, stepping ahead of the boy and shielding him with the bulk of his armoured form.

The boy did as he was told, but gasped as he spied a shadow looming ahead of them at the base of the tunnel.

Brother Apion saw it too, having moved to take point, and aimed his bolter, about to fire.

'It's already dead,' Pyriel informed him, his eyes fading from cerulean blue.

'An Iron Warrior husk,' noted Dak'ir, his vision adjusting to discern the bare metal ceramite and the distinctive black and yellow chevrons marking the armour. 'The same as the redoubts. Advance with caution, brothers.'

Apion lowered his bolter a fraction and led them on.

At the base of the tunnel, the Salamanders found a natural gallery of rock. The machine noise – the whirring of drills and the chugging report of excavators – became louder. Long shadows cast from moving forms in a larger chamber beyond streaked the walls at the end of the gallery.

There were more 'sentries' here – iron-armoured deterrents staged in ready positions abutting the walls. Val'in cowered, the natural fear emanating from the long dead corpses still very much alive for him.

Ba'ken brought him close, leaning down as far as his bulk allowed and whispering, 'Stay close to me, child. The Fire Angels will allow no harm to come to you.'

Va'lin nodded and his mood eased a little as he crept closer to the pillar of ceramite that was Brother Ba'ken.

Dak'ir failed to notice the exchange. His attention was on Apion, who had reached the end of the gallery and was poised at the threshold to the chamber. Dak'ir joined him seconds later and stared out into a wide expanse of rock. Here and there, struts of metal supported the cavern roof above. The empty shells of mining equipment lay strewn about the cavern like a machine graveyard, burned out and discarded once their usefulness had ended. Dak'ir saw boring-engines, bucket-bladed diggers, excavators and tracked drill-platforms. Servitors, slumped over their vehicles or piled up in corpse heaps, were a testament to the incessant overmining.

In addition to the machines, there were three stages, made of metal and lofted a metre off the ground on stout legs. Two of the three were flat and empty. The third was stacked with rotund metal barrels. Dak'ir didn't need to look inside of them to know they were brimming with fyron ore. The third stage was nearest to the source of the machine noise: a short but gaping tunnel shrouded in gloom. The Salamanders had entered the cavern at a slight angle, and through his enhanced eye-sight Dak'ir made out two servitor-driven drilling engines, like the ones the settlers had used in their ambush, and a bulky excavator rig on thick tracks, dragging away the useless rock and earth expelled by the drilling engines' labours. This too was worked by a

servitor, hunch-backed and cable-slaved to the machine
as if it were an integral part of its being. All three
automatons were akin to the ghoul-drones encountered
in the cannon's arming chamber.

The low lighting cast by sodium lamp packs sus-
pended on cables steam-bolted to the cavern roof
framed the grotesque faces of the ghoul-drones evilly.
Their masters were not far away.

Three Iron Warriors stood at the drilling tunnel's
threshold, overseeing the work. They carried combi-
bolters with barrel-mounted sarissa-blades, low slung
on straps around their spiked pauldrons. Chips of rock
scudded off their armour, such was the Iron Warriors'
proximity to the mine face, and they were veneered in
grey dust.

In the distance, a six-wheeled loader transported a
cache of fyron ore barrels on its burgeoning flatbed.
The vehicle rumbled on fat treads towards an opening
at the back of the mine that led into unknown darkness.

A second six-wheeler was on its return journey and
approaching the partially laden stage where another
load of barrels awaited it. A pair of cargo-servitors –
their arms replaced by twin-pronged lifter claws –
shambled into view as the loader closed on them.

In the loader's wake, a group of figures was revealed.

Dak'ir's jaw clenched and he felt a ripple of anger
pass through his body.

Kadai's slayers, the Dragon Warriors, were here.

There were three of them, armoured in blood-red
ceramite that was scaled in places as if the suits themselves had somehow mutated. Their gauntlets ended in
gore-tipped claws and a strong reek of copper exuded
from their bodies. They were once Space Marines, these
creatures; now they were renegades in service to the
Ruinous Powers. Slaves to darkness and damnation.

One wore a helmet fashioned into the image of an ancient saurian beast. Two horns curled like dark red blades from both temples of his battle-helm. A cloud of fiery embers gusted from a snarling, fang-fringed mouth grille in time with the renegade's rapid breathing. Heat haze emanated from the Dragon Warrior, giving his form a sense of unreality.

Another cradled an archaic multi-melta, scarred with kill-markings. His battle-helm was bare but came to a stub-nosed snout that was rendered in bone. Skulls attached to bloody chains hung from his scaled pauldrons and he wore what looked like deep-red lizard hide over his abdominal armour. Dust particles spilled from his armour joints with every movement. To Dak'ir's enhanced sight they appeared like tiny flakes of epidermis and the Salamander was instantly put in mind of a serpent shedding its skin.

The last of them Dak'ir knew well. Flanked by his two warriors, this one's burning red eyes were ablaze as if he were constantly enraged. The smouldering anger was emulated by the scarification on his face, which was a horrific patchwork of burned skin and lacerations. Old welts and tracts of melted flesh ravaged his onyx-black visage. A horn curved from each of his pauldrons and he seized a crackling force staff in a clawed gauntlet.

This was Nihilan, sorcerer and architect of Kadai's destruction.

'Renegades,' snarled Apion, and Dak'ir heard the Salamander's fists crack.

'Ba'ken,' said the sergeant, his gaze never leaving his nemesis. They should have scoured these tunnels days ago. Dak'ir had sensed something here. His visions all pointed to it. Even Tsu'gan had suspected, and still they'd done nothing. Well, now the time for inaction was at an end.

An icon appeared in the visual display of Ba'ken's battle-helm, sent over from Dak'ir's with a single eye blink.

'Target acquired…' rumbled the hulking trooper, moving forward to level his heavy flamer.

The loader had almost reached the stage and the ghoul-drones were approaching it when a gout of super-heated promethium streaked across the chamber and ignited. The spear of flame burst through the pair of drones, setting them ablaze, but that was merely a glancing blow. Its intended target, the loader itself, exploded a few seconds later as its fuel cells were cooked and the volatile liquid within went up spectacularly. The loader was cast into the air and flipped over, the flaming wreckage crushing the still burning ghoul-drones and destroying them in a raging conflagration as it landed hard.

'Salamanders, attack!' roared Dak'ir as they charged into the cavern, bolters screaming.

The Iron Warriors were closest and reacted quickly. One was not quick enough however, as Dak'ir's plasma bolt took him in the chest and punched a hole the size of a clenched Astartes fist. Explosive rounds bursting from the traitor's combi-bolter raked the roof and shot out a lighting rig, as his fingers grasped at the trigger with the last of his nerve tremors.

The other two Iron Warriors reached cover and began to return fire, even as the Dragon Warriors started to move into battle positions. Through the gunfire, Dak'ir thought he saw Nihilan laughing.

The Salamanders panned out: Dak'ir, Pyriel and Ba'ken heading right, whilst Apion, Romulus and Te'kulcar went left. Val'in, not wishing to remain in the corridor with the Iron Warrior corpses alone, ran behind the skeleton of a disused loader, bastardised for spare parts, and hid.

'*Anvil*, gain the stage and secure the fyron ore,' ordered Dak'ir over the comm-feed, using the call signs they'd established before entering the emergence hole. Out of the corner of his eye, past the barking reports of bolters, he saw Apion and Romulus rushing between machine husks as they tried to reach the ore platform, whilst Te'kulcar advanced offering covering fire.

'*Hammer*, we advance now!' Dak'ir led the others forward, streaks of flames keeping the Iron Warriors down as they sought to move to fresh cover. Through darted glimpses at the enemy, Dak'ir saw that Nihilan was letting his minions do the work. An incandescent beam seared through a vehicle shell where Pyriel had crouched. The Librarian moved out of its path just in time. Sustained bolter fire came from the other renegade, who seemed to revel in the act of loosing his weapon. He was like a mad dog, straining at the leash.

All the while, the ghoul-drones maintained their incessant mining.

A low rumble struck the chamber, arresting the Salamanders' shock assault. Fragments of rock were cascading from the roof and the metal struts groaned forbiddingly in protest.

Dak'ir fell to one knee as he lost his balance. So did one of the Iron Warriors, lurching out of cover for a moment. Long enough for Ba'ken, who stood steady with his legs braced, to burn him down. A metallic screech issued from the traitor's battle-helm before he collapsed in a smoking heap of charred metal. The violent tremors grew in intensity so that even Ba'ken couldn't maintain his footing. The tongue of fire from his flamer receded.

The Dragon Warriors had gone to ground too. Dak'ir had lost sight of Nihilan, but he could sense his presence. He judged they were just over sixty metres away, about half the width of the cavern. A determined attack once the tremors had subsided would catch them off guard – they could reach the renegades before the multi-melta fired again. As a psyker, Nihilan was unpredictable, but Dak'ir was willing to take the chance. Strategy icons flashed up on the Salamanders' battle-helm displays, conveying the sergeant's plan.

Romulus and Apion were almost at the platform, the lone Iron Warrior protecting it finding his attention diverted by two groups of simultaneous attackers and giving neither the attention it needed. Short bursts of bolter fire from Te'kulcar, lying on his chest and shooting from a prone position for stability, kept the Iron Warrior down so the other Salamanders could claim their objective.

They were stumbling on to the platform when a deep, cracking sound resonated throughout the cavern like the breaking of a world. A flare of light bathed the drilling tunnel in an angry glow, before shuddering cracks split out from it in a jagged line. The cracks widened to a fissure and then a chasm, filled with bubbling lava. The hellish glow from inside the tunnel spread outwards rapidly. It preceded a wave of lava expelled from where the mine face had broken apart and Scoria's lifeblood was flowing.

Buoyed by the force of the wave, the mining machines were thrust from the tunnel. Languishing in the deadly lava stream, they did not last long. Like short-lived metal islands they sank beneath the glutinous morass in moments, their slack-faced drones engulfed with them.

A yawning chasm of lava now stood between the Salamanders and their prey. A thin line of jagged rock spanned it, floating on the surface, wide enough for two Astartes to cross at a time. The violence of the tremors subsided but more cracks were cobwebbing the ground and streams of dust and rock spilled from the roof continuously. This needed to end quickly, before the entire cavern collapsed on top of them.

Romulus and Apion had reached the fyron ore and were securing it to their power armour. Two barrels each was the most they could carry without compromising their ability to fight.

As he bolted for the rocky channel that led across the lava chasm, Dak'ir hoped four barrels would be enough. Just before he'd reached the edge of the lava stream, a flash of hot light burned past him and Te'kulcar's icon in the sergeant's helm display flickered and went out. A glance back showed him the battle-brother was on the ground a few metres from his previous position, part of his torso melted away.

'Get him out!' Dak'ir cried, recognising the brutal effects of the multi-melta. Knowing Apion and Romulus were retreating with Te'kulcar and the fyron ore, Dak'ir raced heedlessly onto the rock channel. Intense heat from the lava flow either side of him prickled at his armour and warning icons flashed up on his display.

Grimly ignoring the discomfort, he was halfway across when the Iron Warrior on the other side emerged from cover. A bark of fire from Pyriel's bolt pistol, the Librarian a few steps behind the sergeant, clipped the traitor's pauldron and gorget, pinning him back.

But then another foe stepped into Dak'ir's eye line.

Nihilan was grinning, a grotesque and bizarre expression given his facial scarring, as his force staff crackled with power. He levelled it at Dak'ir, who could not avoid the shadowy arc lightning that ripped from its tip and struck him full on in the chest. This was the raw energy of the warp, channelled by Nihilan's sorcery. No one could survive such a blast.

Dak'ir cried out, his voice an agonised scream.

CHAPTER THIRTEEN

I
A Black Rock Dies

THE LINE WAS holding. Few Astartes could boast tenacity as unshakeable as the sons of Vulkan. Here, against an unrelenting and seemingly endless horde of orks, the 3rd Company drew upon it like never before.

Heavy guns, aimed from the rear of the Salamanders' formation, softened up the onrushing greenskins, seeking to close with their opponents and exploit their chief strengths: raw aggression and brutality.

But the Salamanders were equally adept, if not superior, eye-to-eye with the enemy. The recently returned flamers exacted a sizeable toll on the orks as they came through the Devastators' fusillade.

Unlike the initial assaults against the iron fortress, the orks were predominantly on foot, supported by their piston-legged machineries, crude analogues of Space Marine Dreadnoughts. They eschewed the wagons, bikes and war trucks of the earlier sorties of their kin. Long-ranged guns were largely absent, too, and instead an expansive melee of chainblades, cleavers and clubs thundered at the Salamanders to bludgeon them into submission.

The orks found only fury and iron-hard resistance where they'd expected red-wreathed death and capitulation. Alloyed together, at almost full company strength and protecting the relatively narrow defile in which the iron fortress was situated, the Salamanders were all but impregnable.

Casualties had been few, and those that could no longer serve the Chapter were dragged behind the stalwart line of armour, their absence accounted for by their brothers.

Tsu'gan gunned open the chest of an ork some ten metres away, downing the brute as if it were an enraged sauroch. Another took its place and he killed that one too with a precise burst to its snarling head. Several more followed, greenskins running the punishing gauntlet of Salamander guns. They were obliterated from view when Sergeant Vargo's depleted Assault squad landed amongst them. The exchange was savage and swift. Vargo and his troopers took to the air on tongues of fire less than a minute later, seeking other foes isolated by their eager bloodlust from the main greenskin throng. Carcasses rendered by bolt and blade, and a patch of scorched earth were all that was left in the Assault squad's clearing smoke.

'Press forward!' The bellowed order of N'keln reached Tsu'gan through the comm-feed as his captain sought to exploit the short gap that had developed through the Salamanders' recent mauling of the orks.

The line advanced as one. Tsu'gan felt the heavy footfalls of the Terminators alongside his squad through his booted feet.

'Unto the anvil, brother-sergeant,' said Praetor, a dark grin upon his face as he swung his thunder hammer towards the next wave of greenskins.

Snorting amusedly at the fatalism of it all, Tsu'gan fired again and his face was lit by the muzzle flare of his bolter. He laughed in tandem with the weapon's roar.

Overhead, the ork vessels streamed like cancerous veins in the sky. The black rock was venting constantly now. Soon there would not be enough of the ash dunes to hold all the greenskins expelled from its craterous surface.

Tsu'gan laughed harder at the thought of it, before his battle hysteria ebbed with a fresh realisation.

As long as the black rock endured there could be no victory here. If it wasn't destroyed soon, they'd all be dead.

Dak'ir was swathed in black lightning, the dark energies from Nihilan's force staff coursing over his armour. He cried out and fell to one knee, fists clenched over his weapons and shuddering against the terrible sorcery.

Vaguely, at the edge of his nulled perception, Dak'ir thought he heard Pyriel bellow his name. His tone was anguished, already grieving. The sergeant's eyes were clamped shut and saw again the Cindara Plateau, his ascent to the summit the final stage of his induction to become a neophyte. The acrid tang of the Acerbian Sea pricked his nostrils and the hot downdrafts of the Ignean caves of his birth warmed his skin.

Then he returned and the wracking pain of the lightning subsided; his nerve endings, previously ablaze, were still and warm. Dak'ir opened his eyes and realised he was still alive.

An amused look crossed Nihilan's face, the power in his force staff receding, before he turned and fell back with his traitorous brethren.

Ribbons of sorcerous smoke spilled upwards off Dak'ir's body as he started to rise, tugged forward in the draft from Pyriel racing past him.

He felt the presence of Ba'ken slowing just behind. Dak'ir staggered to his feet, waving the heavy weapons trooper on.

'Stop the renegades...' he slurred, still mustering his strength.

'I thought you were dead, Hazon,' Ba'ken murmured, before going on after on Pyriel.

'I should be,' rasped Dak'ir, his senses returning. He was about to drive on when he saw the beam of the multi-melta search menacingly out of the darkness. It forced a scream from Pyriel, his shoulder seared by the deadly weapon through his pauldron. The Librarian nearly fell, but managed to hold on.

Gritting his teeth in anger, Dak'ir found Pyriel's attacker. He recognised his shadowy form from the Aura Hieron temple, back on Scoria. He hadn't realised at first, but now he knew – this was Kadai's assassin, the killer of his old captain.

'Ghor'gan...' bellowed Nihilan to the Dragon Warrior with the multi-melta, the rest of his command smothered by the noise of roaring bolters as he and the other renegade drew away into the darkness. The one called Ghor'gan merely nodded and stood his ground. Nihilan was trying to escape.

This could not be allowed to happen. Dak'ir launched himself across the lava stream. It looked an impossible jump, but incredibly he landed on the other side, the heels of his boots scraping at the edge of where the rock fell away to hot oblivion. Ignoring the Iron Warrior, Dak'ir used his momentum to drive on at the Dragon Warrior with the multi-melta. Reacting to the sudden threat, Ghor'gan swung the deadly weapon about, a nimbus of energy already building in its twin-nosed barrel.

PYRIEL WAS NEARING the end of the narrow rock bridge when the last Iron Warrior threw himself into his path. In his mind, the Librarian heard the slow pull, the long metal report of the depressed trigger as the traitor unleashed his bolter at him.

A bolter's velocity is ferociously quick, its rate of fire faster than an eye-blink. Pyriel's mind was faster.

Bolter shells exploded ineffectually against an invisible shield, dense blooms of light rippling in midair with each percussive impact.

Pyriel ran on, seeing Dak'ir land ahead of him on the other side, and reached his assailant. Changing tactics, the Iron Warrior slowed his fire rate to use his sarissa blade. Pyriel had unsheathed his force sword and parried the thrust meant to impale him. With the Iron Warrior unbalanced, he thrust himself and rammed the blade of his eldritch weapon halfway into the traitor's stomach. Plates of ceramite parted easily before the force sword, undone by its shimmering power field, before the Librarian lowered the invisible shield and channelled his psychic might through the edge of the weapon.

At once the Iron Warrior sagged as his soul was sundered, cast into the oblivion of the warp to be fed upon by daemons. Smoke exuded from the traitor's eye-slits and a deep light glowed from within. He screamed, a long and wailing note that echoed somewhere beyond the realm of reality, and sank into a heap, a scored-out husk all that remained.

With the traitor slain, Pyriel looked ahead to his battle-brother.

FUELLED BY FURY, Dak'ir hurled himself at Ghor'gan. The multi-melta's beam stabbed out, but the renegade's aim was off, pressurised into an early shot by the Salamander's headlong assault. It scorched the edge of Dak'ir's battle-helm, the actual beam itself passing a few centimetres overhead. It was close enough to burn through ceramite. It kept burning, melting away at the armour around Dak'ir's head, who wrenched it off before the corrosive effects ate through it completely and started in on his face.

The ruined battle-helm clattered to the ground, half-disintegrated, as Dak'ir hit Ghor'gan with a roar. Swinging his chainsword two-handed, the Salamander tore into the heavy weapon that had ended Kadai's life, shearing it in two.

PYRIEL GOT TO the end of the narrow span across the lava stream before he realised Ba'ken wasn't with him. He turned, with half a glance at Dak'ir hammering at the massive Dragon Warrior, before searching for Ba'ken.

The heavy weapons trooper was retreating back down the rock bridge.

'Brother!' cried Pyriel, a hint of accusation in his voice.

Ba'ken half turned his head.

'I cannot leave him, Librarian,' was his only explanation.

Pyriel was about to cry out again, when he saw that Ba'ken was heading for the boy, Va'lin.

Geysers of fire and lava were breaking the surface of the cavern now, the forked cracks in the earth splitting apart and allowing Scoria's blood to seep through. Va'lin had retreated to one corner of the cavern, keeping his head down and himself well hidden. Thick veins of encroaching lava webbed his retreat route to the entrance and spears of flame shot sporadically from the ground around him. The boy was crouched atop the skeletal frame of an excavator, clinging on for his life and too afraid to move.

In his determination to reach the Dragon Warriors, and perhaps the pain in his shoulder caused by the melta beam's savage caress, Pyriel had failed to hear Va'lin's plaintive cry. Human life was important; Vulkan had taught them that. The Salamanders were protectors as well as warriors.

Ba'ken had heard the boy and was answering his noble calling as a Fire-born of Nocturne.

'In Vulkan's name, brother,' the Librarian muttered. Smoke was billowing into the cavern now and occluded his view. The hulking form of Ba'ken was lost in the grey and black.

Returning his attention to Dak'ir, Pyriel had taken just a step from the rocky span when a forked seam split the ground before his feet and a titanic wall of intense heat and fire impeded him.

Thrown off by the force of the flame-geyser's expulsion, Pyriel had to scramble back up so as not to be pitched into the lava stream. Warning icons flashed red on a status slate in his gauntlet. Tentatively, he went to touch the fiery barrier but withdrew his hand as the heat sensors in his armour spiked. His gauntlet came back badly scorched and partially melted.

Behind the flickering heat, the struggle between Salamander and renegade became an amorphous haze.

'Dak'ir!' he cried, venting his impotency and frustration. There was nothing he could do; the wall of fire stretched the width of the cavern. Dak'ir was alone.

THE DRAGON WARRIOR let the cleaved ends of the multi-melta fall from his grasp, and jabbed his left claw into Dak'ir's neck like a blade, while the other slashed at his assailant's wrist. The Salamander's gorget took the brunt of the blow to the neck, but Dak'ir was stunned and lost his grip on the chainsword when Gor'ghan's scything talons ripped a chunk of ceramite from his gauntlet. The empty thud of the weapon hitting the ground, the churning teeth slowing to a stop, felt like a death knell.

Dak'ir recovered quickly, barely noticing the barrier of fire that had erupted behind him, butting the Dragon

Warrior's helmet and crumpling the nose despite the pain it caused him. Ghor'gan staggered back with a muffled cry of pain, ripping off the helm to reveal a scaled visage as dark as burnt umber and perpetually flaking. He tore at the shards of ceramite embedded in his reptilian face, casting the bloody wreckage aside before flying at Dak'ir.

The Salamander met him mid-attack and the two of them locked together, neither with the strength or purpose to gain the upper hand.

'Murdering dog!' Dak'ir raged, about to spit acid from his betcher's gland into the renegade's face when Ghor'gan stopped him by shoving his forearm under the Salamander's chin and forcing his mouth shut. The caustic bile bubbled over Dak'ir's bottom lip harmlessly.

'Fight with honour,' countered the Dragon Warrior, his voice like crackling magma. In the frantic struggle, Dak'ir noticed a ragged wound, only half-healed, across his neck and assumed this was the reason for Ghor'gan's throaty cadence.

'You possess none,' Dak'ir accused when he'd pushed back the renegade's grip on his neck. 'I know you are the assassin that shot my captain when his back was turned.'

Ghor'gan's face darkened in what might have been regret.

'I am a warhound, like you,' he rasped, then grunted as he tried to seize a hand around Dak'ir's throat. The Dragon Warrior was big, easily the size and heft of Ba'ken, and Dak'ir was finding his strength a severe test. 'I follow orders, even those I disagree with. It is the way of war,' he concluded.

'Pleading for mercy already, renegade?'

'No.' Ghor'gan's answer was flat, his tone almost weary. 'I just wanted you to know before you die.' The Dragon Warrior exerted his full strength, pressing Dak'ir into a crouch, and slipping his claws around his neck.

Dak'ir felt his throat constricting from the external pressure. He raked gauntleted fingers over Ghor'gan's face, trying to leaven his grip, but came away with a fistful of shed skin instead. Ghor'gan snarled at the ragged wound in his cheek but kept the pressure up, extending his arms to force Dak'ir away. The Salamander went for his holstered pistol but the renegade saw the move and smashed him into the cavern wall. White fire flared behind Dak'ir's eyes as hot knives stabbed his side where he'd struck the rock.

'Don't resist,' growled Ghor'gan, almost fatherly, 'Your pain is almost at an end...'

Dak'ir's lungs felt like withered sacks in his chest, as his throat was slowly being crushed. Darkness impinged at the edge of his sight and he felt himself slipping...

He reached out, trying to deny the inevitable. Pyriel was far away, behind the wall of fire. Dak'ir was alone with Ghor'gan, his old captain's killer about to add to his murder tally.

BA'KEN REACHED THE edge of the growing lava pool slowly encircling Va'lin on his island of metal. The boy was choking on the sulphurous fumes and smoke wreathed his tiny refuge. Ba'ken would have to jump. He couldn't make it and return with the boy as well if he kept on his heavy flamer rig. Without a second thought, he disengaged the locking straps and shrugged the bulky canisters off his back, laying them carefully on the ground with the weapon itself.

Muttering a painful litany as he traced his hand lightly across the barrel of the gun he had forged and crafted, Ba'ken rose to his feet and leapt to Va'lin.

'Climb on, boy,' he said, once on the other side. The skeletal frame of the excavator was already buckling under the Salamander's weight, whilst around them the lava crept ever closer.

Va'lin clambered onto Ba'ken's shoulders, clinging desperately to the Fire-born's neck and pauldron.

'Don't let go,' the Salamander told the boy and launched himself back across, just as the lava flow began eating away at the excavator, until in a few seconds it had consumed it.

The molten stream raging through the cavern, bisecting it with a ribbon of viscous heat, had spilled over the rock span. There was no way back to Pyriel and Dak'ir. Ba'ken could scarcely see them through the smoke and falling debris.

He cried out. 'Brothers!'

A spurt of flame erupted from the earth near where he was standing and Ba'ken stepped away, grimacing.

'Brothers!' he bellowed again, his voice swallowed by the cracking of earth, the roar of fire answering.

The end of Scoria was at hand. There was nothing left for this world now. Maybe there was nothing left for Dak'ir or Pyriel either. Beseeching the Emperor and Vulkan for their safe return, Ba'ken fell back reluctantly.

Va'lin was suffocating; the Salamander heard it in the boy's wheezing breaths, his shuddering chest.

Ba'ken turned and made for the exit.

'Hang on,' he said grimly, racing for the tunnel back to the surface.

IN THE MIDST of the fighting, Tsu'gan had thought he'd seen Romulus and Apion return from the emergence hole, a wounded Brother Te'kulcar draped across their shoulders. He couldn't see the fyron ore, but then his view was fleeting in the press of combat.

A full assault was ordered and the Salamanders were pressing the orks with all the flame and fury they could muster. The line was no more; it had given way to probing attacks launched at strategic points throughout the greenskin horde. Witnessed from above, the assaults would have looked bullet trajectories, forcing their way slowly through the dark green flesh of the beast.

Mob leaders, totem carriers, psykers – these were the Salamanders' targets. Cripple the orks' leadership. Show them their mightiest could all fall beneath a Fireborn's flame and blade. Here the Assault squads excelled, Vargo and Gannon conducting raiding attacks on vulnerable positions or leaders exposed by the sudden death or retreat of their brethren.

Thousands of greenskins lay dead for little reply. That said, every Salamander casualty was felt keenly. Fugis had returned to the fight with Brother-Sergeant Agatone. The two fought shoulder-to-shoulder, their courage worthy of even Vulkan's praise. But the Apothecary, as heroic as he was, couldn't minister to all of his fallen brothers. If they survived this fight, there would be much work for Fugis to do in the aftermath.

Tsu'gan had lost sight of them after N'keln's full assault order and he wondered if they fought still.

It was stretched and the ash dunes were like a copper desert now, so stained were they with blood. Tremors wracked the undulating landscape almost constantly and dark lightning ripped strips into the sky as the volcanoes vented. Their voices were a doom-laden refrain to the heavy thunder overhead.

'The world is ending, brother,' roared Tsu'gan. He had not left Praetor's side, although the sergeant's squad had fragmented in the dense melee. Iagon, for instance, was elsewhere on the field of war. Tsu'gan hoped he was still alive.

'A fitting end for us then,' Praetor replied, crushing an ork with a crackling blow from his thunder hammer, 'consumed by smoke and fire. All is ash at the end of days, brother.'

Tsu'gan smiled to himself – it sounded like something Brother Emek would say.

'All is ash,' Tsu'gan agreed and fought on.

Above the rising tumult of Scoria's last storm, just audible over the raging battle, the churning report of metal could be heard echoing from the innards of the iron fortress.

Peaking above the lip of the wall, the stub-nose of the long cannon forged by the Iron Warriors but purified by the Salamanders emerged. Dust and rock was cascading from its metal casing in huge drifts, its pneumatic platform raising it from the depths of the keep to glower imperiously over the surface of Scoria like the metal finger of a dark and vengeful god.

For a moment, a fleeting second only, the fighting slowed as all who beheld the cannon's emergence gaped in awe. Its eye was fixed heavenward as it sought to destroy a black sun.

Fyron-fuelled capacitors charged the air, their throb and pulse emitted as a wave of force as the cannon was empowered and a second later, unleashed.

II
Retribution

DAK'IR'S WORLD WAS darkening. His arms grew heavy as his vision faded to black and his struggles against Ghor'gan ebbed.

'That's it,' he heard the crackling magma voice say. 'That's it, find peace…'

A trembling in the earth below prevented the Salamander's fall into oblivion. When it shook the very ground, its violent insistence threw the grappling Space Marines apart.

Clutching his neck, Dak'ir coughed and spluttered hot, smoky air back into his lungs. The sensation reminded him of Nocturne and the caves of Ignea – it was like breathing in a panacea.

Ghor'gan was getting to his feet as Dak'ir's vision cleared. The Dragon Warrior braced himself against the rock wall as the entire cavern shook. A huge crack ran up the side of it as geysers of scalding steam and fire roared through the slowly fragmenting ground. In places small chasms and crag-walled pitfalls opened up like yawning mouths, their liquid tongues hot and glowing below. The renegade moved around them, stalking towards Dak'ir, determined to finish what he had begun.

'Relent, little Salamander,' he said, his voice low and weary.

Ghor'gan didn't see the combat blade in Dak'ir's hand until it was too late. The blade was only half a metre long but the Salamander sank it to the hilt in the renegade's chest. The precise blow exploited a gap in the ceramite plates and penetrated armour, bone and flesh.

'A life for a life,' snarled Dak'ir. 'My captain must be avenged.'

Ghor'gan's mouth curled in pain; his eyes narrow slits of agony. Even as Dak'ir twisted the blade, searching out vital organs and soft tissue, the renegade fought on and dug his claws into the Salamander's neck.

Dak'ir cried out, aiming a savage punch to the Dragon Warrior's ear even as he shoved the combat blade harder with his other hand. Ghor'gan shifted his head, and took the blow on his much harder jaw instead, but it jarred enough to force him to release his claw.

Blood was dripping off Ghor'gan's extracted talon when a ball of fire rolled through the wall of heat nearby, wreathed in flames and trailing smoke. From it emerged Pyriel, furled within the protective confines of his drakescale mantle.

Out of the corner of his eye, Dak'ir saw Pyriel move to assist him but the sergeant urged the Librarian on as he kept the bulky Dragon Warrior pinned.

'Stop Nihilan,' he roared, his voice hoarse from being half-choked to death. 'Don't let the bastard escape again.'

Pyriel didn't even pause. The Librarian knew his duty and sped on after Nihilan and his brood.

'Just you and I again,' sneered Dak'ir, scenting the sulphur gas streaming from a craterous hole behind the Dragon Warrior. A sudden idea occurred to him. 'You're not Fire-born, are you renegade…'

THE IDLING OF powerful engines throbbed ahead of him as Pyriel thundered down the tunnel after Nihilan and the other Dragon Warrior.

Dak'ir was right – they could not be allowed to escape again. If it had to end here on Scoria then the renegades would die with them. The Librarian could feel peace if he knew that was so.

Too late, Pyriel arrived at the tunnel's terminus. In the expansive cavern before him, a Stormbird was waiting. Its engines were burning with a dull, red glow. The embarkation ramp in the gunship's hold was slammed down. The fang-mouthed Dragon Warrior was ferrying the last of the fyron ore aboard via the six-wheeled loader, his master looking on.

Just before Nihilan turned to see the foe in his midst, Pyriel looked up and realised the roof to the cavern was vaulted. In fact, it tapered several hundred metres up into a narrow chimney that led directly to the surface. Narrow, yes, but wide enough to accommodate the span of a Stormbird if piloted correctly.

A psychic cry ripped from Pyriel's throat as he recognised his chance to stop the Dragon Warriors was already beyond his grasp. He fashioned a bolt of flame from the essence of the warp, channelling it down his force sword to lash at Nihilan. At least he would sear him.

Some fifty metres away, the sorcerer turned and threw up a hasty force barrier against which the fire bolt crashed and dissipated. Behind trailing smoke and eddies of flame, Nihilan emerged unscathed.

The Dragon Warrior then unleashed a psychic riposte. Black smoke boiled across the ground, resolving into tendrils upon reaching the Salamander. The tendrils coiled insidiously around Pyriel's arms and legs, invading the protective aegis of his armour and bypassing the safeguards of his psychic hood. Powerless to prevent it, in a matter of seconds the Librarian was utterly paralysed. Thunderous rage burned in Pyriel's eyes as he regarded his nemesis.

'It's been a long time, Pyriel,' said Nihilan with a voice reminiscent of cracking parchment. 'I missed you on Stratos, brother.'

'A shame,' Pyriel forced a sarcastic reply. He grimaced against the sorcerous hold, trying to unravel it with his mind.

Nihilan walked off the loading ramp almost casually. Despite the raucous engine noise venting around him, his words were strangely clear. 'How long has it been, then? Over four decades for you? I see you have advanced in Master Vel'cona's eyes since then. A mere Codicier, if memory serves, and now a vaunted Epistolary.' Nihilan's burning red gaze swept over the arcane rank sigils emblazoned on Pyriel's armour contemptuously. The sorcerer's mood darkened.

'Still you deny the raw power of the warp,' he breathed, lingering on the flame icon on the Librarian's right pauldron. Enmity, perhaps even jealousy, flared briefly then died like the mirthless smile curling Nihilan's top lip. 'I eclipse your meagre abilities now.'

'Spoken like a true pawn of Chaos,' bit Pyriel, working as much vitriol as he could into the retort. 'You are naught but a plaything for the Ruinous Powers. Once your usefulness has ended they will discard you.'

The amused expression returned.

'I thought it was just the armour of my former brothers that was green. Not so for you of course, Librarian, but then the shade of your eyes make up for it, don't they.'

Pyriel's eyes burned an angry red. He wished dearly he could look upon Nihilan and engulf him within the fire of his wrath.

'If you're going to destroy me, then do it and spare the rhetoric before I expire of boredom.'

That struck a nerve. Nihilan seemed like he was going to give Pyriel his wish. Static blurted from the external vox feed in the hold of the Stormbird, arresting any retaliation.

'Cargo secured, my lord,' came a rasping voice. 'Brother Ekrine is ready to take off.'

Annoyed at the sudden interruption, Nihilan managed to keep his irritation from his voice when he replied. 'Understood, Ramlek. I will be with you momentarily.' He turned his attention back to Pyriel.

'I could smite you where you stand, but that wouldn't be fitting. I want you to suffer before you die, Pyriel. Just like Vel'cona made me suffer when you betrayed my trust.'

Pyriel's jaw hardened – the dark tendrils binding him were weakening. 'Traitors are undeserving of trust.'

Pyriel shook off the sorcerous bonds with a feral shout. Force sword held high, the Librarian launched himself at Nihilan, who merely stepped back into the hold before the ramp was pulled up. Mocking laugher echoed down to Pyriel as the Stormbird lifted and the hold hatch closed with a resounding *clang*. The burst from the gunship's rapidly vented thrusters sent the Librarian sprawling and the Stormbird soaring up the shrinking mouth of the rock chimney, up into the fractious air of Scoria.

Shrugging off the effects of Nihilan's sorcerous attack and mouthing a muttered curse, Pyriel picked himself up and went back down the tunnel to find Dak'ir.

He returned in time only to see the Salamander sergeant and his foe pitching over the edge of a fiery crevice, plummeting down, occluded by smoke and rising ash.

Pyriel gave voice to his pain again.

'Dak'ir!'

THE BLACK ROCK exploded with all the finality and grandeur of a shattered star. At once the blood-red sky flooded with brilliance, a pure white flare that bathed all in its eldritch glow. The flare died but the sun returned with it, weak and yellow but brighter than the forbidding gloom of the eclipse.

Abruptly and violently sundered, the black rock was spread across the firmament. The fragments of its passing became new stars burning in the light of day. Drawn by the gravitational pull of the planet, the stars became larger and larger until they resolved into vast meteorites, swathed in fire and billowing smoke.

The effect of the black rock's destruction on the orks was almost palpable. The horde faltered, its impetus flagging like a ship with its sails abruptly cut. When the jagged balls of fire arcing from the heavens struck, it only compounded the greenskins' despair.

Simultaneous meteor strikes punished the rear of the ork lines stretching back across the dunes. The celestial storm wreaked utter havoc, slaying hundreds beneath the fury of the fallen rocks, and cooking hundreds more in the resultant radiation wave.

Tsu'gan watched this all happen between the ever growing gaps in the fighting. As soon as the beam from the seismic cannon rang out, piercing the sky like a radiant lance, N'keln ordered the Salamanders to stand fast and consolidate. Though stretched and scattered, the Astartes became like green-armoured islands in the orkish sea, turning their bolters outward and brooking no interloper beyond their individual walls of ceramite.

Shoulder-to-shoulder with Praetor and three of his Firedrakes, Tsu'gan couldn't help but stare in awe at the phenomenal display unfolding above. The earth chimed with it, trembling and cracking. Crevices and chasms split open, swallowing orks in their thousands. Those not falling to their doom in the abyssal darkness were consumed by rushing lava torrenting into the air.

Booming thunder pealed from the volcanoes, louder and somehow final as they erupted with hellish force.

Praetor's laughter rivalled their bellow. The skies were darkening with smoke and ash. Soon artificial night would resume once more.

'When fire rains from the sky and ash smothers the sun, it is the end of days,' he shouted.

Tsu'gan's gaze was still fixed upon the turbulent heavens. 'That is not all the heavens bring, brother.'

Praetor followed Tsu'gan's outstretched finger.

The belly of a ship emerged slowly through the billowing smoke clouds. Tsu'gan was put in mind of a giant predator of the deep emerging from a mist-wreathed ocean. Tiny meteorites arced past it on fiery contrails as it hovered a thousand metres above the surface. The backwash of massive ventral engines pressed down upon Tsu'gan despite its altitude. It was an Astartes strike cruiser.

Argos raised his body up out of the ventral thruster conduit in the enginarium. He stretched the stiffness out of his back, eased the knots from his tired muscles and rolled his shoulders beneath his pauldrons to coax back some mobility. He had done all he could.

The fourth, still non-functional, ventral thruster bank was prepped as exhaustively as possible. The machine-rites had been observed, the correct unguents applied and offerings dedicated. His throat was hoarse from the litanies of function and ignition he had performed in concert with his Techmarines. The Master of Forge was a part of this ship; he felt its malady and he knew its moods. If they could replace the parts they'd lost and needed, it would achieve loft. Once free of the dunes, the *Vulkan's Wrath*'s main engines would do the rest.

The comm-feed in his battle-helm hissed and spat with static before Argos heard Brother Uclides, one of Sergeant Agatone's squad tasked with escorting the human civilians aboard the ship.

After undertaking a cursory geological analysis, Argos had determined that the planet's tectonic integrity was nearing imminent disintegration. Prudently, he had given the order for the auxiliary and all still living casualties to be secured aboard the ship for safety. Those injured who could not be moved were given the Emperor's Peace and enclosed in medi-caskets for later interment into the pyreum.

'All of the Scorian settlers are aboard, Master Argos. What are your orders?'

Argos was about to respond when he noticed the radiation spike in the atmosphere detected by the ship's still functioning sensors, relayed to him through his direct interface.

'Go to the fighter hangar and help prepare the gun-ships,' he answered, changing his mind when he assumed the black rock had been destroyed. Apart from the servitors, the Salamander was alone, having already despatched the other Techmarines to the Thunderhawks still locked in their transit rigs. 'Our brothers will be in need of immediate extraction and conveyance back to the *Vulkan's Wrath*.' Uclides communicated his obedience and cut the feed.

Argos was about to climb out of the sunken thruster access conduit when the ship's vox-unit crackled into life alongside him. Uclides would have used the helmet comm-feed. The signal originated from outside of the ship.

'Brother Techmarine Argos: 3rd Company, Salamanders Chapter, aboard the *Vulkan's Wrath*,' he began, observing protocol. 'Identify yourself.'

A clipped voice responded with all the warmth and smoothness of rusty nails.

'This is Brother Techmarine Harkane of his most noble lord Vinyar's strike cruiser, *Purgatory*. In the name of the Emperor, the Marines Malevolent bring you salvation!'

BROTHER-CAPTAIN N'KELN'S ORDER to stand fast had kept his forces out of bombardment range and the worst hit areas of the meteor shower. The celestial storm had all but abated now and the greenskins, though battered and severely reduced in strength, still lived and fought.

During a brief lull in the battle, N'keln took stock of his surroundings. Mounted upon a high dune with his Inferno Guard and Sergeant Agatone, who had emerged alongside them with Fugis when they'd returned to the battlefield, N'keln surveyed the carnage. He saw tiny knots of Salamander armour out amongst the thrashing horde, lit by controlled bursts of bolter fire or plumes of igniting promethium. Their rear was anchored by the Devastators still. Lok was in able command, several hundred metres distant since the advance. The Dreadnoughts both functioned, prowling the edges of the Salamanders' deployment zone. Ashamon had lost his heavy flamer and meltagun but he continued to pound on the orks with his seismic hammer. Amadeus was wholly intact, but with several deep gouges in his protective sarcophagus where the greenskins had attempted to forcibly exhume him.

N'keln estimated they had lost approximately thirty-three per cent of their original number. He didn't know how many of those casualties would fight again. In light of the ork masses it was a lower rate of attrition than he'd expected. The greenskins, in contrast, had died in their thousands. A slew of carcasses lay strewn across the dunes, slowly decaying.

The company banner, held aloft by Malicant, began snapping violently in a sudden downdraft, drawing N'keln's gaze upward. Above them, the brother-captain saw the long, grey ventral hull of a ship he recognised. Fraught with interference, the comm-feed in his battle-helm opened.

N'keln listened intently to the voice of Brother Argos as he relayed exactly what Harkane on the *Purgatory* had said to him. Towards the end, the captain's face became grim.

'Tell him he has my word,' he replied, jaw clenched. He cut the feed and ordered the warriors around him back into the fight. N'keln suddenly needed to vent his wrath.

PYRIEL RAN TO the edge of the crevice where he'd seen Dak'ir fall, expecting the worst. Peering over the edge, through smoke and flame and heat, he saw it was a short drop into a bubbling lava pool. Ghor'gan's armour was slowly disintegrating in it, along with the rest of the Dragon Warrior. There was no sign of Dak'ir.

Then the smoke and steam cleared slightly and Pyriel saw him. Dak'ir was climbing up the rocky face of the crevice and had almost reached the top. Pyriel reached down and dragged him up just as the lava flow pooled high enough to swallow up the corpse of the renegade completely.

'You are adept at cheating death, brother,' Pyriel remarked. His tone was an ambivalent mesh of relief and thin-veiled suspicion.

Dak'ir only nodded, too exhausted to speak for the moment.

The cavern was crashing down around them. Fire wreathed it and falling rocks and spills of dust fogged the air. Nowhere was safe to stand now, with fresh chasms opening from the webbed cracks that littered the ground and lava plumes spewing capriciously from the bowels of the earth. They had to get out, yet the way to the tunnel was blocked.

'Nihilan…' rasped Dak'ir as a geyser of steam erupted nearby.

Pyriel shook his head. The Librarian's dark gaze betrayed his anger.

'Stand close,' he said after a moment. Pyriel was tired too – breaking Nihilan's sorcerous hold had been taxing. He tapped into what psychic strength he had left and opened the gate of infinity.

SCORIA WAS DYING, and in its despair sought to take those upon its surface with it to oblivion.

The earth tremors were a constant rumbling now as they presaged further cracks opening up in the doomed planet's bedrock. Entire sections of the dunes were collapsing, sending greenskins in their thousands to fiery death in the rising lava streams below. Smoke wreathed the battlefield as if it were a gigantic pyre, the warriors locked in combat upon it fighting to avoid the touch of the flames. Spurting lava threw red and umber shadows into the greying haze, its glow grainy and diffuse in the clogged air.

Even the iron fortress had started to crumble. A few minutes after Elysius and Draedius had quit the keep a wide crack ran up its centre, splitting the bastion in two. Then several errant meteorites had struck it. A broken tower thrust up into the murder-red sky like a shattered femur, another was rendered a sullen stump. Walls partially collapsed, a yawning chasm in its courtyard, the iron fortress hung open a half ruin.

As far as he was from the site of its destruction, and though he could barely see it through the billowing smoke, N'keln sensed fear emanating from the iron fortress – fear and angry denial. The end of Scoria meant the end for whatever fell entity possessed the bastion's catacombs. Fire would cleanse it at last, after all.

N'keln heard the thunder ripping across the sky. It came in the form of gunships, both Salamander and Marines Malevolent. Through the thick grey smog, he thought he traced the flight path of receding engines venturing out to evacuate his battle-brothers.

Occasionally, bright lances of energy surged through the smoky cloud layer blotting out great swathes of the sky as the *Purgatory* unleashed its guns on distant mobs of greenskins. The grey veil lifted for a time as the heat of the strike cruiser's cannons burned it away, only for it to return moments later in the wake of their fury.

The orks were dying in droves and N'keln ordered a final push for victory, reinforced by what squads Vinyar had deigned to assist him with. The compact, agreed under some duress, with the Marines Malevolent captain still rankled but there was little other choice.

Upon N'keln's reluctant concession, a squadron of Stormbirds had roared from the *Purgatory's* fighter bays headed straight for the crash site and the *Vulkan's Wrath*. Aboard were Brother Harkane and several other Techmarines and servitor crews. With them they carried the machine parts necessary for Argos to repair the fourth ventral thruster bank and give flight back to the Salamanders' strike cruiser.

The Marines Malevolent had also secured the crash site. Between them and the Salamander forces still on the field, the remaining orks were being rounded up and destroyed. For that, N'keln was grateful.

The fight all but over, the captain had become estranged from his warriors and stood upon the field of war surrounded by smoke, seemingly alone. Grateful for the solitude, he heard the sounds of battle ending: the sporadic bark of bolters, the errant flash of flame or the desultory orkish roar of vain defiance. The greenskins were defeated. No more dark splinters from the sky, no more brutish ships making landfall. It was done.

Overhead, the Thunderhawks blazed, ferrying Salamanders back to the *Vulkan's Wrath*. He made a mental note to commend Brother Argos for his foresight and prudence in this matter. Even as fire rained from the sky with the last vestiges of the meteor storm and the world shuddered in its final death throes around them, the sound of Salamanders chanting drifted to N'keln on a hot breeze.

They echoed his name.

Prometheus victoria! N'keln gloria!

It was an old Legion custom, this shouted accolade, borrowed from their Terran cousins. N'keln was humbled by their respect and laudation.

His heart swelled with warrior pride as he watched the *Vulkan's Wrath*, visible despite the distance and the smoke, rise from the dunes, rock and ash cascading off its surface, aloft once more.

It was time to leave at last and return to Nocturne. N'keln hoped the ancient power armour suits and the geneseed of Brother Gravius might yield some revelations as to the fate of the Primarch yet and perhaps reveal the purpose of the Tome of Fire bringing them to this doomed world. For now, he was content with victory and the defeat of his enemies.

N'keln was about to raise Argos on the comm-feed to congratulate him and request extraction, when a burning pain flared in his side. At first, the captain wasn't sure what had happened until he was stabbed again and felt the knife dig deep. Incensed, he made to turn to confront his would-be assassin, but was stabbed again and again. Blood flowed freely from the wounds where the knife had exploited the gaps in his power armour, half-ruined from the incessant fighting.

Biological warnings appeared on his helmet display as his armour notified him, belatedly, of the danger he was in. Hot agony raked his side and he fell forward, his body starting to numb. The weapon, still beyond N'keln's sight as was his attacker, wrenched from his flesh and a half gasp, half cry betrayed the captain.

Mind reeling, his gushing blood painting his fingers red, N'keln tried to comprehend what was happening. Orks still moved in the smoke, bent on petty vengeance. Had one of them managed to sneak up on him, aiming for a pyrrhic victory of sorts?

Struggling to breathe, his lungs punctured and smoke billowing around him, N'keln ripped off his battle-helm. Forcing his body up, he staggered onto his feet as the blade went in again. He tried to fend off the attack, still unsure where it was coming from, but could only slump onto his back.

At last, N'keln looked up and saw the face of his attacker. The captain's blood-rimed eyes grew wide. He tried to speak when the thick, orkish blade was thrust into his exposed neck. Blood bubbled up into his throat and all that escaped his mouth was a watery gurgle. N'keln's fists bunched briefly before the weapon was rammed into his chest and his primary and secondary hearts.

The captain of the Salamanders died with rage in his eyes and his fingers curled into talons of impotent hate.

The sounds of his victory and the chants of his name faded in his ears as blackness overtook them...

FUGIS MOVED THROUGH the dense fog of smoke, despatching wounded orks or administering the Emperor's Peace to the fallen and extracting their geneseeds. A faint cry echoing through the murk got his attention and he followed it through the grey world around him.

Upon a bloody dune of ash he found Brother Iagon. The Salamander was clutching the ruined stump of his left hand, trying to staunch the gory flow. Three dead ork corpses were strewn around him. A fourth body lay partially hidden by the rise of the dune, having tumbled into a shallow depression in the ash. Its boots were marred with grey but glimmered green underneath.

For now ignoring Iagon, whose eyes were urging him to go to the other body, Fugis rushed to the edge of the dune and saw N'keln, his rigored faced locked in fury, lying dead below.

Distraught, the Apothecary half-clambered, half-fell to the base of the depression where the slain captain lay. He was checking for vital signs, knowing really he would find none, when the rest of the Inferno Guard arrived on the scene.

Praetor and the Firedrakes, along with Tsu'gan and some of his squad joined them. It was the veteran Terminator sergeant that broke the disbelieving silence.

'In Vulkan's name, what happened here?' A barely tempered rage affected the Firedrake's voice as he directed his questioning first at Fugis, then at Iagon.

Iagon was shaking his head, as Fugis relayed his ignorance of the heinous act to Praetor and went to the other Salamander's assistance.

'I saw them... moving through the smoke,' Iagon's reply was broken by painful pauses as Fugis worked at cauterising the terrible wound. 'Three of them, clad in stealth... and closing on the captain,' he went on. 'By the time I could reach him, N'keln was already dead. I slew two of them without reply, when my weapon ran empty and the third took my hand. I finished it with the stock, but I was too late to save him...' Iagon's voice trailed away, his head downcast.

Praetor regarded the bloodied bolter, its stock caked in gore, and the demolished face of the ork nearest the wounded Salamander. The other two carried bolter wounds, blood-slicked cleavers half-gripped in their meaty fists. Iagon's armour was spattered with dark crimson.

Grave-faced, Praetor nodded slowly and turned his back on the tragic scene. He opened a force-wide band on the comm-feed and issued a full retreat order. All he said in addition was that Brother-Captain N'keln had been incapacitated and that he was assuming full command of the mission.

DAK'IR LEARNED OF Captain N'keln's death sitting in the Chamber Sanctuarine of the Thunderhawk, *Fire-wyvern*. A melancholy mood descended upon the troop hold of the gunship as the black news filtered through to all. First Kadai and now N'keln – Dak'ir wondered what fate was next for 3rd Company.

He and Pyriel had emerged onto the battlefield in a maelstrom of lightning and noise. The nauseating effects of teleportation faded swiftly faced with the immensity of the burgeoning cataclysm about to destroy Scoria. A Thunderhawk was already hovering to land nearby. Dak'ir remembered feeling slightly aggrieved that he had not had a chance to fight alongside his battle-brothers against the orks before the evacuation. But there was no time for introspection.

The boarding ramp of the *Fire-wyvern* clanged open as soon as it touched down. Dak'ir, Pyriel and several others in the vicinity embarked without a word. Moments later, they were airborne and tracking across the ravaged ash desert slowly being consumed by fire.

It was only a short journey to the *Vulkan's Wrath*. Their pilot, Brother Hek'en, voxed through to the troop hold, reporting that the strike cruiser was before them on the horizon, aloft and ready to take them off the doomed world.

Muted cheers greeted this news, tempered by the earlier communication from Praetor that he had assumed command and N'keln was down. Scattered word from Salamanders still out in the field followed swiftly, confirming that their captain was actually dead.

Gazing out of the occuliport in the side of the armoured gunship, yet to assume his transport harness, Dak'ir was saddened further when he saw the ground tear apart. He imagined the inert form of Brother Gravius, lava billowing up and rolling over the ancient Salamander, swallowing him under its fiery depths. The entire world was burning, waves of magma like tsunamis cascading over the fractured surface of Scoria turning it into a gelatinous sun.

Dak'ir turned away and found Pyriel staring at him. The rest of the Salamanders had their heads bowed in remembrance. The Librarian's expression was anything but grieving. It told Dak'ir that the Epistolary was thinking about how Nihilan's sorcery should have destroyed him, but left the Salamander sergeant barely scathed. It was not possible. And it was then that Dak'ir realised it wasn't over for him, that there would be a reckoning upon their return to Nocturne.

EPILOGUE

'DON'T THINK OF me as a fool, Captain Vinyar...' The deep and resonant voice of Chapter Master Tu'Shan filled the vast Hall of the Firedrakes on Prometheus with its authority and power. It was an inauspicious start to their initial meeting.

Vinyar stood stock still and silent, a prudent move given that he was in the throne room of another Astartes Chapter, facing their liege lord having forced one of his dead captains into a compromise he did not approve of but had no choice but to honour.

'I know you and your troops were tracking the *Vulkan's Wrath*,' the Regent of Prometheus continued. 'How else could you have heard its distress beacon and responded in such timely fashion, offering aid but only for the extortion of war materiel.'

Brother Praetor and a squad of Firedrakes looked on with barely restrained anger. The Marines Malevolent had tainted Brother-Captain N'keln's sacrifice with compromise. They had outstretched the hand of salvation in return for the arms and armour they had wished to 'liberate' from the *Archimedes Rex*. Vinyar it seemed was bent on re-appropriating what he felt was his by right – a necessity for his warmongering in the Emperor's name.

If the small retinue of warriors he had brought with him, indeed, the captain himself, felt anything at this show of aggression, they, to their dubious credit, did not show it. But nor did they dare speak whilst the Salamanders Chapter Master admonished.

'I do not believe in coincidence or even providence,' he told Vinyar, leaning forward in his throne to emphasise the point. Tu'Shan lowered his voice and there was a trace of very real menace in it. 'If I thought your intention by tracking my ship was to exact some petty revenge for the *Archimedes Rex*, then you and I would be having a very different conversation to the one we are conducting now, brother-captain.'

A charged silence filled the Hall of the Firedrakes, Tu'Shan allowing his gaze to burn into Vinyar for a few moments before he signalled to the shadows.

A grav-sled emerged into view, lit by the fiery sconces blazing on the wall that hinted at the dozens of glorious banners lauding the deeds of the 1st Company. Apart from that, it was an austere chamber with a throne and several archways leading off into darkness.

The Marines Malevolent had followed the Salamanders all the way back to Nocturne. Vinyar's display of audacity was as bold as it was incredible when he insisted on being given an audience with the Chapter Master before the war materiel was handed over to them. Tu'Shan had agreed without preamble, keen to set eyes on this upstart dog of a Space Marine captain.

The grav-sled was but the first in a long train. Accompanied by a stern-faced Master Argos and three of his Techmarines, the sleds accommodated all of the bolters, armour suits and other munitions the Salamanders had taken from the *Archimedes Rex*.

As the grav-sleds slowed to a halt, Master Argos and his coterie stepped back into the shadows and were gone from the chamber once more.

'We Salamanders are warriors of our word,' there was a snarl to Tu'Shan's tone this time, as his patience began to ebb, 'but I promise you personally that this is not an end to it, *Malevolent*. You have earned the ire of a Chapter Master this day, and that is not a thing to be taken lightly.'

Vinyar absorbed all of this and merely bowed. His body language was almost unreadable as was his expression, unhelmeted as he was before the Regent of Prometheus. But Tu'Shan detected an arrogant mien about him, a disdainful swagger in his deferent movements that riled him.

'Get out,' he growled, before he was forced to do something with the rising anger in his marrow.

The Marines Malevolent left without ceremony, escorted by Praetor and his Firedrakes.

Tu'Shan slumped back onto his throne once he was alone. A sequence inputted on a slate worked into the throne's arm resulted in a hidden door opening in one of the flanking walls. Inside the vault, lit by more sconces, were the suits of power armour recovered in the catacombs of Scoria. Arrayed in rows, yet to be tended and polished as revered artefacts of war, Tu'Shan scrutinised them. The vial containing Gravius's extracted geneseed was nearby, encased in a cryo-tank, its glass confines rimed by liquid nitrogen hoarfrost.

A voice that hummed with power came from the darkness.

'You wonder why the Tome of Fire directed us to Scoria, if this is all we were meant to find,' said Master Vel'cona. The Chief Librarian of the Salamanders did not need his prodigious psychic talents to guess the Chapter Master's thoughts.

It wasn't a question and Tu'Shan didn't answer. Instead he looked. Something had caught his attention. It was, at first, just beyond his reach. But as he pored harder, he began to see... For in the arrangement of the armour in Legion formation, Tu'Shan discerned the fragments of a symbol prophecy. It was only visible when the armour was viewed together, at a certain angle, the components of the hidden shapes confluencing to produce a whole that only then possessed meaning.

Even after those conditions were met, only a Chapter Master had the necessary cognition, intellect and insight to recognise it.

'What do you see, my lord?' asked Vel'cona, the faint sound of his approaching step betraying his eagerness as he realised Tu'Shan had started to read...

'A great undertaking...' the Chapter Master's eyes narrowed as he replied, '...A momentous event... Nocturne in the balance... A low-born, one of the earth, will pass through the gate of fire.'

'The prophecy speaks of one amongst our ranks,' breathed the Librarian. 'I know of him.'

'As do I,' the Chapter Master returned darkly.

'Does it bode well or ill, my lord?'

Tu'Shan turned to face him, a stony expression etched upon his regal countenance.

'He will be our *doom* or *salvation*.'

The Regent of Prometheus allowed a pause before going on.

'Master Vel'cona,' he said. 'Brother-Sergeant Hazon Dak'ir: watch him very closely.'

The Chief Librarian's eyes, fathomless pits of knowledge, blazed with fire. He nodded then bowed, before slipping away into the darkness.

Tu'Shan returned to the armour suits, scrutinising them, trying to discern further clarity in their esoteric message.

'Watch him…' he repeated to an empty room, lost in thought. 'Watch him closely indeed.'

DAK'IR HAD MET Ba'ken on a sandy rock plateau overlooking the Pyre Desert. Few had come to observe Brother Fugis as he made the 'Burning Walk'. Usually, it was not done. The pilgrimage, undertaken by a Salamander, was a spiritual journey, its inception supposed to be conducted in isolation as was the trial itself. Ordinarily, the old or the afflicted went on the Burning Walk. It was a way, according to Nocturnean custom and the Cult of Prometheus, that a warrior who had not died in battle but could fight for glory no more could claim some dignity and even myth in his last days. Fugis, like few others before him, had requested special dispensation to undergo the trial as a way to restore his fractured spirit. Dak'ir knew of none amongst the Chapter who had ever returned from the undertaking. Their bleached bones lay beneath the scorching desert now, he reckoned, the distant places of the Pyre a grave marking in more than name alone.

By treading the Burning Walk, Fugis was an Apothecary no longer. He had given up his power armour and his other Astartes trappings. He wore a sand-cloak now, with breathable mesh underneath, and a dust-scarf was wrapped around his neck and mouth. A specially modified Nocturnean hunting rifle was slung across his back – for he had given up the right to wield the holy bolter – and he carried a machete-knife strapped to his forearm and scant supplies of water. They wouldn't last long. After that, he'd have to find his own way to survive in the desert.

His natural successor was nearby, standing alone upon an adjacent outcrop of rock, head bowed and eyes closed in silent contemplation. Brother Emek had

been saddened to leave his squad brothers, but the
needs of the company outweighed sentiment and the
Master Apothecary of the Chapter was to train him in
the healing arts. One half of Emek's battle-helm was
painted white to reflect his status.

A last plateau, the farthest distant of the three, held
Agatone. He acknowledged the pair with a slight tilt of
his head. As the soon-to-be captain of 3rd Company,
his was a legacy of blood and a heavy burden. It
showed in the weight of his downcast eyes.

Soon Fugis had gone from sight, just a shimmer on
the hazy desert horizon. 'A long deserved honour,'
uttered Dak'ir after a long silence.

It took a moment for Ba'ken to realise he was referring to him and the sergeant's rank sigil freshly worked
upon his armour by the Chapter artisans. By contrast,
Dak'ir's battle-plate was unadorned, stripped completely of its previous honours – a sergeant no longer.

'I can think of no one better to lead the squad than
you, Ba'ken,' he added, clapping a comradely hand
upon the hulking Salamander's pauldron.

'Aye, it's true,' Ba'ken replied.

They both laughed out loud at his mock arrogance,
but their moment of levity was short-lived and eventually painful as it reminded them both of all they had
lost and would never regain.

'The company is breaking,' muttered Ba'ken, giving
in to melancholy. 'You bound to Pyriel's service. Emek
joined to the Apothecarion. My brothers, ash in the
pyreum,' he sighed, 'Even Tsu'gan–'

'Agatone will restore its strength,' counselled Dak'ir.
'He builds upon a solid foundation. Both Kadai and
N'keln have a worthy successor.'

A shadow fell across them, interrupting the former
sergeant.

'Brother Dak'ir.' It was Pyriel.

Ba'ken knew this was coming and bowed curtly to the Librarian before leaving them.

'I sensed the power in you long ago, Hazon,' Pyriel confessed, walking up to the edge of the plateau and staring towards the seemingly endless desert. Behind him, the dull and faraway sound of the volcanoes boomed across the sun-scorched heavens.

'What you did against Nihilan's sorcery...' he began, mastering his exasperation before he turned back around. 'It was nothing short of miraculous. It should not be. *You* should not be,' he said, drawing closer. 'Over four decades a Space Marine and your latent potential has only just surfaced.' He left a short pause. 'You are unique, Dak'ir. An enigma.' Pyriel turned away again, finding regarding the hellish sun easier. 'Chaplain Elysius wanted you conditioned, even branded and censured – I opposed it.'

'So what happens now?'

'You are to accompany me.'

'You don't need them for me to do that,' Dak'ir replied, indicating the pair of hulking Terminators that had just lumbered into view at the Librarian's bidding.

'Don't I?' Pyriel asked, facing him. 'You are a mystery, and like all mysteries a shadow of suspicion hangs over you, but I will lift it if you prove worthy.'

'And how will you know that?' Dak'ir's tone betrayed his impatience.

The Librarian's response was pragmatic. 'After your trials, if you live, you will be deemed worthy.'

'Worthy for what?'

The cerulean flash returned to Pyriel's eyes by way of dramatic gesture. 'To be trained by me,' he said.

Dak'ir heard the engines of a ship growl into life. A dust cloud was billowing from below, where the landed vessel awaited them.

'Where are you taking me, Pyriel?'

The Librarian smiled, but it did not reach his eyes.

'To the Librarius on Prometheus, and an audience with Master Vel'cona.'

TSU'GAN FOLLOWED A long and rocky path of darkened coals towards a great gate. From high above, swept up in the shadows of a mountain cave, sat Iagon, watching him.

Bitterness filled the Salamander's heart. He clenched his fists tightly.

'I killed for you…' he hissed.

Iagon's dreams and plans were in tatters. He had been left behind by his would-be patron, even after the way was open for Tsu'gan's ascension. Except, he *had* ascended, but to the vaunted ranks of the Firedrakes and not the captaincy of the 3rd Company, Iagon his chief aide. Brother Praetor – Iagon resisted a pang of jealous anger – had petitioned for his promotion, impressed by Tsu'gan's actions on Scoria: his courage and battle-ethic, his leadership and prowess. The sergeant of the Firedrakes did not know the brittle tool he had inducted into his ranks. Iagon had been tempted to inform him of Tsu'gan's penchant for masochism, his destructive inner guilt, but that would be all too easy.

Hero worship had turned to hatred in Iagon's heart. He wanted Tsu'gan to pay the dearest price for betraying him.

Ascending a rocky stair, Tsu'gan entered a small amphitheatre. It was meant to be a sacred place; only the Firedrakes or those destined to become one were allowed to set foot on this part of Nocturne. Iagon cared not. He was not followed, nor seen. He had to see this.

Ominous thunder shook the open structure into which Tsu'gan had disappeared and a flash of light blazed out from it and then died as the teleporter was activated and Tsu'gan was on Nocturne no longer.

Iagon sat for a while, allowing the after-flare to fade from his vision, when he heard a pattering on the ground and thought it was rain. When he saw the pool of redness at his feet, he realised it was blood, dripping onto the ground from his clenched gauntlets. He'd seized his fists so tightly that he'd pierced them and dug into flesh.

He blinked, not seeing his own blood there for a moment, but the blood of others... Iagon tried to wipe it clean but it clung to him and spread instead.

Frantic now, slowly coming unhinged, a plaintive wail emitted from his mouth and he fled. Only one thing would calm his dark soul. It yearned within him. A single thought.

Vengeance.

ABOUT THE AUTHOR

Nick Kyme hails from Grimsby, a small town on the east coast of England. Nick moved to Nottingham in 2003 to work on White Dwarf magazine as a Layout Designer. Since then, he has made the switch to the Black Library's hallowed halls as an editor and has been involved in a multitude of diverse projects. His writing credits include several published short stories, background books and novels.

You can catch up with Nick and read about all of his other published works at his website: *www.nickkyme.com*

WARHAMMER 40,000

ASSAULT ON BLACK REACH

THE NOVEL

Buy this book or read a free extract at www.blacklibrary.com

NICK KYME

UK ISBN 978-1-84416-718-0